8/09/11

Glasgow Kiss

Alex Gray

W F HOWES LTD

This large print edition published in 2009 by
W F Howes Ltd
Unit 4, Rearsby Business Park, Gaddesby Lane,
Rearsby, Leicester LE7 4YH

1 3 5 7 9 10 8 6 4 2

First published in the United Kingdom in 2009
by Sphere

A CIP catalogue record for this book is available
from the British Library

ISBN 978 1 40743 489 6

Typeset by Palimpsest Book Production Limited,
Grangemouth, Stirlingshire
Printed and bound in Great Britain
by MPG Books Ltd, Bodmin, Cornwall

FSC
Mixed Sources
Product group from well-managed
forests and other controlled sources

Cert no. SGS-COC-2953
www.fsc.org
© 1996 Forest Stewardship Council

This novel is dedicated to Chris
with much love.

The Lord is my light and my salvation:
whom shall I fear?
The Lord is the stronghold of my life:
of whom shall I be afraid?

Psalm 27 verse 1

PROLOGUE

Her lips were still warm when he kissed them, petal-soft, unyielding. It was like kissing a child's lips at bed time: he could remember that sensation, recalling vividly how the drowsy breath exhaled in a tiny shudder.

But the girl made no response even when he let his finger run across her cheek, down to the corner of her mouth. He could still see traces of pink gloss smeared over the tiny ridges that crossed her parted lips, smell her familiar scent; hands cupped across his nostrils, he breathed in the sweetness mingling with his own sweat. The sun filtered through the leaves, warming his back, filling him with a deep sense of peace as if the world understood his longings and had colluded to bring about this ultimate satisfaction. A kiss, just one kiss: that was all he'd ever wanted, all he'd ever desired.

When he finally looked into her eyes, wide with horror, he had to look away. He turned, hand on his mouth to stop the sound coming out, shaking his head in disbelief. Looking at these eyes spoiled everything.

Now he was angry with her again. She would

1

have to be punished for what she was doing to him.

A dog barking in the distance made him stand up, alert, knowing there was little time to lose. With a final glance at the shallow grave, sunlight-dappled under a canopy of trees, he wiped his hands on a tussock of grass, smoothed down the creases on his jeans and walked further into the woods, his footfall silent on the soft earth.

CHAPTER 1

They were walking a little apart now. Her face was in profile, half shaded by the over-hanging trees so that he could not make out her expression, though from time to time he would sneak a glance to see if she was looking his way. Her long pale-golden hair was twisted into plaits, leaving the cheekbones naked and exposed. It should have made her seem like a child but instead she looked older, more remote, and Kyle wished she'd left it loose as she usually did, burnished and glimmering in the afternoon sunshine.

It hadn't always been like this. They'd walked through Dawsholm Park loads of times, some-times hand in hand, dawdling by the grass verges, snatching the chance to have a quick kiss. But now, Kyle thought gloomily, these halcyon days were over. Halcyon had been Kyle's favourite word last term. His English teacher, Mrs Lorimer, had explained that it derived from a Greek story about a mythical bird that in the middle of winter made its nest floating upon the Aegean seas. The bird had magical powers to make the waters calm and the winds drop. Kyle loved that story and had used the word in his own mind to describe his relationship with Julie. He'd even dreamed of them once – floating together like that bird, side by side, waves lapping gently against their boat.

Something made him shiver suddenly and the girl turned to him, a question in her eyes.

Kyle shook his head, too full to speak. She was still watching him and must have seen the bob of his Adam's apple as he swallowed back the tears.

'All right?' Her voice was full of concern, but not for what was happening between them. Not for that.

'Aye, fine,' he replied but failed to stifle the sigh escaping from his chest. Would she stick with him out of pity after seeing his battered face? Part of him wanted to have Julie around, her warmth and loveliness blotting out the misery of the last two days. But deep down he knew he'd lost her long before his father's release from prison.

'Kyle?'

'What?'

'D'you want to talk about it?' She had stopped walking now and was looking at him, frowning. 'It might help . . .' Her voice trailed off in an unspoken apology.

Kyle shrugged. He hadn't talked about it to anyone though he'd done a fair amount of listening. His gran's house had been full of talk: recriminations, wild accusations and shouting. But that was because women did that sort of thing.

4

And because Kyle was Gran's favourite, the youngest of her three grandsons. His brothers and his gran: they all had something to say about what Tam Kerrigan had done, and not just to him. That was one reason why he was here, with Julie, to escape from all of the talk. But also he'd been interested in the bit about the murder victim, in spite of everything.

What happened to a dead person at a post-mortem examination? He'd looked up stuff on the net, reading in a detached way about incisions and bodily fluids, not really making a link with the dead man his father had killed. Even the illustrations on the Internet site hadn't put him off. It was like selecting bits of vacuum-packed butcher meat from the supermarket shelves and not seeing the animal they'd come from. Not like in the school trip to France where you were in no doubt about the origin of your dinner. One of the lassies had nearly thrown up that time someone had served up a chicken with everything still attached, the yellow claws curled over the platter and the head all to one side; you could imagine its squawk as the neck had been wrung.

'Kyle?' Julie's voice broke into his thoughts and he looked up, seeing her staring at him, a tiny crease between her eyes.

'Och, I'm okay,' he told her, then dropped his gaze, unable to bear the kindness in her face. 'The bruises'll be gone in a day or so. Probably by the time we go back to school,' he added.

'Are you going back right away?'

Kyle shrugged again. 'Why not? Can't see what good it'll do me to hang around the house.' He paused to let the unspoken words sink in. Keeping out of the house meant keeping away from his father.

They walked on again in silence but this time Julie reached out for his hand and he took it, feeling its warmth, glad to have her there. It would be okay. There might be folk staring at him, curious to know the truth behind what the papers said about Tam Kerrigan, but if Julie was there, even as a friend, he'd manage all right. All summer they'd talked about the advantages of being in Fourth Year, both excited, dropping the pretence of being too cool to show it. His mouth twisted at the memory. That had been another person, a young carefree creature whose whole life had stretched before him like an open road. Now that person was dead and gone, his boyhood behind him for ever.

CHAPTER 2

Maggie Lorimer groaned as she picked up the enormous pile of folders and staggered along the corridor to her class-room. In-service days had their uses but sometimes they simply consisted of a different sort of housekeeping. Take these Standard Grade folios, for example. She'd spent hours collating them all and working out what else the kids would need to complete their course. This was a pretty average group, Maggie thought, seeing the first name on the top folder: Julie Donaldson. Aye, the lassie worked hard right enough but she spent more time staring out of the window than concentrating on her work. Maggie shook her head. A lot of them expected grades far beyond their capabilities but she did her best for them anyway.

'Staff meeting downstairs. Right now. Manson wants to see everybody.' Maggie whirled around to see her friend, Sandie. The Business Studies teacher was making a face as she spoke. 'Must be about the Kerrigan thing.'

Maggie nodded distractedly, dumped the folders on the nearest desk, grabbed her handbag and followed Sandie along the corridor that joined the Department of English at one end with Business Studies at the other. When Maggie had first come to teach at Muirpark, her classroom had been right at one end of their department, next door to Sandie's. Their proximity had developed into a friendship and now Maggie Lorimer couldn't imagine a working day without Sandie Carmichael's ready wit bemoaning the amount of administration that they had to endure.

'Is James Kerrigan coming back to school for Sixth Year?'

'Don't know yet. Anyway, look at you! You'd think you'd been in the Bahamas all summer instead of . . . where was it? Skye?'

'No.' Maggie shook her head, making the dark curls fall across her face. 'We were in Mull. In this fabulous wee cottage. Had a brilliant time. Then spent the rest of the holiday out in the garden. Oh, and we've got a cat—'

But Maggie Lorimer's eager flow of chatter stopped abruptly as both women turned the corner and came face to face with a tall man striding towards them.

Eric Chalmers possessed the sort of physical attributes that would make any woman stop in her tracks; his blonde hair was swept forward into a boyish quiff and his smile revealed a pair of dimples that could disarm the most hardened members of staff, and often did.

It was Sandie who spoke first. 'Manson wants us

8

all downstairs. Meeting, Now,' she said, catching her breath as if she had been running.

Eric raised his eyebrows. 'Any special reason?'

'The Kerrigan kids. Has to be.'

'The Kerrigans? Why? What's happened?'

'Eric! Surely you must be the only person in the country who doesn't know about this.' Maggie tut-tutted. 'Kyle and James's father's been released from Barlinnie. Don't you remember? It was a verdict of manslaughter at the time so he's only served eight years.'

'He murdered some thug in Drumchapel,' Sandie added darkly. 'But the victim's family have been making angry noises about lack of Victim Support and the injustice to them of Kerrigan's early release. It's been all over the papers and on the telly. How come you haven't seen it?'

'Ah!' Eric fell into step with the two women. 'Not been quite in this world the past few days,' he admitted. Then his face broke into another hundred-watt smile. 'Ruth had a wee girl!'

'Aw, congratulations!' Sandie's arms were flung around the other teacher's chest and before he could protest she had landed a kiss on his cheek.

'That's lovely news, Eric. How are they both doing?'

'Fine. We've called her Ashleigh. Both sets of grandparents wanted biblical names but we just liked that one,' he said.

Sandie raised her eyebrows but refrained from making her usual caustic comment about Eric's father and father-in-law, both Church of Scotland ministers. It was common knowledge among his friends at school that Eric was a grave disappointment to his family for not following his father into the ministry. Instead he had chosen to train as a teacher of Religious Education and his enthusiasm and charisma made him one of the most popular members of staff in Muirpark Secondary. His own name, he had told them once, had been in memory of the famous runner-turned-missionary Eric Liddell. Somehow the kids had got wind of this and it was not uncommon for them to hum the theme tune of *Chariots of Fire* whenever they passed him in the corridor. Eric, being Eric, just laughed which endeared him to the kids all the more. A surprising number of them turned up for his Scripture Union club on a Thursday after school and he'd taken groups to the SU camps during the Easter and Summer breaks.

They had reached the main hall now and the murmur of voices told them that the meeting had not yet begun.

'What d'you think?' Sandie began to whisper to Maggie as they took their seats. But her words were lost in a general clearing of throats that heralded the entrance of Keith Manson, Muirpark's head teacher. A short, stocky man in his mid-fifties, Manson was nonetheless a figure of authority, his bull neck rising from a frame that was pure muscle. He'd been an amateur boxing champion in his day and still lent a hand at a club in Drumchapel that boasted a steady stream of successful youngsters. One of them had even been picked for the British Olympic team. Never one to smile, Manson's expression was a customary mixture of belligerence and world-weariness, and his legendary temper kept both staff and pupils wary of him.

'Right then,' the man's voice boomed over the assembled staff. 'You can guess why we're here. I'd like to be able to say welcome to you all, hope you had a refreshing break, but frankly those sorts of platitudes will have to wait till a better time. This morning I've got more important things to say to you all.' Manson broke off to stare over his staff. The ripple of talk had died abruptly and the teachers who sat watching and waiting were as quiet as a First Year assembly.

'Unless you've been on a different planet you'll all know that Kyle Kerrigan's father has been released from prison.'

Sandie shot a glance at Eric and was rewarded by a sheepish half-grin.

'It's a terrible business for a young boy like Kyle. He was only in Primary Two when his father was locked up. Now he has to cope with all of this hoo-hah that's going on in the papers. Whether the courts were correct to mete out the sentence they did is not for us to decide. Our responsibility is to the pupils in our care and right now that means Kyle.' There was a pause during which an undercurrent of muttering broke out. 'And no, before anyone asks, James will not be returning to school.'

Maggie listened to the collective sigh of relief from the teachers around her. James Kerrigan had been trouble with a capital T and his departure from Muirpark Secondary was good news. But the assembled staff quietened again as Manson continued.

'Kyle is now back living in Drumchapel with his father and brothers but I have approved a placement request from his grandmother and he will be continuing his education here. I just wanted you all to be aware of the situation and to keep a friendly eye on the boy. He's never been any trouble to us and has never come into the orbit of Strathclyde's finest, I'm glad to say. Speaking of which, congratulations are surely in order for a certain Detective Chief Inspector?' he added as an aside, directing his gaze at Maggie. She felt the colour rise to her cheeks as a few people turned and stared. Her husband, DCI William Lorimer, had been involved in a sensational murder case over the summer months, a case that had also made newspaper headlines.

'Oh, and would you see me after this meeting, Mrs Lorimer? As Kyle's year teacher I'd like a word with you.'

Maggie felt her heart sink. She'd expected it but it was still a horrible thing to have to endure. Being Kyle Kerrigan's year teacher had been a joy for the past three years. He had grown from a shy wee boy into a genuinely nice lad who wasn't

12

afraid to speak out in class. And the fact that English was his favourite subject had made their relationship all the better. Maggie had been looking forward to being his Standard Grade teacher again this year.

'The *gentlemen* of the press will be here later this morning,' Manson continued, deliberately making the word sound dirty. 'I must advise all of you to steer clear of them unless I have particularly asked you to give some sort of comment regarding Kyle. They are bound to target some of his pals, so be on the lookout for anyone hanging around the school gates. The janitors have been told to turn them away and a letter is being sent out to parents advising them not to give any interviews.' Manson scowled as he spoke. 'We can't stop them, of course,' he added, looking around as if to catch any one of his staff who might be thinking of supplementing their salary with an exclusive. 'But I hope common sense and decency will prevail. I want Kyle Kerrigan treated with respect, not wrapped up in cotton wool.' There were a few laughs at that statement: Kyle was one of Muirpark's sporting hopes for the future, his prowess in the boxing ring making him a clear favourite with the head teacher. 'Let him get on with his schoolwork. A sense of normality is probably the kindest thing you can give him right now.' He paused again, nodding to them all. 'That's all you need to know just now. A staff memo will be circulated as and when any other matters need to be discussed.'

Manson glanced at his watch. 'We'll reconvene for this afternoon's staff meeting as printed on your agenda. Right, that's all.' The head teacher's fists grasped the lectern in front of him and one by one the staff moved out of the school hall.

'Good luck!' whispered Sandie as she left.

Maggie gave her a weak smile and turned to follow Manson, who was already striding out of the hall.

Keith Manson's office overlooked the main recreational area, its windows facing south. He was known for opening these windows and booming at any late-comers to school, sending them scuttling across the expanse of tarmac. But today the playground was empty and free of the usual crisp packets and sweetie papers that were the bane of Bob-the-Jannie's existence. Maggie glanced out of the window as she took her seat in front of Manson's desk. Beyond the perimeters of the school were rows and rows of tenement buildings, their chimney tops fading into the distance. Today was grey and drizzly, the rain clouds blotting out the hills beyond the river Clyde and the low pressure was already giving Maggie a headache. By lunchtime it would likely be a two-Disprin affair, especially if Manson was on his usual booming form. Rumours about his deafness were legendary. Some said he'd been injured in a knock-out, resulting in his hearing being permanently impaired. Whatever the truth of the matter, Keith

14

Manson's normal speaking voice was several decibels louder than the average person's, a trait that served to increase his formidable status.

He cleared his throat and shuffled a few papers on his desk – signs, Maggie suddenly realised, that betrayed his nervousness. Curious to see such unexpected body language from their normally stern head teacher, Maggie relaxed back into her armchair, clasping her hands around her knees and watching Manson's face.

'I've never encountered a situation quite like this before,' Manson began, his eyes focused on the paperknife he was now fiddling with. 'Of course we've had bereavements, some sudden, but not circumstances . . .' His voice tailed off in a sigh.

Maggie's eyebrows rose in surprise. Big, bluff Manson lost for words?

'Your husband is no doubt used to things like this,' he said suddenly, staring at Maggie. 'But it's not something a teacher expects to come across in their career.'

Maggie nodded, feeling a trifle foolish. What did he want her to say? That she was accustomed to death in all its grisly forms? Bill told her things about his cases, of course he did, but usually he spared her the more lurid details.

'A pupil's father being a murderer, you mean, Mr Manson?' she asked.

Manson nodded his head, his eyes wandering back to all the paraphernalia upon his desk. 'It was a horrible business. Do you remember it?'

'Yes, vaguely. Bill wasn't involved in that case, though.'

'Sweeney, the victim, was out late at night near a pub when he was set upon by Kerrigan. That's one story. Kerrigan pleaded self-detence and there was enough to suggest that Sweeney had initiated the fight. Had a knife on him. Kerrigan left him to bleed to death in some alleyway.' Manson's voice was bitter. 'Nobody saw a thing.'

'There was quite a bit of forensic evidence,' Maggie murmured.

'Be that as it may, we have a seven-day wonder on our hands now that the papers have chosen to make a thing of Kerrigan's release. Must be stuck for real news,' he growled. 'Anyway, our job is to ensure that Kyle is kept as free from gossip and speculation as possible. I meant what I said about keeping life normal for him. What I want to ask you is to try to keep the lad as busy as you can. Give him jobs to do, things that will take up his free time, stop him from thinking too much.' He gave Maggie the famous Manson Gimlet Stare.

'At least the PE department gives him plenty time for his training,' Maggie offered.

'Aye,' Manson replied. 'We could go down in history if things work out right for Kyle Kerrigan.' His expression softened. 'Boy's got the makings of a real champion.'

Maggie closed her classroom door and leaned against it. For a couple of days it would be a haven of peace and tranquillity till the kids returned on Thursday. She looked around her room and smiled. This was her private domain, her own wee world. Even after a teacher exchange programme when she'd been away for several months she had returned to the same classroom. She walked across to the window and stared out for a moment looking over the rows of tenement rooftops, their slates slick with rain. To her right there were trees screening the bowling green and cricket pitch, a view she enjoyed during the winter months when the trees were bare and she could sometimes make out the shape of distant hills peeking in between the chimney tops. But not today. After the longest, hottest summer the city had ever known, the rains had finally come and Glasgow was now blanketed in a misty drizzle.

The Detective Chief Inspector's wife gave herself a shake. There was such a lot still to do before term began, so she'd better get a move on. But first she ought to give some thought to Kyle Kerrigan. Picking up the Fourth Year timetables, she spread them out in a fan until she saw his name. A quick glance showed Kyle's subject choices; English, French, Physics, Maths, Geography and Chemistry were all slotted into different periods of the week. If Maggie's predictions were correct he could gain top passes in all of his subjects next session. And then he'd be well placed to sit five Highers; easily enough to take him into Glasgow University. Kyle had spoken to Maggie about wanting to read

English Literature, a fact that had secretly delighted her. She had loads of lessons already prepared and was looking forward to taking this top class, with one eye firmly on next year's Higher exam.

But what would happen now that the boy was back in Drumchapel? Would his father encourage him just as his grandmother had? Somehow Maggie doubted that. The older boys had been so different, she mused. Thomas had left school with no qualifications other than an aptitude for getting out of difficult situations: the eldest Kerrigan boy had been the sort who'd made arrows for other more gullible lads to fire. And James had been the bane of her existence last year: thank the Lord he'd decided not to come back for Sixth Year.

Kyle was so unlike them: a keen sportsman and a lad with lots of academic potential. And was that all to change now with his father's release from jail? Maggie's lips tightened in a thin hard line. The boys' mother had died of cancer shortly before her husband's conviction. And hadn't his Defence made plenty of that? she thought cynically, remembering a newspaper article about Kerrigan's shortened term of imprisonment. The Kerrigan children had become victims, too, she told herself: no mother and a father fresh out of Barlinnie.

Life wasn't fair. Surely she should have learned that by now.

CHAPTER 3

The Argo Centre was really an acronym for The Saint Andrews Recreation and Games Organisation, a fact that almost everybody in Drumchapel had long forgotten since its construction back in the seventies. Glasgow humour being what it was, it was referred to affectionately as the Aggro Centre.

Drumchapel itself had started out as an escape for slum-dwelling families to a newer, fresher life outside the city. The post-war years had been a time of high ideals and lofty aspirations. Close to the leafier suburbs of Bearsden and Knightswood, the City Fathers had hoped to create a social housing programme that would lift its citizens up to emulate their more affluent neighbours. The planners who had shared this vision were ultimately disappointed to see parts of it develop into the sorts of ghettos from which its original residents had tried to escape. Now its population had one of the highest levels of unemployment in Glasgow and drug dealing was rife within its streets.

The Argo had been built to try to relieve some

of the social problems of Drumchapel's youth, namely giving them somewhere to go and something to do. And it had been successful to varying degrees. Wee girls in pigtails and leotards regularly tapped their way from the baby class right through to senior level, some even going on to the famous dance school at Knightswood Academy. But it was their boxing club that had gained most prestige over the years. Several Scottish champions had learned their skills at the Argo under the fierce eye of Dave Savage, himself a former gold medallist.

Kyle Kerrigan aimed a series of jabs at the punchbag suspended from the ceiling. Around him the lads were sweating, some doing star-jumps, others press-ups, a few like him were battering their demons out against the solid leather bags.

'Change!' Dave yelled out and the boys moved around the hall, star-jumpers taking their turn at the bags, others stifling a groan of relief as they stood upright. The smell of sweat lingered in the air as Kyle ignored Dave's command and kept his eye focused on the bag. Jab. Jab-jab. Jab-jab-jab. His hands flew out in a rhythm, his eyes narrowing as if the dark blue bag was indeed an opponent to be watched and feared. At fifteen, Kyle was one of the older boys in the boxing club. Most of the lads were twelve or thirteen, wiry wee fellows and whippet-thin. Kyle had been just like them, devoted to the sport and ambitious as hell, not understanding why so many of the big boys who were really, really good had drifted away from the twice-weekly training.

'Girls!' he'd heard Dave snort in disgust when some of the dads had been talking. He supposed it could be, though he'd never let his friendship with Julie affect his sport. Some of the older lads were winching right enough, but it was more than that. James and Tam, his older brothers, had mocked his loyalty to the boxing club.

'Away an' rin roon that hall. Much good it'll dae ye!' Tam had spat at him earlier that evening. 'Cannae say I ever needed tae learn tae fight,' he'd added with a grin that had made James laugh.

'Tam could pit the heid in tae onybody roon here. Nae fancy footwork fur him, eh, Tam?'

Kyle had picked up his gym bag and left, their taunts ringing in his ears. Maybe that's why some of the older lads had given up; it wasn't cool any more to go down the Argo when your nights could be filled with the sorts of stuff Tam and James got up to. Tam Kerrigan was number one dealer round their bit and James looked set to follow in their older brother's footsteps. Not that James wasn't clever. He'd managed to find an apprenticeship with his pal's father who was a master joiner, and that was a good sort of trade to follow. Joiners were dead well paid, James had boasted when he'd told them he was leaving school. But money didn't last long in Jamesey's pockets and Tam's preferred trade was much more lucrative.

21

Kyle aimed his punches at the bag. One for James. One for Tam.

'Change!' Dave commanded and he glanced over his shoulder at a star-jumper eyeing up his punchbag. Reluctantly Kyle let his arms fall to his sides and he moved away to let the boy have his turn.

Standing against the cream-painted brick wall, Kyle Kerrigan watched the boys go through their paces. Most of them wore jogging pants and T-shirts, some revealing their affiliation to a particular football club, something that could give away their religious upbringing. But such things were ignored inside the Argo. Sectarianism had no place here. You were a boxer first and left any of that stuff outside. Saint Columba's boys mixed happily with the Proddy boys on Mondays and Thursdays; what their teams did the rest of the week was immaterial. Besides, these lads were all keen on the boxing. Footie wasn't their first love.

He watched as Dave put on a head guard that matched his dark red boxing gloves and beckoned one of the smaller boys into the ring. The lad had the same determined expression on his face as they all had when facing an opponent: tight, screwed-up brow, mouth firmly shut, teeth clamped against a gum shield. (Dave was always going on about keeping your mouth shut so your jaw didn't get broken.) Kyle saw the boy's feet drag one way and the other as Dave put him through his paces, correcting his footwork, making him jab, keeping him coming at the big man who put himself up as a human punchbag for all these aspiring boxers.

Kyle's eyes wandered across to Gordon Simpson. At seventeen, Gordie was the oldest boy in the club and had had the most fights. A tall, thin lad with a buzz cut above his pale face, Gordie always looked as if he'd come out of the Bar-L, as Barlinnie was affectionately known to Glaswegians. But it was no prison pallor; Gordon suffered from a funny kind of skin disorder and couldn't stay in the sun without masses of special cream on. This past summer must've been a nightmare for him, Kyle thought; day after day of scorching hot sun. He'd gone up the park with his pals, laid on the grass, mucked about with a football, his own skin turning a continental shade of brown. He'd felt funny when some of the lassies he recognised from his class at school had shouted out insults at him that were really compliments in disguise.

'Right. Kyle. Gordon.' Dave waved his gloved hands in the air and someone set the clock back to zero.

Gordie gave a weak grin as he faced the younger boy. He might be older and taller but everyone knew that Kyle Kerrigan was the one with the makings of a true champion.

As Kyle approached, fists bunched, eyes straight ahead, he could sense the other lads and their fathers gathered around to watch as if it was something a bit special. Balancing on the balls of his feet, Kyle threw the first punch and saw Gordie's head jerk to the side, but not before his glove made contact. He would not hurt him but he'd make sure that his jabs went home, keeping his own guard and not letting Gordie near him.

The three-minute bell sounded and the boys tapped each other's gloves then ducked under the ropes.

Kyle nodded to the coach who gave him a grin of approval. Dave wasn't given to praising his lads, but you knew when he was pleased. The boys moved out of the way so the older men could dismantle the ring and put it away till the next training night.

Outside, the dusk was growing and Kyle was grateful for the slight cool on his skin as he turned out of Halgreen Road towards his own bit. School began tomorrow. He shrugged. It wasn't so bad and he'd see his mates again. Muirpark was somewhere to pass the time till he could be back here. Kyle cast a backward glance at the Argo, its door scabbed where generations of wee neds had kicked it. Tucked in amongst the rows of houses, it looked shabby and run down but each time Kyle Kerrigan arrived at that familiar entrance it was like he was coming home.

CHAPTER 4

The squeezing sensation in his head came back stronger this time and he slumped into the armchair, feeling its metal frame bite through the thin cotton covering. He shifted a bit until his back moulded against the seat cushion. If he just sat still for a minute, took a few deep breaths, it would pass. It usually did. Eyes closed, he let himself drift, let the feeling overwhelm him. Morphing into gossamer, he floated: insubstantial, light and bright . . .

Outside the buzz-saw sound of garden machinery cut through the pale threads that kept him dangling up above the chair, and brought him crashing down again. He opened his eyes, head thumping now, examining his surroundings. The room he was in should have been so familiar. The furniture hadn't changed since he'd left; it was the same mismatch of rubbish that he'd known all his life. A flicker in his brain made him see how things had been the day she had moved in. That had been a summer's day too, sunshine spilling into the room making everything seem bright and gaudy. Even the tired brown armchairs could have been described as russet, he supposed. The wallpaper was still the same brown-and-cream pattern of overlapping loops (whose repetitions he'd counted over and over again), the dingy white lampshade still hanging at a rakish angle. He'd never bothered trying to fix it. She had seen the place as a temporary stopping-off point, nothing more.

Anna had wanted a place by the seaside. She'd talked about it as they lay on top of the bed that first afternoon, the dust fairies (her expression) flickering in the still air above them; how they'd get a wee place of their own, how she'd do it up. He'd listened, never saying a word, imagining the sound of waves murmuring on a distant shoreline, sea birds pecking among the pebbles.

But the house had changed and that old, easy familiarity was gone for ever. The bookshelves were empty for a start. Where were the rows of the *Reader's Digest Omnibus* and all those ancient discards from the local library? He remembered their faded linen spines and the faint whiff of dust. But now there were just three empty shelves, their original varnish scabby with age. Had he sold them? Thrown them away? A sense of panic began to creep into his thoughts and he had to shake his head to dislodge it. It didn't help to remember everything.

He looked around, trying to see what else was different. They'd put a peephole into the front door. The man who'd helped him with his stuff had remarked on it. 'Keeps you safe,' he'd said. That was the sort of thing they were fond of telling him. Keeps you safe or Concerned for your welfare: these were their favourites. He didn't care. They were really only anxious to be seen to be following the guide-lines that some clown had decided to set in place. They were like wee puppies, tongues lolling out of their mouths, eyes hopeful for a crumb of praise, or even a thank you. Mostly he ignored them but some-times, just for sheer devilment, he stared them out, then, just as their gaze had dropped, he'd say it. Thank you. Gravely, sonorously, he'd say it, catching the doubt in their eyes as they tried to gauge if he was being sincere or sarcastic.

He was glad when that one had finally left today. It had taken all of his patience not to give the man a good slap as he'd twittered on about how this worked and how that worked. It was his own home, for Christ's sake! Not some mangy bedsit he'd never clapped eyes on before.

The headache was subsiding now. There was no need to take any medication. There was no need to do anything at all, simply rest and relax, relax, relax, relax . . .

CHAPTER 5

Julie Donaldson, her long blonde hair caught by a sudden gust of wind, stood on the pavement, waving and waving until the Range Rover was out of sight, the ubiquitous Jane Norman schoolbag slung across her shoulder. At the end of last term Julie had hung around, waiting for Kyle to appear, but she wouldn't be doing that any more she told herself, turning to pick out the staff-room windows, wondering if *he* was there.

Now she could see some of the girls in her own year group and her special pal, Samantha. Julie waved at her, her pace quickening. From the corner of her eye she spotted two young lads in the reception area staring but she just ignored them. Let them stare, she thought as her friend grabbed her in a hug. She was done flirting with stupid wee schoolboys.

'See you later.' Samantha turned to catch her older brother's eye before linking arms with Julie. A group of other Fourth Years were already bearing down on them, their girlish voices becoming louder as each tried to outdo the other.

'See you, Tim.' Julie gave Samantha's brother a

wee smile, gratified to see him blush. It was cool being one of the seniors now. And maybe certain people would take her a bit more seriously.

More pupils streamed through the gates, following the girls and their friends towards the school buildings. Over in the staff car park, doors slammed shut as teachers arrived to begin their working day. Some members of staff did arrive on foot, though, and the kids instinctively moved away from them; engaging in conversation with a teacher was just so uncool. A tall young man, a slim document case under his arm, stopped to ask directions from one of the younger girls. Her face colouring up, the pupil pointed to the main entrance then rejoined her pals and much sniggering as the man followed her directions. There were always new teachers or students at the start of the autumn term and this one wasn't at all bad looking, they thought, measuring up his appearance against their favourite pop stars.

'Don't we have to wait till Manson gives us the okay?' Kyle asked. The Fourth Year lads were milling around the PE block, sneaking a look down the corridor that led to the place that everyone had been talking about: their Fourth Year common room. It was evident that the boys were keen to inhabit one of the rooms that were given as a special privilege to senior pupils, but still respectful, in a kind of fearful way, of their head teacher.

29

'Aye, I think we have to have assembly first. Let's go and see if the team lists are up, eh?' one lad suggested.

Kyle let himself be carried along with the others but he kept looking over his shoulder, hopeful of seeing Julie. They'd not spoken since that day in the park, though a couple of text messages had passed between them, and Kyle was anxious to see how she'd behave towards him.

'Hey, you're playing with us this term, Kerrigan!' Ali, a whippetthin Pakistani boy who was the First Eleven's best striker, clapped him on the shoulder.

'Let's see!' Kyle pushed his way to the notice-board and looked. Ali was right. His name was there, in the middle of an alphabetical list. For a moment he simply stared at it. He wasn't all *that* good at footie, he knew that. Second Eleven was where he expected to be until at least Fifth Year. So what were they playing at? Had he done better last year than he thought? Or had his name been added to this list for a different reason? Kyle listened to the congratulations from his mates with a few insults thrown in for good measure. But while he pretended to be pleased and even faked a grin, his overwhelming feeling was one of puzzlement.

'Off to the bog,' he said, turning on his heel and heading for the boys' toilets across the corridor. He left them still crowded around the noticeboard, commenting on names and dates, only Ali looking after him with a strange expression on his face.

Inside the cubicle, Kyle slumped forward, head in his hands. He didn't want to be in the First Eleven football team. Didn't want to be here. And even if Julie was all over him like a rash, Kyle suddenly knew that it wouldn't change a thing now that his father had come back into his life.

Morning assembly on the first day of a new term was split into three parts due to the number of pupils that could be accommodated in the main hall. While the juniors were being given Keith Manson's annual words of wisdom, the other year groups drifted into their year teacher's classrooms. It would be some time after morning interval before Maggie's group was taken downstairs for their turn.

'Good morning, nice to see you all.' She beamed as she closed the door, the bell signalling the official start to the school year. 'Oh, Jessica, sorry,' she added, opening the door again to admit a tall girl who glided into the room. Jessica King smiled vaguely and drifted towards the back. Jessica had never been on time for school as long as she had known her and Maggie guessed that it had ceased to bother the girl around the end of Secondary One. Her disrupted education, caused by her family's many moves from country to country, meant that she was the oldest student in the class yet she remained quite unconscious of having the sort of cosmopolitan glamour that her contemporaries lacked. Maggie watched the girl sail past the desks,

31

oblivious to the boys whose eyes automatically followed her. They couldn't help it, Maggie thought, nobody could. At sixteen Jessica was everything a teenage boy fantasised about: long dark hair (still damp from this morning's shower), porcelain skin, huge blue eyes framed in lashes that looked too thick and luxuriant to be real (they were) and a poise that came from a gene pool that had spawned generations of gorgeous women. Jessica (she had not shortened it to Jess and never in a million years would she answer to Jessie) sat at the back of the room next to Amanda Hamilton. Maggie considered them for a few moments; they were like two Arab mares, manes tossed back, bloodlines showing an elegance of breeding. But where Jessica took her appearance for granted, Manda was different. It wasn't that the red-haired girl craved attention, Maggie thought, more that she enjoyed warming herself in the sun of admiring glances.

Kyle Kerrigan was sitting on the far side of the classroom, next to the wall. He was leaning his head against it now, eyes on the magazine that the boy next to him had spread over the two desks.

'Timetables,' Maggie announced briskly, handing them out around the room. 'You will see that there are a few gaps,' she paused at the outbreak of cheers and grinned, 'but they'll be filled up with plenty for you to do. Remember we've got Charities' Week to organise this year so you'll need time for all of that, then you have to arrange your own Christmas ball.'

'When do we get into the common room?' someone asked.

'Later on today,' Maggie replied. 'Once assembly's over the janitor will come up and give you the keys.'

'And can we do anything we like to it?' another voice demanded.

Maggie raised her eyes to heaven. The janitor grumbled long and hard about having to white-wash the senior common rooms every year, but he did it anyway, covering each successive year group's graffiti so that the walls were blank slates for more creativity. 'Anything within reason,' she murmured. 'You'll still come here for registration every morning after the first bell and I'll be here if anybody needs to see me.' She made a conscious effort not to look in Kyle Kerrigan's direction though she could sense his eyes were trained on her. His face bore traces of bruising, something that might well have happened in the boxing ring but for some reason those scars had made Maggie shiver and wonder exactly who had inflicted them.

'Right, next thing to do is to elect a form captain. Someone who is always at school *on time*,' she continued, deliberately looking at Jessica and producing a few grins. 'Anybody want to volunteer?'

'I'll do it.'

Maggie raised her eyebrows then pasted a smile on her face as Kyle's hand went up. 'Okay. All in favour?'

A forest of hands shot up, not one of them going

to deny this boy anything he wanted, not even a minor distinction like being Fourth Year form captain. Maggie nodded. 'Fine. Sorted. Thanks,' she said, but somewhere deep inside she had a queasy feeling that Kyle Kerrigan had sussed them all out. In fact, now that she looked his way she could see that he was watching for her reaction and, as she caught his glance, she blushed.

Jackie Montgomery smiled at the man as he raised his hand to say goodbye. Nice chap, she thought absently. Well mannered, too, not like some of the teachers here who treated the secretaries as though they were an inferior species. And such a lovely speaking voice, Jackie mused, watching as he pushed open the swing doors. She could've listened to him all day. Pity he'd only come to deliver some papers from the agency. The secretary shook her head and made a face. Probably had a wife and three kids at home, she decided gloomily; all the good-looking ones seem to have been snapped up early. Anyway, now that the Muirpark kids were back she'd have her work cut out with no time to daydream about passing strangers.

When the morning interval bell rang, Maggie hoped Kyle would stay behind, talk to her as he'd usually done last term, but he was one of the first to leave the room and Maggie was left with the feeling that somehow she'd let him down. Or was

Kyle simply trying to avoid any discussion about the return of his father?

The clatter of feet in the corridor died away as one by one the rooms emptied. Maggie sat, relishing a few moments of quietness. Arching her back, she stretched then relaxed, massaging the muscles below the nape of her neck. A glance at her watch showed she'd need to stir herself if she wanted a morning coffee. The English base several doors along had facilities for making tea or coffee but she preferred the buzz of the staffroom two floors below, where she could join her friends from other departments.

The stairs were empty and her heels sounded distinct and hollow as Maggie made her way down but she paused, mid-stride, when she suddenly heard shouting coming from the floor below. What on earth? As she leaned over the banister, the sounds became louder, more insistent: a girl's voice screaming abuse, then another voice, one that she knew . . . Maggie moved forward, sensing trouble.

'I hate you!' the girl cried out, bursting through the door from the first-floor corridor.

Later Maggie would try to recall exactly what had taken place but at that moment all she saw was an angry, tear-stained face and blonde hair flying as the pupil stormed down the final flight of stairs. Then the door opened again and Eric Chalmers stood there, his face chalk-white.

'No, Julie. Don't do this!' he called. Then,

stepping forward as if to follow her, the RE teacher stopped dead, seeing Maggie Lorimer standing just above him. The look Eric gave her was one of sheer bewilderment, then, with a shake of his head, he slipped back through the door.

Maggie hovered on the stairs, uncertain whether to follow the girl. Or should she go in to see Eric? Standing there, dithering, she simply couldn't decide. Was it any of her business? a little voice asked and, as if in answer, she moved on down, letting her feet take her towards the staffroom.

Later she would come to regret her moment of indecision.

But by that time the evil that had been let loose would have seeped into every corner of Muirpark Secondary School, destroying so many lives on its insidious journey.

CHAPTER 6

'Thank you, sir.' Detective Chief Inspector William Lorimer put down the phone and allowed a grin of pleasure to spread across his face. It was a face that had seen too much human suffering and over the years the frown lines had deepened, making him appear constantly at odds with his world. But the smile changed such an impression in an instant, lighting up the keen blue eyes and softening the determined jaw. Lorimer did not often indulge himself in moments of self-gratification but this one was well deserved. To have news that he was to receive an official commendation was a little bit special, after all. The murder case had almost ended in disaster, and Lorimer was human enough to give a shudder at the memory of facing that mad gunman at close quarters.

His hand hovered over the telephone again, then dropped. She'd be in some meeting or other. Besides, it would be better to tell her face to face when they were both home tonight. Lorimer's case-load was as busy as usual but there was no reason for staying on too late. He leaned back in his chair, surveying his surroundings. He'd been DCI in the Division for a good few years now and was comfortable in this room. Too comfortable, maybe, a small voice told him; a voice that reminded the DCI of his wife, who insisted his promotion to Detective Superintendent was long overdue. Lorimer let his eyes wander over the maps of Glasgow and the Van Gogh prints that he'd hung to remind him of a world outside his own, then realised he was searching for a space to put the commendation. He wasn't a vain man but this was a matter for genuine pride and his team deserved the reflected glory such an accolade would bring. So he would display the certificate, not somewhere in-your-face but – he let his eyes roam around – yes, over there above the filing cabinets. That would do. It was directly behind him so he didn't have to look at it day in, day out. But anyone who was seated opposite would be reminded that DCI William Lorimer was a hands-on sort of person, not the type of senior officer who wallowed in a morass of administration.

'Sir?' The voice interrupting Lorimer's thoughts made him whirl around in his chair. He blinked for a moment then the grin reappeared on his face.

'Didn't recognise you without your uniform, Annie,' he joked, making the woman blush. Annie Irvine had recently realised her ambition of joining the CID and now she was standing there in his office, almost a stranger in her smart new trouser suit.

'I see Tulliallan's worked its magic, then,' he went on, referring to her recent training course at the Scottish Police College and instantly the tension was broken as his newest detective constable grinned back at him. They were lucky to have kept her, he suddenly thought. Irvine might have been sent anywhere within Strathclyde once her promotion had come through. And now that Niall Cameron had stepped up to detective sergeant, this was just the icing on Lorimer's cake.

Then the telephone rang again and DC Irvine stood still, uncertain whether to stay in the DCI's room or withdraw. Hovering there as Lorimer answered, she saw the change in his face immediately; the laughter lines around his mouth disappeared and the lips became thinner, a bitter line that immediately told Annie Irvine that something grim was being relayed to her boss.

'Right,' he said, then put the phone down, rising from his seat and turning to Irvine.

'A missing child,' he said. 'We need to get cracking.'

The orange cat looked up expectantly, tail erect, as Maggie emptied the tin of food into its plastic bowl.

'There you are, Chancer, at least one of you comes home in time for dinner.' She sighed, placing the cat's food onto a mat on the kitchen floor. It was a humid evening and she had left the back door open to air the place. Leaning against the kitchen counter, Maggie Lorimer gazed out into the garden. The rain had stopped now and a weak shaft of sunlight made diamond sparkles on the grass. Somewhere unseen amidst the trees a blackbird sang, its liquid notes piercing the murky air. The headache that had persisted all day was now a dull throb but listening to the bird's pure, clear song seemed to soothe all her sore places.

She'd already prepared all of tomorrow's lessons so the evening ahead was hers to enjoy. If Bill had been home . . . Maggie gave a shuddering sigh. What hell must that young mother be going through? Somewhere out there a wee girl was lost. Snatched from the pavement outside her own home. A huge number of officers had been deployed in the search and DCI William Lorimer had his own team scouring every likely corner in his patch of the city. It was times like these when Maggie truly appreciated her husband's job. So what if another night went by and she was left to her own devices? All those lonely hours were worth it if he could do something that would reunite that little family.

One of the local children had noticed a car draw up, had seen a woman pull the child in, then watched them drive away fast. Maggie shook her head as if to make the image of that moment disappear. There was nothing that she could do about it. Asking herself who would do such a wicked, wicked thing was futile and knowing what lengths a paedophile might go to only compounded her misery. Sometimes being a policeman's wife gave too much insight into certain crimes, she thought sadly. An overactive imagination didn't help either. Maggie's eyes fell on the small pile of books she'd bought at the Edinburgh Book Festival. A good read would take her mind off this matter, at least for a wee while, she decided, picking up one of the new titles that had taken her fancy.

When the doorbell rang, Kim was out of the chair like a shot, hope making her eyes gleam.

'Ms Fraser?' Two people stood on her doorstep, a man and a woman. She didn't recognise them, hadn't remembered seeing them earlier on, but Kim Fraser knew by that flash of warrant cards that they were plain clothes police. Letting her hands fall weakly by her sides she took a step backwards and nodded. 'Aye. Come in.'

She'd been going to ask them if there was any sign of . . . but the words died on her lips as soon as she saw their faces – closed and weary. Kim Fraser had become an expert on reading faces in the last few hours: she'd seen eyes that regarded her with a kind of wary sympathy, and searched them for any sign that told her something, anything about their opinion on finding Nancy. They hadn't found a thing. Kim slumped back into the armchair, her fingers wrapped around Nancy's rag doll, a scruffy wee toy that was worn with handling. They were saying something but she couldn't respond, hot tears melting her cheeks, strangling a voice that had grown hoarse with weeping.

★ ★ ★

The morning sky was stained with shafts of pink against the banks of grey, a new day beginning when a further search for the missing child could begin Lorimer leaned against the windowsill for a moment, looking out at his garden. The trees were motionless at this early hour and there was no sign of life. It was that time between night and day when the world seemed to be holding its breath. Then, somewhere from the depth of the trees, a collared dove began its monotone cooing over and over into the cold air.

She could still be out there, he told himself. With somebody. They'd made little progress during the long hours of darkness but now daylight held a promise of renewed effort. But also the awareness that every minute ticking by meant a growing fear for the little girl's safety.

He unbuckled his belt, letting his trousers fall where he stood, and slipped into his side of the bed. A few hours' sleep were essential if he were to be sharp enough for what lay ahead. Beside him Maggie murmured in her sleep, her body warm and drowsy beneath the duvet. Resisting the urge to caress her into wakefulness, he turned on his side, drew his knees up and closed his eyes. He forced himself into that dark familiar place, letting his mind escape for a short while, banishing thoughts of Nancy Fraser and of what might have happened to her.

★   ★   ★

The dream returned and he knew what lay ahead. The tunnel beckoned him forwards and, in the way of dreams, he found himself helpless to resist. As always, the walls were covered in thick green slime that lost its colour as the darkness swallowed him up. And then the sense of terror closed in on him and he was unable to breathe, choking in the dense blackness, panic suffusing his senses, bringing him to his knees where he acknowledged this awful weakness, hiding his eyes from the suffocating walls and roof that were closing in on him, hearing his own voice cry out.

Even on waking the tears were real, as was the feeling of shame that swept over him. How could he be so unmanned by a dream? It was as if somewhere in the deepest recesses of his soul his one weakness had been found out by some fiendish spirit sent to mock him. *You're claustrophobic,* it seemed to taunt him, *you're scared of the dark narrow places, aren't you?*

Lorimer lay on his back, letting the images recede, grateful that other thoughts came thick and fast to obliterate this nightmare, thoughts of a small girl and her weeping mother. But even as he sank back under the duvet, he could feel the sweaty dampness on his chest, a physical sign of his continuing frailty.

CHAPTER 7

The sound of the alarm drilled into her brain, her hand already reaching to stop its noise even before she was properly awake. Maggie groaned softly, rolling back beneath the warm bedding, cuddling into her husband's side. She hadn't even noticed when he had come home, Maggie thought to herself. Must have been sound asleep for once. Wrapping her arms around his chest, she fitted her naked body to his, feeling a stirring as he struggled against the depths of sleep. Just a couple of minutes, she thought, no more or she'd doze off again and be late for work.

The memory came to her, hauling Maggie from slumber more effectively than any alarm: Julie Donaldson charging down the stairs away from Eric – and that expression on his face that Maggie simply could not fathom. Guilt? Fear? Or had it been a sort of puzzled disappointment? Sitting up now on the edge of their bed she tried to analyse what she had really seen. But somehow the image in Maggie's mind kept shifting to the one of Eric's shining face when he'd told Sandie and herself about the new baby. That was Eric as he usually was; a 'shiny, happy person' Sandie Carmichael called him and she was right. He was always smiling and cheerful, a fact that didn't endear him to all of the staff. There were some at Muirpark Secondary whose blacker outlook was thrown into sharper relief by the young man's sunny attitude and who curled a cynical lip at his Christian way of life. Maggie gave a shudder. Thank God she'd been the one to see that little incident, not one of the older, hard-bitten lot who might have read something salacious into it.

As she dressed for work, Maggie remembered that Julie Donaldson was one of Eric's unlikely Scripture Union kids. Had she been at his summer camp? And if so, what on earth had prompted that weird outburst?

'And, dear Father, please let us remember Nancy Fraser. Let whoever has taken her feel compassion for the little girl and her family and let her be safely returned to them. Amen.'

An echo of amens sounded around the classroom as heads lifted just in time to hear the morning bell.

'Right. Registration. Thanks for coming and see you all at prayers tomorrow. Keep bright!' Eric Chalmers nodded to each pupil as they filed out of his room, answering their smiles with one of his own. But when the last of them had left and the place was empty and quiet, Eric Chalmers chewed his lower lip, a caring expression clouding his features. What on earth was it like for that family? He thought of baby Ashleigh. How could anyone steal a child away from its mother like that? It didn't bear thinking about. But they had thought about it in prayer, had interceded for their welfare, handed it over to God. Eric shook his head. There was nothing a mere schoolteacher could do but pray. Giving it over to the Lord was all he could do. That, and encourage the kids to do the same.

She hadn't been to prayers this morning, Eric thought. No surprise there, really, after the way she'd come on to him. How did it feel to be fifteen and have a crush on your teacher? He'd tried to reason with her, but Julie wasn't a reasonable sort of girl. The power of her rage had astonished him. He'd grabbed hold of her wrists after she'd lashed out at him, trying to subdue the passion that was at work in her. But instead of calming her down it had made things worse. Julie had begun to shout and scream and before he knew what was happening she was out of his room and flying down the stairs.

He had a few minutes' respite before the first period began but as Eric Chalmers closed his eyes to pray that Julie Donaldson would come to her senses, the words simply wouldn't come and he was left instead with images of her tear-streaked face and her protestations of how much she loved him, ringing in his ears.

From his classroom window Eric could see the pavement that ran around the school disappearing down to the busy main road beyond. An elderly man was walking slowly behind his little dog, a nondescript mutt that bore some passing resemblance to a terrier. He stopped to let another man pass him by, giving a friendly nod. Life was all so normal out there, Eric thought, staring at the two men.

As if the teacher's thoughts had reached out beyond the school railings, the younger man looked up, pausing for a moment, his eyes searching for something. Eric shrugged. Maybe he'd been a Muirpark pupil in years gone by?

Then the bell rang out, breaking the spell, and the man resumed his walk as Eric turned away from the window, the moment forgotten.

The headlines screamed out from every newsstand in the city that morning. Nancy Fraser was still missing and every hour that passed suggested that it would be a tiny corpse that would be returned to her grief-stricken mother. Not that the journalists had written such a thing outright, but it was there just the same – a feeling, an unspoken thought in everyone's mind, suggested by a turn of phrase or a memory of other, bleaker outcomes in child abduction. People read what the papers wanted to tell them. Not good news, not the hours of sheer slog that had kept many officers away from their own homes and families, trawling woods and parkland for signs of the missing girl. Nor did they have any inkling about the extent of the investigation, the masses of Internet files that had been screened to see if any similarity existed between this abduction and any others in the UK.

The vehicle that had been spotted by a neighbour's child was a white hatchback but beyond that the description was sadly lacking. The older girl, who had been kept off school that day, had been shown picture after picture of cars similar to the one she had seen but, instead of focusing her mind, the pages and pages of images had proved confusing. Now the police were left running around, looking for other sightings of the white car, hopeful that another more reliable witness would come forward.

Kim Fraser snatched the telephone off its hook at the first ring.

'Hello?' The question dangled there, breathless and full of anticipation.

'Tom Scott, the *Gazette*. May we—'

Kim clicked the voice into silence, tears welling up in her eyes. She'd hoped and prayed that someone would phone her with news of Nancy. Even with a ransom note, though God alone knew how a single mother on benefits could stretch to the demands of a kidnapper. That nice woman from the Police Family Liaison had told her it was highly unlikely that anyone had taken Nancy for money. But she'd also skirted over the alternatives;

some dirty gang of paedophiles who wanted to film her Nancy doing horrible things . . . no, she wouldn't let her mind go down that route. Safer to think of some other woman taking her child away; some poor soul who couldn't have children, maybe? Nancy might be with a person like that right now, being spoiled with toys that Kim couldn't afford to give her.

The tears flowed for real now, every memory of Nancy's short life unfolding like a length of film: falling pregnant when she'd still been at school, leaving home and setting up here in this wee council flat with Robbie; the hollow empty feeling when he'd walked out and left them both, Nancy a mere six months old and Kim still wanting to be a teenager in love; the struggles between her parents and the social workers when all of them seemed intent on taking Nancy away from her, then these last couple of years when things had settled down and she'd been able to make this place a home for them both, even gaining a modicum of approval from her neighbours who all said what a grand mother she was and how nice she always kept her wee girl.

Now these neighbours would be asking themselves if Kim Fraser was such a good mother after all, if her child could be left playing on the pavement instead of being upstairs in the flat. But Kim had just gone round the back to hang out a basket of washing. She'd seen Nancy skipping through the close with the other kids – had heard the sound of their laughter – they'd wanted to watch all the bigger boys and girls walking to primary school, all shiny with excitement on their first day back.

If only Mrs Doherty hadn't leaned out of her window and started to tell Kim about the new entry system . . . how many minutes had she spent listening to the old woman before Sally MacIlwraith had rushed out onto the green?

Kim closed her eyes, still hearing the words, 'Nancy's mummy! Come quick!' The child had grabbed Kim's hand, dragging her, bewildered, to the pavement where three other toddlers stood staring down a road that was now empty of any cars, especially a white hatchback containing her struggling daughter.

It wasn't her fault, Kim told herself, hugging her knees to her chest. If the entry system had been fixed then the kids couldn't have slipped out without at least one grown-up in tow. And Sally was such a sensible wee lassie, even if she was aye at the doctor's with that chronic asthma. The papers were full of condemnation for the state of the flats; vandals had ripped the heart out of this place and the Council was fed up repairing the damage. It didn't matter to them, did it? It was only folk like Kim Fraser, a single mum who didn't contribute anything to the economy, who lived there. Scum, that's what they were being called. You made a mistake when you were sixteen and spent the rest of your youth paying for it. Now they wanted to ask her – what? For her life story?

Kim shook her head jerking the tears from her wet cheeks. That wouldn't bring Nancy back, would it?

Detective Constable Annie Irvine stood aside as her colleague, John Weir, knocked on yet another door. They'd been at this all morning, along with a few uniformed officers from Cranhill police station. There was a knack to this sort of work, she knew, and her sidekick, DC Weir, just didn't have it. Annie groaned inwardly as the door opened and a man faced them, his unshaven face and rumpled trousers testament to the probability that they'd dragged him out of bed.

'Whitisit?' the man mumbled as Weir showed him his warrant card.

'Sorry to trouble you, sir.' Weir's upbeat expression was surely hurting his face by now, thought Irvine. 'We're making house-to-house inquiries about a missing toddler.'

'Aw, richt. Thon wee lassie frae the next close?' The man's eyes seemed suddenly that bit less bleary. 'Heard aboot it the morn when ah came aff ma shift, so ah did.'

Annie listened as the DC went through his usual spiel then yet another door was closed and they drifted across the landing to the next tenement flat where the tartan-backed nameplate showed the resident to be a D Lindsay. They were getting nowhere fast, Annie thought gloomily. Nobody had seen a thing.

51

'Yes, oh, police?' As soon as she caught sight of their warrant cards the elderly woman standing in the crack of doorway behind a security chain gave a simpering smile. 'Is it about the wee girl? Come on in, will you,' she added, sliding the chain off and opening the door wide. 'A cup of tea?'

Annie and Weir exchanged glances and Weir shrugged. 'Why not? Thank you, Mrs Lindsay,' Weir added.

The old lady wagged her finger. 'It's Miss, Officer, not Mrs,' she told him. 'Never did find my Mister Right,' she added with a schoolgirlish giggle.

Inside the flat Annie could smell the distinctive odour of lavender furniture polish, and images of her late granny's own house with their long-forgotten memories came rushing back. They followed the old woman down the hallway and into a room so reminiscent of a bygone age that it might have come out of a Victorian film set. Annie had heard the tales about people from her granny's day keeping their front rooms for 'good' but, apart from the museum in the People's Palace, she'd never seen this for herself, until now.

'Make yourself comfortable and I'll bring you through the tea. Just made some scones this morning, I'm sure you're ready for a wee break,' Miss Lindsay rattled on, 'then I can tell you all about poor little Nancy.'

Annie and Weir looked at one another as the old dear left the room. 'D'you think she really has any information?' Annie asked.

Weir shrugged his shoulders. 'Who knows? She strikes me as a bit of a lonely old soul. Maybe she just wants our company. Mind you, she's not daft – keeps her chain on the door.'

'It's not the most salubrious area of the city,' Annie told him drily.

While they waited for the old lady to return with their tea, she looked around the room. A front parlour, she knew, used to be kept for special occasions: visits from the clergy, Christmas and New Year celebrations. They could add a house-to-house call by CID in the twenty-first century, she thought drily. The room looked as if it hadn't been used for years, though Miss Lindsay must have kept it well dusted for every piece of china on the mantelpiece gleamed in this subdued light. And it wasn't just any old tat, Annie realised, crossing the room for a closer look. The little figurines arranged in ones and twos looked like Staffordshire pottery and she was willing to bet they were the real thing. It was a dismal morning, with rain mizzling down on the streets outside and only a dull light coming from the large bay windows, their heavy green velvet drapes partially obscuring the four rectangles of glass. All the furniture was dark too, adding to the general air of a room that had been preserved from a different era: an upright piano stood against one wall, a large picture of a dreary Highland glen above it, the three piece suite in its original bottle-green uncut moquette, only relieved by the beige antimacassars with their crocheted edging, one placed carefully over the back of each chair, three on the settee. Even the fireplace looked as if it had been there since the late-nineteenth century when these tenements must have been built, she mused. Brass firedogs and a beaten-brass log basket lay on either side of the empty hearth, a black hole that looked as if it hadn't seen a proper fire in years. The policewoman glanced around the room but failed to locate a single radiator. She shivered at the thought of what this room must be like in winter. No wonder it looked like it was scarcely ever used.

'There you are, my dears, something to warm you up.' Miss Lindsay was suddenly there beside them and setting down a tray on a highly polished mahogany table next to the window. 'What do you take? Milk? Sugar?'

Annie watched as the old lady lifted a silver pot, her hand steady as she poured out the tea. She might be old, the DC thought to herself, but she seemed to have all her faculties about her.

'Nancy Fraser,' Weir began, after Miss Lindsay had sat down to face them both, satisfied that they were each holding a tiny patterned plate with a well-buttered scone.

'Yes, I'm so glad you came today. I just wasn't sure what to do. I mean,' she leaned forward confidentially, 'you can't just knock on the poor girl's door and tell her what you think you've seen, can you?'

Annie laid down her cup, the saucer rattling

faintly. 'What do you think you saw, Miss Lindsay?' she asked.

For a moment the old lady's face showed a shadow of doubt as she glanced from one visitor to the other. 'Well, you like to be *sure*, don't you? I mean, it would be awful if I was wrong.' She tailed off, her fingers grasping the handle of her teacup as if afraid that they might begin to shake. 'I saw the wee girl being taken away in that car.'

For a moment nobody spoke, then John Weir cleared his throat and smiled encouragingly at the old lady. 'Maybe you'd like to tell us exactly what you saw, Miss Lindsay,' he said, then, laying down his plate, he took out his Blackberry and prepared to make notes.

'It was the first day of school, you know,' she told them. 'I always like to watch the wee ones in their new uniforms walking down the road. Some of the younger children from the next close were out on the pavement watching them as well. I'd just taken a look down the street to see if any other children were coming when this car drew up.' She paused, looking expectantly at them both.

This pause, wondered Annie, was it for dramatic effect?

'A woman got out, lifted Nancy up and put her in the car. Then she drove off!' Miss Lindsay's eyes gleamed with triumph as she leaned back, watching them intently.

Irvine could almost feel John Weir's desire to catch her eye. Were they being given a story by an old lady who wanted some small excitement in her lonely life? Or were they actually hearing the truth from a credible witness?

'Can you show us exactly where you were standing at the time, Miss Lindsay?'

The old lady rose to her feet and crossed to the large bay window. 'Right here. You get the best view of the whole street from here. Come over and see for yourselves.'

She was right, Irvine thought. The view from this upstairs flat took in the entire block, from one end to the corner where it merged with the main road. Looking across at the rows of windows showing a glimpse of curtain or a pot plant on the sill reminded her of something. Then, suddenly she had it – Avril Paton's famous painting of tenement blocks in Glasgow, *Windows in the West*, where you had some sort of voyeuristic insight on lots of people's lives.

'That's where they all go to catch the school bus,' Miss Lindsay told them, pointing downwards. 'You can't see it from here; it's a few yards along the main road.'

'So all the parents would be out of sight,' Weir said, looking over the old lady's shoulder.

'That's right,' she agreed, turning to face him, her eyes bright with suppressed excitement. 'They'd all gone by then and the wee ones were playing just at the close mouth. I could see Sally MacIlwraith with Nancy and some of the other children when the woman drove up in the car.

Perhaps I was the only one to see what happened,' she added hopefully.

'We haven't completed all our visits,' Weir told her sharply.

Annie gritted her teeth in annoyance at her colleague when she saw Miss Lindsay's face fall. That was no way to gain the confidence of a witness. DC Weir might be her senior in CID by a few months but it hadn't given him better people skills.

'Perhaps you were,' Annie encouraged her. 'Now can you tell us exactly what you saw?'

'Well,' the old woman looked a bit doubtful now, 'you can only see the tops of heads from here, of course, but I could see it was a woman right enough. She looked young. Had red hair, the sort that comes out of a bottle. Bright, you know what I mean. What d'you call that stuff?' She had turned to Annie now, her hand flapping back and forth as if she were holding an invisible wand that would magically bring back the forgotten word.

'Henna?' Annie suggested.

'That's right, really bright and shiny her hair was, and curly, quite long too.' She brushed her shoulders lightly. 'Down to here, I'd say.'

'Did you get a look at her face?' Weir asked.

'No, I told you, you can't see from up here. Not unless they look up. And she didn't. She just bent down to Nancy. I thought she was just talking to the child', she added, turning to the policewoman, 'but then she picked her up and put her into the

57

car. It all happened so quickly, I thought Nancy must have known her. That it was meant.' She swung back to Weir, an imploring expression in her eyes. 'How was I to know the woman was a stranger?'

'So it wasn't until you heard the news that you realised what you had seen?'

Annie's eyes sparked angrily at the patronising sound in Weir's voice. He obviously thought that Miss Lindsay was nothing more than an attention-seeking timewaster. The old lady's mouth hung open, an expression of horror on her face.

'You mean if I had let someone know—?'

'Don't worry.' Annie patted her shoulder, glad that the woman had misinterpreted Weir's insinuation. 'You've let us know now. That's what matters. Now, do you think you might recognise the car she was driving?'

Detective Constable Irvine looked as if she were seething as she sat beside her neighbour. The rest of the team had come up with zilch so Dorothea Lindsay's witness statement was all that they had to add to Sally MacIlwraith's version of events. So far Weir had rubbished the old lady's account, laying it on thick how decrepit she was and that she was, in his opinion, simply milking the situation for her own benefit.

'What was your impression, DC Irvine?' Lorimer spoke quietly, neither dismissing Weir's report nor obviously deferring to the other officer.

'I thought she was telling the truth,' Annie blurted out. 'It made sense. All the other parents were down at the bus stop or in the back court. Young Sally said as much too, didn't she?'

'But there was no mention of red hair. Surely the kid would have remembered that detail?' Weir protested.

'She certainly hasn't picked out any specific types from all the images she's been shown,' DS Wilson added.

'We could try again. See what she makes of pictures of red-headed women,' Annie suggested, 'including ones with henna-dyed hair.'

'Right.' Lorimer smiled. 'That's an action for you to follow up, DC Irvine.' He nodded towards her, seeing a blush of pleasure spread across the woman's face. Any detail like this was vital in the early stages of a case; it narrowed the huge area of possibilities into something a bit more manageable.

'We've had several sightings of a white Mazda hatchback that was in the area. I want each and every one of you to see if there are any links between the owners of these cars and the list of women under investigation,' Lorimer rapped out. Members of his team looked back at him, each face sombre. Some cases gave rise to a modicum of levity, but never one involving a child.

'The search has spread out now to the woods next to Dawsholm Park and the Vet School. We're still hoping that she might be found safe and well,' he added grimly. 'Right. Everyone report back here by five o'clock. Tomorrow's press conference will include a live televised plea from the child's mother. *If* she's still missing,' Lorimer added. He gave a curt nod before the officers dispersed. Anyone looking his way might see a flint-faced senior detective simply dishing out orders, but those who knew him better could sense his anguish. Childless himself, Lorimer could nonetheless empathise with the agony of loss that the young mother was going through. And he could even understand how another woman, deranged with grief, might have snatched little Nancy Fraser away from her own home. Hadn't he seen Maggie go through the terrible pain of miscarriage, time and time again? Each one harder than the last until their decision to leave things as they were – a marriage where there would never be any babies now.

Julie Donaldson linked her arms with her pal, pulling her towards the shrubbery.

'Got something to tell you.' She smirked, watching Sam's face as the two girls walked out of earshot from the rest of their group. Morning break had brought the pupils out to the playground in huddles; some younger boys were kicking a football about whereas the girls were mostly grouped together in chattering cliques, sly glances being cast at anyone outside their orbit.

'What is it?' Sam Wetherby shrugged off her

friend's hand, dropping her school bag onto the ground. 'Did you get off with someone at SU camp, then?' she said, rolling her eyes.

Julie's dark eyes snapped. 'What's it with you and Scripture Union?'

'Och, nothing. Keep your hair on.' Sam attempted a smile as she saw Julie's mood change. The last thing she wanted was her pal going off in the huff with her. 'Come on, then, tell us what it is.'

'Shouldn't really,' Julie mumbled. 'Might get him into trouble.'

'Jules!' Sam squealed. 'Don't tell me! You've done it, haven't you? I mean, really done it?' Sam's eyes were on her friend's face now, a mixture of awe and anticipation in their expression.

'What if I have?' The tone of pretended nonchalance was all part of the game; she'd tell Sam but wanted to let her wheedle it out of her if she could.

'Go on, who was it? One of the seniors? Someone in Tim's class? Not Kenny Turner?' Sam spoke in a breathy undertone, thrilled and shocked at the same time.

'Promise you won't tell. Promise!' Julie had grabbed Sam's arm, her grip fierce on the thin white cotton sleeve.

'Hey!' Sam pulled away, rubbing the sore place where Julie's nails had left their impression. 'Okay, I promise,' she said, seeing a sudden change in her friend's face. Julie was scared. That was something she'd remember later on.

Cupping her hand over Sam's ear, Julie whispered eagerly then stood back, her eyes shining as she watched the disbelief in Samantha Wetherby's face.

'It's true,' she said, nodding. 'Honest to God.'

'What are you going to do about it, then?' Sam asked, a frown of doubt creasing her forehead. 'If that's really true then he should be fired. It's against the law,' she added pompously. 'Anybody can tell you that.'

For a moment Julie looked blank then as Sam picked up her bag and began to walk away, she pulled her back. 'It *is* true,' she said. 'Only . . .' Her voice trembled and she shook her head, tears starting up in her eyes.

'Jules.' Sam was back at her side, a new tone of concern in her voice. 'What happened? What *really* happened?'

'Oh, Sam.' Julie flung herself into the other girl's arms, sobbing now for real. 'It wasn't proper sex. He raped me.'

Maggie Lorimer glanced up as the whispering began. This close-reading test had to be done today in order to gauge exactly what level her Standard Grade pupils were going to achieve. At the back of her room she could see the two heads bent together: Samantha Wetherby and Julie Donaldson, the girl she had seen tearing downstairs away from Eric. Clearing her throat in an exaggerated manner caught their attention and she noticed with relief that Samantha moved away. The last thing Maggie wanted was to reprimand them in the middle of a test. But just as Julie glanced up at her, Maggie caught something in that girl's expression that she didn't like at all – a knowing, self-satisfied little smile that was hiding something. For two pins Maggie would have wiped that sly look off her face, but experience told her to let it pass and preserve the peace and quiet for the rest of the class.

When the bell rang Maggie called out, 'Stop writing now, please. Make sure your names are on the papers and hand them down to the front.'

As Julie and Samantha passed her at the class-room door Maggie was tempted to pull them back. What was all that whispering about? Maggie wondered, watching the two girls walk along the corridor, seeing Samantha sling an arm around Julie's shoulders as if she were consoling her friend. There was something going on, that was for sure. And it had absolutely nothing to do with their English close-reading test.

CHAPTER 8

It was only the second day of term but already Kyle felt as if the summer holidays were a distant memory. *Write about the best thing that happened to you during the holidays*, the teacher had asked them. Their regular maths teacher hadn't left any work and the man at the front of their class was from the English department, covering just for this period. Mr Simpson was okay, really, a bit old and frayed at the edges but a good sport and always ready for a bit of a laugh. A short bald man, Simpson had the sort of merry face that Kyle associated with Christmas. Put him in a red suit and he'd make not a bad Santa Claus. Kyle had been in the top maths class at the beginning of June when the official new term had begun and they'd gone up to Fourth Year. But his teacher wasn't here this period. Had some sort of meeting, Simpson had told them. He supposed it would be okay doing English during a maths period, since they were expected to be working towards a really good folio this year. He was glad the older man wasn't his regular English teacher. Simpson always took the dunderheads, the ones who weren't expected to go on to gain any useful qualifications like Advanced Highers. The bright kids in Mrs Lorimer's class were the ones who would rise to these lofty heights in Sixth Year, maybe go on to university. Would that be him in a couple of years' time if he worked harder at his other subjects? Or did his ambitions really lie elsewhere?

He chewed his pencil. The other kids seemed to be really into this bit of writing, Kyle thought, glancing at his classmates bent over their jotters, earnestly scribbling away. They'd probably be telling all about holidays in Spain or Florida. He'd overheard plenty of them boasting about family fortnights that always seemed to have been some- where with sun, sand and sex, if you believed them. He grinned to himself; they wouldn't be letting their teachers know anything about their quick fumblings down on a darkened beach. But what could *he* write about? The only place he'd been apart from his gran's in Partick was to Dawsholm Park, near the Vet School. And being back home with his da, of course, though that was the last thing he'd ever write about. Then it came to him. The Argo. He could write about that, surely? *The best thing that happened to you*, Simpson had written on the old chalk board in his fine, sloping hand- writing. He'd had a great fight that night, hadn't he? Scored more points off Gordon than he'd ever done before. And it had been a proper fight, not just a three-minute bout. With growing excitement, Kyle began his essay: *The best thing that happened to me . . .*

★　　★　　★

'Whit ur ye doin?' Da had pulled his jotter away before Kyle even realised he was in the room.

'It's homework. I've to finish it for the morrow,' he replied, willing his da to hand back the blue-covered jotter. It was still in pristine condition, with just his name and English section on the front. By Christmas it would probably be covered in doodles and graffiti like everyone else's but for now it was clean and fresh, and Kyle didn't want his da to muck it up. 'Can I have it back?' he muttered.

'No yet, want tae see whit ye're doin. Ah'm no havin any snotty teacher tellin me ah dinna take an interest,' he sneered.

Kyle's heart sank. His father had never attended any of Muirpark's parents' evenings in his life, but the boy remembered how his Year teacher, Mrs Lorimer, had pointedly reminded him about the one coming up this term. Kyle's face had been bruised enough lately, the old man taking his temper out on his youngest son. He'd not be letting on about a parents' night to Da, that was for sure. Kyle shuddered to think of Tam Kerrigan sitting with his teachers, glowering at them, inwardly sneering at their correct pronunciation. Mrs Lorimer meant well enough, he knew, and was simply doing her job but most of the teachers didn't have a clue what really went on nowadays in the Kerrigan household. Only Finnegan in PE seemed to understand Kyle and the kind of home-life he was now leading.

So Kyle held his tongue and waited for his father's reaction. The old man's lips were moving as he read the couple of paragraphs Kyle had managed to write so far, his finger tracing each line. Old man Kerrigan's education must have been pretty patchy, Kyle thought suddenly. And he'd never taken any opportunity to try to improve himself in the jail, had he? All his stories about the Bar-L were big-man stuff, if you accepted half of it: wheeling and dealing with the Glasgow gangsters who had gained a notoriety that the likes of Kerrigan aspired to. That was the only kind of education his father had gained.

'What's this? Who wis ye fightin? How did ah no hear aboot it if it wis that special? Eh? No tellin yer auld man whit ye're up tae? How's that, then?'

The swipe came before Kyle had time to duck, a hard blow catching him just below his right eye.

'Wee nyaff!' His da threw the jotter on the floor and shambled off, cursing as he went. Kyle caught the tail end of his muttering as he disappeared down the hall, 'No bliddy son o mine . . .'

Sitting on the edge of his bed, one hand against the stinging pain, Kyle trembled, hearing the familiar words. *No son of mine*, his da had said often enough since he'd been home. And was it true? Kyle didn't feel as if he belonged in this family of drunkenness and drug dealing, but was that really what Da meant? Or had he actually been fathered by another man?'

Kyle turned slowly to face the wardrobe door with its rectangle of mirror. He lifted his head, considering the boy that stared back at him. Fit, he was certainly fit, he told himself, appraisingly. Beneath the washed-out black T-shirt he saw a muscular pair of shoulders that gave him the appearance of the man he might become, strong and ready to defend himself. Kyle's eyes stared at the face in the mirror; it wasn't a weak face, though the full lips and thick eyelashes were sort of girlish. They'd ragged him about being a cute wee boy in primary school but he'd grown into his looks now. His skin was clear and fresh, not acne ridden like Tam's had been all through his big brother's adolescence. The figure in the mirror was stroking his chin and he could feel the stubble, a testament to his burgeoning manhood. His forehead creased, leaving eyebrows like twin arcs above a pair of sea-grey eyes as he came to the same decision as the boy in the mirror.

One day, he thought, his jaw hardening, one day Da would come on to him and he'd give him back everything he deserved.

Dawsholm Woods were beginning to look tired of summer, Kyle thought as he watched a chestnut leaf float silently onto the path. Everything was too full, blowsy and dusty, the air thick with thistledown. There was a smell of decay and something rotting within the trees, maybe a dead animal that hadn't been cleaned up by foxes and magpies. He wrinkled his nose in disgust. They were into the second half of August already and soon all the deciduous trees would turn russet and brown, carpeting the walkways. As a wee boy Kyle had

68

loved to kick his way through the fallen leaves, hearing them crunch beneath his sturdy shoes. And he'd gathered chessies, made conkers, rattled them against the ones made by his pals, glorying in the frosty evenings when Hallowe'en and Guy Fawkes Night came around again.

Now the thought of darkening nights and shorter days simply depressed him. Summer had meant time spent with Julie or mucking around in Gran's back garden, waiting for Da to get out. It was, he thought, a symbol of all that he had lost. He kicked a pebble into the long sweep of grassy under-growth, a fierce anger beginning to burn through his veins. Why did he mind so much about Julie? Couldn't he be like his pals and play the field with other girls? There were plenty who would go out with him; being in Fourth Year had given them all a new kind of status. Even the girls in Third Year wanted to hang out with them.

But, try as he might, he couldn't forget those moments when Julie had deliberately caught his eye across the classroom. A wee flirt, he'd told himself, and there were other names for girls like her. But the image of the girl with her long blonde hair and knowing smile made Kyle aware of the hard-on tightening his jeans and he allowed his mind to savour just how he might assuage these feelings of hopelessness.

CHAPTER 9

It was the robin trilling its note deep within the hawthorn bushes that made Maggie realise that summer was waning. That distinctive sound, clear in the morning air, was redolent of frosty mornings and the crispness of autumn leaves underfoot. August might still be summer across in Florida where she'd spent so many months teaching, but here in Scotland there were hints, like the robin, that the seasons were changing. Even the hills were different, their flanks clad now in sweeps of purple as the heather came into flower. It wouldn't be long before the bracken turned from green to tawny brown, weaving the landscape into muted shades of tweed. Yet there was always something about a new term at this turn of the year that made Maggie Lorimer feel fresh and ready for new challenges. She'd felt the same even as a young child, school bag over her shoulders, new pencils rattling in their tin box, new school-shoes shining like polished conkers. For Maggie it hadn't been the excitement of seeing her friends again so much as the thrill of learning new things and having a different teacher who would take her another step along what was becoming an adventure.

How many of her own pupils ever felt like that? Maggie wondered, closing the back door on a cold wind that wafted in from the garden. Kids these days were far too aware of their appearance ever to let down their guard and admit to being enthralled by something as uncool as a school subject. She flicked the switch on the kettle, listening to its faint hum as the water heated quickly. Bill must have taken a cup before he'd left, she thought with a pang. He'd let her sleep a bit more as he'd left early for work. Maggie smiled. Och, maybe he'd be back tonight at a reasonable hour. Then her smile straightened out as she remembered why he'd slipped out before she was even awake. That poor wee girl. What sort of night had her mother spent? And had she been able to sleep at all? Maggie poured boiling water into the pot of redbush tea, the steam fogging up her glass-fronted cabinet, her mood soured now.

Then she heard it again – the robin's whistle right outside her kitchen window, pure and fresh like every new morning. And a strange feeling of optimism surged through her. They'd find that little girl. Of course they would.

'Juli-ie! C'mon, you'll be late for school!' Mary Donaldson shouted up the stairs. But there was no answering reply, no, *Okay, I'll be right down* or even a muttered, *Keep your hair on*, a phrase that

Mary always pretended not to hear. With a sigh, the woman clumped up the two short flights of stairs, several treads creaking under her weight.

'Julie, you need to get down or you'll miss the bus!' Mary scolded through the door to her step-daughter's room. She waited just a moment before turning the doorhandle and peering into the darkened room. Blinking against the darkness, Mary could see the curled shape on the bed and in two strides she had crossed the room, flinging open the curtains, her only reward a muffled moan deep within the duvet.

'It's nearly eight o'clock. You'll be late for school!' Mary protested, tugging a corner of the bedding so that Julie would have to face the light.

A mumbled response came as Julie turned away from the window, hands over her eyes.

'What? What are you saying?' Mary demanded. 'Come on, get up right now!'

'M'not goin to school,' Julie's voice intoned.

'Oh.' Mary stood back, temporarily at a loss, her fingers letting go of the duvet. 'Why? What's wrong?' she faltered, unsure now, the usual guilt kicking in. What if she'd missed something obvious? Should she have shouted at Julie like that if the girl wasn't well?

Then to Mary's astonishment her stepdaughter sat up and looked at her with a plea in her blood-shot eyes. 'Mary, if I tell you, promise you won't tell Daddy?'

★   ★   ★

72

It was well after nine o'clock and two pots of tea later that Mary Donaldson finally let Julie go back to bed. Frank had gone long since, his job down at the docks demanding an early start every day. Lucky it was her own day off, Mary thought, though *lucky* wasn't exactly how she felt right now. She'd have to tell him, promise or no promise. If what Julie was saying was the truth, then her father had every right to know and to do something about it. Mary Donaldson's hand faltered as she reached for her mobile phone. Frank hated being disturbed. But a call would have to be made just the same. This wasn't something she could easily keep to herself.

Mary bit her lip anxiously as the tone rang out, fearing what he'd say, worried that he would be angry about a call at work.

When she finally heard his voice, a sob broke from her throat. 'Oh, Frank,' she cried. 'Can you come home? Something's happened to Julie!'

As head teacher of Muirpark Secondary School, Keith Manson had to perform many unpleasant tasks. The buck, as he was fond of saying, stopped right here in his room. However, there was one of his deputies whose remit was dealing with staff issues and that deputy, Jack Armour, was sitting across from him, arms folded, a look of suppressed fury on his face.

'I cannot and I will not allow such idiotic accusations to be levelled at someone whose integrity is so impeccable!' Manson thundered.

'It's happened and nothing you or I can say will make it unhappen,' the man opposite declared wearily. 'Once the parents have made their complaint then it's official. You know that as well as I do. Whether Julie Donaldson is a lying little bitch is neither here nor there. An official investigation has to take place.'

'Eric Chalmers doesn't deserve this,' Manson rumbled.

'Neither did half of the martyrs of the early Church if we're to believe all that's been said down the centuries,' Armour replied drily.

'He's just become a father, for goodness' sake!'

'Maybe Ruth will appreciate him being at home for a while, then,' Armour continued. 'Look, Keith, we have to do our job. Have to be *seen* to do our job. We can't take sides in this. Eric'll have to be suspended. On full pay, of course. Let me talk to him, explain that we have no option. Give him time to sort out his response to the official inquiry team.'

'What about the parents?'

'Well, we can hardly tell them that we think their darling daughter is a scheming, conniving wee madam, can we? We have to play this fair for all concerned.'

'How about suggesting the girl sees a doctor?'

'To see if she's *virgo intacta*? That's taking a bit of a risk, surely? I'll bet loads of them in that year group have had it off. Even the ones in Eric's Scripture Union group,' Armour added to himself, hoping Manson couldn't hear him.

'I still think we're overreacting,' Manson replied, thumping the desk in front of him.

'Well, there's nothing we can do about it now. The Donaldsons have got till tomorrow to put their complaint in writing. Maybe a heart-to-heart with their precious daughter will uncover the truth before then.'

'I hope you're right,' Manson replied. 'I bloody hope you're right.'

'But are you sure?' Mary Donaldson asked for the umpteenth time, sitting side by side with her step-daughter on the couch. Beside them a half-empty box of Kleenex gave testimony to the storm of weeping that had accompanied Julie's story. Mary bit her lip. It was too late now, anyway. Frank had phoned the school, demanding to speak to the head teacher while Mary had watched Julie closely, looking for any sign that the girl was making the whole thing up. It was a classic case of attention seeking, she'd tried to tell Frank. An only child who was constantly vying for her father's attention, Julie hadn't been the easiest of stepdaughters over these last four years. Mary had tried hard, patiently giving her best and even succeeding at times, but Julie would never accept her as Mum. She would always be Mary. A nice person who had happened to marry her widowed father and make him happy and who didn't cause too much friction between parent and child, that was all.

But something was gnawing away at Mary Donaldson even as she put an arm around Julie's heaving shoulders, a doubt worming its insidious way into her thoughts. Had she been too lenient with this child, was that it? And if so, was she partly to blame for this ghastly situation? That Julie had had sex with a teacher was just too incredible to believe, yet Frank had swallowed it hook, line and sinker, raving on about filthy religious maniacs who preyed on innocent young girls. Her hand stroked Julie's upper arm and she felt the girl's sobs shuddering. But, try as she might, Mary couldn't believe that the nice young man who had collected Julie in the school minibus had taken advantage of her stepdaughter in the graphic way she had described to them.

'Eric, can I have a quick word?'

Eric looked up from the book cupboard to see Jack Armour standing in the doorway of his classroom.

'Sure, come on in.' Eric waved a friendly hand and straightened up. A visit from the deputy head was nothing to excite his imagination but Jack had a sombre look on his face that made Eric wonder. 'What's up?'

Jack's sigh and his pursed lips should have been signs that all was not well, but it was avoiding eye contact that made the first alarm bells begin to ring.

'Jack, is there something wrong?'

'Aye. I hate to spring this on you, but we've had a complaint about you from a parent.'

'A complaint about *me*?' Eric laughed, stepping back in surprise. 'What on earth—?'

'It's Mr Donaldson,' the deputy head began. 'He says you, you . . . Julie told him that you and she . . . Oh, God, it's a load of nonsense of course but we have to follow the correct procedures . . .'

'Jack, what are you trying to tell me?' Eric stood up, suddenly aware of the other man's discomfiture.

'Eric, Julie Donaldson told her parents that you sexually assaulted her at SU camp this summer.'

'*What?* But she can't have!' Eric's jaw dropped and he stared, speechless, at the man who was obviously finding it difficult to meet his eyes.

'I'm afraid she did. Look, we know it's a load of bullshit, Eric, but that's not the point. We have to be seen to be doing the correct thing, so . . .'

'So, what happens to me now?' Eric's voice came out in a whisper as he leaned against his desk, one hand gripping the edge.

'I'm afraid you'll have to be suspended.'

It was odd, Eric thought, being in the car park and leaving school when inside the building his colleagues were working away. There was little noise at this time of the morning, even the playing fields were empty he saw, looking across at the expanse of grass and blaize, only the constant hum of traffic beyond the rows of grey tenements. The man

77

paused, his fingers holding the ignition key. What would Ruth be doing right now? He thought back to those few precious days before term had begun, remembering how he'd helped with everyday chores: hanging out washing, shopping for groceries, cleaning the kitchen, never for a moment grudging time spent being useful to her. Maybe if he'd taken the two weeks' paternity leave? But they'd discussed it, knowing how important the beginning of term was for the pupils. Ruth hadn't minded in the least and now Eric wondered if she'd welcomed the chance to have time alone with Ashleigh. How would she feel when he came home now burdened with this news?

Coming to a decision, Eric turned the key and released the handbrake. He wouldn't go home, not just yet. There were things he had to think about first, not least how he was going to tell Ruth about Julie.

Eric eased his car over the speedbumps that lay between the school and Dumbarton Road. The whole area had been traffic-calmed and now drivers had to weave in and out as 'No Entry' signs appeared at the mouth of every second street, slowing them down to a perpetual second gear. At last he spotted a gap in the traffic and signalled left, heading towards town, passing the entrance to the Western Infirmary then the Art Galleries at Kelvingrove. On a sudden impulse, Eric took a left and drove along Kelvin Way, the University of Glasgow towering high above him on one side.

He'd been so happy there, following his dream of studying theology and then, of course, meeting Ruth. They'd grown up together, he mused, slowing down at the junction where the old student union curved around the end of University Avenue. And he felt that few people in this world understood him quite as well as the woman who had become his wife.

The Church was always open, even on a weekday morning. Although the main building dated back to Victorian times, there had been numerous additions tacked on to it, providing services like a daily nursery and a drop-in coffee bar. And it was outside one of those extensions that Eric parked his car. Posters on the door told of the many weekly activities: the Jam Gang, Men's Fellowship, Anchor Boys, and Mothers and Toddlers, all brightly illustrated in primary colours. Inside he was faced with a row of tables, leaflets stacked up neatly below more posters depicting Christian Aid and a Mission to Malawi. A group of young African kids with shining eyes grinned shyly out of one of them, a dust-coloured hut behind them. In the centre a white man in a bush hat hunkered down, his arms around the two nearest children. Eric swallowed hard. That could have been him, if he'd made a different decision. The mission field had always held a fascination for him. It would have been a challenge. And I wouldn't be in this situation now, he told himself.

He pushed open the door, hearing the sound of a guitar and childish voices chanting a familiar song, *I can sing a rainbow, sing a rainbow* . . .

'Hello!' Jim's eyebrows raised as he caught sight of him with the unspoken question, What are you doing here at this time of day?

Eric tried to smile and waved a hand towards the crowd of small children and their parents surrounding the man with the guitar.

Perhaps something in his expression told Jim that here was a friend in need, for he stood up, put the instrument aside and clapped his hands.

'Right, everyone, it's time for juice and fruit. Linda's in charge today. I'll be back in about fifteen minutes.' The group dispersed to the far side of the room where tables and small chairs had been set out, the older children whooping and running, their feet stamping noisily on the wooden floor.

Jim led Eric back out into the reception hall, one hand on his friend's elbow.

'Something's up,' he said quietly. 'You look terrible.'

Now that he was here, the enormity of what was happening overwhelmed him and sudden tears sprang into his eyes. For a moment he couldn't speak, terrified that he was going to weep, and simply shook his head.

'It's okay. Nothing's so bad that it can't be taken to the Lord,' Jim told him.

'I know,' Eric whispered. 'It's just . . . a shock, I suppose.'

'And you want to talk to me about it, right?'

Eric nodded, took a deep breath and relayed all that had happened since the start of term.

'But why would she tell such a lie? I mean, we were friends. She knew she could come and talk to me, confide things in me. And she did.' He looked at Jim with puzzled eyes. 'She was so happy at camp, always the first to be involved, singing her heart out whenever we had chorus times. What did I do to make her hate me?'

The Reverend Jim Bowyer looked into his friend's eyes; he'd never seen the man like this before, hurt and bewildered. Eric Chalmers was the most upbeat person he knew.

'You didn't do anything, pal, that was the trouble.'

'What do you mean?'

'Ach, I've seen it before. Young love. A lassie has a crush on you and thinks you should behave as if you were her boyfriend – hold hands, give her a kiss when no one's looking.'

'But I'm a married man! How could she expect me to do things like that!' Eric protested.

Jim smiled sadly. 'Teenage girls don't think straight. Surely you should know that by now. You've worked with them long enough. Raging hormones,' he added, raising his hands in a hell-fire-and-brimstone-preacher style.

Eric laughed, in spite of himself.

'That's better,' Jim said, clapping him on the back. 'I'm sorry you have to go through all this nonsense, but it'll all blow over. This girl—'

'Julie,' Eric supplied.

'Julie. She'll come to her senses eventually. The school will probably give her a hard time when they find out she's been making it all up.'

Eric shook his head, staring at a spot on the floor. 'I can't believe that her parents actually want to bring charges against me,' he said. 'That's one of the things that hurts the most, to have lost their trust.'

'And you'll regain that trust,' Jim assured him. 'Any doubts they have now will be swept away once the girl tells the truth.'

'Maybe, but mud sticks,' muttered Eric.

'Ach, man, can you not remember what the scriptures tell us?' Jim admonished him gently. '"The world will make you suffer. But be brave! I have defeated the world!" Has God ever let you down?'

Eric's shake of the head made his friend clap him on the shoulder once more. 'Well, then, go home and see Ruth. She'll stand by you, you know that.'

'Thanks, Jim. I knew you'd say the right things. You always do.'

Outside the air seemed fresher and Eric took large gulps, steadying himself before he headed back across the city. He'd dipped into a Slough of Despond, Jim had told him, using the image from *The Pilgrim's Progress*. But now he had been rescued and the way was ever upwards. Raising his eyes to the clouds scudding past the church

82

spire, Eric wanted to put up a prayer, to thank God for Jim's friendship. But his stomach was knotted with gnawing acid, making his mouth twist suddenly. Everything had been so perfect; why did she have to go and spoil it all for him now?

Raging hormones, Jim had said. Eric smiled ruefully. Were they so terribly sinful? And wasn't Julie just a misunderstood teenager who needed a bit of comforting?

'That's right, Chalmers. C-H-A-L-M-E-R-S. Fine. No bother.'

The journalist put down her telephone, aware that the voice on the other end of the line had sounded almost cheerful. She sensed another story at Muirpark Secondary, some political friction between members of staff. Well, it would still be there if ever she wanted to dig a bit deeper. This fellow hated the RE teacher's guts, that was for sure. Barbara Cassidy rubbed her hands gleefully. Another swipe at the religious establishment would go down well in the *Gazette*. The public's mood was ripe for outrage against the Church. That recent coverage of a priest and several small boys had provoked a fair ding-dong of correspondence on the letters page, just what the editorial team demanded. A few more phone calls and maybe even an interview with this guy, Chalmers, and she would have a cracker of a story.

CHAPTER 10

'It's not all right,' Lorimer barked into the phone. 'It's not all right at all. A daily bulletin is simply going to cause more misery for the mother.'

As he listened to Davie Mearns, the Police Press Officer, the DCI tapped the edge of his desk with an impatient finger. Nancy Fraser was a missing person, not a tasty morsel to be fought over by the nation's newshounds. Okay, they would be holding a press conference, but that was all he was willing to concede at the moment. In the wake of the Madeleine McCann case, every British police officer was at pains to show just how efficient their system was. No stone would be left unturned: Lorimer could trot out that familiar cliché with the best of them. Public confidence counted for a hell of a lot in this job, especially where small children were concerned. Davie had recently been promoted to Chief Police Press Officer and was a little over zealous at his job, in Lorimer's opinion. Wanting a daily report on Nancy Fraser was just not on, at least at this early stage, he told himself. Yet the man had a point: What they don't know they'll simply make up, he'd told the SIO. Well, that was a chance Lorimer was willing to take. Once the mother had faced the newspaper people maybe that would satisfy them for a while, then they could let Lorimer's team get on with the job of finding the child.

'Did you hear about Eric Chalmers?' The woman smirked over her coffee mug as Maggie rummaged in her pigeonhole for any notes that might have been left in the staffroom during the day.

'Oh, yes, he's got a wee girl now. Ashleigh, they've decided to call her,' Maggie replied. Why on earth was Myra Claythorn taking an interest in Eric? As a self-promoting disbeliever in anything other than her own importance, Myra regularly disparaged anything that smacked of religion, particularly Christianity, and was always ready to rubbish any of Eric's innovations at school, like his Scripture Union Club.

'Not *that*,' the other teacher told her, a gleam of triumph in her eyes as she realised Maggie was oblivious to this latest piece of news. 'Your precious friend's been having it off with one of his own pupils at that summer camp of his! Been suspended!' Myra's smile gloated over Maggie as the full horror of the woman's words hit home.

'Julie Donaldson,' Sandie told her as they walked together out across the car park. 'The father's called in and he's going to make a formal complaint. Jack Armour's told Eric to go home.'

85

'He's already been suspended?'

'We think so. Manson's wanting a full staff meeting tomorrow morning.'

'Yes, I know. I got the note in my pigeonhole. What about Julie?'

'She's been told to come into school as usual tomorrow. Manson's not going to miss her and hit the wall, believe you me. Bet it'll all be over bar the shouting this time tomorrow.'

'I hope so,' Maggie replied doubtfully. But, try as she might, that knowing smirk on Myra Claythorn's face was something she was finding hard to erase from her memory.

'I can't believe it,' Ruth said, running her fingers through her husband's blonde thatch of hair. 'Why on earth would she say something to hurt you?'

Eric's sigh seemed to reach his boots. 'She came on to me at school yesterday. Said some pretty stupid things. I . . .' He shook his head as if reliving the memory. 'I pushed her away. Not violently,' he added hastily, seeing Ruth's look of alarm. 'I hardly touched her. Well, only to stop her grabbing hold of me.' He groaned aloud. 'Why did she make these horrible things up? I mean, how could anyone think I'd behave like that with a pupil?'

Baby Ashleigh's cry made them both look up. The tiny scrap in their nursery had begun her nightly bawling session. Ruth sighed and rose from her seat.

'Don't. Let me bring her down. You stay there,' Eric told her gently.

Watching him leave the room, Ruth Chalmers told herself for the hundredth time how lucky she was, how blessed to have a husband like Eric. They'd been so blissfully happy since Ashleigh's birth; it was as if a halo of golden light had surrounded them all. Now this silly little girl had gone and spoiled it all. And maybe put Eric's career into jeopardy.

She was so tired, almost too tired to think. Too tired to pray? Ruth closed her eyes, bent her head and spoke a few words into the silence. And when the door opened and Eric came in cradling the baby in his arms, she was able to give him a smile that was full of trust and love.

Nobody ever came in without knocking. That was the rule she'd established ages ago, when Mary had first come to stay. The white painted door lay between Julie and the rest of the world, she thought; it was a barrier between now and tomorrow. The girl bit her lip. What would they all say? Would they call her a slag? Or would there be enough shock value to gain her some sympathy? Sam had believed her. Eventually.

Remembering her reaction to Sam's initial scepticism, Julie swallowed hard, feeling the prick of tears under her hot eyelids. She couldn't lose Sam. They'd always been there for one another, she told herself, the cliché echoing characters from her favourite TV soap opera.

Julie lay back on her bed, legs splayed, feeling

the cold cotton of the duvet against her bare calves. What would it really be like with him? She held the image of Eric in her mind: his smile, the way his eyes crinkled up at the corners. Making him real, coming towards her, whispering things she wanted to hear, touching her . . . She shivered in anticipation as her imagination took her further and further into the story and her hand strayed towards the hem of her skirt. Would he lift it gently like this? Let his hand creep upwards to where she was wet and eager for him? Julie let out a whimper as the images came faster and thicker, her body hot and demanding.

Then that other image came back, the one where he looked at her, grim and unsmiling, telling her what a mistake she'd made, that he didn't love her like that at all. Julie sat up suddenly, pushing her skirt back down.

Eric Chalmers would never humiliate her like that again. Never. She'd make sure of it.

CHAPTER 11

When he woke from the dream, he found that his body was slick with sweat. Breathing long deep breaths, he let his eyes focus on what was real in the room: the lampshade on the ceiling, the stippled plaster-work, the tops of the curtains where one hook was missing and the material sagged forwards like a drunken woman's dress, open to show her tits.

He kept on breathing, deliberately, slowly, the way he'd been taught to calm himself after one of his episodes. It was all right now. It was just a dream, that was all. There were no arms pinning him back, no eyes staring up at him accusingly. Just a dream.

Closing his eyes he saw her again, the fear and shock as he leaned harder against her windpipe, heard the snap below his knee, felt at last her body yielding below his own. Then . . . but before he could remember the next bit, he opened his eyes and threw back the covers, pulling one corner of the sheet to wipe the sweat from his chest. He'd get up, wash, have some food and go about as if it was a normal day.

It would be fine. The daylight was just behind those curtains. It promised a new beginning where everything in the past was like the dream already fading from his sight.

'D'ye hear the latest? That wee slag Donaldson's got Mr Chalmers into trouble. *Says* he sexually assaulted her.'

Kyle Kerrigan slowed down to keep pace with the group of Fourth Year boys who were heading towards the milling area, listening intently to their conversation.

'How d'ye know that?'

'Archie's faither's a mate o Mr Donaldson. Telt him in the pub, didn't he?'

'That's pure garbage. Julie Donaldson's makin it all up. Bet you. Wis she no goin wi you last term, Kerrigan?'

Kyle shrugged as if to distance himself from Julie, from their gossip, but his heart was thumping nonetheless.

'Well, we've got Chalmers second period,' the lad persisted. 'See if it's true or no, eh?'

Kyle peeled off from the group and made towards the PE base where Finnegan would be hanging out. Finnegan (Mr Finnegan to his face) was one of the few bright spots in Kyle Kerrigan's life at Muirpark Secondary these days. The PE teacher had recognised early on that the lad was well above average at sport and it was Finnegan who had made it his business to foster that talent. As he entered the covered walkway that led to the sports block, Kyle glanced up at the workout area,

90

his personal haven where he spent as much time as he could get away with. It was a narrow rectangle boxed off from the upper floor of the PE department, filled with rowing machines, exercise bikes and various types of weight-training gear. Strictly speaking, anyone using the equipment had to be supervised by a member of staff but Finnegan let Kyle have free run of the place so long as he was somewhere on the premises.

The knock on the door of the PE base was answered by a rumbling cough as a tall thin man appeared. His pock-marked face creased in a grin as he saw Kyle.

'C'mon in. Want a cuppa tea before the bell goes?'

'Aye, why not.' Kyle moved into the square room with its different bits of kit arranged along hooks on the wall, his nose twitching at the scent of new-cut grass coming through the open window. The PE staffroom looked out onto the vast playing fields that were the envy of every other secondary school in the district. Muirpark had been one of the lucky new builds of the seventies when spare land had been snapped up by councils eager to showcase their commitment to education. The site had been considered for private development but, in a rare moment of altruism, the City Fathers had given it over to their children. Now Muirpark, complete with an ex-boxing champion as its head teacher, was regarded as one of the schools most likely to produce tomorrow's sporting heroes.

Finnegan busied himself with a teabag and hot water from the kettle jug as the boy gazed out over the flat land between the back of the school and a line of trees that helped to screen a row of red sandstone tenements beyond. His eyes traced the line of the running track that curved around the three pitches; one for rugby, and two for hockey and football. Before the holidays there had been cricket nets out there on the faraway field, the assistant janitor acting as part-time groundsman, rolling the turf into a green sward. Kyle had jogged around that park, winter and summer, more times than he could remember.

'Here, take it before the first bell.' Finnegan was handing him a white mug emblazoned with a green shamrock. Kyle nodded and sipped the tea. He wanted to ask Finnegan about Chalmers – that's what he'd really come over for – but somehow the words were lost and he remained silent, looking at the green vista out there. How could you ask another teacher about something like that?

The bell broke into his reverie and he put down the half-finished tea, nodding his thanks.

'Want a work-out after classes?'

'Aye, thanks. I've got PE last two anyway,' Kyle reminded him.

'So you have. Right. See you later.'

Kyle picked up his rucksack, left the PE base and began to run across the playground back towards the main building. Heart scarcely thumping, he took the stairs two at a time until he came to his own form-room door. Mrs Lorimer was just closing it but smiled at Kyle in a friendly way as she caught sight of him.

Kyle slung his bag under a desk and slumped back against the wall, his eyes taking in the rest of his classmates. The boys who'd been talking about Julie were at the back, sniggering among themselves. Of Julie Donaldson herself there was no sign. And she'd been off yesterday as well. Samantha Wetherby was sitting near the front, pretending to be absorbed in one of her jotters, but even from this distance Kyle could see she was uneasy, shifting in her seat, glancing up at the classroom door as if she were expecting her best mate to appear. She knew. She *knew*. Kyle could tell.

Mrs Lorimer was calling the register now and when she came to Donaldson there was an outbreak of giggles from within the room and a snort from one of the boys at the back. Her swift, sharp look around the room showed Kyle that his registration teacher was annoyed. Had she heard, then? And was it true?

Kyle considered this carefully. He'd known Julie since primary school. She was a daft wee lassie, so she was, but not so daft as to let some teacher have his way with her. And it had been nice hanging out with her for these few weeks, even when she'd come out with some right bizarre stuff. Fanciful. That's what Miss Galbraith had called her in Primary

Four. Was she like that still? Even after their brief liaison, the boy realised he didn't have an answer for that. Kyle raised his hand as his name was called out then sank back into his slouch. Och, it was just some unfounded rumour. Chalmers was a cool guy, everyone knew that. Surely?

Morning interval had never been like this before, Maggie thought, glancing around the crowded staffroom. Many of the staff simply headed for their own departmental bases for a swift cup of something caffeine-related that would keep them going till lunch. But today they were all there, waiting for Manson to appear. The note had appeared in their pigeonholes late yesterday afternoon so most of the staff had only picked it up at registration. A matter of importance, it had read. She'd had a free period just before morning break but the pile of jotters on her desk had kept her from slipping downstairs to the office to see if she could wheedle any information out of the secretaries.

'D'you think he'll tell us that Julie's making it all up?' Sandie wondered, one eyebrow raised in speculation. Maggie shrugged, sipping her coffee, glad she'd managed to reach the head of the queue where the auxiliaries were being kept busy dispensing drinks, a steamy mist escaping from the huge urn behind their counter.

Then Manson was there, his squat, almost malevolent presence hushing the buzz of talk.

Every eye was on his face as he spoke. Whatever it was, that grim expression betokened bad news of some description. Maggie shuddered, fearing the worst.

'I have to tell you all that Eric Chalmers has been temporarily suspended as from yesterday,' Manson began, raising his hand to quell the sudden sounds of disbelief that rose like a wave from the assembled staff.

'An accusation from a pupil has meant that we have to carry out a serious investigation into Eric's conduct.' He paused and in that pause cries of protest and outrage emanated from various parts of the room. Clearing his throat, Manson continued, 'It has been claimed by Julie Donaldson of S4 that Eric sexually assaulted her during the Scripture Union's summer trip.'

Maggie stood, speechless, feeling the colour drain form her cheeks. She wasn't hearing this. She couldn't be. Okay, so Myra Claythorn had told her already in that malicious way of hers, but hearing it like this from Manson . . .

'Of course there may be absolutely no substance to this accusation, in fact I personally have great hopes that this might be over as soon as it has begun,' Manson rumbled, glaring around him as if to defy anyone who was of a different opinion. 'Eric Chalmers has been told to stay away from school for his own benefit and I'm sure Ruth will find plenty for him to do,' he added, eliciting the first murmur of laughter. 'So, no gossiping about this outside school and, unless you have anything cogent to bring to the investigative process, no speculation either,' Manson growled. 'I'm sure we'll see this young lady well chastised for bringing the good character of one of your colleagues into disrepute. Meantime, there'll be 'please takes' to cover Eric's classes. I'm sure you'll all enjoy the spiritual benefits,' he added with a hint of a grin. 'That's all.'

A storm of talk broke out and Maggie felt a hand on her sleeve.

'Are you okay? You've gone chalk white,' Sandie said, guiding her friend to the nearest free chair.

Maggie shook her head, afraid to speak.

'What a hell of a shock!' Sandie went on. 'Poor Eric! Just not what he or Ruth need right now. Stupid bloody girl! What's she on about?' Sandie's voice rose in indignation.

Maggie looked up as she felt someone brush past them. It was Herriot, one of her least favourite colleagues, a disaffected biology teacher whose career had stalled long since and who was simply marking time till retirement.

'No smoke without fire, eh? Know what they say about these religious types,' he sneered into their faces, his voice only loud enough for Sandie and Maggie to hear.

'What?' Sandie's outrage came too late as Herriot had already slipped out of the staffroom and away from anyone who might verbally slap him down.

'How can he say such a thing? Horrible little man!' Sandie fumed.

But, looking around them, Maggie caught sight of a few other faces that were clouded in uncertainty. Maybe horrible Herriot wasn't the only one to think Eric guilty of this accusation.

And what about herself? After seeing what she had seen, could she really say that there was nothing between Eric and this girl?

CHAPTER 12

He saw her from the opposite side of the road, just as he was coming out of the flat. Head down, she was walking slowly towards him, her blonde hair a stream of light against her face. He stood still, following her with his eyes as she drew nearer, trying to see the outline of her jaw, the bow shape of her lips. When she crossed the road and looked up, not seeing him standing there, it was as if something within him had been released and he let out his breath in one long exhalation. Then he turned away from the close mouth, letting his feet take him wherever it was that she was going to lead.

Julie sat stirring her coffee, watching the froth swirl close to the lip of the cup. It wouldn't do to let it spill over the edge. That would look so uncool. Besides, someone might be watching her, seeing her for the truant schoolgirl she really was, not the young woman she was pretending to be. Mary had told her to go into school as normal, face up to whatever was waiting for her there, but she'd bottled it at the last minute. Instead of joining the usual crowd of Muirpark kids at the bus stop, Julie had turned and headed towards town, stuffing her tie into the bottom of her bag. Now she was sitting outside Tinderbox, her favourite coffee bar, the sun making dimples of light on the silver-topped tables. She'd ordered her coffee, trying to make eye contact with that sexy barista, the dark-skinned guy with eyes like treacle toffee, but he'd hardly registered her presence. Fine, Julie had told herself, she wasn't bothered anyway, but as she'd carried her brimming cup outside, she'd scowled, the barista's lack of interest rankling.

There weren't many people about yet; through the open doorway she could see a couple of youngish blokes with their laptops open in front of them – too well dressed to be students – and to one side there was a woman reading the *Gazette*. Closing her eyes, she thought about what would be going on at school right now. Registration would be well over and they'd have begun classes. Nobody would really be missing her, would they? Except Sam, a wee voice reminded her; Sam, who had cried against Julie's shoulder after her dad had walked out on her mum.

Julie opened her eyes and sneaked a look at the *Gazette*'s front page, scanning the first few lines. They hadn't found that wee girl yet, then. She sighed deeply, the news making her feel even worse. Julie swallowed hard. She couldn't let her emotions show in such a public place. Here she was thinking about real tragedies that made her own situation seem tawdry by comparison. Taking a sip of the hot coffee steadied her and she leaned back, wondering how the people round about her could just go on with their daily business as if nothing really mattered. Maybe that was the secret of being grown up: looking cool and pretending not to feel anything at all.

She saw herself reflected in the plate-glass window, a slim figure in black, newly washed hair gleaming in the morning sunshine. Nobody would take her for a school kid. Would they? Her black skirt and high-heeled shoes could just as easily be the garb of any of the students working in the last weeks of their summer holidays. Maybe she could be mistaken for a new student looking for a place to stay? Her mind took her to the tobacconist's shop further down Byres Road where a mosaic of postcards gave out details of rooms to let, flats to share. If only she could be that person, eager to begin afresh, away from the restrictions of school and home . . .

She looked at the bottom of the cup in surprise, realising she'd hardly tasted any of it. Too late now, and she wasn't going to be like one of these naff women who scraped the dregs of their cappuccinos with the metal teaspoon. With no plan as to where she was going next, the girl rose from the table, knocking against it and making the cup clatter in its saucer. Awoken from her reverie by her own childish gaucheness, Julie turned abruptly towards the corner, seeing with some relief that the light had just changed to green.

As she fled across the junction she took no notice

of the other pedestrians who came in her wake, nor was she aware of one particular man whose eyes followed her along the street all the way to Hillhead Underground station.

He had seen her coming, bright as a summer angel, and known at once that she was the one. It was as simple as that and he'd smiled to himself as his feet took him after her, watching her progress along the street. When she'd finally stopped at the coffee bar he had waited patiently, reading a paper just inside the doorway, out of her line of vision. The moment she had crossed the street he had ambled after her, his long legs easily keeping pace a few yards behind. Even the Underground had posed no particular problems. They had waited together among the other people standing silently on the platform. She was so close that he might have reached out and touched the back of her thin white blouse. His fingertips tingled at the thought.

The sooty smell from the tunnel and the whoosh of air as the train approached caused a fluttering in his stomach and he remembered what it was like to be a small child again, full of anticipation for a treat to come. The carriage was half-empty so he let her sit down before selecting a place several seats away; she could see him only if she turned around and stared at all the other passengers. But instinctively he knew she was too sophisticated to do that; she would be like everyone else and keep herself closed and contained, wrapped in a mystery.

The train rocked back and forth as it sped through the darkened tunnel, his lip curling in distaste at the nearness of all those other bodies crammed up next to him. Making human contact was an avoidable transgression if you could sway with the motion.

The train slowed down at Kelvinbridge and he watched to see if she'd stand up and get out, but when she remained seated he guessed she would be going all the way into town. Buchanan Street, probably; three more stops. As he let his eyes gloat over her, he noticed her fingers rummaging in that black leather shoulder bag, then saw a small movement across her lips as she drew out the mobile phone. Sitting back as the train began gathering momentum on its shrieking journey, she fiddled with it, an expression of concentration on her soft, young features. Texting, he realised. It was far too noisy to try to actually talk to anyone. Biting his lip, he thought about this. He should have reckoned on a mobile phone. They were like bodily appendages on the young; well, he would just have to perform some delicate type of surgery to remove it from her. Smiling at the metaphor he set his mind to the task ahead.

Julie looked at her watch, trying to remember what class she would have been in. It was still too early in the term to have memorised her timetable and it was past morning interval so she'd missed a chance to speak to Sam. She'd just have to text her instead, reassure her that she was fine and just dogging it for a laugh. They'd gone up to Buchanan Galleries loads of times during the holidays, dawdling at all the clothes shops, trying stuff on and screaming with laughter whenever they'd found something utterly bizarre. That was their current catchphrase, *utterly bizarre*, and they spoke it in a pseudo-posh voice, collapsing into helpless giggles and clutching one another. Julie's mouth twitched into a tiny smile at the memory. Even when Sam had been in a mood, they'd still gone into town, mooching around the stores from Buchanan Street down to Argyle Street and the St Enoch Centre. Sam liked to sit in Princes Square, watching all the people, whereas Julie was always itching to be on the move, to see what was in the shops, coaxing Sam to try things on.

In town, she texted Sam, *c u later. XXX*. That would do for now, she thought, snapping the mobile shut and slipping it back into the wee pocket inside her bag. She'd call her at lunch-break. Julie frowned suddenly. Was this the one day of the week when Sam had a different break from her? Muirpark had such a huge pupil population that there was a staggered lunchtime, half of the pupils timetabled for an earlier lunch. It had been okay last year but now they were in Fourth Year it didn't always work out. *Was* this the day? Julie simply couldn't remember. She'd try anyway and hope to catch Sam between classes if necessary. Now she would sit and anticipate a stroll around the town.

Catching sight of herself in the darkened glass, she saw a school leaver all ready and eager to begin university. She would be going in to buy all the stuff she needed for her course, wouldn't she? Great big lined-notepads for lectures like the ones Mary used for her night-school class. And clothes. New stuff that made a statement, saying that here was someone out for a good time. She wouldn't think about school. About him. She was past all of that now and there were things to do today, places that a new university student would want to see. A sudden thought struck her. Maybe she could actually go up to Strathclyde? Check it out before the official university term began? The other Julie stared back at her – older, more knowing – and she suppressed the self-satisfied smile, forcing herself to feign the nonchalance that an older girl would certainly feel.

Julie-the-student-to-be let the carriage rock her back and forward in a hypnotic rhythm, quite unaware of the eyes that were trying to translate every phrase of her body language.

CHAPTER 13

'We won't give up until Nancy is found,' Lorimer insisted.

'D'you think she's dead?'

DCI William Lorimer swallowed back the angry response he wanted to make to the question. What an insensitive little bitch! He glowered at the journalist, seeing her red mouth turned upwards in what was meant to be a smile but was more like a sneer. How could any woman, reporter or not, form a question like that when the child's mother was sitting in front of them, nervously twisting her hands and throwing glances his way as if begging him to make it all stop. Well, that was just what he bloody well would do. He'd had quite enough of the national press for one morning.

'That's all, ladies and gentlemen,' Lorimer replied, the merest hint of stress on the word ladies. Barbara Cassidy was no lady, just a nasty little hack grubbing for dirt. His gimlet stare at the reporter made others turn and look her way. Cassidy, he was glad to see as he ushered Nancy's mother away, had the grace at least to blush.

Or perhaps those twin spots of colour were simply temper at being so publicly thwarted?

'You did well,' Lorimer told Kim Fraser as they left the room where a backdrop of larger-than-life-sized photographs of Nancy had gazed down at the reporters. 'A public appeal like that can only help to push things forward.'

'But the newspaper people . . . ?' Kim trailed off, unwilling to voice any allusion to that last crass question. She wanted to ask him. Of course she did. Any young mother would be desperate for the reassurance that the Senior Investigating Officer could provide. Especially if he thought her daughter was alive. But that was something Lorimer simply couldn't give her.

'We've got teams out right now scouring the city, Kim,' he said gently. 'There are door-to-door inquiries as well as officers looking in more remote places where Nancy might have been left.'

'D'you think she's—?'

'There's no point in speculating one way or the other. Kiddies have gone missing and been found several days later, alive and well. You just have to keep on hoping.'

Lorimer heard himself speaking and hated the sound of such platitudes, but knew fine that was exactly what Kim Fraser wanted to hear. He couldn't very well quote the other statistics about children whose wee corpses had been turned up after as little as forty-eight hours.

'You will find her, won't you, Mr Lorimer?' Kim

was looking at him as though he were the only person who could make a difference to her world, eyes full of trust for the man who was organising the search for her daughter.

'We're doing everything we can, I promise you,' he replied, steering Kim in the direction of the Family Liaison room where she would be given a cup of tea before someone took her home. An older woman was waiting for them, her bleached-blonde hair swept back into a ponytail, huge gold hoops dangling from her ears. Kim's mother, Lorimer realised, noticing the resemblance between the two women.

'Aw right, hen?' Mrs Fraser asked, taking a tentative step towards them, eyes flicking over Lorimer, unsure of this tall policeman and his serious expression. He saw Kim let herself be folded into her mother's swift embrace, then she was standing looking back at him, lip trembling.

'You'll let us know when you have any news?' The young woman looked at him, her eyes wide with an appeal that let Lorimer see how young and defenceless she really was. Under that brave exterior, Kim Fraser was just a wee Glasgow lassie herself, still needing her mammy.

'Of course,' he replied, forcing his face to create a reassuring smile. Then, with a nod to both women, he turned and briskly walked away as though to show them that he was eager to be back at work on the job of finding little Nancy Fraser.

It was a hellish job whenever something like this

happened. Triple murders and pub riots were a dawdle compared to the anguish of seeing a mum squeeze her emotions dry over a missing child. So far they'd not found very much but what little there was had been offered up for public consumption. Nancy's wee friend had been helpful enough in giving them the lead of a white car, and the laborious task of visiting each and every potential owner of the vehicle was still ongoing. They'd had her in a second time and even shown photographs of types of Mazdas whose redhaired female driver might have snatched the girl. And yes, Sally had agreed – her little face screwed up in a frown of concentration – she thought that the lady did have hair that colour as she pointed to a picture showing a woman with henna-dyed hair.

The task of hunting down known paedophiles had begun the day after Nancy's disappearance, a discreet line of inquiry that was being kept strictly under wraps for now. Lorimer and his team had to walk that fine line between observing civil liberties and making visits to the men on their register. All known sex offenders in their area had been contacted; their DNA profiles were all held on the national database. It was a painstaking job made even harder by keeping it from the papers. Sadie, the wee dragon in the police canteen, had her answer for them all: 'Castrate the bastards! That's whit ah'd dae tae the lot o them!' she'd growled when the news of Nancy Fraser's abduction had filtered down to her domain. But the reality was a lot more delicate than Sadie's politically incorrect suggestion. Just one smart-mouthed officer could provoke a convicted paedophile to run to the *Gazette* in the wake of a vigilante attack, screaming that his human rights were being trampled underfoot.

The possibility that Nancy had been snatched by a recently bereaved parent was harder to investigate but that was what Lorimer was working on, now that the appeal had been broadcast on national television. Back in his own room, Lorimer drummed his fingers on the edge of his desk, thinking about the sort of person who might take a child away from its own home and leave her mother worried to distraction. What sort of personality . . . ? Just as the thought was beginning to form, Lorimer picked up the telephone and dialled a number that he knew off by heart. It rang out twice then he heard a familiar voice, which made him smile for the first time since he'd left home that morning.

'Rosie? How are you? Still keeping your feet up and reading all these novels Maggie gave you?' Lorimer leaned back in his chair, swaying slightly from side to side as he heard the woman's chatty reply. Doctor Rosie Fergusson was currently on sick leave from her job as a consultant forensic pathologist at the University of Glasgow, a job that had brought her into close contact with Lorimer on many occasions. They had a good working relationship, the pathologist always ready to supply what information she could whenever a particularly difficult case of suspicious death arose. But it was not Rosie that he had wanted to call, despite the pleasure that listening to her voice always gave him. She was so lucky to be here and everyone was grateful that the feisty little blonde was going to be back at her work before the year was out.

'Is Solly around?' he asked.

'Ah, I see. After my other half, are you?' The note of amusement came across and Lorimer could hear her calling, 'Solly! Phone for you!' as she turned away from the telephone.

'Hello?'

'Solly. How are things?'

'Lorimer,' the voice on the other end of the line sounded relieved, 'thought it might have been one of my postgraduate students. Some of them are particularly needy at this stage in their work,' he sighed.

'Well, sorry to disillusion you but I wanted to pick your extensive brains just as badly.'

There was a silent pause while Dr Solomon Brightman considered this. The DCI was well used to Solly's long pauses, although they could still irritate him whenever he was looking for a particular response.

Dr Solomon Brightman had come into Lorimer's life one spring day when he had been at a loss to solve the murder of three young women whose bodies had been dumped in a Glasgow park.

From being resentful of an expertise that he'd not fully understood, Lorimer had come to admire the behavioural psychologist whose skills had been useful in helping to solve those multiple murders. And the forensic side of Dr Brightman's work was not simply a tool that Lorimer lifted and laid without thought for the man himself. Solly was a Londoner who had embraced the city of Glasgow as his permanent home and had become as much a friend as a colleague. Not only had the psychologist's initial involvement brought him into close contact with Strathclyde Police, but it had introduced him to Rosie.

'The Nancy Fraser case?' Solly ventured at last.

'Got it in one.'

'Not the happiest sort of investigation for you,' Solly remarked.

'You can say that again. I've just been with the mother making a public television appeal. Grim.' Lorimer heard himself sigh. 'Anyway, we're following several lines of inquiry, one of which is to investigate the possibility that the girl's been taken by someone who may recently have lost their own child. We've got a few documented cases from way back though I have to be honest they were all babies, not kids as old as Nancy. I wanted to run that idea past you to see if you would come up with any aspects of that sort of female behaviour that could give us something to go on.'

The silence at the other end might make anyone else wonder if the line had been cut off, but

Lorimer knew that Solly was taking his usual ponderous time before replying.

'I could certainly give you some case studies on the subject,' the psychologist replied at last. 'If that's what you want.'

Lorimer ran a hand through his hair. At this point what he wanted was for someone to come forward and tell them where Nancy Fraser was. But any pointer in the right direction would help.

'Okay. Thanks. But if you wanted to have a wee chat about the case, I'd be happy to see you. Unofficially, of course,' Lorimer added. The costs of this case were already spiralling and his superintendent was making noises about financial effectiveness. Paying for the services of a forensic psychologist just wasn't on unless events dictated otherwise.

'Can you spare some time this evening? Bring Maggie up?' Solly suggested. 'I'm sure Rosie would be delighted to see you both.'

'See what I can do. Call you later. Thanks,' Lorimer replied, hanging up as a familiar figure entered his room.

Detective Superintendent Mark Mitchison shot a questioning look at his DCI then let his eyes flick over Lorimer as though inspecting his appearance. Whatever he'd hoped to find (and possibly criticise) just wasn't there. Lorimer had taken extra care with his formal suit and had worn a sober tie that was the right side of funereal.

'This morning's appeal. No problems?' the

Detective Superintendent asked in a tone that suggested that his confidence in Lorimer handling the media was less than complete. It was true that certain journalists had rubbed Lorimer up the wrong way in the past and he'd had his own way of sorting them out, but an occasion like a public appeal for a missing child would never be one of them. A meeting with the Assistant Chief Constable was the only thing that had prevented Mitchison from doing the appeal with Kim Fraser himself. He wasn't averse to pulling rank in a case even when the DCI was Senior Investigating Officer.

'None whatsoever,' Lorimer replied smoothly, swinging in his chair in a manner deliberately calculated to annoy. There was no love lost between the two men and many officers still grumbled about the decision that had promoted Mitchison over Lorimer. Still, a decent working relationship was usually maintained by Lorimer's strategy of avoiding his senior officer whenever humanly possible.

'Right.' Mitchison paused as if he wanted to say more then turned away abruptly, his jaw tight with tension.

Lorimer let out a sigh of relief once the door was closed. Some days he'd have happily upped sticks and transferred to another division. He'd even seriously considered a vacancy in the recently formed cold case unit but the thought of leaving behind a team of officers who regarded him as much more than just their boss made him realise what he'd lose in the process. If promotion came, then fine. Right now he had far more immediate concerns, in the shape of a missing child.

Rosie smiled as she felt his fingers caress her hair. 'Anything interesting from the big man?' she asked.

Solly bent down and cupped her face in his hands, kissing her gently on the lips. 'Just wanting to talk about a case,' he murmured.

'Anything gory enough for my taste?' she replied, laughing.

'If you mean is it a murder case, well . . .' Solly tailed off, a crease appearing between his dark eyes.

'It's not the Nancy Fraser case, is it?'

'Why is it that a beautiful woman like you brightens up at the mention of serious crime when her lover is trying to distract her?' Solly gave a mock sigh, twirling a lock of Rosie's blonde hair around his finger.

'It *is* the Nancy Fraser case! What's Lorimer's take on it?' she asked, sitting up and snuggling against Solly's shoulder.

'I think he's hoping for a happy ending,' Solly replied quietly.

Rosie looked at his face. He had turned away from her but even so she could read the pain etched around his mouth. Her darling man, she thought suddenly. All of his training had led him to conclude that, statistically, this little girl was probably dead already. And such knowledge hurt someone as sensitive as Dr Solomon Brightman.

'Come here,' she whispered, shifting nearer to him. She couldn't change what was happening out there, where small children disappeared from their own doorsteps, but perhaps she might just be able to change that expression on Solly's face.

CHAPTER 14

It was one of those days when every period seemed to last an eternity, Kyle thought to himself. Why he'd thought of taking Geography last year simply defeated him. The teacher's voice droned on and he'd long since lost the thread of the lesson. The prospect of lunchtime and then double PE last thing was all that kept him awake. At last the sound of the corridor bell galvanised him into motion as the entire class scrambled towards the door, heedless of the teacher's instructions: 'Walk don't run.'

Everyone belted down the corridor, Kyle grinning as if he knew his taller frame and turn of speed would keep him out in front and near the head of the dinner queue. As he sped past Samantha Wetherby he could heard her swearing at her mobile phone. And at Julie. Pounding along the corridor, it crossed Kyle's mind to wonder just what Sam's best pal was up to. 'Too feart tae show her face,' one of their classmates had declared loudly at registration that morning. Mrs Lorimer had looked up at that but hadn't said a dicky bird, probably just as well. None of the teachers would be on Julie's side, would they? He agreed with them, but only just. Had there been anything going on at SU camp? Eric Chalmers was a big heart-throb to loads of these impressionable wee lassies. *Had* he taken advantage of her? There was plenty of speculation going on in the Year areas, much sniggering about Chalmers playing away when his missus had been up the duff. But did anyone really believe that? Was it not all daft talk?

But then again, Julie had finished with Kyle right after her return from the Scripture Union camp . . .

Kyle slithered to a halt, his trainers squealing on the vinyl floor of the dining hall. A chicken and veggie wrap, that's what he'd have – any thoughts about Mr Chalmers and Julie Donaldson disappearing as he concentrated on a fifteen-year-old boy's all-important task of filling his belly.

'Oh, that's better,' Sandie declared, slumping into the staffroom armchair, legs stretched out in front of her. 'First night at badminton. Why do I do it? Everything hurts!' she complained.

'Och, you'll be used to it in no time,' Maggie assured her. 'You're always worse at the beginning of term.'

'True,' Sandie admitted, wincing a little as she rolled her shoulders. 'What a morning I've had, though. See that Fourth Year? Hopeless! Haven't a clue about basic accounts.' The Business Studies teacher picked up a crumpled brown paper bag from the low table. 'Food! At last!' she sighed.

'Still, they're all computer literate, that must help,' Maggie offered.

'Sometimes. Though they'd rather be playing daft games than setting up spreadsheets.' Sandie dipped a wedge of cucumber into the pot of hummus she'd brought for lunch. 'And Miss Julie Donaldson's absence wasn't helping any. Even when the stupid wee cow isn't here she's causing trouble. Could hardly get them to shut up about it.'

'D'you think she's dogging it?'

Sandie snorted. 'Course she is. Manson told me that the stepmother was telephoned at her work. Says Julie left the house to go to school this morning. That wee madam's going to get hell from him whenever she decides to show her face!'

Maggie nodded silently. It certainly didn't look good for the Fourth Year pupil. All the talk throughout school was about Eric's suspension and Julie's sudden failure to attend school. The period before lunch Maggie Lorimer had been holding forth on Harper Lee's classic novel *To Kill a Mockingbird*. Put yourself in his shoes, she'd told her class. That's what Atticus Finch had told his daughter. Now Maggie wondered about the truant schoolgirl. Could she put herself into Julie's shoes, walk around in her skin and try to understand what was going on in that adolescent head? Maybe they were all too bound up in their loyalty to Eric, too horrified to contemplate that there might just be some grain of truth to the girl's accusation. And was it fear of the staff's condemnation that had made Julie cut classes today?

Maggie Lorimer let her mug of tea go cold as she stared into space, hardly listening to the chattering voices around her. It was etched in her mind, that moment when she'd heard Julie's anguished cry and seen the look upon Eric's face. And now, what was she supposed to do about it? a little voice asked.

'What?' Kyle looked at Finnegan in disbelief. 'No PE? Why the f—?' The boy swallowed the oath, a warning look from the teacher's face stopping him in time.

'Can't be helped, son.' Finnegan shrugged. 'Two of the staff called in sick this morning and we've already got periods docked to cover Mr Chalmers' classes.'

'But sitting inside on a day like this . . .' Kyle felt tears of angry frustration prick his eyelids. 'Can I no just go up to the workout area myself?'

Finnegan shook his head, watching the boy closely over the rim of his coffee mug. Kyle lived and breathed sports. He was a bright lad and had a good future before him if his grades were anything to go by, but at a time like this any enforced classroom activity would be purgatory for him. Those PE periods provided a precious escape valve for the youngsters, especially this lad. Kyle's family background was pretty dodgy with his brutish alcoholic father and an older sibling who was a known drug dealer. The boys from Drumchapel had been attending the school in Partick simply because their grandmother lived here and she was the one secure element in their lives. Granny McGarrity had battled for years with various well-intended folk from the Social Work department and had done a pretty good job in times past of protecting the three lads from the worst excesses of her son-in-law. All three had stayed with her during Kerrigan Senior's latest spell of detention at Her Majesty's pleasure. Nowadays, although there was always a room in Chancellor Street for her favourite grandson, Kyle still made his way back each day to the flat in Drumchapel, some notion of family loyalty binding him to the place. The teachers in Muirpark had been careful with this boy, nurturing his undoubted talent. Finnegan was not the only member of staff to see that Kyle could break free from the spiral of crime that had threatened to overwhelm the boy and several others like him.

Kyle closed his mouth and a mulish look came over his face that Finnegan recognised. Trouble ahead, the PE teacher told himself.

'Can I come up after school, though? Have a workout?'

Finnegan's sorry shake of the head made the boy jump to his feet, his metal chair falling backwards with a bang.

''S not fair!' he cried then turned and barged out of the PE base, leaving the upturned chair behind him, a visible mark of protest.

The teacher watched Kyle run across the playground, his rounded shoulders an eloquent statement of the lad's disappointment. Finnegan sighed. The start of this term had brought nothing but problems: all the publicity about Kerrigan's early release from prison, Eric Chalmers' suspension and now this. Kyle Kerrigan's day being spoiled might be small beer compared to what other people had to put up with, but teenagers didn't rationalise such things, especially ones whose home lives were hellish to begin with.

Kyle looked at his watch. Nearly three hours sitting in a stuffy classroom. No way! He glanced beyond the deserted playing fields to the road where a fast-food van was doling out greasy lunches to a string of kids. The bus stop was just around the corner. If he sidled around the van and just kept walking . . . The idea took flight and Kyle found himself shouldering his knapsack, already fingering the school tie that would be whipped off the minute the school building was out of sight. So what if he was missed this afternoon? Mr Finnegan might even cover for him if he was lucky. Kyle thought about the chair lying on the floor of the PE base and a spasm of guilt churned inside his stomach. Wasn't Dave Savage always telling him to keep his temper in check?

A good boxer always had self-control. Kyle gritted his teeth. He'd let himself down. But there was no way he was going back to school today, he decided, dodging round the burger van, his nose twitching from the smell of over-cooked fat.

It was as if fate had taken a hand in his decision. Just as he approached the bus stop, a number twenty drew up and Kyle hopped on and paid his fare.

'Not at school this afternoon, son?' the driver enquired.

Kyle reddened. Damn! He'd forgotten to take off his school tie. 'Dentist appointment,' he improvised swiftly.

The driver's raised eyebrows told Kyle exactly what he thought about that mumbled reply. Shuffling to the back of the bus, the boy slumped into a seat, his bag on his knee. He'd go all the way into town, he thought. Once there he'd decide what he wanted to do. For now escape was enough.

'She's where?' Tim Wetherby looked askance at his little sister.

'In town,' Sam admitted.

'Everyone says she's bottled it,' Tim said. 'Can't say I'm surprised. I mean, giving out all that pure crap about Chalmers. I mean, Sam, come on!'

Samantha hung her head, hair masking the doubt on her expression. 'I dunno. She was awful upset the day before yesterday . . .'

'Och, Julie Donaldson's the biggest drama queen, Sam. You know it and I know it,' Tim told her.

They were standing in a corner of the playground beneath a shaded walkway. The text to Sam's mobile had been the only communication from Julie and somehow that had hurt. Why hadn't she called her? Properly. It wouldn't have taken much time out of her day. What was she doing anyway? In town. What was that supposed to mean? Sam's thoughts whirled around but failed to come up with any sort of solution. She'd cried night after night after Dad had left and Julie had been there for her each morning, on the telephone or actually coming round to the house. Now things had changed.

'She's been really good to me since—' Sam began, a break in her voice. Abandoning any sort of worries about looking cool, Tim put his arm around his wee sister as he sensed the tears about to fall.

'It's okay, wee yin. Julie's a big girl. She'll take care of herself. Wait and see. It'll all sort itself out. Mr Manson'll make sure it does.'

'D'you really think so?' Sam lifted a tear-stained face. Her big brother sounded so sure. Tim had changed in recent days, Sam realised looking at his profile, the sharp jaw ending in that determined Wetherby chin. He was so like Dad, she thought with a sudden pang of recognition. Was that why her big brother seemed so much older?

She'd thought it was just because he was one of the Sixth Years now. Or maybe with Dad gone Tim was trying to take his place as the man of the house. That's what Gran had called him last night.

'Aye, you're probably right. Guess she'll call me tonight, eh?' Sam pulled away and searched in her bag for a paper hanky. 'Right, better go and tidy up. See you.' She attempted a tremulous smile and Tim grinned at her. In that fleeting moment Sam caught sight of the old Tim, the happy-go-lucky boy he had been before all this horrible stuff between their parents had happened. Then the moment was over and he was striding away from her towards the door that led to that holy of holies, the Sixth Year common room.

Glasgow city centre was more crowded than Kyle had anticipated. The unexpected bonus of more sunshine after a few days' interlude of rain seemed to have brought out the shoppers in force. A group of old ladies clad in light rain-jackets of varying shades of beige (as a concession to the summer weather) were standing staring at a window display; as he passed them he saw one point at something and declare, 'An awfu price' in reproving tones. Kyle grinned. It could've been his granny, the old dear sounded dead like her.

He'd left the bus at the corner of Renfrew Street and now he was walking past the steps leading up to RSAMD. The Royal Scottish Academy of Music and Drama was one of many cultural institutions of which the city was rightly proud. Kyle's class had been taken to a student production of *Twelfth Night* before the end of last session. He'd moaned like the rest of his class, sure that any play of Shakespeare's would bore him out of his box, but much to his surprise he'd actually enjoyed it. A comedy, the teachers had told him, but somehow he hadn't expected it to be so bloody funny or the actors to be so very, very good. The bus trip on the way back to school had been great, with everyone shouting out lines from the play in daft voices. Mrs Lorimer, who'd organised the event, had even joined in at one point. Kyle glanced up Hope Street towards the Theatre Royal. He'd been there just the once, at primary school. Some Roald Dahl story, he forgot which one. His two recollections of the place were of the myriad lights that made the gold-painted balconies glitter and, once those lights had dimmed, wondering how the band underneath the stage could possibly play in the dark.

Crossing as the wee green man appeared on the pedestrian lights, the boy made his way further into the heart of town, instinct taking him towards the Glasgow Royal Concert Hall that dominated the hill above Buchanan Street. He passed the verdigris-green statue of Scotland's first First Minister, Donald Dewar, and began walking past Buchanan Galleries. There were some young lads, not much older than himself, sitting on the stone steps tucking into their lunches; watching one of them take a bite from a huge baguette made Kyle's mouth water. His own lunchtime snack was already a memory. Maybe he should've gone round to Chancellor Street. Granny's tins were always full of home baking. A wistful look filmed Kyle's eyes. Och, well, it was too late now. He'd just hang about here till it was time to go home. She'd have just made a fuss anyway, giving him what for when she found he was cutting classes.

There was a Borders bookshop further down the hill; their magazine section was ace and you could actually sit and browse some of the sports copies without being hassled. The shop assistants always seemed too busy to bother so Kyle supposed that most folk eventually bought their stuff anyway. He'd rather keep what cash he had for the bus home and maybe something else to eat.

'Hiya. What're you doing in town, Kerrigan?'

Kyle whirled round. Julie Donaldson was standing right behind him, her bag slung casually over one shoulder.

'Could ask you the same question, Donaldson,' Kyle retorted.

'Dogging it, same as you,' she replied with the beginning of a grin. 'Fancy going for a coffee? There's a Starbucks just over there.'

Kyle felt his face redden. Starbucks' prices were out of his range and he couldn't afford to pay for hers as well. 'Naw, don't like that place,' he lied. 'How about we just go an sit at the back o Borders, eh?'

'If you like,' Julie agreed. 'It's probably a wee bit early for a thae Goths that always hang out there anyway.' She giggled. Kyle shrugged. School was split into so many factions, self-branded as Goths, Emos or whatever. Julie and her crowd certainly didn't favour the Goth look, he knew. They were right girly sort of girls, always on about the latest bands and fashions. Kyle glanced at Julie, appraisingly. Pity they weren't an item any more. She was a nice-looking lassie, with all that long blonde hair and a neat wee figure. Kyle liked to see the ones that kept fit. In his book there was no excuse for a teenager to get all flabby and he hated seeing lassies whose bellies rolled fat over their waistbands. Julie, he noted, was all right. More than all right, he thought, those old feelings suddenly rushing back. Today her lips were a nice pink colour with some shiny stuff making them all glossy. But apart from that she didn't have loads of stuff on her face, not like some of them who painted themselves daft until their grannies wouldn't recognise them. That was one of the things that had made Kyle fancy her in the first place.

'It's pure magic in the sunshine,' Julie said, flopping down on the stone steps beside him.

'Aye,' Kyle replied, suddenly at a loss for what to say. Why had he agreed to chum her? Why on earth hadn't he made up some excuse to go and do something? But her sudden appearance there in Buchanan Street had caught Kyle unawares.

Besides, he sensed that Julie was actually quite pleased to see him and that made him feel good, sort of. Julie Donaldson had been in his class since way back, he could simply regard her as an old pal, Kyle told himself. So that made it all right. There was no sense of her wanting to get back together with him.

Below them, Royal Exchange Square was thronging with afternoon shoppers looking for a rest in one of the many tea rooms on either side of the Gallery of Modern Art, a pseudo-classical building that dominated the area. The sun was warming the old grey stones making the place seem almost continental – the pavements filled with dinky wee tables and chairs outside where folk could sit and blether as they had their lattes or whatever, Kyle thought.

'So, why are you dogging it? They're all saying it's cos you cannae face Manson after what you said about Mr Chalmers.' The words were out before Kyle realised.

Julie gazed at him, her mouth opening to protest.

'Ah cannae see it myself. Chalmers always struck me as a right decent guy, y'know,' Kyle ploughed on.

'That's all you know!' Julie bristled, her shoulders suddenly squared. 'My father's making an official complaint. Chalmers better watch out!'

'Ooh!' Kyle grinned at her, his voice deliberately high and girlish. 'Fourth Year lassie tells tales.' He gave Julie a playful punch on her arm. 'Come on,

Jules, you can do better than that. Why not admit you're on another of these fantasy trips, eh?' Kyle asked, his tone more serious.

'Kyle Kerrigan, you know absolutely nothing about this! And if you did, you wouldn't talk to me like that!' Julie stood up suddenly and lunged at the boy but, caught off-balance, she tripped and landed heavily against him.

It was an automatic reflex, Kyle realised afterwards. His hands flew to her arms and grasped them tightly, taking her away from him.

'Ow! That hurt! You're just as bad as all the rest of them, Kerrigan. Bloody wee ned!' The girl wrenched free from his grasp and swung her bag at him, narrowly missing his right eye. Kyle recoiled but the dark expression on his face made Julie retreat down the steps, still yelling at him. Fists bunched by his sides, the boy watched as she crossed the square, clip-clopping on these silly high heels. Ach, she wasn't worth bothering about, Kyle decided, his mouth turning up in disgust. Behind him he heard an exhalation of breath as someone came out of the bookshop, someone who'd obviously witnessed that little scene. Kyle moved aside, catching a glimpse of a tall woman who shot him a look of disapproval before walking down the steps. His face flaming now, the boy turned away, stumbling back into Borders and the sanctuary of the crowded bookshop.

But the woman was not the only one to have taken in the fracas between them; up above the classical

129

pediment and the fluted pillars of the building, a CCTV device had its grey head turned on the very spot where the argument had taken place, Kyle's mask of fury immortalised on camera for anyone who wanted to see.

CHAPTER 15

It was almost too easy. Of course he hadn't expected to see her with the boy. But the way things had turned out had worked to his advantage.

'Mind if I sit here?' he asked, looking at all the tables around them in the cafe's forecourt, deliberately adopting an air of exasperation.

The girl looked up, a mixture of doubt and surprise in her expression. A swift turn of her head to see the lad was nowhere in sight seemed to reassure her. 'No problem,' she told him, a hint of a smile softening her face. 'It's so crowded here today.' She broke off and he grinned at her, pulling out the metal chair.

'What'll you have?' A dark-haired waitress appeared, her tiny frilled apron tied tightly round the tiniest of miniskirts, long black-clad legs ending in clumpy shoes. A student waiting on tables for the holidays, he surmised, someone who would be here today and gone tomorrow, never remembering the man and girl sitting outside in the afternoon sunshine.

He gestured for the blonde to order first then,

'Double espresso, please,' he replied then, when the waitress had gone off, 'My treat,' he whispered conspiratorially. 'I've just slipped away from the studios for an hour or so. Don't tell.' He placed a finger against his lips and winked at her.

'Oh.' Julie seemed taken aback. 'I can't let you—'

'Least I can do since you let me sit at your table.' He smiled at her. 'You're not keeping it for anyone?'

'No.' Julie hoped the warmth on her face and neck was not a huge big reddie. How uncool would that be? This guy was nice – a bit old, maybe – but nice. Tall and angular with a good head of thick fair hair, he reminded Julie of someone off the telly. He had a good voice, too, like he was maybe an actor or something. A frisson of excitement ran up her spine. That was probably it! Why else would a good-looking man like that be in Glasgow at this time of the day? Away from the studios, he'd said.

'Enjoying the summer vacation?' he asked, pulling a packet of Marlboros from his pocket, taking one and placing it between his lips. He had nice white teeth, Julie saw.

'Sorry, how rude of me. Do you . . . ?' The man offered the packet across the table and Julie took one without hesitation.

'Thanks,' she said, then bent forwards as he cupped a hand around the flame from his match, his fingers just brushing her own. As the nicotine rush left her lungs like a great sigh of relief, Julie sat back, crossed her legs and regarded this man in what she hoped was a sophisticated appraisal.

'Yes, just doing a bit of shopping before I go back to uni,' she lied, swinging her leg up and down. He smiled again and nodded, flicking ash from his cigarette and taking another drag, his eyes hazy and warm as the smoke drifted upwards.

'One latte, one double espresso.' The dark-haired waitress was there and gone in seconds, rushing to take orders from yet another table.

'Cheers.' The man held up his little coffee cup and bent his head to one side. 'To all the pretty students who wish they were as lovely as you.' He kept looking at Julie as he drank his coffee and this time she simply couldn't control the blush that seemed to spread tingling right into the roots of her hair. Just then her mobile sounded and she dipped into her bag, lifting it out. But before she could do another thing, his hand had covered hers, enclosing the phone.

'Switch it off,' he said, another twinkling smile making his dimples deepen. 'Don't let's spoil the moment. It won't last, after all.'

Julie felt the warmth of his hand for just a moment, then it was gone. Obediently she pressed the red button and dropped the mobile back in her bag. Of course, it was bad manners to use phones in company. That was what Mary was always going on about. She'd call Sam back later. *And* she'd have something interesting to tell her,

Julie thought, tossing her hair back and smiling conspiratorially at the man.

'What's your name?' he asked suddenly. 'No, don't tell me, let me guess. Must be something special. No parents could have looked at such a baby and given her an ordinary name. Francesca, Susannah . . . Angelica. Yes. That must be it: Angelica. Tell me I'm right,' his voice pleaded even while his grin told her he was teasing.

Julie suppressed a giggle, shaking her head. Was he in films then? All these names were redolent of fame and this man looked as if he did indeed spend time with such female goddesses. Suddenly plain old Julie Donaldson seemed a bit of a let-down, so horribly dull.

'Juliet,' she replied. 'Juliet Carr,' she improvised swiftly, a silver BMW suddenly in her line of vision as it swept along Queen Street only yards from their table.

'Well, Juliet Carr,' he began, his tongue fondling the name as if it were something he could actually taste in his mouth, 'how would you like to give up university and do something much more exciting?'

CHAPTER 16

'**D**arling, I'll get her. Just you relax.'
Ruth tried to let her body sink into the squashy cushions of the settee, her hands clasping over the place where Ashleigh had been. It was an automatic gesture, but now instead of the rounded bump she felt only a roll of post-baby fat. Tears of self-pity sprang to Ruth's eyes. She'd had such a nice figure when they'd married and now it would be ages before she'd be her old slim self again. Closing her eyes, Ruth felt her whole body stiffen as Ashleigh's cries became ever more distressed. Each time the baby woke, screaming, it was as if a reflex action occurred, galvanising Ruth into action, some instinct telling her to pick up the baby, shush her gently and see what she could do to placate the little scrap of humanity that had turned their world upside down. She'd fed and changed her less than half an hour ago, so what was wrong this time?

'She's tired, wee lamb,' Eric announced, cradling their daughter as he brought her into the lounge.

His large hand looked enormous supporting her

tiny head, Ruth thought. He was so strong; her strong tower, she'd called him just this morning.

'Tell you what. Why don't I take her for a ride in the car? She'll go to sleep in her carrier and then I can put her down for the night. Good idea?'

Ruth nodded silently, a smile of pure gratitude crossing her lips. 'What a pet you are. Thanks, love,' she told him.

'And get some rest. I don't want to come home and find you've been doing the ironing or anything. Remember what the doctor said.'

'Promise,' she agreed and put her hand on his arm as he bent to brush her hair with his lips. 'You're so good to me, Eric. Thank God you're here.'

'Well,' he cocked his head to one side, grinning ruefully, 'maybe God does work in mysterious ways after all. Could be he intends to have your husband at home just for a wee while.'

'You should have put in for paternity leave,' Ruth mumbled then her face split in an enormous yawn and she snuggled deeper into the corner of the settee, her head already lolling against the arm rest.

Eric Chalmers looked down at her for a moment then, as Ashleigh began to whimper once more, he placed his little daughter gently into the baby carrier and took her out of the room.

A ride round for half an hour might do the trick, he thought. It would also help to clear his own head for the meeting scheduled tomorrow. A risk assessment was not enough prior to suspension. This accusation of sexual assault was serious and merited an interview with the police in attendance. As Eric strapped the baby safely into the back seat, he thought about Julie. She was once a wee thing like that, and not so terribly long ago, either. What had gone wrong? He closed the car door as quietly as he could manage then, before turning the key in the ignition, Eric thought again about the pupil who had caused him so much heartache. How could she have done this to him after that glorious time they'd spent at SU camp?

It took only ten minutes before Ashleigh quietened down and Eric knew she would be sound asleep. So, go home now? That's what he really should do, but as the car turned the round-about at the foot of the hill he began to think about what lay back there for him: Ruth's tired, patient face and days, weeks perhaps, of interminable emptiness, suspended from a job he loved. For the first time, Eric Chalmers knew a pang of loss and regret so strong that his jaw hardened and the mouth that had laughed with so many of his pupils became a thin, unsmiling line. What on earth was he going to do now? Then panic began to rise like a tidal wave, threatening to overwhelm him. What would happen to them if he lost his job? And in such circumstances that he'd never find another?

He needed time to think, to decide what he had to do. The Vet School was nearing on his left as the car crept back uphill, Dawsholm Park a little way beyond. It was a favourite place of theirs and he'd planned to take Ashleigh there in her pram one day. The road ahead blurred with sudden, self-pitying tears; if his worst imaginings became reality then everything he'd worked so hard for might be snatched away from him.

Kyle gave the tin can a vicious kick, sending it rattling along the pavement. Why the hell had he blurted out that stupid question to Julie? It had just caused a bigger fuss and he'd felt so self-conscious slinking away from the city after that. Hadn't folk been looking at him as if he was some kind of yob? His toe found the can beside the scrubby verge and he lashed at it again, kicking it across the road where it clattered under a car. Hands in his pockets, Kyle trudged up the road, rows of brown tenement houses hemming him in on either side, cutting off the crepuscular blue of the sky. He'd been hours returning from the town, preferring to walk rather than take a bus. Being close to other people was something he just didn't want right now. Hopefully no one would be at home and he could raid the fridge and sit and watch telly on his own for a bit. His belly grumbled again, reminding Kyle that he hadn't eaten since lunchtime.

At last he came to his own close and turned in, shoving open the heavily scarred wooden door. The place was supposed to be secure but the outside gadget with all the wee buttons had been ripped out ages ago and nobody seemed to care if it was replaced or not. A couple of kids were scuttling about on their plastic scooters as he rounded the corner to head up the three flights of stone stairs. It was Tracey-Anne from the ground floor and her pal, Ellie, both four-going-on-fourteen with big eyes that had knowing looks far beyond their years.

'Hiya Ki-yul,' one of them called out in a sing-song voice. 'Hiv ye been away with yer girlfriend?' The pair of them broke into daft giggles.

'Youse shouldnae be out this late. Where's yer mammy?' Kyle scolded, his words assuming their own dialect. Then seeing Tracey-Anne stick her tongue out at him he laughed and started up the stairs. The mammy would be down the boozer, like as not, and some older kid would be inside watching *Big Brother* instead of minding the weans.

Kyle fitted his key in the lock as quietly as he could. Reaching the sanctuary of his bedroom could be like a military operation if he wanted to avoid his da. The noise of the television told him immediately that someone was home. Creeping down the long, narrow hall, Kyle peeped into the darkened room and ducked back out immediately. Da was slumped in front of the screen, his back to the living-room door, watching football on Sky, a can of lager in one hand and the usual bottle of Bell's on the floor by his side. With the sound turned up and the images flickering across the screen, old man Kerrigan hadn't noticed a thing.

The boy moved like a cat as he slipped into the kitchen, opened the fridge and extracted an opened pack of ham, a jar of pickle and the remains of a pizza. He was thirsty, too, and there just might be a bottle of ginger lurking inside the larder. Yes! Grasping the bottle neck with two fingers, he held his food against his chest and tiptoed back up the corridor to his own room. The sound of his father shouting made him freeze for a second until he realised that someone on the telly had scored and the stream of four-letter words was merely the old man voicing his approval.

Kyle let out his breath and slipped into the bedroom that he was supposed to share with Tam. His older brother spent most of his nights with a lassie nowadays and Kyle welcomed the peace and quiet it gave him. He sat down on the unmade bed, smoothing a bit to make it more comfortable, then made a start on the cold pizza. The congealed cheese was rubbery in his mouth. Kyle didn't care; it was better than nothing and nothing was what he'd had for most of the day. He ate swiftly, swigging from the ginger bottle to wash it all down, then gave a belch of satisfaction once everything was finished.

Replete, the boy lay back, arms tucked behind his head. God, he was tired! Kyle smiled; he should be safe from his da now that the old guy was well on the way to being bevvied. Well, at least he'd made it back and no one had seen him come in.

Had he known what lay ahead, Kyle Kerrigan would not have been congratulating himself on the prospect of being left all alone with nobody to say where he was and what he was doing that night.

CHAPTER 17

'How did you find the time to escape from the case?' Maggie asked as they settled into Lorimer's ancient dark blue Lexus. The leather seats creaked as she stretched to buckle up her seat belt, then seemed to emit a small sigh as she sank back, stretching out her bare legs.

'Done all we can do for now. There's still a team of uniforms working the surrounding areas and night shift will call me if there are any major developments.' There was a moment's pause, each of them realising what sort of developments he had meant. 'Think we can class this evening as work of a sort, though, don't you?' Lorimer tried to give her a grin that creased his eyes, making Maggie feel a familiar tingle. For two pins she'd have stayed home and gone to bed early; that look in her husband's eyes told her he was thinking along similar lines.

'Love you,' he said, sliding a hand over her thigh then looked ahead of them as the big car swung into the road.

His wife caught his hand and gave it a squeeze in reply. Never mind, a night out at Solly and

Rosie's would be just fine. Bed, if not sleep, was still a delicious prospect some hours away.

Maggie gazed out of the window as the countryside sped past. Late August here in Scotland's West Coast meant harvest time and following that long, dry summer the fields had become creamy with swathes of barley and oats, many having been baled into squat rolls and wrapped in aquamarine plastic. A hen pheasant erupted from the hedgerow as they drove by, a nervous wreck of a creature flapping mindlessly to the safety of adjoining pastureland.

'Daft bird!' Lorimer commented, an indulgent smile hovering upon his lips. It would've been a different story if he'd hit it, Maggie knew. He might be the tough Detective Chief Inspector who was used to reducing hardened criminals to tears but her husband was a sentimental soul when it came to wildlife. Every flattened hedgehog by the roadside made him wince and Maggie had learned long since not to remark on roadkill if she could help it.

At last they were in the city and driving up from Woodlands Road towards the graceful curve of houses where the forensic pathologist lived with her fiancé. Lorimer eased the car into a nearby space then walked around to the passenger's side to open the door for Maggie. She could feel his eyes on her slim legs as she swung them around on to the pavement. Then his hand was searching for hers as they made their way towards the front door. This almost felt like a night out, though she knew from previous experience that the conversation would inevitably turn to shop talk.

'You made it!' Rosie opened the door wide and gave Maggie a hug. 'Wondered if His Nibs would be able to come up with all that's been going on,' she added. 'Come on in. Solly's just opening some stuff he bought in the KRK store. Nibbles with attitude,' she added, rolling her eyes.

Maggie just laughed. Their men both enjoyed the delights of what had become known as Curry Valley, Glasgow's legendary eastern cuisine, and the KRK store was well patronised by Asians who had made this part of Glasgow their home.

'Something to drink?'

'Just something soft,' Lorimer replied. 'I'm driving.'

'Well, I'll be joining you. Still on *tons* of medication,' Rosie said, screwing her pretty nose up in disgust. 'How about some lime juice and tonic? At least that way it'll feel as if we might be drinking gin.'

'Well, I'm happy to hit the harder stuff.' Maggie grinned. 'A proper G and T, thanks. Plenty of ice. It's really warm tonight, isn't it?'

'Ah, lovely. Here we are.' Solomon Brightman emerged from the kitchen bearing a tray of small bowls. Maggie looked up at him appraisingly. Anyone meeting the psychologist for the first time might be excused for taking him for a foreigner, so exotic was his appearance. That dark, luxuriant beard and those twinkling ebony-brown eyes fringed with impossibly long lashes seemed to belong to a person from some distant land. Or from another time, Maggie mused to herself; Scheherazade might have told a story concerning a sage who looked just like Solly.

'You're all right, Maggie?' he asked, turning as if he had felt her gaze on him.

'Never better, Solly,' she assured him, raising her glass in his direction. For a long moment Solly simply smiled at her as if he could somehow see into her mind and read her thoughts. It was a disquieting habit of his and Maggie often wondered just what the psychologist made of her, an ordinary schoolteacher who had hitched her star to the legendary DCI William Lorimer.

The evening sky deepened into a luminescent blue, Venus sparking her flint against the burgeoning darkness as the talk drifted towards the missing girl. Maggie, her limbs heavy with sudden sleepiness and too much gin, sat up a little bit straighter, suddenly conscious of just how important Solly's input might be to the case.

'Let's leave them to it,' Rosie whispered, nudging her friend's arm. 'Got something to show you next door.' And with a wink, the pathologist led Maggie out of the lounge and into the spare bedroom.

As soon as Rosie threw the light switch, Maggie saw it.

'Wow! You're certainly using your recuperation to good purpose! That's . . .' Maggie, suddenly lost for words, took a step towards the old-fashioned wardrobe where an open door revealed a full-length wedding gown. The dress shimmered in the light, illuminating a thousand tiny seed pearls scattered over a fine web of creamy lace. 'That's . . . that's like something out of a fairytale,' she said at last, a sigh in her voice.

'You like it, then?' Rosie grinned. 'Solly's forbidden from coming in here unless I let him.' She laughed. 'Good old tradition. Never let the groom see his bride until she has him at the altar.'

'So you've set the date?' Maggie hardly looked at her friend, so taken with gazing at the exquisite dress. Full skirted with a tiny waist and satin straps, she could already imagine this wedding gown on Rosie as she floated down the aisle.

'Yep. December twenty-sixth. Stick it in your diary and tell that man of yours he'll be on a different kind of duty that day.'

'Oh? How's that, then?'

'Well. We thought you two might just be our witnesses.'

'Oh.' Maggie failed to hide her surprise. 'You're being married in the registry office.'

Rosie laughed. 'Well, to start with at any rate. It is just along the road, after all. We will have all the family up for a traditional Jewish shindig, though. Can't have their boy selling out on them completely,' she added. 'But there'll be a few Scottish elements as well, never fear.'

★   ★   ★

Lorimer looked at the psychologist and frowned. 'You're sure about this?'

Solly nodded. 'I found all of these case studies in our department. The Prof is quite happy for you to have them. They are copies, naturally.'

'Good of you,' Lorimer muttered, turning over the sheets of paper within a pale grey folder.

'There's one in particular that I thought you might find interesting.' Solly bent over Lorimer's shoulder, thumbing through the file. 'Yes, here it is. If you read this you'll see the patient was incorrectly diagnosed at first as having Munchausen's by proxy.' Solly made a face. 'There were some high-profile offenders round about that time and every Tom, Dick and Harry wanted to put the Munchausen's label on them. But this was a bit different, as you'll see.'

The psychologist straightened up then wandered over to the stereo to change the CD. Soon the strains of Elgar's *Enigma Variations* commanded one part of his attention as Lorimer read the case study.

It was chillingly familiar. A child exactly Nancy Fraser's age had been snatched from near her home by a woman in a car and driven away. Lorimer glanced at the date; it had happened more than a decade before and in a small Lancashire town, the names of the victim, her family and the snatcher all quite unfamiliar to him. The child's mother had been a single mum, her home a rented flat in a sink estate not unlike the one where Kim

Fraser had been trying to raise her daughter. A massive police search had ensued. Lorimer nodded to himself: so far it all tallied. Then his eyebrows rose as he read on.

'She gave the child back?' He looked at the psychologist in surprise.

Solly nodded from his chair beside the bay window, his dark head outlined against the sodium glow from the city lights. 'Took her right to her own front door. Waited until the mother appeared then apologised to her.'

'And gave herself up to the police,' Lorimer continued, reading on. 'After which she was detained in a secure mental hospital where she was eventually diagnosed as suffering from a delusional disorder.' He looked up. 'Where is she now?'

Solly smiled sadly. 'Still there as far as I know. She thought she was the child's grandmother, in her less lucid moments.' He shrugged. 'When she was, shall we say, "seized with a spell of normality",' he fingered the inverted commas in the air, 'she returned the child and asked for help. The names are changed, of course. But the story is perfectly accurate.'

Lorimer tapped his chin thoughtfully. 'Would be nice to think there's a person out there looking after Nancy Fraser.' Then he shook his head. 'But statistically we aren't expecting to find her alive now.'

'I know,' Solly replied softly. 'But if you read to the end you'll find that the Lancashire police expressed quite the same sentiments. Coffee?' he asked, motioning towards the door of the kitchen. 'I suspect our other halves will be a little while. Rosie's bought her wedding dress,' he confided, a shy smile making his handsome features even more boyish than usual.

'That was a lovely night.' Maggie sighed as the car picked up speed. She closed her eyes and Lorimer glanced over at her, savouring the smile softening her face. It was good that Solly and Rosie had one another, good that they were cementing this unlikely pairing. For a moment Lorimer had an image of them both as an elderly couple, laughing together, Solly's mop of hair grizzled with age, Rosie's blonde locks a white halo. And he found himself mentally saying a word of thanks for whatever power had brought the pathologist back from the brink of death after that terrible accident, giving them both a future together.

Following the beam from his headlights, Lorimer stared straight ahead, willing that same power to let him find little Nancy Fraser.

CHAPTER 18

'What exactly are you trying to tell me, Eric?' The tall man stared down at his son, his hawk-like nose and bushy eyebrows making his handsome face harsh and bleak.

Anyone seeing both men together would immediately have seen the familial resemblance; each man had the height and spare frame of an athlete and the sort of facial bone structure that classical sculptors recreated from the finest Carrera marble. But the Reverend Paul Chalmers lacked a certain quality that featured in his son's appearance. Eric had a natural grace that seemed to shine through, as if a light within could not help but illuminate his entire personality.

'I told you, Julie forced herself onto me. The poor girl.' Eric shook his head. 'She's simply infatuated, Dad. She didn't know what she was doing. I mean, teenagers like that . . .' He broke off with a shrug, as if anyone would understand.

'Little tarts, you mean?' Paul Chalmers' sneer made Eric look up suddenly to see his father's curled lip and expression of distaste.

'She isn't like that,' Eric replied quietly. 'Julie's

a lively girl, full of fun. A bit too inclined to fancies, perhaps. But I won't have you calling her a tart, Dad.'

'You seem a bit too protective of her for your own good, Eric,' the minister replied. 'Perhaps there's more to this relationship of yours than you've told Ruth, for instance.'

Eric stood up quickly, facing his father, twin spots of colour in his cheeks.

Paul Chalmers smiled grimly. 'Don't like to hear the truth, is that it?'

'Dad,' Eric shook his head, 'you just don't understand, do you? I have done absolutely nothing wrong, as the Lord is my witness. And if you can't accept my word for it, well . . .' He trailed off, a look of disappointment in his eyes. 'At least the folks at school seem to have accepted what I've told them,' he muttered, turning away and gathering up his jacket. 'I'll be in touch,' he added. 'May God bless you, Dad.'

As his son closed the door behind him, the Rev Paul Chalmers curled his hands into fists, his jaw clenched tightly in suppressed fury. Eric had brought shame on their good name and that was something he would find hard to forgive.

Once out in the fresh air, Eric let his breaths become deeper and slower. Why did his father always make him feel like that? The need to justify himself, to prove to the older man that his son was right to follow this vocation, kept coming to the surface like a sore that wouldn't heal. That his father had never forgiven him for refusing to take up the ministry was one thing, but to suggest that there was some guilt on his part with Julie, well, that simply defied any sort of belief. It had seemed the right thing to do, driving over to the Manse early this morning, letting his father know what was happening. It was not the sort of thing a telephone call could easily achieve. But what had he expected, sympathy? No. There had been nothing like that between them, ever. A simple acceptance that his only son was a truthful man who found himself in an invidious situation was surely not too much to ask. Well, it seemed that it was. And now Eric experienced the familiar sinking feeling that told him he would never be good enough for his father no matter how hard he tried.

As he opened the car door, Eric smiled to himself. Ruth was waiting. And baby Ashleigh. These were blessings that God had provided, a voice in his head reminded him, and he must be glad in his heart. Yet, as he drove along the road, knowing that his wife and child were becoming ever closer, Eric felt a certain sense of despair. The shadow of that wee girl's abduction seemed to hang over the entire city like a pall.

'Let them find little Nancy Fraser,' he whispered, eyes fixed on the road ahead.

Then other words flickered into his mind. *A bit too protective of her for your own good. Perhaps there's more to this relationship* . . . The sound of his father's voice hammered inside his head, drowning out any other thoughts of prayer, especially one for himself.

'Wouldn't *you* want to disappear if you were in her shoes?'

'I don't know,' Maggie Lorimer replied. In truth she was worried. Maybe it was that other case, the little Fraser girl who had been abducted from right outside her front door, that gave her such a feeling of unease, but something cold was turning in the pit of her stomach. Guilt? Should she have told someone about seeing Julie and Eric? Last night Maggie had decided on a course of action but now she hesitated to put it into practice.

'Are you doing anything after school?' she asked Sandie as they hovered outside their respective classrooms.

'Nope. What have you in mind?'

'Thought we could go and see Ruth. I've got a present for the baby. How about it?' Maggie asked, her face creasing into a smile.

'Okay. But can we go via the shops first? I haven't even got them a card yet.'

'Right, you're on. See you later,' Maggie said. They parted company for that interlude of quiet before the first bell brought their registration classes thundering into the corridors.

The daily staff bulletin had Julie Donaldson's disappearance from home as its headline. Her parents had telephoned Manson early on and now everybody on Muirpark's teaching staff was aware of the girl's absence. But was it simply an absence? Maggie Lorimer tried to reassure herself with Sandie's words as she tucked the bulletin out of sight. Would she have done a runner to avoid the situation she'd created for herself? Or, and here that little doubt niggled away at her, had something bad happened to the girl? Oh, come on, fifteen was old enough to take care of herself, wasn't it? Maggie's mind see-sawed back and forward as she considered just what Julie Donaldson might have done. With a sigh, she turned to the cupboard behind her and took out the folder with lesson plans for periods one and two. Poetry with S3, 'Dulce et Decorum Est'. Good old Wilfred Owen would take her away from such everyday problems. There was nothing like the gloom of trench warfare to focus one's mind.

Mary Donaldson stood in the middle of her step-daughter's bedroom regarding the smooth coverlet over the single bed, the slippers tidied neatly under the dressing table and the wardrobe doors closed at last. She'd wanted to pick up the clothes from the floor where Julie had dropped them and hurl them out of the window in a moment of sheer blind fury that would leave her weak and shaking. Instead Mary had picked everything up, putting the discarded items into drawers, onto hangers or into the white metal bin that Julie was supposed to use for dirty laundry. Now all the clutter was tidied out of sight Mary actually felt worse, as if she had somehow been responsible for erasing Julie's presence from the room.

Had it been her fault? she asked herself for the hundredth time. Had she been too hard on the girl, suggesting a fantasy when in fact there really was some substance to her dreadful accusation? Frank was adamant that his girl had been wronged by that Religious Education teacher, but Mary hadn't been so certain.

'I've called the police.' Frank's voice behind her made Mary spin round, her mouth an 'O' of surprise. She hadn't heard him coming up the stairs. How long had he been standing there, watching her, feeling her despair? she wondered.

'Have we phoned everybody?' Mary asked, hearing the thickness in her words, emotion constricting her throat. She put out a hand to touch his arm, an automatic gesture that sought to reassure him as much as it signalled her own desire to be comforted.

Frank Donaldson nodded his head, his shoulders bowed in weariness. Neither of them had slept a wink, rising and dressing at first light after hours of straining their ears for that sound of a key in the lock. He'd driven round looking for Julie after that, then the phone calls had begun, each one producing the same negative result: Julie wasn't there, nobody had seen her since that last day at school. The only whiff of his daughter had come from the Wetherbys; Samantha had had a text from Julie saying she was up in the town, then nothing. He and Mary had tried over and over to make contact with her mobile phone but it was clearly switched off, yet another sign that his daughter was rebuffing all their efforts to communicate with her.

'I called Manson as well,' Frank said, his hands dangling uselessly by his sides. 'Told him Julie had never stayed out like this before.'

'Yes, that's true. I mean, we know Julie's going through this bolshy teenage phase, but she's always let us know where she is and who she's with.' Mary bit her lip to stop from crying, aware that she was beginning to babble, with hysteria not too far away.

'Except,' Frank Donaldson said with a sudden venom that made his fingers curl into fists, 'when she'd been seeing that Chalmers fellow. D'you think he's behind this?'

Mary looked at him, stunned into silence by the accusation.

'For two pins I'd like to know where he lives so I could shake the truth out of him!' Frank's voice rose and ended in a cry of anguish. Mary watched in horror as his tears of rage turned to tears of impotent self-pity.

'It's all right, love,' Mary soothed, her arms around his waist. 'She'll come home, I'm sure she will.' Yet as she laid her head against her husband's heaving shoulder, Mary Donaldson experienced a spasm of anxiety that gave the lie to her own words.

★   ★   ★

156

'Missing fifteen-year-old girl.' DS Niall Cameron waved a piece of paper at his colleague Detective Constable John Weir. 'Father says she was dogging school yesterday. Didn't come home.'

Weir shrugged his shoulders. 'Wonder who she's shagging.'

Cameron frowned. 'That's maybe the crux of the problem. She recently claimed that her RE teacher had sexually assaulted her at Scripture Union camp.'

'So what does this teacher bloke have to say about it?'

Cameron's smile faded. 'We should know soon enough. He's due to have an interview with uniforms this afternoon as part of an initial inquiry. Seems we're invited to join the party.'

Lorimer eased himself back into his chair, a smile hovering on his mouth. Last night had been one of the most enjoyable since Maggie had returned to work after the school holidays. Rosie was obviously recovering well from her operation and enjoying the enforced rest. It had done his heart good to hear the two women chattering about girly things instead of what was happening in the world of pathology. Solly and he had discussed the Fraser case at some length and that had not made such pleasant conversation. Both agreed that it would now take a bit of a miracle to find the little girl alive and well. Too many days had passed for any good news to emerge.

When the telephone rang, Lorimer was still thinking about the previous evening. As he listened, the smile was immediately wiped from his face.

'Where?' he asked. 'Right. I'll have the team over now.' He put the phone down, reached for his jacket and was out of the door in two seconds flat.

'They've found a body,' he declared, entering the open-plan room where several members of his team were sitting at desks. 'Team scouring the woods for Nancy Fraser,' he added. 'So let's get ourselves over there now!'

Lorimer was aware of his heart thumping a rhythm of despair as the big car leapt into the road outside police headquarters. Dawsholm Woods was less than ten minutes' drive away from Nancy's home. As he headed west all he could think of was that young mother's face as she'd turned towards him yesterday, doubt and fear etched so clearly on her features. What the hell was he going to tell her?

'Young white female, mid to late teens. Strangled.' The pathologist lifted up a grimy hand. 'Nothing under the fingernails that can be seen, so maybe we can conclude that it was over pretty quickly.' He glanced up at Detective Chief Inspector Lorimer, who was staring at the body. The girl's face was a mask of agony, eyes and mouth wide open in her final moment of terror. Her head was still thrown back, revealing a series of bruises upon her throat where fingers had cut off her last breath. Lorimer tried to stop himself imagining the scream that had been lost in that moment when all that could have been uttered was a weak gurgling sound as the airways were constricted. Every time he came to a crime scene and saw the body, it happened: his mind would flash back to the moment of death. It was something he had no control over and he'd gradually come to realise that he was trying to see the victim as a flesh-and-blood human being who had been violated, not simply as another murder case. Moments like these kept alive that spurting flame of anger that drove him on and helped him focus on the questions that could lead to a killer.

Her blonde hair was full of leaves and soil from the shallow grave where they had found her, and her pallid skin was streaked with dirt. As he hunkered down there beside the pathologist, Lorimer noticed a shiny red insect emerge from inside the girl's white blouse. It crawled over the edge, stumbling on the ridge of her collar, then hesitated before opening a pair of brown gauzy wings and taking off into the air. His mouth twisted in a spasm of disgust. She was probably crawling with tiny beasties. Swallowing back the phlegm that had gathered in his mouth, Lorimer swept a careful eye over her clothing – she was fully dressed, even down to her high-heeled shoes. That wasn't to say she hadn't been sexually assaulted, though, he told himself grimly. As he leaned in close to the dead girl, Lorimer caught a whiff of decomposition.

'Dan, how long?'

'Oh, she was put here very recently. I'd say she's been dead less than twenty-four hours. Know more later,' the pathologist replied gruffly.

Lorimer nodded. He would be there to see for himself as Dr Daniel Murphy performed the post-mortem and someone else's daughter was subjected to the pathologist's scalpel. His throat tightened as he stifled a sigh of relief. Okay, so it wasn't Nancy Fraser's body but some other poor souls would be grieving just as badly before much longer. He looked back at the girl's body, wondering about the person who had dug the hole out of the dry forest earth. Forensics would be making every effort to look at things like spade marks. Had she already been dead when he'd buried her there? Or was this some sicko who'd been all prepared with a shovel in the back of his van? Such things had happened before and Lorimer was only too familiar with the vagaries of that sort of warped human nature.

Leaving the scene of the crime, Lorimer headed back to the nearest footpath. This wood was full of paths that turned and twisted in a maze-like fashion and he quickly noticed that someone had put in coloured markers to show where each track was leading. Had this been carried out by park rangers? How many worked here and what exactly did they do? These were details he'd have to find out, he thought, even as he eyed the red-painted tree stumps, fearful of losing his sense of direction. Had the killer been so familiar with this place that he needed no such guidance? A local man? One of the dog walkers, perhaps? His head buzzed with questions about the identity of the man who had taken the girl into the woods.

He soon realised that the park had been built on a hillside with several undulations that fell away into the steep sides of the river Kelvin, its waters racing along, a fierce brown torrent that might carry the woodland's detritus miles away. Some paths were made from tarmac, others were mere cinder paths while a third sort consisted of red chips. The path he had chosen led Lorimer deeper and deeper into the quiet of the woodland. Many of the great trees looked like something out of a child's nightmare: their roots snaking green mossy tentacles into the ground, clutching at it cruelly. It would be hard to bury a body in among such a proliferation of tree roots, so had the killer known about this terrain, had it in mind when he chose that quiet spot where the wood ended and the meadowland began?

He came to a halt as the path was suddenly cut off by a barricade where several large trees had been felled, their sawn trunks piled in a heap about five feet high. It probably deterred all but the most eager kids who would enjoy the challenge of scrambling over it but, since there were so many alternative paths everywhere, Lorimer doubted that many people persisted with this route. He turned aside, letting another path take him to the edge of a clearing where more felled trees had been set into neat piles, their snarls of twisted logs arranged in heaps as though waiting for someone to come and light a series of bonfires. In the centre of the clearing a blasted tree stood stark and upright, clinging to the vestiges of existence, but only fungal growths seemed to inhabit this unwilling host. Death and decay lay scattered all around him.

Picking up a stout stick, Lorimer scratched at the leaf mould, noticing the rich burnt umber of the soil beneath, real forest bark that had decomposed beautifully, with fine red threadlike roots within many other root systems. Looking up, he could see that the trees formed a bright canopy of green from the majestic beech and oak. Elsewhere he had passed a stand of Scots pine and some shivering sycamores that would produce yellow leaves come autumn. Would they find her killer by then? The next twenty-four hours were going to be crucial. He stood up and looked back into the wood, listening for the sound of water that might give him a clue as to where he was and which path might take him back to the crime scene.

It was a shorter walk than he'd expected. The trees petered out beside a high wall, its broken stones green with algae, next to the electricity substation where the crime-scene tape fluttered in the breeze. On one side of the wall was a culvert running parallel with the line of trees and disappearing back into the wood, but on this side was a section of grassy field like the corner of a neglected suburban garden. The girl's body had been buried just at this margin, obscured by long grasses, docks and ash saplings. The silence here was only broken by a raucous magpie performing its acrobatics on top of a slender birch tree, oblivious to the activity in this small corner of the park. Lorimer watched it for a brief moment, then his eyes took in the vista of Maryhill with three tall skyscrapers and a cluster of houses spread across the hillside opposite. The path that led out of the woods would take him to the other side of the park, past the recycling facility and a metal barrier. Right now a couple of uniformed officers were stationed there preventing any member of the public from entering.

Had they come into the park from that direction? And was the victim someone who had trusted her companion? Lorimer stood and gazed across the skyline, wishing for answers.

CHAPTER 19

'I can't believe it.' Frank Donaldson slumped forwards, thrusting his head into calloused hands that were used to grappling with heavy machinery down in the Clydeside dockyard. 'I can't believe it's really her.' His voice choked and the family liaison officer proffered a box of tissues, silently letting the father expend his anguish for those few minutes before he could face the outside world. Sometimes the bereaved poured forth a torrent of words, sometimes they clammed up entirely. The officer sat patiently, observing the big man who sat hunched over his grief like it was all he had to hold on to. He'd been white round the gills as they'd led him into the viewing room to make a formal identification. The man had seemed utterly bewildered as he'd gazed at his daughter's body. His whispered 'yes' had been almost a question as he'd turned, gaping open-mouthed at the stranger at his elbow who was trained to deal with such situations. Nothing in Frank Donaldson's life, though, had prepared him for a moment like this.

'What am I going to tell Mary?' he said at last,

looking up at the officer with frightened, helpless eyes.

The family liaison officer drew a deep breath and began to talk him through all the things that lay ahead, hearing himself recite the usual spiel and wondering as he did if the man was taking in a single word.

DCI Lorimer glanced at the familiar figure standing beside him at the window. Iain Mackintosh, the Procurator Fiscal, had come straight down to the crime scene and now both men were watching as the post-mortem was performed on the victim's body at the mortuary. As Dan had already pointed out, the girl had been strangled and now the pathologist was talking them through the external signs of injury before he began the process of examining her internal organs.

'The injuries are concomitant with the assailant having straddled his victim to the ground,' Dan remarked to the other pathologist who was taking notes. It was mandatory procedure this side of the Scottish border, and Lorimer wondered for a passing moment when Dr Rosie Fergusson would be back with her colleagues. Their workload was tough enough at the best of times and she was sorely missed.

'The assailant must have been fairly strong if her ribs are so badly crushed,' Mackintosh observed, cutting into Lorimer's thoughts.

'Yes, and there are visible signs of both carotid

arteries having been pressed, showing that he's grabbed her with both hands. If it's any consolation, the victim will have lost consciousness within twenty seconds,' Dan replied, glancing up at them from his place beside the stainless steel table. 'I think we can say without too much trouble that the injuries causing death were deliberately inflicted.'

Lorimer nodded. Twenty seconds; the longest and most horrific time in Julie Donaldson's young life before someone had finally snuffed it out. Of course it was a clear case of murder, but it never did to assume anything until the pathologist had given his qualified opinion, an opinion that could take Dan into a court of law.

'No signs of any sexual activity, though she's not a virgin. So, not a case of a rape gone wrong,' Murphy remarked as he looked over at the two men.

'A class "B", then,' the Fiscal said quietly to Lorimer. 'It might have been worse.'

'Aye, simple murder,' he replied with a bitter twist to his mouth. There was rarely anything simple about a murder investigation but he knew what Mackintosh was trying to say: had the body been that of Nancy Fraser then the whole case would have taken on a different aspect. Child murder meant the possibility that it was the work of a dangerous paedophile and thus an obvious threat to the public, a class of crime that might have seen Superintendent

Mitchison being appointed as SIO. The wee girl from Yoker was still in his own caseload as a missing person, meantime. They were being careful to ensure that the identity of the victim was being kept quiet for now, though 'the body of a teenage girl' would be allowed as a quote from the police press office. Lorimer was keen to distance the missing toddler from this new case although the locus could not be ignored. And hadn't it been the little girl's body he'd expected to see when the call had come in?

'Want to know what she last ate?' Dan asked as he turned towards the window separating the post-mortem room from the raised area where the two men stood. Taking their silence for an affirmative, Dan began to reel off the stomach contents.

Eric Chalmers tugged nervously at his tie. It was as bad as the time he'd sweated outside the interview room at Muirpark, waiting for his turn. Every prayer he'd sent up last night and this morning had met with a sense of nothingness. There was no feeling of peace, just a disquieting lack of anything at all. Mind you, he'd been wakened several times with the baby and had got up to change her after she'd been nursed, singing softly to her as he paced up and down. 'Amazing Grace' he'd sung, rocking her gently in his arms till she'd closed those tiny eyes and gone back to sleep. So he shouldn't be too troubled this morning; it had happened before when he'd prayed at times of crisis and he knew that, even if he had no sense of a listening ear, God was there with him. It was all a matter of trust. He was being tested, perhaps, made to feel weak and small, just as weak and small as baby Ashleigh. What was it Scripture said? 'Truly, I say to you, unless you turn and become like children, you will never enter the Kingdom of Heaven.' Eric felt something inside him change and his shoulders dropped, the tension in them suddenly released. Everything would be all right. He was bound to be found innocent of their accusations.

When the door opened at last, Eric Chalmers was smiling calmly, his face lifted to greet the men and women whose eyes were fixed upon him.

Detective Sergeant Niall Cameron sat listening as the education committee member quoted the paragraphs dealing with statutory suspension. It looked to him that Eric Chalmers was quite impassive while the education man's throaty voice elucidated every part of the procedure. The head teacher, Manson, had already been told about Julie Donaldson's murder, and of all the people in this room he alone betrayed signs of anxiety. Cameron glanced at him, seeing the fingers stray into his mouth as he chewed his nails, noting the way Manson's eyes kept flicking towards Chalmers. Was he wondering if the man he knew so well could be capable of a crime like that? Since Manson was the only other person who knew about the discovery of Julie's body, the officers could observe the disciplinary meeting objectively before taking Chalmers down to HQ for further questioning. The head teacher appeared to be gritting his teeth and anyone else in the room would suppose that it was his loyalty to his staff making his expression so grim.

'Do you understand the *nature* of the allegations that have been *brought* against you, Mr Chalmers?' The committee man's voice grated in Cameron's ears, rolling his words in a guttural sound that reminded him of a particular preacher who had bored him rigid back home in Lewis.

'Yes, I do,' Chalmers replied with a smile that seemed totally at odds with the gravity of the situation and Cameron couldn't help but think how that smile was going to be wiped off the RE teacher's face before long. But it wasn't a self-satisfied smirk. Cameron wouldn't be able to report it as that, he suddenly thought to himself as if he were preparing to testify in court. It was a genuine sort of smile, as if this man being accused of sexually assaulting a minor was actually feeling a modicum of sympathy for the men who had to deal with the situation. Chalmers was a self-confessed Christian, the son of the Manse (not that that was necessarily any character endorsement) and he had glowing testimonials lying on the table in front of them, all from various authorities, not least the head teacher of Muirpark Secondary.

The hearing came to a close at last and as they all rose, Cameron came forward and rested his hand on Eric Chalmers' sleeve.

'I'm afraid I have to ask you to accompany me, Mr Chalmers. There are more questions we need to ask you at police headquarters,' he added, keeping his voice deliberately low as he saw one or two faces turn their way.

Eric Chalmers raised his eyebrows in an unspoken question and then nodded, looking at his wristwatch. 'Fine, how long will I be? I should let my wife know.'

Cameron gave a shrug and scratched his forehead, giving the impression of the simple plod just carrying out orders. It was a trick he'd learned to carry off several times to good effect, but as Eric Chalmers looked at him sharply he wondered just what was going through the man's mind. Certainly he didn't appear to be a person with a guilty conscience. But appearances could be deceptive, as Lorimer had often told him.

CHAPTER 20

Lorimer's divisional headquarters – a functional, modern concrete block with no pretensions of architectural merit – had been built on the brow of one of Glasgow's many hills. For a new-comer to the place it looked large and imposing, the five stories towering over the pavements, casting their shadow right across the street towards a more graceful line of grey sandstone Victorian townhouses, now used as offices. Situated just to the north-west of the city centre, the Division covered several square miles in a densely built-up area, Lorimer's own room overlooking the buildings that marched down to the river Clyde. It was near enough from Pitt Street, one of Strathclyde Police's three main central offices, and the city mortuary across town to make life relatively easy in terms of fitting in as much as he could to his day. That was the good part about its location. The downside of being so close to Pitt Street was the ever-present worry that one of the senior officers would descend at a moment's notice. Superintendent Mitchison just loved it whenever the Chief Constable or his deputy arrived on the scene but for Lorimer it was usually one more thing elbowing out the really important matters in his case-load.

The DCI pasted a smile on his face as he finally shook hands with the Chief Constable. The remains of tea and scones lay on a table behind him, crumbs testifying to the little celebration that had taken place in Lorimer's honour. Okay, it was nice to have the commendation and the Chief Constable had been very flattering. Maggie would just love hearing how he'd hinted that promotion to Superintendent was surely overdue. Lorimer had tried very hard not to grin or even to make eye contact with Mitchison but he could imagine the latter's teeth grinding as the words of praise had been lavished on 'a most deserving officer'.

Then they were gone and Lorimer could pick up the discarded threads of his day. First off, he wanted to know just what was happening downstairs. Cameron and Weir had brought the teacher in for questioning; Lorimer suddenly felt a spasm of envy for his more junior officers. He didn't often have a chance to get involved with the cut and thrust of interviewing suspects and if promotion to Superintendent did come these occasions would be even fewer. Remembering how he had hated it when his own superiors had interfered in a case, Lorimer stifled the desire to muscle in on Cameron's present task. It would just have to wait and he'd hear about it later.

There was still a lot to be done if they were ever

to find Nancy Fraser, he told himself, opening an already well-thumbed file. Given that he'd been designated SIO in this latest murder case, Lorimer would have to delegate Nancy's case to a more junior officer – someone like DI Jo Grant, for instance – but so far the paperwork was still on his desk. He'd try to run the two cases if it was physically possible but past experience told Lorimer that it simply wouldn't work. Besides, a sense of loyalty to that young mother who trusted him to find her child was warring against the gnawing anxiety that the murder of Julie Donaldson was a bit too close to home, with Maggie having been the girl's teacher. Would that complicate things? Perhaps, but he was managing to cope with this extra workload and so would the other officers involved in these cases.

'Interview beginning at three-twenty p.m., August twentieth.' DS Cameron's lilting voice spoke clearly as the recording equipment hummed into life. Outside the faint drone of traffic could be heard from one small window set high up in the bare walls of the interview room. What air did venture into the box-like room did little to dispel the stuffy smell of the countless unwashed, sweaty bodies that had passed through the place.

Across the formica-topped table Eric Chalmers sat, hands clasped on his lap, his eyes fixed on the men who had brought him from Muirpark Secondary School. On their way across town,

Cameron had formed the impression that Chalmers was a friendly sort of guy; he'd asked questions about the Detective Sergeant's accent then gone on to reminisce about a childhood holiday spent in Harris and Lewis. A more relaxed murder suspect would have been hard to envisage. His avoidance of the subject of Julie Donaldson had been interesting, though.

'You are Eric Peter Chalmers of fifteen Queen's Court, Anniesland.'

Chalmers unclasped his hands and shifted in his seat. 'That's right,' he replied, a small shadow crossing his face as if Cameron's tone was alerting him to something even more serious than the accusation of sexual assault on a minor.

'May I ask you, Mr Chalmers, where you were between five o'clock and midnight last night?' Cameron stared at the man, seeing his head tilt in a questioning frown.

'What are you asking me that for?' he blurted out. 'What on earth has this to do with the hearing?'

'Just answer the question, please, sir,' Cameron continued, his manner as controlled and polite as ever.

'Well, I was at home, of course, with my family!' Chalmers' frown deepened and Cameron had the sense that the man was annoyed. Good. Annoyed would do fine. A wee bit of rattle to his cage might reveal quite a lot.

'For the entire evening?'

Eric Chalmers leaned back, his hand massaging his chin as he considered the question. 'Well, I did go out for a while. Yes, that's right. I'd forgotten about that. I took Ashleigh for a drive.'

'Ashleigh?'

'Our new baby. She's still a bit fretful now that she's home from hospital. My wife, Ruth, becomes quite tired and I suggested that I take Ashleigh for a drive around to see if that would settle her.'

'Please could you tell us approximately what time you left your house and what time you returned?'

'Oh, now you're asking. I'm not sure, actually. It was some time after dinner. About nine? Maybe my wife would remember better. We drove around for maybe an hour or so. I did take a bit longer than I'd anticipated. Thought it would be nice for Ruth to have a break. Ashleigh is quite a wakeful baby, you see.'

'And did she go to sleep in your car?' Cameron gave the faintest of smiles as if he were conversant with the troubles of a new baby, which he was not. But it always helped to seem understanding; creating a rapport with a suspect was usually a good thing to achieve early on. He'd watched Lorimer in action often enough to know that.

'She went to sleep almost right away,' Chalmers replied. 'The motion of the car put her out minutes after we'd left the house.'

'So why didn't you return for, what, an hour?'

Chalmers shook his head. 'I already told you. I wanted Ruth to have a rest. Could you tell me what this is all about?' he added.

'Whereabouts did you drive, sir?' Cameron continued, ignoring Eric's last question.

'Oh, heck, where did we go? Erm . . . well, I drove up the boulevard past Knightswood then back down to Anniesland Cross and over towards Canniesburn.'

'Past Dawsholm Park?' Cameron interrupted.

'Well, yes, I suppose I would have driven past there.'

'Did you go into the park?'

'No. I was driving all the time, I told you—'

'Did you arrange to meet Julie Donaldson at any time last night?'

Chalmers sat back with an expression on his face as if Cameron had physically hit him. Seeing the colour drain from the teacher's face made the DS wonder. Had they come to the crux of the matter, then?

'No,' he whispered at last. 'What on earth has given you that idea?'

'Mr Chalmers, I have to tell you that the body of Julie Donaldson was found in Dawsholm Woods earlier today. We have reason to believe that she died some time yesterday evening. Perhaps during the time you were away from your own home. With your little baby sound asleep in the back of your car,' Cameron insinuated, his hands clasped in an authoritative manner, his stare unflinching.

176

Eric Chalmers said nothing, but his mouth fell open in a gasp of horror, the blue eyes wide with shock.

'Julie's dead?' Eric said at last, his voice barely discernible. Then he swallowed hard. 'What happened?' As the silence in the room gave him no answer, he looked wildly from one officer to the other. 'You don't think . . . ? No, you can't think . . . I wouldn't . . .'

Then, to Cameron's discomfiture, Eric Chalmers put his head into his hands and began to weep.

Glancing across at Weir, Niall Cameron saw a pair of raised eyebrows and an expression that said as clearly as if it had been uttered that the Religious Education teacher was on the point of confessing to murder.

The DCI snatched the telephone off its cradle before the second ring.

'Lorimer?' It was impossible to keep the question out of his voice. Whilst there was no sign of Nancy Fraser there was still the tiniest flicker of hope that she might be found. But the caller was not bringing anything more to bear about the little girl. It was one of the officers in charge of Glasgow's extensive CCTV cameras. Lorimer listened as the woman explained what had been found.

'You'll send us the images, then?' he asked at last.

As soon as he broke the connection, Lorimer was up and out of his room. 'Time to gather the troops,' he said under his breath, striding towards the general office where he hoped to find at least some of the team. Weir and Cameron's action was taking place downstairs, but this new information concerned them too.

Three pairs of eyes looked up as the DCI entered the open-plan room: Irvine, Wilson and DI Grant were all at their desks, but Lorimer was aware of bringing something into the room with him, an almost tangible sense of excitement.

'Nancy?' DC Irvine began and then looked down as Lorimer shook his head.

'Central CCTV cameras have images of Julie Donaldson in Royal Exchange Square,' he began. 'They were taken on the afternoon that she absconded from school. They're emailing them over now,' he added. 'My office. Okay?' Lorimer turned on his heel and retraced his steps, hearing the scrape of chairs as some of the others left their desks to follow him. He could easily have watched the images himself first, but the team deserved to be there. Plus it would be all the quicker to issue further actions if what his caller had described was true.

In a matter of seconds Lorimer had accessed the forwarded footage. There was silence as they watched the grainy pictures, their staccato stop-frame images blinking across the screen. These particular cameras, like many in the city centre, did not have fixed heads but swivelled from side to side like intelligent robots, sucking up visual information as they swept the streets. At first all they could see was the bottom of a flight of steps and a pavement cafe where people were sitting around tables in the sunshine. Then the camera shifted its stance and the whole of the staircase came sweeping into view.

'That's her,' Lorimer said, pointing at a figure on the screen.

'Who's the boy?' Wilson asked, but Lorimer had already raised his hand for quiet and they continued to watch in silence.

At first it looked like any other boy and girl sitting on the steps on a summer afternoon, chatting to one another. Lorimer noted the way the pair sat together. She knew the boy well; there was no great distance between them and she was smiling at him as if he were an old friend. But then things changed. The camera caught a moment when the girl swept her hair back revealing an expression of fury. The boy stood up and so did Julie, yelling something and gesticulating wildly. Suddenly he had her by the arm and Lorimer heard Irvine gasp behind him as she watched the CCTV footage. But the boy caught by the camera didn't strike out as it seemed he might; instead, he yelled something at Julie making her run off down the steps. There was something menacing in the stance of his rigid body: fists clenched by his side. Then he too disappeared from the camera's view.

'I—' Irvine began, but Lorimer shook his head.

'There's more. Wait,' he told her, concentrating on the computer screen. Another figure swam into view, a woman, turning in the direction where the boy had gone, a look of severe disapproval on her face. Then the camera shifted once more and the link was cut.

'Right. That recording was made at two-thirty-five yesterday in Royal Exchange Square, only an hour or so after Julie called Samantha Wetherby to say she was in town. Now we know she hadn't told her pal about meeting anyone, but maybe she wanted to keep that to herself.'

'Good image of the boy,' DS Wilson offered. 'Shouldn't be too hard to find him.'

Lorimer smiled. 'That an offer?'

Alistair Wilson looked up and grinned. 'Why not? Shall I begin with the Donaldsons?'

Lorimer nodded. 'And Muirpark Secondary. He looks school-age, doesn't he? Let's get some of these images frozen and printed off.'

'Hold on a bit, though. Wouldn't chummy downstairs recognise him if he were a Muirpark pupil?' Alistair Wilson suggested.

'Worth a try. Let's hang fire with the parents just now. No need to upset them any more than is necessary. If Eric Chalmers can give us a name it might even be to his own benefit.'

'Here.' Cameron handed a large clean handkerchief to the man across the table, cursing whoever had forgotten to replace the empty box of Kleenex tissues. Carrying a white folded hanky was a habit ingrained from his youth when Ma would tuck one into his blazer pocket. 'You never know when you might need one,' she'd always told her menfolk.

Eric Chalmers blew his nose, wiping away the evidence of his sudden distress. 'Sorry,' he gulped, trying a watery smile, 'I just never thought something like this might happen to her.' He looked at the crumpled handkerchief, a question in his eyes.

'Keep it,' Cameron told him shortly. 'I've got plenty.'

'She was such an innocent wee girl,' Eric began. 'Always ready to join in things. But quite impulsive.' His face clouded. 'She . . .' He broke off, looking down at his lap. 'She thought she was in love with me,' he continued. 'Fantasy stuff; silly wee girl nonsense that most male teachers have to put up with from time to time.'

Studying him, Cameron thought there might have been plenty of times that Chalmers had had to endure attention from teenagers whose hormones were raging around their young bodies. He was an especially good-looking man, the thick blonde hair, that fine brow and blue eyes gave Eric Chalmers the appearance of a young Robert Redford. No wonder Julie Donaldson had come on to him.

'So what did you do about it?' Cameron asked.

'Well, I didn't murder her,' Eric replied quietly.

'The last time I saw Julie she was at school and not very happy with me. I told her not to get any silly ideas about us. Told her I was a happily married man and any feelings she had should be kept for boys of her own age. She didn't like that.' Eric grimaced.

'And you say you did not go near Dawsholm Woods the night she was murdered?'

Eric leaned back, hand on his chin. 'No, I didn't say that. I *was* near to the woods since I drove past, but as I didn't get out of my car then I wouldn't have been in any position to see her.'

'But your only witness is your two-week-old baby, who was sleeping at the time,' DC Weir cut in, a sneer in his voice.

Eric looked at him, the expression on his face changing to one of almost pity.

'No, you're wrong there. I had a witness, the best possible witness. The Lord God knew exactly where I was, what I was doing, what I was thinking and even what I was feeling. And He knows that I am totally innocent of any accusation you can bring against me.' The words were spoken with such firm conviction that John Weir sat back, half-embarrassed.

Cameron wanted to believe the man but there were other ways of obtaining the proof that they required. 'Forensic evidence may help to clarify who was last with Julie and so I would ask you, if you are willing, to supply a sample for us to test, sir?' Cameron glanced across at John Weir as if to verify that this was customary procedure.

Chalmers nodded. 'Of course.'

'Interview ended at four-o-five p.m.,' Cameron intoned for the record. 'Let's get you off to see a police doctor, shall we, sir?'

But as the door opened, Cameron saw DS Wilson looking over his shoulder for the Religious Education teacher. 'Need a minute of his time, Niall,' he whispered. 'Can we go back inside?'

'Sorry about this, sir,' Cameron said, one hand on the man's arm.

'Just a routine matter,' Wilson began, a reassuring smile on his face as the door to the interview room was closed once more. Seating himself where Cameron had been a moment before, the Detective Sergeant placed a picture in front of Eric Chalmers.

'Can you say if you recognise this person?'

Eric drew the picture towards him, nodding. 'Yes. Everybody knows him. That's Kyle Kerrigan. Muirpark's sporting hero. Got the makings of a real boxing champion, that boy.' For a moment he bit his lip as though another thought had occurred to him. Then a look of alarm crossed his face. 'Nothing's happened to Kyle, has it?'

'Thank you, Mr Chalmers,' Wilson replied and got up, sweeping out of the interview room without so much as a backwards glance, leaving the men staring after him with puzzled expressions on all of their faces.

CHAPTER 21

It had been a long day and now this staff meeting was going to make it even longer, Maggie grumbled to herself, shoving a bundle of photocopied poems into the desk drawer. Three-thirty was the official end of the school day but Maggie, like many of her colleagues, usually stayed on until just before five o'clock. Having her own classroom to prepare lessons and carry out the never-diminishing mountain of administration was a huge bonus, though she still carted piles of marking home most nights.

As she walked along the middle corridor a familiar notice caught her eye.

YOUR ATTITUDE CAN MAKE A WORLD OF DIFFERENCE.

Manson loved having these sorts of things around the school; they were meant to give the kids some kind of lofty ideals but Maggie had long since ceased to notice them, suspecting that the same applied to most of the kids. Yet today this one had leapt out at her. Could her own attitude make a difference? Would being fiercely loyal to Eric (and saying nothing about seeing him with Julie) help to reinstate the teacher to his rightful place in Muirpark Secondary? The hearing had taken place earlier in the afternoon but Maggie had been teaching right through from lunchtime so she'd been unable to discover how things had worked out for Eric. That was surely what this meeting was about.

Taking a seat at the back of the assembly hall, Maggie looked around for Sandie, but she was nowhere to be seen among the rows of teachers. The woman next to her shifted sideways in her chair with a sniff, as if by coming in late Maggie had somehow committed an offence. It was Myra Claythorn. Maggie stifled a groan. One of the senior staff, Myra was a teacher who was not well liked by either the pupils or her own colleagues, given the acid tongue that could flay a child into tears. Maggie had tried to feel sorry for Myra after the death of the woman's husband, but had to admit that she'd failed miserably. Myra was simply one of those vexatious persons that 'Desiderata' urged one to avoid, especially as she clearly had it in for poor Eric. Now Mrs Claythorn was staring straight ahead as if Maggie no longer existed, her thick ankles tucked under the chair, arms folded under her ageing bosoms.

Manson had taken the platform and even from the back of the hall Maggie could see that something was wrong. The head's normally ruddy complexion had a grey hue to it and he looked as if he had aged ten years since the beginning of term.

'I have to apologise for asking you all to stay behind today, especially those of you who have had to make other arrangements to pick up children,' Manson began.

Maggie Lorimer's heart sank. It wasn't like Manson to be all nice and considerate like this. What had happened?

'I have most distressing news to pass on to you all.' The head teacher's voice broke suddenly and he put a handkerchief to his mouth, prompting a murmur from the assembled staff. Had Eric been sacked? The question was on everybody's lips.

Manson raised a hand for silence and the ripple of talk died away.

'One of our Fourth Year pupils, Julie Donaldson, has been found dead in suspicious circumstances,' he said, taking a deep breath as gasps of horror echoed around the hall.

Maggie felt sick. She'd heard enough from her husband over the years to know what suspicious circumstances meant. Julie had been murdered.

'Strathclyde Police has asked me to keep this within the school. Though obviously it will be in the news before much longer,' Manson continued, his voice becoming stronger. 'But I urge you all to resist any overtures from the media. Details about Julie's life here and the recent accusation of sexual harassment will no doubt come to the fore. But,' he paused, the familiar gimlet eye roving over them all, 'I would like to think that no member of Muirpark staff would be so crass as to speak to the press. Julie's parents are having a difficult enough time as it is without that.'

'What about the pupils?' someone called out.

Manson pursed his lips together before answering. 'Can't do anything about them or about their families today. But I would ask all registration teachers to have a word about this first thing tomorrow. Emphasise just how bad it will be for the Donaldsons.'

'You mean appeal to their better natures?' another voice retorted sarcastically. Maggie turned to see who had spoken and saw Herriot's sneering face sitting a few places along from her. Glancing at her neighbour, Maggie was appalled to see a similar expression. Had they no sense of pity?

'What about Eric?' This time a woman had posed a question and Maggie Lorimer was relieved to hear Sandie's voice coming from somewhere down at the front.

'Mr Chalmers is helping the police with their investigation,' Manson replied quietly.

Immediately the hall erupted in an explosion of talk.

'Always thought he was too sweet to be wholesome.' Myra Claythorn had turned to Maggie with a bitter smile on her face. 'All that religious claptrap!'

Maggie Lorimer wanted to punch the woman

187

straight in her smug face, watch the shock as she reeled backwards off her seat. It took all her self-control to keep her voice steady as she replied. 'In this country we consider people innocent until they are tried and found guilty in a court of law,' she countered.

'And that won't be long for pretty boy Chalmers!' Claythorn exclaimed with something approaching relish.

Maggie shook her head, not deigning to reply any further. The woman was pure and utter poison and anything she said would be wasted on her.

The meeting was breaking up and Maggie almost ran to the front of the hall, seeking out her friend.

'Oh, Sandie.' Maggie's voice caught as the two women clasped hands, their thoughts unspoken: what was going to happen to Eric?

'Well, should we go?' Sandie asked at last, dropping Maggie's grasp.

Maggie looked at her blankly.

'We were going to see Ruth, remember?'

'Oh, help! I completely forgot.' Maggie bit her lower lip guiltily.

'Think she might be glad of some company right now,' Sandie suggested, threading her arm through Maggie's and leading them away from the knots of men and women that had gathered around the hall.

Queen's Court was situated to the west of Anniesland Cross, its small modern terraces dwarfed by two rows of dark red stone tenements that curved around from Great Western Road towards the dual carriageway that climbed up past the Vet School into the leafy suburbs of Milngavie. They'd taken Sandie's car, an elderly Audi that was the Business Studies teacher's pride and joy. 'Half the house and all of the motor!' Sandie had announced gleefully on the day that her divorce settlement had been finalised. A quick stop at a baby shop in Partick had allowed Sandie to purchase a tiny dress and matching cardigan for baby Ashleigh.

'Right, here goes,' Sandie announced, switching off the ignition and nudging her pal's arm. 'You first, Mags. She knows you better.'

Raising her eyebrows at this blatant untruth, Maggie nevertheless made sure that she was out of the car and at the Chalmers' front gate in front of Sandie.

Standing there, listening to the dying echoes of the doorbell, Maggie wondered not for the first time if they were doing the right thing. Would Ruth be pleased to see them or was this simply an intrusion into her privacy?

A noise at her back made her turn to see a couple walking towards the garden gate.

'Mrs Chalmers?'

'No. This is the Sheridans' now. Chalmers moved away last week. We're here for the housewarming.' Sandie had spoken quickly before Maggie could even begin to gather her wits. A swift glance at the man and woman hovering over the privet hedge, their eyes full of questions, told Maggie what her friend had already grasped: reporters. Somehow they'd got wind of things already.

'Oh, right. Know where they moved to?' the man asked.

'Haven't a clue. Sorry. Oh, hiya Mary, can we come in?' Sandie pushed Maggie forward as a bewildered-looking Ruth Chalmers opened the door, then closed it behind her, leaving two puzzled-looking journalists checking their Blackberries.

'What's going on?'

'Can we come into your kitchen, Ruth?' Sandie was already steering the young mother away from the front of the house.

A thin wail came from upstairs and before anyone could explain, Ruth smiled an apology and left them in the hallway.

'Okay, Mrs Lorimer. What do you say to a nice cup of instant coffee?' Sandie breathed out a sigh of relief as they wandered into the dining room of the little terraced house that led to a bright airy kitchen.

'Yes, please, though I could murder a gin and tonic right now,' Maggie muttered, her voice muted. She glanced out of the dining-room window and saw the two reporters climb into a red car.

'Come on!' Sandie hissed. 'Don't let them see you staring or they'll guess I've thrown them a wobbly!'

Ruth Chalmers' kitchen was kept surprisingly tidy for a couple whose lives had recently been disrupted by a new baby. The work surfaces and pale cream units were spotless and from each wooden doorknob little fabric hearts of red gingham had been suspended. Through the kitchen window Maggie could see a line of washing fluttering in the afternoon breeze. Baby dresses that looked like dollies' clothes hung in a row beside a variety of other tiny garments. She bit her lip, keeping back a sudden wave of self-pity that threatened to overwhelm her. If only . . .

'Here.' Sandie handed her a mug of coffee. 'It's not all it's cracked up to be,' she added, following her friend's gaze. 'Smelly socks under the bed can put you off them for life.' She grimaced. Maggie smiled. Sandie's sixteen-year-old, Charlie, was going through what she knew to be a typical teenage phase and his mum never tried to pretend that her boy was anything other than a pain in the neck.

'Aw, Ruth, she's gorgeous!' Sandie had turned away and Maggie put down her coffee mug as baby Ashleigh was brought into the kitchen.

'Thanks. We think so too, but we are biased after all. Coming through? Time for a feed, I'm afraid.'

The three women moved back into the lounge at the front of the house, Ruth cradling her baby who peered wide-eyed from the folds of a woollen shawl. Once seated in a comfortable chair, Ruth undid the buttons of her blouse and in moments they were rewarded with the sight of Ashleigh feeding contentedly at her mother's breast.

'Fair takes it out of you, but I do love nursing her,' Ruth told them shyly. Certainly the new mum looked relaxed and happy sitting in the rocking chair, her feet up on a low stool. 'She's a right hungry wee baby, has us up loads during the night, bless her,' Ruth told them.

Maggie forced a smiled. Eric's wife ought to be cocooned in her own little world right now. Claims against her husband must have upset them both dreadfully, she thought, noting the dark circles under Ruth's eyes. The woman was exhausted and probably not just from Ashleigh's constant demands.

'It was awfully nice of you to come today.'

Sandie shrugged. 'Och, couldn't let this wee one grow any bigger or she'd never have fitted this outfit,' she said, proffering the hastily bought gift bag.

Maggie resisted the temptation to raise her eyebrows at this blatant lie. Her friend was proving pretty adept at the art of sweet deception. 'Here,' she said, rummaging in her own capacious bag, 'thought this might be useful,' then handed over the tissue-wrapped package containing a soft, pure-woollen blanket.

'Oh, thanks, girls. This is lovely.' Ruth's eyes softened. 'Why don't you undo them for me? Got my hands a bit full,' she continued, her pale cheeks flushed with pleasure.

It was while Maggie was unwrapping the gift that the question was posed, making her freeze, pink satin ribbon trailing onto the floor.

'Sandie, why did you call me Mary?'

They had waited until the young mother had finished nursing the baby, Sandie prevaricating all the time. But then it had all come out: Julie's death, Eric's putative involvement and the narrow escape from the two reporters at the Chalmers' front gate. Ruth had sat quite still, listening as the women had taken turns to explain. Then, with a shudder that seemed to convulse her whole body, she'd begun to cry. A pot of tea later, they'd talked round and round the subject, never wavering in their belief that Eric was innocent. Then, before they had left, Ruth had stood up, her voice surprisingly strong: Remember to pray for Julie's family, won't you? She had even managed a watery smile, leaving Maggie and Sandie feeling a little bit humble. It was almost dusk when they heard the door close behind them.

'God, that was awful!' Sandie slumped into the Audi and looked across at Maggie. 'D'you think we were right to tell her?'

Maggie Lorimer made a face. 'Don't think we had much choice, did we? You'd spun her enough yarns to make one great big web. She had to know sooner or later, though.'

'But shouldn't Eric—'

'Eric's not home yet and we don't know what's happening down at the station.'

'Can't you phone Bill?'

Maggie shook her dark curls. 'No. It's bad enough that it's my school that's linked to this new case. A conflict of interests might upset things.'

'But you don't know if it is his case yet, do you?' Sandie persisted.

Maggie sighed heavily. 'No. But d'you know what? It wouldn't surprise me if his name's already on it.'

And as the big car gathered speed away from Queen's Court, Maggie pondered on the horror of Julie Donaldson's murder, the likelihood of her husband being Senior Investigating Officer and the problems that could lie ahead for both of them.

CHAPTER 22

'He's no here, wee toerag. Whaddye want him fur anyway?' The man who stood blocking the doorway looked up at them belligerently, his rheumy eyes full of hatred. The polis were the enemy round here, especially in a flat that was listed as the permanent address of one of Drumchapel's known drug couriers. Tam Kerrigan had jinked his way in and out of trouble, often thanks to Kerrigan Senior – who now faced the two policemen. The old man swayed slightly then held on to the door as if to hide the fact that he was the worse for drink, a gesture that could have been taken as further barring the officers' entry.

'Got a warrant?' he sneered. Then clocking the glance that passed between the officers, Kerrigan began to close the door. 'Piss aff. He's no here.'

John Weir stuck his foot in the doorway. 'Where is he then?'

Something in the detective constable's tone made Kerrigan's eyes flit nervously from one of them to the other. Then he shrugged as though he was conceding defeat. 'Ach, maybe he's doon the Aggro. It's a boxing night.'

'Thank you Mister—' But as soon as Weir moved, the door was firmly shut in their faces, leaving them standing staring at one another.

'Okay, the Argo it is, then.' Weir nodded. 'But we'll maybe be back before long,' he added, jerking a thumb in the direction of the Kerrigans' flat.

Kyle thumped the dark blue punchbag, his eyes concentrated on a point directly in the centre. School had been a real drag and everyone was talking about how Julie had dogged off again. All day Kyle had rerun the scene on the steps of Borders bookshop, asking himself over and over why he had been so tactless. She was a daft wee lassie, that was all. No real harm to her. But her face, darkened with rage, was one that the boy simply couldn't erase from his mind.

That he'd still fancied her had come unbidden into Kyle's mind more than once and now he tried to dismiss the thought, lashing out at the punchbag as if that could cure this feeling of unease.

It was the sudden silence that made Kyle turn around, rather than the sound of his name. Then he was standing alone, everybody's eyes directed towards him. All activity in the room had ceased, the boys watching Kyle from their positions on the floor mats, the adult helpers suddenly standing still. It was as if everyone was holding their breath, waiting for Kyle to make the first move.

'What?' he asked, dropping his gloved fists to

his sides as the two strangers began to walk towards him.

It had to be his da. They wouldn't be so quiet otherwise. What had he got up to now? Kyle glanced at the two men in the front seats. They'd shown Dave their warrant cards, asked if they could take Kyle down to the police station. Then everything had moved in slow motion: getting the gloves off, picking up his bag, someone else handing him a white towel he didn't remember bringing with him, and following the two men downstairs to the waiting car. He was aware of a burning sensation in his ears and knew if he could look in a mirror he'd see them red and tingling, the way they always went when he was nervous.

'What's happened?' he ventured at last, leaning forward to make himself heard above the engine noise. They were travelling quite fast down the boulevard and Kyle could feel the road bumps jar his stomach. No. He wouldn't throw up. Swallowing hard, Kyle repeated his question. 'What's going on? Can you no tell me? Is it my dad?'

'We need your help with something, son,' one of the men replied. 'It'll all be explained once we're at the station.'

Kyle sat back, folding his arms. Load of rubbish. It wasn't Da, then. He swore softly under his breath. Must be Tam or Jamesey. But why bother to drag *him* down the cop shop? Kyle bit hard into the remnants of a much-raggled fingernail, anxiety making him draw blood. Jamesey. Had to be him. One of the policemen whispered something to the other and cocked his head in Kyle's direction. Catching the moment, Kyle knew then that it was serious. Had something happened to his brother? And if so, why wouldn't they tell him? And where was Da? As the car sped towards the West End of the city, past the concrete finger of Anniesland Cross, past rows of elegant terraces then down towards the university, the questions multiplied until Kyle's head hurt.

Then the car stopped and one of the men was helping him out, taking his arm. So he wouldn't run away? Or was he being nice, preparing him for bad news? Kyle glanced at their faces but nothing he saw gave any clue as to what lay ahead as he climbed the steps into the police station.

'He's in there,' DC Weir told Lorimer. 'Seems in a bit of a sweat. Dead quiet most of the time, though.'

'Okay, the police surgeon's still here and can take a swab from the boy. See if we can make it quick.'

Lorimer's manpower was sorely stretched with some of the team still on the Nancy Fraser hunt alongside officers from various divisions throughout the city, and others that he'd chased home before another day dawned. The beginning of any serious case was a balancing act; manpower had to be deployed right away and sometimes for long stretches at a time but keeping his officers sharp meant giving them a chance to go home, see their families, get a decent kip. It wouldn't be the first case to have suffered from officers so weary that they made basic errors of judgement. And Lorimer didn't want any mistakes made now. That was why the SIO himself was opening the door to Interview Room Two, where Kyle Kerrigan sat waiting.

'We've sent for your father, Kyle. He'll not be too long,' Lorimer began. 'Would you like a cup of tea?'

The boy's eyebrows shot up, revealing pale grey eyes fringed with long lashes and an expression of feigned nonchalance as he shook his head. Lorimer understood. He was the polis and this was a lad whose family had form. He wanted to try to win the boy's confidence, if he could, before Kerrigan Senior made his appearance. He'd hand the interview over to DS Wilson when the father arrived, maybe sit in to see how things progressed, but first the DCI wanted to see the boy for himself.

Kyle's whole body showed signs of strain, his shoulders nearly up around his ears; it was natural given where he was right now. As Lorimer cast his eye over the boy he saw a good-looking young-ster. There was a small scar below his right eye, just visible under a fading suntan, and his brown hair was swept to the side, slick with sweat, revealing a furrowed brow. If that generous mouth had been capable of smiling right now, Lorimer reckoned that Kyle Kerrigan would be quite a heartbreaker.

'Been to the boxing tonight, have you, Kyle? I believe you're pretty good in the ring.'

'Who told you that?' Kyle's head came up and his nostrils flared suddenly as if he'd had to take a deep breath.

'A teacher you know: Mr Chalmers from Muirpark Secondary.'

Kyle's frown deepened. 'Chalmers?'

It was obvious that the boy was genuinely puzzled.

'Are you sure you don't want something to drink? Water maybe?'

'Aye, okay,' Kyle replied, never taking his eyes off Lorimer for a single moment. The DCI was acutely conscious of those grey eyes boring into him as he stood up and poured water from the litre bottle into a plastic cup. This boy was a boxer, trained to focus on his opponent and that was exactly what he was doing now. But Lorimer didn't want to be cast in that role so he shifted his chair to one side and made the boy turn sideways to face him.

'We can't go into all the details of why you're here, Kyle. The law says you must be in the presence of an adult member of your family before we talk to you.'

'So why's he no here now?' Kyle shot out.

Lorimer shrugged and smiled, leaning back in

his chair and clasping his hands behind his head. 'Och, this is just a wee informal blether. Thought I'd keep you company while we're waiting for your dad to arrive.'

Lorimer's smile seemed to be working. The boy lifted the water to his lips, taking his eyes off the policeman for a moment. In truth Weir could have picked up old man Kerrigan and brought him in with Kyle. It would have saved time and manpower but Lorimer had wanted these few minutes alone with the boy. It might be important to see what he was like without a drunken father shouting the odds.

'School's started again, hasn't it?' Lorimer began.

'Aye.' Kyle made a face.

'Och, the summer holidays aren't long enough,' Lorimer went on. 'See, over in the USA, they have three whole months off.'

'S'that right?'

'Aye. Don't start back till September, most of them. No bad, eh?' The DCI let his accent thicken: it was a mark of Glaswegian solidarity and might help to gain the boy's trust.

Kyle grunted his reply and Lorimer stifled a grin. He was boring the pants off the lad, but that was a good ploy to use if he were to become more relaxed.

'All these summer schools and activities. Don't you have these in Muirpark?'

Kyle shrugged and looked down at his hands, seeing something far more to his interest than this policeman whose line of small talk was becoming irritating.

'Thought Dave Savage took some of his lot up to Fort William on trips. Or am I getting that mixed up?' Lorimer put his forefinger to his chin as if he was trying to remember something.

'How d'you know Dave?' The boy's head was up again, suspicion in his eyes.

'Friend of a friend used to box with Dave. Kept in touch.' Lorimer smiled as though he'd said nothing out of the ordinary. In truth he'd heard about Dave Savage from Maggie's stories about Keith Manson's boxing days; the head teacher was a supporter of Savage's boxing club.

'Oh.' Kyle's face lost some of its hostility. 'Right. Aye, we went up there last summer.' The boy's expression changed at once, memories softening his mouth, a smile just teetering on the edge of his lips. 'It was great,' he added.

'I bet,' Lorimer enthused. 'I love it up that way myself. Tell us about it,' he said with a wee shrug that was meant to let Kyle know they were just passing the time.

'We did loads of stuff, canoes an everything.' Kyle had sat forward and he betrayed an excitement that lit up his whole face.

In that moment Lorimer found himself warming to this boy.

But before he could continue there was the sound of loud voices outside the door and then DS Wilson came in with Kyle's father.

The change in the boy made Lorimer's mouth contract into a grim line. Kyle suddenly seemed smaller, cowering into himself, his eyes darting towards the door and Lorimer could read the fear in them. It didn't take a degree in psychology to see that this boy had probably been abused by his father. The man belched suddenly as if showing his contempt for his surroundings and the reek of alcohol wafted around him like a poisonous cloud. Swallowing his distaste, the SIO stood up, conscious of towering over Kerrigan.

'Thank you for coming in.' Lorimer had grasped the man's hand and ushered him into a seat before he could say a word. 'Now that you're here we can ask Kyle some questions that may help us in a case we're investigating,' Lorimer told Kerrigan, his best bland expression allaying any opposition from the man. 'Tea?' he added as though Kerrigan was a special visitor who must be catered for. The DCI's disarming manner seemed to do the trick and he had the satisfaction of seeing Kyle's father lean back in his chair, a tentative grin on his wasted face.

'Aye, milk and two sugars, hen,' Kerrigan called after the WPC as she left the room. 'Aw right, wee man?' he added, turning to Kyle. 'Whit's he done?' he asked Lorimer. 'Hey, dae ah know you?'

'Detective Chief Inspector Lorimer,' he replied, smoothly, watching the doubt cross Kerrigan's features. The older man shook his head. 'Mibbe. Cannae mind.'

From the corner of his eye he could see Kyle's mouth opening as he made the connection. Lorimer. His teacher's husband.

'We need you to be present when we talk to Kyle,' Lorimer reminded him. 'As he's a minor.'

'Aye, okay.' Kerrigan nodded. 'Oh, ta, hen.' He looked over his shoulder as a paper cup was placed before him.

'Kyle,' DS Wilson began, 'we have reason to believe that you met Julie Donaldson in the city centre yesterday afternoon.'

The blush that spread over Kyle's neck told them what they had wanted to know before he could reply. 'Aye.' He swallowed hard. 'Aye, I just ran into her.'

'You didn't have any plans to meet up, then?' Wilson did not try to disguise the surprise in his voice.

'No. No. We just ran intae one another. In Buchanan Street. That was all.'

Wilson raised a sceptical pair of eyebrows at him. 'Not quite all, Kyle. We've got CCTV footage that shows you having a fight with Julie in Royal Exchange Square.'

Kyle made a face. 'Aye, well. She had it comin, didn't she? She'd made up some daft story about one of the teachers in our school. I asked her about it and she got mad.'

'Did you follow her? See her later on yesterday evening?'

Kyle frowned. 'No. See her? No. Julie doesnae stay round our bit. She's from Crow Road.'

204

'Where did you go after your altercation with Julie?'

'My . . . oh, when we fell out, d'you mean? Och, she stomped off. Didn't see her after that. I just mooched about then went home.'

'You spent the evening in your own home?'

Kyle glanced nervously at his father. 'Aye. Aye, I did.'

'Presumably your father can vouch for that?' Lorimer interjected.

The pause lasted just a fraction too long before Kerrigan nodded. 'Aye, aye o course I can. Was watchin telly wi me a night. 'N't that right, son?'

Kyle sat frozen, staring at his father as if the man were some sort of alien species. What had his father been watching? Which teams had been playing last night? 'Went tae bed early,' he mumbled.

'Sure you didn't go up to meet Julie Donaldson in Dawsholm Woods?' DS Wilson snapped open the jaws of the trap, inviting Kyle to walk in if he wanted to.

Kyle's face paled and he fidgeted with the edge of his jumper. 'Julie? No. I don't go down there wi lassies . . .' Then the boy reddened at his own lie as a sneer appeared across his father's face.

'Better wi lassies than always up at thon boxing club. Mair natural,' he spat out, the contempt on his expression clear for everyone to see.

'If we could ask you not to interrupt, please, Mr Kerrigan,' Wilson told him severely. But it was too late for Kyle.

'Why shouldn't I be a boxer? Better than being a drunken bum or a druggie like Tam!'

Lorimer jumped up just in time to prevent Kerrigan lunging across the table at his son.

'Drunken bum? Whit sort of wey's that tae speak tae yer faither?' Kerrigan struggled against Lorimer who held his arms close to his sides. 'Wee toerag! After me standin up fer ye! Ah didnae see him at a last night!' he blurted out, eyes wild as he glared at Kyle. 'He could've been out a night as far as I know!'

'But I wasn't,' Kyle stammered, 'I was at home, in bed. Honest,' he added, his eyes pleading with each of the officers in turn. 'Whit's all this about, any road? Has something happened to Julie?' Kyle's hands were on the edge of the table now, his father totally ignored, fear making the boy's eyes widen.

'The body of Julie Donaldson was found today in Dawsholm Woods. We have reason to believe she was murdered,' Lorimer told him.

In the silence that followed his words Lorimer could hear Kerrigan's heavy breathing and the whimper that escaped from Kyle's throat. He watched as the boy swallowed back his tears, his Adam's apple rising and falling.

'If we could take a mouth swab from Kyle, for elimination purposes.' Lorimer had let Kerrigan go and the man nodded, bewildered at this latest turn of events.

'She said it was true,' Kyle whispered at last. 'And I didn't believe her . . .'

'What's that?' Wilson asked.

'She said Chalmers done it to her. But I told her she was making it up. That's why she got so mad at me.'

Lorimer looked the boy up and down. Here was a strong young man, a boxer, who was perfectly capable of strangling a girl as slightly built as Julie. And his father wasn't covering for him after all. Why?

'I think you'd better tell us the whole story, Kyle,' Lorimer suggested, crossing his arms and leaning back into his seat as though preparing for a long night ahead.

CHAPTER 23

Kyle stared up at the ceiling, his eyes tracing the delicate hairline cracks in the paintwork. They had just appeared one day, for no apparent reason. This house had simply aged, that was all. The process of decay happened to things as well as to people. Death, that was just a word, wasn't it? And what did it signify: the end, the finish, a label to stick onto that transition between a flicker in the brain and eternal nothingness. Julie was dead. Finished. The wee girl who'd played with him in primary school, argued with him, sent him daft text messages: that person was gone for ever. Snuffed out.

He imagined Mrs Donaldson crying every night. That was okay. She should cry. It was right to grieve for the stepdaughter she'd loved. Kyle had kept his tears to himself and now he lay, dry-eyed, wondering about the mysteries he'd never thought about before. Something had piqued his curiosity and in a rash moment he'd gone into the school library, scouring the shelves for some philosophical wisdom. That's where he'd found it, Sartre's great work *Being and Nothingness*. A lot of it was hard going but Kyle had ploughed on, seeking something, anything, that would give him some kind of an answer.

Now Kyle imagined the scene: policemen with dogs scouring Dawsholm Woods. He remembered the sunlight on the summer leaves, the walks with her, the squirrels scampering across the woodland floor, the perfect quietness when he'd returned there alone.

Julie was nothing now. Her spark of being had been extinguished and the terrible storms of weeping by her friends and family were for who she had been and for their own loss, not that empty body in the mortuary. Kyle's interest was aroused once more. What exactly had they done to her? How did they actually open her up? What did they look for? And was their examination quite dispassionate? Suddenly a wave of longing came over him and he wanted to be there, white-coated, scalpel in hand, seeking answers to difficult questions; not about life and death but about facts that the tissues and organs might reveal to one who was trained to see and understand. Pathology might make some people shudder, but it held a fascination for him that he couldn't quite explain.

Maybe it was because the dead couldn't hurt you, Kyle told himself. Only the living posed a threat.

Three in the morning was the dead hour. Lorimer turned the ignition key, cutting off the engine's noise, and sank back. He needed these few minutes before he could open the door, haul himself out of the driver's seat and walk towards his front door. It was something that was happening to him more and more these days; the later he returned, the longer he wanted simply to sit there and let his body relax against the leather that had moulded itself to his shape over the years.

They'd let Kyle go back home with his father after their time had run out. Six long hours he'd spent, trying to prise open the boy's defences. Six hours of battling against the father's outbursts, working to regain the boy's confidence only to see it disappear like grains of sand trickling through an hourglass. And where had it got them? He'd certainly obtained a clearer picture of the relationship between the boy and his father; Kyle's cowed manner and the old man's belligerence told the two police officers plenty. The boy's grandmother seemed to be the only stable force in Kyle's life. So why had he gone back to live in Drumchapel when he could have stayed with the old lady in Partick instead? That was something Lorimer had tried to ask, in an oblique way, but Kyle had clammed up completely on the subject.

Julie's death seemed to have come as a shock to the boy. Nothing that he had seen earlier on had told the SIO that this boy was hiding a guilty secret of such proportions. But he might well have been the last friend the girl had spoken to, face to face. And there had been something in his manner when they'd mentioned Dawsholm Park that had made Lorimer raise a mental eyebrow; Kyle had not been entirely truthful. The youngest Kerrigan had seemed relieved when they had called a halt, but the way he had walked out to the police car taking them home, three paces behind his father, gave Lorimer serious misgivings.

Now he sat with the window rolled down to feel the cool of the night air against his face, as if it might awaken something in him. There was insufficient evidence to hold Kyle Kerrigan and Eric Chalmers, though when the results of both swabs were reported things could change dramatically. If either of their DNA matched the samples obtained from Julie's body or the scene of crime then an arrest could be made. And Kyle was a boxer, a strong lad, Lorimer reminded himself; it was quite possible for him to have strangled the girl.

Lorimer shivered then gave the ignition key a half-turn and let the electric windows close. It was time to catch a few hours' sleep. Somewhere out in the darkness was there a killer lying awake, pondering the nature of his crime? Or had the act been conceived by a mind that could slough off any feelings of guilt and remorse? And if so, was there a danger that the killer might strike again?

He remembered the kiss. Her lips had been warm and unyielding, parted after that final muffled cry.

If he closed his eyes he could feel it all over again. His body quivered with a longing to be there touching her face, stroking her hair, whispering words to which she could never respond. 'Juliet,' he'd crooned, taking her shoulders in his hands, pulling himself on top of her. 'My Juliet.'

Suddenly a voice echoed in the darkness and his eyes flew open in a panic. The word trembled in the still air of the room. Juliet. Had he spoken her name aloud?

Wiping the sweat from his neck, his hand travelled downwards, fingers searching. His cock felt soft as he touched it, a wrinkled, unresponsive slug. Turning on his side he bunched his legs up, curling into himself, fist in his mouth to prevent the howl of despair escaping from his soul.

CHAPTER 24

Frank Donaldson hadn't slept a wink. Lying beside Mary, listening to her softly snoring, he envied her and cursed himself for his male pride. Take pills? Not him. Yet, now with morning showing through the gap in the curtains, Frank wished he had been able to obliterate the last few hours and the questions going round and round in his head.

It had to be Chalmers. There was no other explanation. The man had gulled their Julie into joining his wretched club, taken her away on that trip of his with smiles and a fanfare of jollity that Frank saw now as false and sickening. Chalmers had groomed her, wasn't that the word they used? He'd seen something he wanted and he had taken it, simple as that. And when Julie had had the sense to tell them what had happened, well, he must have panicked. And he'd been suspended, hadn't he? Frank had seen to that, at any rate, he told himself with grim satisfaction. But being out of school, maybe that had given him the opportunity to see her, lure her away from her home and . . . Frank stopped, his imagination refusing to go any further.

If Chalmers had been charged with her murder, they'd know soon enough, wouldn't they? Waiting, that's all he seemed to have been doing for days. Waiting for Julie to come home, waiting to find out where she was and now waiting to hear if the police had caught her killer.

Frank slipped out of bed, his feet finding the cold laminate floor and, putting on his dressing gown, he headed along the corridor to the bathroom. As he pissed into the porcelain bowl, he thought back to the time when he and Jeanette had been trying for a baby. He looked down at his penis, his manhood. It had served to transform their lives, hadn't it? Had helped to create Julie, their only child. Jeanette had been overjoyed when the baby had been born. Frank shook the remaining droplets into the pan before hugging the dressing gown around his body. Pity she'd never survived long enough to see the lovely girl Julie had become . . .

He tried to stop the sound, his fists covering his mouth, but it was hopeless and he sank to his knees, the howl resonating off the bathroom walls.

'I don't want anything.' Frank pushed his plate away, hands across his eyes. Then he heard the scrape of a chair and Mary was close to him, arms around him, holding him tightly as if she never wanted to let him go. They stayed like that, neither of them speaking, giving in to their mutual need for comfort, until a noise outside made Mary break away from her husband.

'It'll be the paper,' she said, rising to fetch it from the hall.

Frank looked up, wanting to say, *Just leave it, stay here with me*, but the words remained in his head, unspoken.

'Oh, Frank!' Mary came into the kitchen, one hand against her mouth, holding the *Gazette* a little away from her, fearfully.

'What is it?'

Instinct told Frank what he was about to see before he even read the headline.

SCHOOLGIRL MURDERED: POLICE QUESTION MEN

A pupil from Muirpark Secondary School was found brutally murdered near Dawsholm Park yesterday. Julie Donaldson, aged fifteen, had been missing from school and home on the day of the murder. Sources close to the teenager say that she was upset following allegations that one of her teachers had sexually assaulted her during a school camp holiday. The teacher in question, Mr Eric Chalmers, has already been suspended on full pay pending an inquiry. Police have questioned two men overnight, both of whom have been released. It is believed that Mr Chalmers had been asked to accompany police officers to their divisional headquarters immediately after a preliminary investigation by the

education authorities into his conduct but left some time later.

Frank Donaldson, fifty-two, broke down in tears as he spoke about his daughter. 'Julie was the light of our lives,' he said. 'She was a happy girl who had lots of friends. We simply can't understand why anyone would want to harm her.' Mr Donaldson went on to say how much he and his wife appreciated the overwhelming support from members of the community, especially Julie's immediate school friends and their families.

No arrests have yet been made and the police are still asking for anyone who saw Julie on the afternoon or evening of August nineteenth to come forward.

Barbara Cassidy, senior reporter

Frank stared at the column, reading it over and over again, then looked up at Mary, his lower lip trembling.

'They've let him go?' Then his face crumpled and he drove one fist against the newspaper. 'They've let him go!' he screamed.

Mary backed away, heart pounding, as the stream of obscenities left her husband's mouth. This would do no good at all. Frank had it all wrong, she was certain of that, just as she was sure Julie had made up the whole sordid little story about that nice young man having attacked her. Mary Donaldson was no expert on human behaviour but she'd been around long enough to know the difference between a decent man and a bad one. Mr Chalmers hadn't done what Julie said he had. And he surely had no hand in her killing.

Frank's face was red with fury as he thumped the wall with his hand, leaving a mark. Mary shivered. The man who stood there filling the kitchen with his frustration and grief was far more likely to vent his anger against another human being than Julie's teacher ever was. But there was no way this side of eternity that she was going to express that particular thought.

The *Gazette* had done their dirty work for them, Maggie thought, pushing the newspaper deeper into her satchel. Already crowds of kids were huddled together in their different year areas and she could practically feel the tension in the air as she strode across the playground towards the main building. A few heads turned her way, and she caught their appraising glances. It was the detective's wife they saw, not Mrs Lorimer of the English department. Most of them would know by now, Muirpark Secondary's bush telegraph having done its work. It would help to make life a little easier for the registration teachers, but there might still be kids who hadn't heard the news and were still to be shocked by Julie's murder. And there were bound to be questions, particularly from her articulate Sixth Years who would want answers from her.

She made a face. Being the wife of DCI William Lorimer had given Maggie a wee bit of notoriety following her husband's successful apprehension of a multiple murderer, just weeks before term began. Then the *Gazette* was full of praise for the senior officer who, unarmed, had faced down the gun-wielding killer. But all news was short-lived and today's would surely fade out as soon as someone was arrested.

Maggie Lorimer clenched her teeth as she walked along the glass-sided corridor that overlooked the playground. It wouldn't fade out so quickly for those poor parents, for Julie's friends. Or, she reminded herself, for Eric and Ruth and their families. Bill was never slow to remind her just how many victims there were whenever a murder was committed. And looking down now at the kids trooping in to the sound of the bell, she told herself that there was going to be one hell of a lot of young folk numbered among the victims today.

Maggie's eyes were drawn to the frieze of pupils' work that one of her colleagues had mounted on the corridor wall and she slowed down to read some of their offerings. It was early in the session for anything new to be displayed. A smile twitched at the corners of her mouth as she took in the 'First Impressions of Muirpark Secondary School'. S1 had not pulled any punches. These kids seemed unafraid to criticise any aspect of their new regime, she thought, noting their opinions on everything from school dinners to the amount of books they had to carry from class to class. Maggie was so absorbed that she didn't notice him at first.

'You've heard, then?' Tim Wetherby, one of Maggie's Sixth Year boys, stood just outside her classroom door, barring her way. Maggie took one step back so that none of her form class could see them together. If Tim wanted to talk then it would be in private, away from any curious eyes.

'Naturally, given that my husband's in charge of the case.'

'And you've seen *this*.' Tim pulled a copy of the *Gazette* from behind his back.

'They're trying to make it look like Mr Chalmers murdered Julie, aren't they?'

'Trial by media is something we should be used to by now,' Maggie replied cynically. 'Not that I'd condone it for one minute,' she added. 'The press has its uses and can be positively helpful when reporters cooperate with an investigation. But,' she shrugged and made a move towards the classroom door, 'some of them don't always look at it that way. Some of them', she gave a deliberate glance towards the headlines on Tim's paper, 'are far more interested in the kudos of getting to a story before anyone else. Anyway,' she said, tilting her head to one side, 'your sister must be in a bit of a state. I take it she's not in today.'

Tim dropped his gaze. 'Yeah, Mum thought it best if she took a bit of time off. It's been hard on her . . .' He trailed off, reluctant to voice the

219

problems between his parents that had no doubt reached the ears of his teachers.

Maggie put a hand gently on his arm. 'Tim, it's been hard on you both. The school understands that and given this tragic event—' She broke off, biting her lip. 'Well, let's just say that there will be professional counselling services offered from today. And everyone can take advantage of them. Do you know what I'm saying?'

The boy's head flew up suddenly. 'Me and Sam don't need a shrink to sort us out, thanks. We're doing just fine.' And shaking off her hand, the boy held open the classroom door to let Maggie enter, a small courtesy designed, she was sure, to demonstrate just how in control he was.

The door closed behind him and for once Maggie felt trapped inside her own room. Even the familiar things like her favourite posters and the daft cartoons she'd pinned beside her desk failed to comfort her. Every eye was upon her, waiting.

She swallowed hard and took a deep breath.

'Many of you already know about Julie Donaldson,' she began. One or two of them looked puzzled and Maggie knew she was going to have to spell this out.

'I'm terribly sorry to have to be the one to tell you this,' she said, her voice softening as she was suddenly all too aware of the vulnerability in some of these young faces. 'Julie Donaldson – your classmate – has been found dead in Dawsholm Woods.'

A gasp from the back of the classroom told

Maggie that for at least one person this was news and she broke off for a moment, letting the awful news sink in.

'For those of you who saw this morning's *Gazette*, you will also know that the police have been questioning two people already.' Maggie paused again, looking around at the kids she had known for the last three years. They were young adults now, looking ahead to university in a couple of years and the prospect of a good career. Perhaps it was the frieze outside on the wall but she had a sudden memory of that first day she'd had them all assembled here, their faces turned to her, uncertain of what life would be like for them at Muirpark. She felt some of that same uncertainty now and wished she could offer the warm assurances she'd given them way back in First Year.

'I know you'll want to ask me questions, but can I say something first?' Maggie heard her voice, confident and assured, as if it was coming from somewhere else, belying the nerves churning in her stomach. 'My husband is the Senior Investigating Officer in Julie's murder.' She took another deep breath as one of the girls began to cry. 'What I wanted to say was that I can't divulge anything about the case that isn't in the public domain, so don't ask me. Please. Mr Lorimer is bound by codes of confidentiality. I'm sure you appreciate that.'

A few murmurs arose and Maggie saw some heads nodding, though she lacked the courage to look at

Julie's closest friends; she could imagine what they must be feeling. A swift glance to her left showed the place where Kyle usually sat was empty this morning. But she mustn't mention his involvement.

'One of the things mentioned in the paper is Mr Chalmers' suspension.'

Some muttering could be heard towards the back of the class but Maggie pretended not to hear it.

'Please remember,' she said quietly, 'this is a newspaper, selling stories, not a definitive judgment by a jury of fifteen people. It's a sad fact of life that you have to learn not to be gulled into believing everything a newspaper tells you. Your teachers here will keep you all updated about this awful tragedy. And if anyone needs to talk to me in private, well, you know I'll be here whenever you want me.'

The muttering had ceased now though there were still soft sounds of weeping from a couple of the girls. Normality – Maggie thought, remembering Manson's mantra – give them some shape to their day. Then she raised an arm towards the girl at the very back of the class.

'Jessica, since Kyle's off today would you mind taking the register down to the office. Thank you.' Maggie let them begin to talk among themselves as she busied herself with ticking off names on the beige record book then writing down the names of pupils missing from her class. When she came to D for Donaldson, Maggie bit her lip, trying hard to conceal the pang of dismay that she felt.

Once Jessica had left, Maggie came round to the front of her desk, perching on the edge as she usually did. 'The school will be visited by police welfare officers today,' she told them, 'and there is also the opportunity for professional counselling, should anyone feel the need for that.'

'Mrs Lorimer?' Manda had raised a languid hand. 'Is it true that Mr Chalmers has been arrested?'

'In the light of the accusation Julie made, Mr Chalmers was questioned by police, Amanda. That's not the same as being arrested.'

'Helping the police with their inquiries.' One of the boys offered the well-used phrase.

'Exactly.' Maggie nodded. 'And any of you can do the same if you have any information about Julie's disappearance. Anything can be useful to the police, no matter how small or insignificant you might consider it to be,' she told them, grimacing as she realised her words echoed every episode of *Crimewatch*. But at least she had diverted their attention away from Eric.

As the bell rang for the end of registration and the Fourth Year trooped out, Maggie wondered at her last words to them. Was that tempestuous scene between Julie and her RE teacher big enough and significant enough to share with the police? And would it be her courage or her loyalty to Eric that would fail her?

Kyle woke up, the pain in his face throbbing. How he'd managed to sleep after last night was anyone's

223

guess. If it hadn't been for Jamesey coming in and pulling his da off . . . Kyle gave a groan as the memory flashed vividly back to him, his father's curses ringing in his ears. The words had hurt him almost as much as the blows. Did he think he'd actually murdered his own school pal? He was mad, that was true enough, Kyle told himself, but surely not mad enough to believe that? There's always wan, the old man had shouted, and yer maw always a bad streak, he'd yelled. Kyle had lost it then, had lashed out at the old man, but he'd been battered stupid instead. He sat up, fingering the swollen skin below his eyes where it hurt most. He'd have a couple of keekers, he thought, blinking painfully.

Kyle suddenly remembered the tall policeman with those penetrating blue eyes who had looked at him as if he could see right into his mind. He could sort out his da if anyone could, he thought. Why couldn't he have been born to a man like that? Life just wasn't fair.

'Ye awake, wee man?' Jamesey stood in the doorway, one hand holding a dinner plate full of bread and jam. 'Ye want wan?' he added, nodding towards the pieces, his own mouth already full.

Kyle shook his head. The very thought of eating turned his stomach and even watching Jamesey's jaws masticating the thick wedges of bread brought a sour taste of bile into his mouth. 'Wouldnae mind some Irn Bru, though,' he muttered.

'Aye, well, see if therr's ony left,' his brother replied, moving out of the room. The sound of the fridge door opening and shutting was followed by a metallic snap as Jamesey tore off the widget.

'Here ye'are,' he said, holding out the can. 'Phenomenal!' he added, grinning stupidly.

'Great,' Kyle gasped between gulps as the orange liquid slid down his throat. ''S better. Thanks.'

Jamesey settled himself on the edge of the bed. 'Whit was a that aboot last night, then?'

Kyle didn't reply, tilting his head back and pretending to drink the last drops from the can though it was already empty.

'Mean, th'old man wis fair ragin wi ye. Cannae blame him, righ'nuff, huvin tae go doon the polis fur ye. Dinna tell me ye were at the skag, eh?' The older boy nudged Kyle slyly, his gap-toothed grin creasing his unshaven face. He could be a moody bastard, Kyle thought, but he had his better moments like now when he was trying to be nice. James Kerrigan had a certain sort of charm whenever he smiled, a fact that he used to his advantage and not only with the lassies. He'd talked his way into the prospect of a good job since leaving school, though Kyle was certain Jamesey could have gone on to college if he'd wanted to. Now his big brother was well in with Tam, the eldest of the three boys and the district's main drug dealing thug who was the spitting image of their father.

'Jamesey,' Kyle began, 'see what he said last night. About my mother?'

225

'Ach, ye dinna want tae listen tae thon garbage, man,' Jamesey snorted in disgust.

'Aye, but is he serious?' Kyle persisted. '*Is* he no my real father?' He paused, awed by the enormity of the idea. 'D'you know anything about it?'

James scratched the side of his nose for a moment then sniffed. 'Aye, well, he's said it aften enough, since he came hame, hasn't he? Mibbe ye should look it up at the registry. See yer birth certificate, eh? They cannae stop ye now, can they?' The older boy slid his bottom off the bed and began munching on another piece of bread. 'See'f it wis me ah'd gie him a right doin. Glasgow kiss. Like that. Oof!' James lunged his head forwards imitating the blow. 'Nane o yer Queensberry Rules, kiddo. Dae him right.' James gave him a wink and sauntered back out of the room.

Left alone once more, Kyle considered his brother's words. Jamesey and Tam had been brought up to admire street fighters like old man Kerrigan. They'd carried blades since primary school and like their father they wouldn't hesitate to use one if they had to. That's what had landed Kerrigan and his hot temper in the jail and Tam, so like his father in every way, could easily end up there too. But Jamesey? Kyle shuddered to think of it. The middle boy ducked and dived; he'd always preferred talking his way out of trouble to raising his fists.

Why was it, then, that *he* wasn't like the other men in his family? Kyle had never known that aptitude for violence, had never wanted to get into knives or stuff; boxing, now that was different. In the ring he was a calculating animal, padding around its cell, waiting for the moment to strike out at his opponent. It was a sport, not a way of knocking someone's brains out, he thought disgustedly. He could no more batter the living daylights out of his father than fly in the air.

Then the irony of his situation suddenly struck home: Kyle Kerrigan might have the makings of a boxing champion but he'd never have swung a punch in anger. So how could they believe he was capable of Julie's murder?

CHAPTER 25

A heron flapped noiselessly over the estuary, the morning light turning the underneath of its wings to gold. Because it was still so early, the clouds were tinged with pink, trailing grey shadows in their wake above an eggshell-blue sky. It was one of those mornings that gave false promises, the light shining on the river dazzled the eye; 'too bright too early' had been her mother's favourite saying for such a start to the day. So they had come before breakfast, mindful of the forecast telling of rain coming in from the Atlantic; Ireland would see it first, that darkening of the skies, obscuring the horizon's sand-coloured light and this expanse of blue arcing overhead.

They'd taken a taxi down to the river's edge; her car had been a write-off after the accident and Solly didn't drive. The taxi driver had stared at them curiously, thinking them mad no doubt as he'd left them there with a promise to return in an hour, the dark bearded man and the slight blonde wrapped up in a long beige cardigan. She smiled at the memory, snuggling against Solly as they sat looking over the Clyde. Just a few miles downstream, yet it was so different from the sluggish waters that coursed through the centre of the city. Rosie gave a huge sigh that prompted Solly to raise questioning eyebrows, but she merely shook her head and gave him a reassuring smile; the sigh had been one of pure pleasure at being able to breathe fresh air that was tinged with just a hint of autumn chill and to stare out across the sandbanks where hundreds of birds were foraging for food, beaks pecking in the slate-coloured mud. Occasionally an oyster-catcher would flap noisily from one patch to another, disturbing that large group of birds with long red legs. What were they? she wondered, taking a mental note of their appearance. Lorimer would know, Rosie suddenly thought; he was such a keen bird-watcher. He saw other things with his sharp blue eyes too, she mused, things that many people would miss. The sigh she gave now was not one of contentment, but rather the longing to be well again, to be fit for work and part of an ongoing case where her expertise as a forensic pathologist gave her such satisfaction.

Perhaps he'd caught something in her mood for Solly's arm came around her shoulders, hugging her closer, and she let her head sink gratefully onto his shoulder, glad to have his strength while still mourning her own weakness. It would take time, the surgeon had warned her. She'd been lucky, so many of her fellow medics had stated once they'd known the extent of her injuries and how close she'd come to the brink. Rosie shuddered and Solly rubbed her arm as though to warm her. It was something they didn't talk about any more. What was the point? She had a future to think about and that was reason enough to feel positive, wasn't it?

But the thought of Detective Chief Inspector Lorimer and the missing toddler had been planted into her mind now and Rosie's eyes no longer saw the shifting clouds or the change in the hills as the shadows lengthened. Her work had taken her into many distressing situations before and she had enough imagination to see just what that young mother must be feeling: such pain, such terrible, unbelievable pain.

It was the sort of pain that nobody really understood. A pain so deep inside that it couldn't be touched, let alone seen or felt. Last night he had woken to find moonlight streaming through the curtains, even though he'd closed them against the night; the brightness had seeped into the room, insidious like his pain, making him want to shed his skin as though he were a snake. It didn't belong to him, this covering over his bones. It itched and irritated him beyond human endurance, making him feel a restlessness that had driven him from his bed to pace up and down the house, going from room to room in the half-dark, never able to hide from that all-seeing, unforgiving moon. Raging with thirst, he'd gulped water poured straight from the kettle then wiped his mouth, feeling his swollen lips and the dry patches where he had bitten them over and over in an effort to keep from screaming. A sudden chill had crept over his flesh and set him sneezing, the sound making him wake properly to realise that he was shivering uncontrollably. Wrapping his arms around his naked body, he'd shuffled hastily back to the warmth of his bed then, whimpering, curled onto his side, foetus-like, hiding from the all-seeing moon.

Now he lay sweating, remembering the horrors of the night. No one could ever feel what he could feel, see what he could see: his pain was his alone, no matter how much other people tried to tell him that they understood. Could they crawl inside his skin? Inside his head?

Only another bright angel could soothe away this sort of pain with an everlasting kiss.

It was hard to see the world outside going about its business: children chattering noisily as they were led to the bus stop, just as they'd done on the morning when Nancy had been snatched. That her own life had stopped didn't seem to matter to anybody else; the world still turned on its axis, night becoming day and such sleep as she managed disturbed by nightmares of monsters doing dreadful things to her daughter. Kim's eyes were dried and flaky with so much weeping, their lids red and sore where she'd rubbed them over and over. How could daylight appear and life still go on like this? She clasped her cold hands together as yet another child ran laughing past her window. With every passing day a sinking in her heart told her she would never see her Nancy again. Kim slumped into a chair, too weak to stand and watch the morning parade of kiddies going to school, their tiny hands held by watchful mothers. As the tears flowed down her cheeks, she didn't even bother to wipe them away; they were part of her now, like this hollow, cancerous pain that grew inside her. She'd even given it a name. Despair.

Mum had tried to comfort her, but it was all just a torrent of words raging over her, making her think too much about what might have happened. It was the not knowing that killed her heart, and the realisation that she was a bad mother. That was what everyone would be saying, she thought, castigating herself for the hundredth time. If she hadn't let Nancy go out the front . . . Kim bent over, rocking back and forth as the keening cry of pain was torn from her lips.

Maggie Lorimer hummed along to the jingle on the radio, one eye on the traffic streaming along on either side of her. Just a wee bit further ahead and she'd signal, make for the inside lane and prepare to turn off the motorway. It was a routine she had honed to such perfection that she sometimes thought the car could drive itself to school without her help. It was one of these mornings that made you feel good to be alive, she thought, bright and blue with just a sweep of white cloud above the city skyline. Despite the awfulness of the previous days, she couldn't help but respond to this feeling of newness and opportunity. Maybe the kids would feel it too, she told herself hopefully. She had a timetable full of interesting topics for them today, things to take their minds off the twin subjects of playground talk: Julie Donaldson and Eric Chalmers. Manson had been spot on when he'd told them to keep Kyle Kerrigan occupied in the wake of his father's release from jail; who'd have thought that such instructions would soon be extended to the entire school? The head teacher was right, though; school work was the best possible panacea for the sort of anguish the kids were facing and Maggie Lorimer had prepared some of her favourite lessons. Old Possum's 'Growltiger's Last Stand' for her First Years, a strip cartoon exercise of *A Midsummer Night's Dream* for S2, then that board game she'd invented on *The Cone-Gatherers* for her Intermediate Ones. Hands-on stuff, it would also keep them mentally challenged and away from any thoughts of what was happening in the world of crime and detection.

That was a problem for their teacher, though. Both of her worlds were in collision: Muirpark and home. Despite the fact that his wife was a member of staff, DCI Lorimer was still the SIO on this murder case. He'd been told that Maggie's inside knowledge might prove useful so there had been no expression of a conflict of interest. Well, that was Strathclyde Police's take on the case, but it didn't stop her feeling uneasy about her own husband coming into school. She was so engrossed in her thoughts that she hardly noticed the traffic being swallowed up by the Clyde Tunnel. The roar of cars echoed as they swept down under the river, the curving tunnel walls glistening like the innards of some ancient worm, its spine a white light against ribs of darkness. Then they were out again into a fresh morning, the sky bright above tree-lined avenues of red sandstone houses, the very air charged with respectability. Maggie preferred this route, winding in and out of these affluent West End terraces until she came back down to Partick and the bumpy ascent to the school gates. The Expressway might be quicker, but by now she'd had enough of being immersed in lanes of traffic. Besides, she liked to look at these houses with their neatly-trimmed hedges and twin bay trees either side of the front doors. She enjoyed this part of the journey best at Christmas, for all the residents appeared to purchase real fir trees, huge affairs placed in the windows and lit up for all to see.

The thought took her back to Jenkins' *The Cone-Gatherers* and the spite and hurt that the book had contained. There had been a death in that story, too, and anger and grief. She had to stop at the lights and in those few moments her eyes fell on a billboard outside a newsagent's shop. **WHAT HAPPENED TO JULIE?** The headlines shouted at her. Maggie bit her lip as she drove the final part of her journey. Would she really be able to give them something to take their minds off this tragedy?

'Mr Chalmers would have wanted us to keep going,' the Sixth Form girl said, her voice sweet with what she hoped was an understanding tone. The younger kids all gazed up at her, respecting her position as their House prefect. Mr Chalmers had been Head of Clyde House but now he wasn't there and rumours were flying around the school about why he had gone.

'You know we have all this fundraising to do and that our chosen topic this term is Malawi? Well, let's show the other houses that we can do better than they can. Agreed?'

A faint chorus of 'yes' made the girl shake her head.

'Come on, you can sound a bit more enthusiastic than that!' She smiled, egging them on.

'Yes!' came back stronger this time, a few First Years sitting cross-legged at the front showing a genuine eagerness.

Maggie Lorimer, sitting at the back of the gym hall, nodded her approval. Frances Lane was doing a grand job with Clyde and she'd make sure that the girl's efforts were recorded in any House report she'd be writing. Eric would have been proud of her, she thought wistfully. Muirpark was a product of the seventies' expansion of comprehensive secondary schools when directives about what constituted good teaching practice had been implemented across the entire country. Successive head teachers had grafted on their own ideas, one of them being the House system. Each House had been named after Glasgow rivers: Clyde, Kelvin, the White Cart and the Molindiner Burn, though the latter was in truth a mere trickle under the necropolis. It had once been frowned upon by some parents as too middle class but the Harry Potter books had succeeded in popularising Muirpark's arrangement of splitting the pupils into four different houses. One up for children's literature, Maggie had thought, on overhearing a particularly enthusiastic Primary 7 boy during their orientation day before the summer holidays.

The bell rang just as Frances was ending her spiel about charities and several hundred feet clattered out of the gym hall towards the playground and the main building.

'Walk!' a voice commanded and Maggie glanced across at Jack Armour, the deputy head, who was covering Eric's House duties. Things were settling down to a semblance of normality, she thought.

It could be just an ordinary day in any ordinary school were it not for the piles of shop-bought flowers heaped by the school gate and their hand-written messages of condolence. That was something none of them could pretend to ignore.

PC Brian Maxwell was almost enjoying the swishing sound of the damp grasses against his boots when his feet slipped and he had to throw out a hand to steady himself. They'd fanned out in a line again this morning, tracking an area near to the Vet School, uniformed officers with their heads down, still intent on their search for the missing girl. Maxwell stood up sharply, fishing around with his stick to see what had caused this sudden depression in the earth. They were trained to be alert to the least little difference in the terrain and although it was probably no more than a rabbit hole, he would look just to make sure.

At first sight it looked like a tree root exposed by an animal burrowing deep within the soil, but when he dropped to his knees for a closer look, PC Maxwell's mouth dropped open in horror. There, at the end of what he'd taken to be a thin dark root, were smaller twig-like bits splayed out in the unmistakable shape of a human hand.

'Hoi! Over here!' His voice came out clear in the morning air despite a hoarseness that was clogging up his throat. They'd all been looking for a corpse but none of them wanted to be the one to make this discovery.

Dr Daniel Murphy crouched beside the area that had been excavated within the woods. It was not so very far from that other crime scene where Julie Donaldson's body had been found, but one look at this showed that the victim had been placed into its grave years before. The forensic archaeologists and botanists were going to have a field day

237

with this one, he told himself, scraping more dirt away from the skeletal remains. Two corpses found while looking for a missing toddler, Dan shook his head; what were the statistical chances of that happening? Still, it would make for an interesting real life story when it came his turn to lecture to Glasgow University's evening course on forensic medical science. Rosie Fergusson usually took a couple of the classes but Dan was looking forward to filling in for her during her sick leave. Flashes popped around him as the SOCOs took photo after photo at the scene of crime manager's direction; every image would be needed to build up a true account of the discovered corpse, especially if this new case ever made it into a court of law. Hours of work lay ahead of them even before the remains could be moved and so a large white tent had been erected, covering the site and its nearby surroundings. Overnight rain had left the grass sodden and there were puddles in the yellow mud where the heavy machinery from the construction of the new Vet School buildings now lay useless until the police were finished with this scene of crime. When that would be was anybody's guess and there had been more than a few grumbles from the foreman in charge of the project.

Dr Murphy did not turn around as the man came into the tent and hunkered down beside him.

'Lorimer? Aye, thought it'd be you. Bit of a co-incidence, isn't it?' Dan glanced sideways at the shadowy figure next to him. 'Mind you, our Rosie always tells us that you don't like to believe in coincidences, isn't that right?' The Irishman's voice had a hearty quality to it that was at odds with the macabre setting.

'I don't,' Lorimer told him shortly. 'And I'll be much happier once you've taken this back to the mortuary and we can see everything more clearly.'

'Ah, you're right there, Detective Chief Inspector. We haven't found the skull yet, but I think meself it can't be far away,' Murphy replied cheerily, pointing towards the half-dug grave with one gloved finger.

The day had brightened by mid-morning, giving the illusion of a warm summer's day to come. But since noon, grey clouds had obliterated any trace of blue and now the first fat drops were falling on the tarpaulin covering the shallow grave. Lorimer sat back on his heels, feeling the sweat trickling down under the white boilersuit. As he looked out, he could see the perimeter fence had long since been cut through to make space for the heavy plant that had cleared part of the woodland floor where the new Small Animal Hospital would be built. The area below the construction site ended in a muddy culvert, marking a natural barrier between the flat ground and the steep slope running parallel to the path above. It was an ideal hiding place: there was plenty of grass and moist soil that would be easy to dig, unlike the upper area with its tangle of tree roots. The slope itself must have hidden the killer from view.

To his left lay the Vet School, a cluster of pale buildings with one grey brick edifice towering over the rest of the outbuildings. Despite all the upheaval caused by the builders, the university's life still went on and Lorimer could see a woman and a young man tending to a piebald horse where it stood in one corner strewn with piles of straw, their eyes fixed on the animal rather than on what was happening within the crime scene tent.

It had been a lot of work for the SOCOs, but worth all their painstaking effort. Now the grave had been properly excavated, showing the dark layers of subsoil beneath the lighter topsoil and possibly much, much more besides. These spade marks would come up particularly well, he thought, looking at the sides of the hole; grass and flowers had returned to grow on top though these species would be examined and compared to the other flora round about to see what they might reveal. They'd sieved for ages, taking care to preserve each and every piece of evidence, especially the bones. As the rain continued to patter down on the roof of the tent, Lorimer felt the sense of a job well done. Now it would be down to pathologists and forensic scientists as well as the archaeology team at Glasgow University's specialist unit to make sense of all of this.

★   ★   ★

It was hours before the grave had given up all its contents and now the DCI was standing a little behind the pathologist in the mortuary room, both men gazing down at the pile of bones that had been reassembled into what should have been an entire skeleton. One of the femur bones was missing, probably taken by a fox, Dr Murphy had suggested, though after careful digging the skull had been recovered. The depression on the ground had been caused by the body sinking deeper into its grave as decomposition had taken place, Murphy had explained. Foxes might well have uncovered bits as they'd foraged for food. Lorimer had swallowed hard, not wanting to imagine the process. But it did explain why the constable had tripped in the hollow.

'It'll take time, but once we've examined the bones there'll be more information to tell us when she was murdered and left to rot in that place.'

'Now *I* look on this as a possible murder, certainly a suspicious death, but is there any actual evidence to show that?' Lorimer asked.

'Oh, yes,' Murphy replied cheerfully, 'D'ye see that?' He pointed towards the area between the skull and the upper torso. 'One snapped hyoid bone,' he announced, 'she was possibly strangled. And look at these.' His hand circled the upper part of the skeleton and Lorimer saw what he meant; the ribcage had been badly crushed.

'Perhaps something heavy was laid on top of her? Weighing her down?' Lorimer suggested;

playing devil's advocate was one way to glean more information from the pathologist.

'No, no, we would be able to see differences on the actual skeletal remains; this one's been buried in soil, nothing more. We'll have the botanists' report to confirm that, of course.'

'How long do you reckon she'd been buried?'

'Hm, you want me to give a reasonable estimate at this stage?' The pathologist cocked his head to one side in response to the DCI's question. 'Certainly less than five years.' He leaned forwards. 'See the tags of soft tissue here and here?' Murphy pointed with his scalpel. 'Shows she's not been there all that long, really. Decomposition in a Scottish soil might take a few months or even a couple of years, depending on the time of year she was killed.' He shrugged his broad shoulders. 'We'll know more once we have samples under the microscope; the percentage of nitrogen in the bones helps us to be more specific about how long it's been since she died.'

'Can you give any indication yet of the victim's age?'

Murphy stepped back a little from the surgical table as though appraising a work of art. 'Mm, she wasn't elderly, that's for sure. No wisdom teeth had developed and from the size of the bones and the shape of her pelvis, we'd probably give a range of between fourteen and twenty. Glad we found the skull intact,' he announced gleefully. As Murphy glanced up at Lorimer, the DCI had the distinct impression that the pathologist was as delighted about this discovery as a small boy with a new toy to play with.

'Right, let me know when you're done here and how long the other reports might take. Any chance of a facial reconstruction, do you think?' Lorimer gazed at the skull lying at the top end of the steel table, its jaws wide open, reminding him too horribly of the expression on Julie Donaldson's dead face. But Murphy had simply shrugged again, a gesture that irritated Lorimer and made him wish not for the first time this morning that he was working alongside Rosie Fergusson, instead of this great bear of an Irishman.

As he turned away from the post-mortem room, Lorimer's thoughts turned to the ongoing work near the Vet School; he'd already authorised aerial photography to be carried out around the twin crime scenes and instructed a geophysics team to begin work on the areas surrounding both graves. GPR could give detailed images of the manner in which the graves had been cut whilst other archaeological techniques might show how the corpse had been deposited and what methods had been used to backfill the body. Plus, there was always the chance of discovering further burial sites in the area.

Standing outside on the pavement once more, Lorimer looked across to the expanse of Glasgow Green and took a deep breath, glad to be in the open air. Coming out of the mortuary he always had the feeling of being tainted with death, as if the smells of the place still clung to his clothing. It was part of his job to be close to the dead and to see for himself what atrocities had been perpetrated upon their remains; it helped firm his resolve to find their killers. He glanced back at the doorway: the body of Julie Donaldson lay in the chiller room, only one of several corpses stacked neatly away until such times as they could be released for burial. Lorimer nodded to himself. Despite the time between each murder, he wondered whether those two girls could have met their deaths at the hand of one man and one man only. And the thought was hardly in his head when he wondered just what Dr Solomon Brightman might have to say about them.

'I would think so.' Solly nodded his head. 'The place where he's hidden them is probably sufficient in itself to tell us that,' he added.

The two men were sitting on a bench in Kelvingrove Park, a short walk away from Solly and Rosie's flat. The West End shimmered beneath them, the setting sun glimmering off the rows of parked cars along Kelvin Way, the stark outline of Glasgow University's tower black against the pale evening sky.

'What sort of man would do this, d'you suppose?' Lorimer asked, adding swiftly, 'I guess our killer *is* a male?'

'Oh, yes,' Solly returned, abandoning his usual

thoughtful pause so swiftly that Lorimer glanced sideways at the psychologist. His face was partly in shadow but there was no mistaking the resolution in those composed features, nor the slight nodding of that head of dark, curly hair. 'That's one of the easier things to say about the perpetrator. There is probably some sexual motivation, though that's not as straightforward as it seems . . .'

This time he did tail off, his gaze somewhere beyond the view below them.

'I shouldn't really be asking you at all, off the record and all that.' Lorimer tried to elicit some further speculation from his companion but Solly simply continued to stare ahead of him, his thoughts evidently taking the psychologist back to that densely wooded Glasgow park.

CHAPTER 26

'They're ah religious nutcases! I'm telling you, sex-mad fiends, that's whit they are!' Arthur Pollock laid down his can with a decisive flourish as if to emphasise his point. 'Your wee lassie wis jist wan o his victims, mark ma words, Frank.'

Frank Donaldson nodded, his can of lager still clutched firmly in one massive fist, its contents barely touched. Arthur, his brother-in-law, had come to offer condolences on behalf of the family – Jeanette's family – and Frank hadn't had the heart or the strength to turn him away. Mary had brought through a bowl of crisps with the cans then disappeared quietly, leaving Arthur to his opinions about Eric Chalmers. Opinions she didn't seem to be expressing much herself, Frank thought suddenly.

'Any word o the funeral, son?' Arthur asked.

'No.' Frank dropped his head, trying to stifle a sigh of resignation. 'They don't let us have her back until . . .' He broke off, shaking his head as further words refused to come.

''S'awright, son, we all understand whit ye're

goin through, Mary and yourself,' Arthur said, patting Frank's back, his voice immediately lower and kinder. 'We cannae believe it either, poor wee Julie. Ah mean, whit sort o animal wid dae that tae a wee lassie?'

Frank shook his head again, wishing that Arthur would simply finish his drink and leave him in peace. But he couldn't do that, could he? There were proprieties to follow in death as in life and this seemed to be one of them, putting up with visits from his daughter's close relatives. After all, the man sitting next to him on the settee was Julie's uncle. He'd probably see more of the Pollock family in the next few weeks than he'd done since Jeanette's funeral. The groan that came from Frank Donaldson's throat expressed this realisation as much as the sheer wall of misery that continued to surround him.

'Och, man, it's terrible, jist terrible. An the polis huv let him go an all. Can we no dae onything aboot it? Frank? Can we no?'

'What're ye saying, Arthur?' Frank raised his head and looked more closely at his brother-in-law. The man next to him might be small in stature with only a ring of hair surrounding his bald pate, but the older man was a wiry wee fellow still and Frank could see his eyes shining with the sort of fervour that he had just been decrying. Then he watched as Arthur Pollock lifted up his can of beer, tipped it back and finished the last dregs before crushing it tightly in his fist.

'The polis huv'nae arrested him, right?' Arthur Pollock shook a commanding finger in the air. 'And why no? It's as clear as the nose on yer face that the man's guilty, d'you no think?'

Frank Donaldson sat up straight as he saw the gleam of menace in his brother-in-law's eyes. 'Go on,' he said slowly.

'Seems tae me we hiv tae dae somethin aboot it wursels, know whit ah mean, son?'

'DCI Lorimer speaking.'

The woman's voice came across the line, hesitantly, stumbling over her words as if she wasn't quite sure what to say.

'This is Mrs MacIlwraith speaking. It's my Sally. You know, the wee girl who saw Nancy bein taken. She says . . . says she's seen something, like . . . you know the wee round things they pit oan car aerials? Mickey Mouse heids? There wis wan o them oan that car that took Nancy away.'

'Is she sure?' Lorimer's eyebrows rose in a mixture of hope and scepticism.

'Aye.' Mrs MacIlwraith's voice rose in a note of indignation. 'Sure she's sure. She seen wan oan a car roon oor bit.'

'Right, I'll pass this on to the investigation team. Thanks very much for calling, Mrs MacIlwraith. Tell Sally her information is much appreciated.'

Lorimer swung on his chair for a moment, considering. So, Sally MacIlwraith had remembered something else, something that might just help to

248

nail whoever had snatched little Nancy Fraser; it wasn't much, but every last detail counted in this case. He could just imagine the child's excitement as she pointed out the tiny Mickey Mouse head on the end of the car's aerial, suddenly telling her mother as the vehicle passed them by. And she was certain the white car had sported one just like it. It would help to date the car, Lorimer thought, since most modern marques had retractable aerials these days.

Then the DCI was seized by a moment of sheer gloom that this had come too late to be of any use. And the case wasn't even under his control – he'd delegated it to DI Grant. But could this little bit of information make any difference now? And what were the chances that the person who'd taken the child away still held her somewhere, alive?

'Dad, it's me, Eric.' The silence that followed made the young man uneasy. Blaming him for being suspended from school was one thing, but surely—

The sound of a throat being cleared showed he was still there on the other end of the telephone line at least.

'What do you want?'

Eric sat down suddenly, the weariness in his father's voice making him falter in his resolve. What did he want from his dad? Sympathy? Understanding? Or merely an acknowledgement that the bond between father and son was strong enough to withstand this latest horror.

'Have you read today's paper?'

The grunt in reply was one of assent.

'Dad,' Eric began slowly, 'I had absolutely nothing to do with Julie's death. You must believe me.'

Again a silence followed his words, making Eric break out in a sweat of apprehension.

'No son of mine could ever be capable of such an act,' Paul Chalmers replied at last, but there was such controlled anger in his tone that Eric wondered at whom the minister's emotion was directed. 'What are you going to do about it?'

'Do?' Eric frowned, then his face cleared as the answer came to him. 'Well, what I always do in difficult circumstances, Dad. Pray, of course. As I'm sure you'll be doing as well. It's what you always told me when I was little, isn't it? "Prayer changes things",' Eric answered, trying to keep the sarcasm out of his voice.

'That's not what I meant,' Paul Chalmers snapped. 'I meant how are you going to clear your name?'

Eric paused, considering not only his father's words but the peremptory tone of his voice. 'I don't know, Dad,' he said at last. 'I really don't know.'

Maggie sat down behind her desk and put her head into her hands, the words still ringing in her ears. How could they say such things? How could any sane person actually say that Eric Chalmers was capable of taking someone's life? The voices in the staffroom had been raised to angry shouts between those who were supporting their colleague and those who had him tried and sentenced already. Maggie had snatched up her lunch and run back up the two flights of stairs to the sanctuary of her own classroom, unable to stay a moment longer and listen to their tirades. Teachers – of all people – should know better, she thought angrily, the blood pounding in her ears. In front of Maggie lay the remains of her lunch; a half-eaten sandwich for which she no longer had any appetite. Usually she needed something to sustain her through the afternoon but hunger had been replaced by an acidity of rage gnawing away inside her. How could they? Eric was the gentlest of men, a loving husband and probably the best of fathers, as well as being the sort of teacher who drew kids to him like a magnet.

Maggie shuddered. That trait in his character might well be used against him now. She could imagine the things his detractors might say: how he was over-friendly with the kids, how he was always smiling and joking with them. Overfamiliar, they'd say instead of simply acknowledging that Eric Chalmers was a born teacher who wanted to do his best for every child in his care. What had the police team made of him? she wondered, making a mental note to ask her husband. Surely these men and women with their expertise in reading the human character would have seen him for what he truly was? Yes, that must be the case, Maggie nodded to herself, feeling better; otherwise, why would Eric have been allowed to go free?

Her hand still shaking with emotion, Maggie reached for a carton of apple juice and drew it towards her. As she sucked from the tiny plastic straw, an image from the Chalmers' home came back to her – baby Ashleigh at her mother's breast, a tiny helpless infant nurtured and protected against the storm that was raging around her parents' world. And maybe the little one would never know about the terrible things now being said about her father; maybe it would all blow over once the real perpetrator of this vicious crime was caught.

At first she thought it was a car door banging but the second thump was followed by the sound of breaking glass downstairs, making Ruth jump. Instantly the baby began to howl, the source of milk suddenly snatched from her toothless gums.

'Sorry, wee one,' Ruth whispered, swinging the infant over her shoulder, covering up the naked breast with her free hand. Heart thumping, Ruth crept over to the nursery window just in time to see the figures of three men running away from her front gate. Then there was a raised hand and a missile hurtling towards her. She stepped back as the rock made contact with the window, crashing its way into the room, leaving a gaping hole surrounded by a spider's web of cracked glass.

At Ruth's scream the baby's howls redoubled, forcing the young mother to retreat into the safety of the upstairs corridor. Cuddling the baby with one arm, Ruth picked up the handset and dialled 999, her mouth open with shock.

Frank Donaldson slowed down, his chest heaving from the unaccustomed exercise. Ahead of him, Arthur and young Eddie Pollock stood waiting at the end of the lane. The van was across the dual carriageway, parked next to the garage, an easy place for a quick getaway.

'Awright, lad?' Arthur clapped him on the shoulder as Frank drew alongside the two men. 'That wis good, eh?' His brother-in-law's eyes were alight and even young Eddie was standing grinning like an idiot.

'Aye,' Frank replied shortly, though what he was feeling was far from good. The sight of that young woman's face at the window with her wee baby had sickened him. How had he been talked into this mad exploit? As he staggered across the midsection of Great Western Road, his feet slipping on the wet grass, Frank Donaldson already knew the answer to that one: too much drink and a hasty temper, twin ingredients in a recipe for disaster.

'Think she saw us?' he panted.

'Naw, nae chance. We wis too damn quick fur her!' Arthur replied. 'Lucky the man wisnae in. Eh?' His brother-in-law gloated as they dodged the traffic and headed for the van.

Frank Donaldson merely nodded in reply. Lucky? The man he'd come to avenge hadn't been there and now all he felt was a sense of guilt at his cowardly actions. What if Mary was right after all? He knew she hadn't believed Julie's story about the teacher. Her silent and anxious looks had told him as much. Frank bowed his head into his chest as he sat in the back of the van. But someone had killed his little girl and if it wasn't Eric Chalmers, then who was it?

'We've had a call through from Anniesland,' DC Irvine informed her boss. 'Mrs Chalmers has reported an attack on her property.'

'Is she all right? Where's Chalmers himself?' Lorimer asked.

'She's had a hell of a fright,' Irvine replied. 'A couple of uniforms are with her now but they thought we'd better know what was going on,' she added grimly. Every last person in Glasgow would be aware of the serious case involving the teacher, thanks to the morning papers. 'We don't know where Mr Chalmers is,' she admitted. 'His wife left a text message for him though.'

'Great,' replied Lorimer grimly, 'just what we don't need: some vigilantes taking the law into their own hands. Does she know who it was?' And when Irvine shook her head he made a face and turned back to the mass of paperwork on his desk. This was the sort of mindless reaction that a less than scrupulous newspaper could provoke.

He'd been through several battles with the gentlemen of the press before now, coming away each time with a harder attitude towards the fourth estate. Just putting Eric Chalmers into the same paragraph as the death of Julie Donaldson was tantamount to suggesting he was responsible for the girl's murder. As yet, there was no sign of a forensic report but perhaps they'd know later today if Barbara Cassidy's article had any shred of credibility. Lorimer found himself hoping that Chalmers' DNA swab proved negative – that would wipe the smile off the journalist's face. But, he asked himself, would it also mean that blame might fall on the boy, Kerrigan?

Her First Years could be pretty demanding, but Maggie had already found a rapport with them and, as they filed into the classroom, she was met with an occasional friendly grin. Kids that age didn't dwell too much on the bad things in life, maybe, and as she counted heads sitting at desks Maggie Lorimer could see that there was nobody missing from class. That was good. Her Fourth Year class was decimated, many pupils having opted for the advice given by the counsellors; Take time off to nurse your wounds, as Sandie had put it sarcastically. No teacher enjoyed disruption to their routine, but this was different and Maggie had drawn her friend a dark look of disapproval.

'Right,' Maggie began, 'who can tell me the name of the pirate cat?'

Several hands shot up and there were audible murmurs of 'Growltiger'.

The dark-haired woman facing twenty eleven-year-olds smiled at them. This was what she needed, what they needed: to slip into a writer's make-believe world and escape for a while from their own. Mentally she blessed her favourite poet and his quirky collection; *Old Possum's Book of Practical Cats* had served her well over the years.

As the afternoon wore on, the smile on Maggie Lorimer's face gradually disappeared. The First Years had been a tonic after that desperate scene in the staffroom but subsequent classes were less inclined to knuckle down to work, and it was with some relief that she welcomed the bell at the end of a weary afternoon. Maggie rubbed her eyes, not caring if the last traces of mascara were being smudged into dark circles. God, she was tired! The tension in that last class had worn her out. The kids had regarded her warily, no doubt wanting to ask the forbidden question about Eric: 'D'you think Mr Chalmers—' But Maggie's insistence on normality being restored in every lesson precluded such gossip coming from them. Sometimes it was hard being so firm, especially as she was the sort of approachable teacher the kids could talk to whenever a problem arose: Mrs Lorimer was famous for the ever-ready box of Kleenex tissues inside her desk drawer. But this was different. Even if Manson hadn't insisted on it, Maggie would have gone down this road of concentrating on classwork as a diversion from the horrors of recent days. She'd doled out plenty of homework too, giving herself extra loads of marking into the bargain. Ah well, she thought resignedly, it was for their own good, and it would give them all a head start with this year's folio work.

Maggie's gaze drifted out of her classroom window. The trees were beginning to turn already, no doubt helped by the dry summer, and hints of red and yellow told of the changing season. It would soon be time to roll out that wonderful poem of Keats', 'Ode to Autumn'. It had been one of the best teaching poems she'd ever used. 'Season of mists and mellow fruitfulness . . .' Maggie quoted softly to herself, then grinned as the next line came to her, bringing with it a memory from her own school days. Miss Livingstone, her English teacher, had been off for a few days one October for a wedding and Maggie never forgot the teacher's clever remark: 'I'm a *close bosom friend of the maturing son.*'

Miss Livingstone had also taken Scripture Union, Maggie remembered. A tall woman with prematurely grey hair and a kindly smile on her long face, she'd played choruses on the piano and encouraged them to study their bibles. Eric had told her that a lot had changed in SU since then but the choruses seemed to be the same anyway.

As Maggie's eyes fell on the rows of empty desks

in front of her, she could clearly recall Julie sitting whispering to her friend, Sam Wetherby. If she'd only known what was going to happen, she'd not have felt so annoyed at the girl. That was her last memory of Julie – leaving the classroom and being comforted by her pal. Maggie blinked away tears of remorse as she thought of the young girl. Oh, if only she could turn back time she would have said something kind to Julie. But it was too late for regrets now.

A sudden thought came hard on the heels of her sense of contrition: what kind of guilt must Eric Chalmers be feeling?

As he sat rocking gently in Ruth's nursing chair, Ashleigh cuddled in his arms asleep at last, Eric gazed around the room. The nursery had been decorated with a frieze of animals from Noah's Ark, not because it was a biblical image but simply because they'd liked the vibrant colours and all the jolly cartoon animals parading behind a white-bearded Mr Noah. It was gender neutral, too, a fact that had counted when they'd made the decision to wait until the baby was born to see if it was a boy or a girl. Now that the blinds were drawn against the damaged window, it was a soothing sort of room: the pale yellow walls dancing with shadows cast by the mobile turning slowly above the baby's crib. The fresh, clean lines of the white nursery furniture with its wicker baskets full of baby paraphernalia were now a source of pride, given that he'd sweated over the flat-packs this summer. Eric glanced up at the light shade suspended from the ceiling – a hot air balloon, its miniature aviator a Paddington Bear rescued out of the flotsam of his own childhood.

Somewhere downstairs, Ruth was preparing their evening meal and he should really be thinking about laying the baby down in her Moses basket until she woke again demanding her next feed. Just one meal enjoyed together would be a little respite from Ashleigh's constant demands, if she would stay asleep. Eric shook his head, smiling: time spent here alone with the baby was so very special. He looked at his daughter's tiny downy head and marvelled at how perfect she was: her baby skin quite flawless, her rosy mouth an exquisite Cupid's bow. Such loveliness was breath-taking. No wonder Jesus had said, 'For of such is the kingdom of God.' Her innocence contrasted so sharply with all the errors of mankind. Whoever had made this mindless attack on their home had failed to touch the baby. In years to come she'd change from this state of grace, Eric thought with a pang of regret, those feathery eyelashes would be brushed with mascara, those lips smeared with artificial gloss.

Then suddenly he was remembering Julie; her long blonde hair swept back and the carefully made-up face, so pretty yet so vulnerable, and that expression in her eyes when she'd said how much she'd hated him.

Eric felt as if someone had dealt him a blow, so physical was the pain. He stifled the moan that wanted to escape from his lips.

But if he felt this way, a little voice chided him, what on earth was it like for Frank Donaldson, suffering the loss of his only child?

She was still awake when he came into the room, taking his shoes off as quietly as he could so he wouldn't disturb her. Maggie heard the clothes falling on to the carpet then the duvet swishing as her husband slipped in beside her. Her hand reached out for his and she felt its warm clasp as the fingers closed over her own. For a moment they lay there, not speaking, each wrapped in their separate thoughts. He gave one small squeeze and the handclasp was released, then Maggie felt him turn on one side, ready for sleep.

Biting her lip, Maggie knew that if she couldn't tell him now, then she never would.

She rehearsed what she would say: 'I've got something I have to tell you.' But even as the words came into her head, Maggie Lorimer's courage deserted her. Sleep wasn't going to come easily either, she knew, tossing and turning as her conscience niggled away at her. Heaving a sigh that she hoped wouldn't disturb her husband, Maggie slipped out of bed and headed downstairs to the kitchen.

As she filled the teapot with boiling water from the kettle, Maggie gave an enormous sigh. What was it that had kept her from telling her husband what she had seen? Was she beginning to have doubts about Eric? At the end of the day it might make a difference, but right now they were depending on forensic evidence to show whether Eric had been present at the crime scene, Bill had told her. So here she was, shivering in her scanty nightdress, making tea, that panacea for all ills. *The cup that cheers but not inebriates*, the illustration on her tea caddy proclaimed. Maybe she should put a wee tot of whisky in it, Maggie thought wickedly, her sense of humour reasserting itself.

'Couldn't sleep?'

His voice made her spin round as she groped in the refrigerator for milk.

'No. Lots on my mind,' she said, conscious of her breath coming in short panicky bursts as if she'd been running.

'Me too. Any chance that pot would stretch to another cup?'

She'd had her chance to tell him of the scene between Julie and Eric, but now, safe and warm under the bedclothes, Maggie tried to banish it from her mind.

They'd talked for ages, about Eric mostly: what he was like at school, what she thought of him, the sort of nice wholesome couple he and Ruth made. And he'd listened as she'd let all her frustration out about the rumourmongers on the staff who'd so upset her.

'It isn't fair!' she'd murmured, snuggling into his shoulder. 'Why do people think such horrible things?'

And Lorimer, feeling the emotion gradually ebb from her as sleep at last took its toll, wondered at her words. Why did some folk always assume the worst? Even among his own colleagues there were those who aired their negative opinions freely. He could tell from John Weir's face that the young DC had already decided on Chalmers' guilt; religion had a way of dividing people, he'd told Maggie gently.

And just because she protested her friend's innocence didn't mean she was right, though he was tactful enough to keep that little thought unsaid.

CHAPTER 27

They'd found the second body close to the Glasgow Veterinary School, just at the margin of their search, near to the building site that was to become the new Small Animal Hospital. The perimeter fence between the park and the Vet School had been diverted from its original demarcation months ago, the burial site now within the University's new boundaries.

The third body was nowhere near the site of the other two.

Using geophysics had paid off; the disclosed grave in its hiding place deep within a screen of rhododendrons would almost certainly have been missed otherwise. Lorimer breathed a tiny sigh of relief; Mitchison had been carping on about the expenses mounting up in this case so now there was at least some justification for the series of modern police techniques that he'd set in motion. No murder investigation was ever cheap. There was always a careful balancing act to determine how much could be spent to achieve real progress and, now that it looked as if he had a multiple killer on the loose, Lorimer would be demanding even more resources.

So that was why he was standing inside the white tent with Dr Solomon Brightman by his side on this bright autumn morning.

'All right?' Lorimer asked quietly, seeing the psychologist put a folded handkerchief delicately to his mouth.

Solly nodded back, his eyes turned towards the hole in the ground that was becoming deeper by the minute as the white-suited woman below them carefully scraped away the mud and earth from around the body.

'It's more recent than the last one,' Lorimer said, following Solly's gaze. 'Still has some remnants of clothing. That should be helpful.'

He noticed the man beside him swallow hard and knew that it was only by sheer effort of will that the psychologist was not throwing up outside in the bushes. That keen intellect was unfortunately combined with a weak stomach and Solly Brightman's presence inside the tent was one more sign of how seriously he took his work, wanting to observe as much as he could before he began determining a profile.

'We've not found any parallel in the entire UK for something like this,' Lorimer told him. His team had already scoured HOLMES, the nation-wide database that kept scrupulous details of murder cases on record, searching for a similar sort of MO in the hope that their killer could be identified. It was unlikely that any former killer would be at liberty to carry out these murders, though; most were either incarcerated in prisons or high-security mental hospitals, and there didn't seem to be any unsolved cases that resembled this one.

'Looks like she's been strangled,' Lorimer went on. 'The position of the head . . .' He tailed off as Solly nodded again. They could see the open mouth; the woman's last gasp could have been a scream cut off by vicious hands.

'Like the others, there's been no attempt to cover the body with anything else – no blanket or anything – only earth dug up from the forest floor. Just how prepared was he, I wonder?' Lorimer said, thinking aloud for Solly's benefit. 'Must have had a spade ready at hand; see these marks on either side of the grave? Just like the last two. Can you imagine it?' There was no reply from the psychologist, however. What was going on in that dark head bowed so silently beside him? Was Solly seeing the same scenario? A car somewhere, not too far away, a shovel or spade in its boot, the intention to kill and bury his victim all part of the killer's pattern of behaviour.

'There's no easy access to a path,' Lorimer continued. 'He'd have had to walk back to his car from the Maryhill entrance or over at Switchback Road then return to bury the victim. Wonder if he did it straight away,' he mused, glancing sideways at Solly. 'Or would he wait until nightfall?'

'It would be too much of a risk to leave the corpses exposed,' Solly replied at last. 'Your forensic people say that the murders took place in the woods and there's no sign yet that this one will be any different.'

'Not bringing them here in the boot of his car, then,' Lorimer said.

The two men stood silently for a minute, each remembering the first case that had brought them together. Three young women had been brutally killed and mutilated then dumped in St Mungo's park. But that killer was now in a secure unit and whoever had perpetrated these new crimes certainly wasn't copying his MO.

'No. It's not like the St Mungo murders, is it? He simply dumped them; there was never any attempt at burial.' Lorimer pointed towards the open grave. 'If Julie Donaldson and the other two women had been killed elsewhere then *their* killer would have chosen a safer burial place. Think of the bodies found in the gardens or under the floorboards of the killers' homes.'

'And even though he's buried them in out-of-the-way places within the wood, it's still close to human habitation.' Solly lifted his head and indicated the muted sound of traffic beyond the Vet School. 'Anyone might have found those girls. And he didn't want them found,' Solly murmured to himself as if he was already trying to probe the killer's mind.

'Why use the same area, then? If he's not a risk-taker?'

'That's what makes this so interesting,' the

psychologist replied, watching the slow progress of uncovering the human remains a few feet away. 'He knows what he's doing on one level; on another he may seem to display quite normal behaviour.' He turned to look up at Lorimer. 'How else would he be able to lure these young women to their deaths?'

'So we're dealing with a psychopath.'

Solly smiled sadly and gave a non-committal shrug, but the Senior Investigating Officer's face had grown grimmer as the scenario played itself out in his imagination. Who was this killer: a madman with periods of lucidity or an apparently normal person with bouts of manic behaviour?

He shivered suddenly, wondering if the school-teacher who was so loved by his pupils might actually be hiding a terrible secret. His mind ticked off the men who had got away with multiple murders in the past, men whose home lives had seemed quite normal on the face of it but whose actions betrayed the evil deep inside. At least, he thought, they should be able to eliminate Kyle Kerrigan; especially if the DNA from each body showed a common set of strands. Lorimer looked up as a gust of wind blew some dried leaves on to the roof of the tent. How long had this woman been lying here, surrounded by the elements? Had foxes smelt her decaying corpse? Or had they slunk past the hidden grave night after night, foraging for other food? And what was the story behind her death?

★　★　★

The statistics in the missing persons register made grim reading: every year in the Strathclyde region alone more than sixteen thousand people went missing. Some would have chosen it that way, deliberately cutting themselves off from their past for reasons of their own but many, he knew, must have met with tragedies that were still to be uncovered. The records were further complicated by so many foreign nationals coming to work or study in Scotland for relatively short periods of time, some of them slipping through the bureaucratic net that struggled to contain them all. Who were they, these two young women whose decomposed bodies now lay in Glasgow City Mortuary? The forensic pathologists were working their socks off trying to find identification that could match up with a woman whose relatives were anxious to find her. The third victim was, like the others, a young female, possibly around eighteen to twenty, maybe even younger. Each girl had been strangled and there were signs of compression on their rib cages, showing a similar MO. Not only that, but the way each grave had been dug indicated that it had been done by the same perpetrator. What was left of the latest body's clothing was now undergoing intensive forensic examination and Lorimer fervently hoped that there would be something that would show who she had been and where she had come from.

His team's actions today included a search of Eric Chalmers' home and car as well as interviewing the close relatives and friends of the Donaldson family. Multiple killers were sometimes known to their victims and if Lorimer could find a link between anyone in Julie's circle and these other murders, then this case could really be pushed forward. Meantime, Solly Brightman was looking for the type of criminal mind behind these acts of murder. Lorimer could only hope that the psychologist might come up with a profile that fitted someone who was already within the net he had cast around this area of Glasgow.

'Do you realise just how much this is all costing us?' Mitchison's voice rose in a crescendo of disbelief, waving the figures for the ongoing case as close to Lorimer's nose as he could. 'Profilers don't come cheap these days, you know.'

'I do, actually,' Lorimer replied, keeping his tone as level as he could manage. He'd like to have taken the man by his Armani lapels and shaken him. What price can you put on the lives of three young women and bringing their killer to justice? he wanted to demand. But with Mitchison it paid to be cool and distant, a tactic that suited the DCI perfectly. His superior officer would just love Lorimer to lose his temper, any excuse to record one more black mark against the man whose presence within the Division irked Mitchison so much. They'd never rubbed along since Mitchison had been promoted over Lorimer's head and the officers within the Division continued to show a marked partiality towards their DCI. He should probably have moved by now, Lorimer thought absently, tried for promotion elsewhere within Strathclyde or further afield. And it might come to that yet, but real life – in the form of serious crime – had a habit of getting in the way of any plans he might make for his own career prospects.

'I'm not happy that you took so long to hand over the Fraser case,' Mitchison began again, his eyes cold with suppressed anger.

Lorimer sighed, not caring to hide his feelings this time. 'I thought we'd agreed on this,' he said, shaking his head slightly in disbelief. 'Kim Fraser *wanted* me to continue as SIO and I wasn't about to let her down with a thump. DI Grant has taken over the running of the case now but I still have an overview of the proceedings.'

'Sounds a tad egoistic to me,' Mitchison scoffed. 'You're not the only senior officer who thinks they've been endowed with people skills.'

Lorimer felt his jaw tighten; he wouldn't rise to this bait. It simply wasn't worth it.

'Public opinion in the shape of the press might easily turn against us if it looks as though we're giving up on finding Nancy,' Lorimer reminded his superintendent.

A gruff noise in Mitchison's throat that might have been the sound of acquiescence was all the response Lorimer had before one final glare was shot in his direction. The DCI's sigh of relief as the door closed behind his senior officer was tempered with a sense of irritation. With two major cases ongoing among his team, Lorimer didn't need his time wasted like this. And surely Mitchison knew that?

'Strathclyde Police,' the man had announced, showing his identity card and a paper that he said was a warrant to take the car away for examination.

Eric Chalmers stood in his doorway for a moment, his brain trying to focus on what was going on. 'But why . . . ?'

'Got orders to take this vehicle away, sir. All part of our inquiry. If you'll just sign this receipt and let me have the keys, that's right, just here.'

It was over so quickly that Eric still stood on his doorstep, a feeling of unreality sweeping over him as he watched the stranger back his Fiat out and drive away, followed by the second officer in a black Citroën. The sound of his baby's cry made Eric turn back into the house, but before he closed the door a flash of curtain from across the street drew his attention to the fact that at least one of his neighbours had been watching this little scene. Part of him wanted to slam the door shut, but another more mischievous side urged him to put up two angry fingers. Eric Chalmers did neither, closing the door quietly and making his way upstairs with a heaviness in his step that was nothing to do with yet another sleepless night from Ashleigh's constant crying.

'What is it?' Ruth looked up from where she was

standing by the baby's changing mat. 'Someone at the door?'

He looked at her pale face, as sleep-deprived as his own, and shook his head. 'It's okay. I'll tell you later. Can I do anything to help?'

'I've a load of baby things to get from the supermarket. Can you drive over for me?'

With a sinking heart, Eric shook his head, suddenly aware that he had no car to fill with the endless lists of stuff that seemed so necessary for this tiny person. And now he was going to have to tell his wife exactly why that was.

'Do I have to?' Samantha Wetherby lifted a tear-stained face to her mother.

'Yes, darling. You must tell us everything you can,' Mrs Wetherby said, her own eyes brimming full of unshed tears.

'It'll help us find whoever did this to Julie,' the policewoman explained gently. 'Just tell us who else Julie had been going about with over the summer, where she had been hanging out, that sort of thing.'

Sam looked from one woman to the other, her expression still full of doubt. Then, swallowing hard, she gave a little nod. 'Julie was seeing Kyle,' she whispered. 'But they'd broken up.'

'Kyle Kerrigan?' Mrs Wetherby sat up ramrod straight. 'That boy whose father was in prison for murder?'

Sam rolled her eyes, ignoring her mother's tone

of disapproval. 'Kyle's been in our class since Primary. We've known him for ever,' she added, clicking her tongue in exasperation.

'When exactly did she split up from her boyfriend?' The policewoman's tone was even, not betraying any sign that she may have hit upon something that might make her SIO's eyes light up.

Sam shrugged. 'Can't remember. After she'd come back from camp, I think.'

'And had they been an item for long?'

'Not really. Just since the end of last term. He'd got off with her at the Third Year disco.' Sam shrugged, feigning a nonchalance that was at odds with her white face and trembling hands.

'I wouldn't have thought he'd have been Julie's type,' Mrs Wetherby stated, arms folded across her thin chest, 'a boy with that kind of background.'

'Mu-um!' Samantha protested. 'Kyle's okay. Just because . . .'

'Perhaps you could tell me about the places Julie went over the summer holidays?' the policewoman cut in, sensing the tension between mother and daughter. 'And a wee cup of tea would be very welcome, Mrs Wetherby,' she added, smiling. A quiet word with Samantha was what she needed right now, without an overwrought mother putting in her tuppence worth.

'I remember when she told me . . .' Samantha broke off, frowning. 'When she told me about Mr Chalmers . . .' The girl looked up at the

273

policewoman. 'Julie looked scared,' she said at last, her lower lip trembling. 'And I didn't know why.'

They were sitting at the kitchen table, Maggie pouring tea into two mugs that were decorated with dancing sheep, a holiday souvenir from one of the craft shops in Mull. Lorimer watched as she laid down the teapot, her slender fingers uncurling from its handle. Everything about Maggie was fine and graceful, he thought; from those high cheek-bones and her slight figure down to the bare feet that were swinging back and forward as she sat sipping her tea. Yet, like so many women, Maggie Lorimer failed to see just how lovely she was, choosing instead to focus on what she thought of as her bad points: a tumble of dark, unruly hair, those small breasts Lorimer loved that she lamented as being too unwomanly and long slim feet that turned shoe shopping into a terrible chore. The very fact that she was so unaware of it was part of her own loveliness.

'How are the kids at school? Still a lot of tension?'

Maggie gave a sigh. 'You'd think the school routine would help. A bell after every class, you know. Gives a shape to their day. But some of them . . .' She trailed off, shaking her head. 'There's one girl in my Fourth Year English class. Kept her head on the desk all through the period,' Maggie told him. 'Couldn't see her face but we all knew she'd been crying.'

Lorimer nodded, covering her hand with his own.

'She's been off school, like some of the others in Julie's year group.'

'But wise parents sent her back before she made her depression worse sitting all day in her room, I suppose,' Lorimer said.

'You're right. It's horrible, though, this silence in registration class instead of the usual load of noise. Never thought I'd hear myself say that.' She grinned weakly. 'Even some of my S4 boys are actually tackling their work in a meaningful way.'

'So it's not all bad, then.'

'I'd feel better if you weren't on the case,' Maggie blurted out, then looked away as she saw the tight line of her husband's mouth.

'It was decided there was no serious conflict of interest,' he said in clipped tones that made Maggie realise he was trying to contain his temper.

'But nobody asked me!' she protested.

'You weren't part of the decision-making process,' Lorimer began.

'And why not? I know these kids better than most folk,' she stormed at him. 'I've been Julie and Kyle's registration teacher since First Year as well as their English teacher! Doesn't that count for something?'

'Look,' Lorimer said, 'I understand how this is affecting you. Of course I do. But wheels have to be set in motion like every other case. I have to appear as dispassionate as I can here for the sake of good objectivity. Don't think I can't feel anything for these kids, though,' he added, taking Maggie's hand in his.

For a moment it seemed that she would pull away from his grasp, but she didn't. Maybe she realised she'd been overreacting. Not seeing things from his point of view.

'Just today we heard that a careers woman is coming into school,' Maggie told him, a flag of truce waving in the deliberate change of subject.

'An outsider can be a big help at times,' Lorimer said, his voice gentle with relief that the spat between them seemed to be over. 'It's something to focus their minds away from all of this. When does she start?'

'Next week. We've drawn up a timetable for her to interview all the S4 pupils. I'll be keen to see just what they all decide to do. Visits to the careers fair will be the next thing to tackle.' She sighed.

Lorimer listened as she talked on, sipping his tea, not saying much. It had been his decision not to let Maggie know the latest information about Kyle Kerrigan and how the boy might well be back in the frame for the murder of Julie Donaldson. *And only Julie.* It had happened before: a series of killings that they assumed to be the work of one person turning out to be quite different. But how could the teenager's death fail to be part of this larger inquiry?

Lifting his mug, Lorimer drained the last of the

tea and rose from the table, a faraway expression in his eyes.

Maggie clicked shut the dishwasher, pressed the start button and leaned against the sink. The sound of the evening news was coming from the room next door. More murder and mayhem in some other part of the world, she thought cynically. Was he watching it, or was the sound simply a background noise to drown out the worst of his thoughts?

She was well aware that there were things about this case that her husband was leaving deliberately unsaid. They were both skirting around the subject. I have to fit in some extra time to do a little bit of sleuthing, she might have told her husband. But this was treading in a delicate area. To make enquiries among the pupils, however discreet, was perhaps going against the very authority that her husband represented.

Yet, however much she tried to justify her plans to herself, Maggie Lorimer realised that she was being driven by a sense of guilt. Whether that was a feeling born of doubts about Eric or the knowledge that she ought to have owned up to witnessing Julie's passionate anger that day, she didn't rightly know. What she did know was that if she could find out something, anything, to exonerate the RE teacher, it would assuage all of these guilty thoughts.

CHAPTER 28

She heard the footfall behind her just as she turned into the street. It was becoming darker now and already the sodium glow from the street lamps was making yellow puddles of light on the pavements. Don't turn round, Jessica told herself. That's what he wants you to do.

There was a large, glass-fronted shop opposite so she gave a quick glance left and right to check for traffic, then hurried across the street. The shadowy figure that had dogged her steps for the last ten minutes hesitated then Jessica could only hear one set of feet pattering along the hard tarmac, her own high-heeled boots that were hastening her ever nearer to home.

As she fitted her key into the lock, Jessica could not resist turning to give a quick glance behind her. Was that a shadow by the trees across the road? Or was it a figure standing stock-still, watching her? Shivering, the girl slipped into the empty house and closed the door firmly behind her. The ringing telephone made her scurry through the long hallway into the darkened kitchen.

'Hello?' Her voice was breathless.

A small pause that seemed to open up a black space in her head was followed by the click of a handset being replaced. Had it been a wrong number? But why not ask for someone by name? Why that infinitesimal sigh of nothingness? Jessica put down the telephone, the cold wrapping itself around her as she crept towards the front of the house once more.

Sliding along the wall of the living room, she peeked out into the night. That shadow by the trees had vanished. Shouldn't she feel relieved that her pursuer had gone? Biting her lip to stop it trembling, Jessica visualised him walking away somewhere out in the darkness, mobile phone in his pocket and a sense of satisfaction on his invisible face that he'd succeeded in frightening her.

She yanked the curtains closed, a sense of outrage making her heart beat faster. It had to be someone from school, some idiot boy trying to scare her. How else would they know her number? Or that she'd be all alone in the house, her parents away on business?

Her mind only half-aware of what she was doing, Jessica went from room to room, turning on every light, banishing every trace of shadow until she came at last to her own bedroom that looked out towards the street. Jessica stood just inside the doorway, hesitating, her hand on the dimmer switch. This was her sanctuary, her safe place. Should she announce her arrival in the room by turning on this light too? What if he was still out there, watching? The wall opposite her window glowed with the reflection cast by the street light; would she be seen slipping across the room? With a muffled sob, she flung herself down on the bed, pulled off her boots and scrambled under the duvet, not bothering to undress.

For several minutes she heard nothing but the thumping of her own heart. And then the phone began to ring once more.

CHAPTER 29

'Her name is Miss Munro. She is going to be interviewing you all later today and tomorrow for careers guidance, so make sure you have plenty of questions to ask her,' Maggie continued, her eyes taking in all the expressions on the faces of her Fourth Year pupils. Announcing the arrival of a careers officer along with all the other administrative details was being met with the usual bored indifference by most of them; Amanda and Jessica were deep in conversation about something, heads down and whispering behind their smooth curtains of hair. Only Kyle Kerrigan seemed to be sitting up a bit straighter, his eyes glued to Mrs Lorimer as if he could see right through her. Did he see her as his teacher any more or had she become a different figure of authority simply by being DCI Lorimer's wife? Maggie shivered, aware that she was already having misgivings about meddling in affairs that were rightly her husband's.

As they filed out after the bell, Kyle hung back.

'Yes, Kyle,' Maggie began briskly, trying to hide the anxiety that was gnawing at her innards.

'This careers officer,' Kyle began, then paused, biting his lower lip.

Maggie looked at him for a moment. What was wrong? Why was the boy acting so nervously?

'Would she know anything about forensic medicine?'

'Why?' Maggie frowned. 'What do you want to ask her?' Was this something to do with Julie? A sense of pity swept over her. Following the girl's tragic death, had they lost sight of the need to take care of this troubled boy?

'I'm . . . you might not like this, Mrs Lorimer.' Kyle hesitated, a flush of red gathering at his neckline. 'It's just that . . . you know how we talked about me doing English at uni? Well, I've kind of changed my mind about doing English past Fifth Year.' His voice tailed off in a mumble.

Maggie felt her shoulders relax as the truth dawned on her. 'You want to concentrate on your science subjects instead so you can study forensic medicine? Is that it?'

The boy nodded, suddenly looking like the fifteen-year-old that he was.

'You've certainly had good marks in physics and chemistry, Kyle, and though I must admit I'm sorry you won't be following my subject, there's no reason why we can't see our doctors being well read in contemporary literature.' Maggie twinkled at him and was rewarded by a tentative grin.

'So this careers woman . . .'

'Miss Munro,' Maggie supplied. 'She'll give you

all the information you'll need. In fact,' Maggie hesitated as a sudden thought struck her, 'I have a friend who is a consultant forensic pathologist. Would you like me to ask her if she'll give you some pointers? She's actually off her work for a while, so maybe she would have some time to speak to you. What do you think?'

The answering beam on the boy's face was enough. 'That'd be great, Mrs Lorimer. Thanks.'

And as Kyle sped off down the corridor to his next class, Maggie allowed herself a long exhalation of relief. Her own silly conscience was all that had made her think – what? That this boy had guessed she was doing some snooping of her own into Julie's murder? Maggie shook her dark curls. Too much imagination: that was all that was wrong with her. Gathering up the papers on her desk, she watched as the noisy movement of pupils in the corridor outside began to disperse to the next class.

She would talk to the kids, to Julie's friends, although that was easier said than done. There was always the Scripture Union club, she remembered. And a chit had been put into all their pigeonholes asking for someone to fill in for Eric while he was away. Maggie looked thoughtful for a moment. Could she do it? Surely it was simply a matter of singing a few choruses and giving Bible readings? And she was good at reading aloud, wasn't she? The kids were always saying how she brought stories to life for them. Yes, she decided.

If no one else had offered yet, Mrs Lorimer would step into that particular breach; she had to start somewhere after all and Eric's SU club was as good a place to begin as any.

The corridor leading to Eric's room was painted a pale, cold blue. Maggie glanced absently at the wavy line where some naughty child had taken a pencil for a walk along it, the curves suddenly taking an upward flow and breaking off: she could just imagine the offending pencil being pocketed as a teacher turned the corner. She paused outside the RE teacher's room. It wasn't fair, Maggie told herself for the hundredth time. There was no way the man was guilty of any terrible crime. He'd never interfere with an underage pupil, nevermind try to silence her in the most evil way. Eric just wasn't like that. But is that simply what you want to think? a little voice asked. Was she trying to convince herself of Eric's innocence simply because she couldn't handle the idea of actually knowing a killer? Suddenly she recalled the personal accounts of a particular serial killer's life from his friends. He'd been quiet but harmless, one had reported; a little brusque sometimes but never in a million years had anyone thought him capable of such terrible acts of cruelty, others said.

Brushing down her skirt as if she were ridding herself of these thoughts, Maggie stepped into Eric Chalmers' classroom. Somewhere in his filing cabinet she would find the SU folder.

There it was, decorated by a single silver cross stuck on the front, the words Scripture Union written in Eric's flowing hand. The contents consisted mostly of sheets of paper with lists of names and little mini sermons that he'd headed 'stories', but as Maggie flicked over the sheets, a few photographs fell out on to the desk. Curious, she picked them up.

At first Maggie was shocked to see Julie's face laughing out at her from the group surrounding Eric. Then the feeling was replaced by one of immense sadness. She should still be here, laughing or crying, making a nuisance of herself whispering in class, flirting with the boys.

'Oh, Julie,' Maggie Lorimer said softly, turning the photos over one by one, her eyes picking the girl out as she posed on the beach, smiled with the rest of the group or made daft faces for Eric's camera. But it was the final photograph that made Maggie take a sharp intake of breath.

It might have been taken by a professional portrait photographer, this picture of a young girl – no, Maggie thought, correcting herself – a young *woman*. Julie was sitting sideways, long blonde hair flicked casually over one shoulder, her eyes focused on the cameraman, a look of sleepy sultriness in her eyes and a smile that could only be described as sexy. Had Eric taken this? And if so, why had he kept it here in this folder? Maggie turned the photograph over but there was nothing written on the back. It was so out of keeping with these other images of youngsters having fun, larking about at SU camp, that Maggie found herself shivering.

Then another thought occurred to her and she looked back at the group photos, her eyes scanning each pupil to see who had been at the summer camp. One by one, familiar faces looked out at her until she came to the tallest boy standing right at the back. It was Kenny Turner, one of her Sixth Years. Kenny? Maggie raised her eyebrows in surprise: fun-loving, football-daft Kenny Turner? Well, that was a turn-up for the books, seeing him at SU camp. Maggie cast her mind back to her class's subject choices; she was sure Kenny didn't take RE, so why had he been at Eric's summer camp? Slowly Maggie laid out the photographs and examined them more carefully until she found what she had been looking for. Yes! That group photo with Eric in the centre didn't have Kenny in among them, so had he been behind the lens? And if so, had this photo of Julie with those come-to-bed eyes also been taken by Kenny?

Maggie Lorimer experienced a little frisson of delight at her discovery. Maybe her idea wasn't quite as mad as she'd thought and perhaps she had the makings of a decent detective after all.

He heard his name spoken aloud, the words punctuated with a question mark, words spoken by the taller of the two men outside his door. They stood with polite expressions on their faces, betokening something other than the usual salesman trying to offer double-glazing or a new kitchen. And the other one, gazing keenly at his face, told him that it wasn't the Mormons either. Besides, he knew exactly who they were. One of his neigh-bours, passing the ground-floor window, had caught sight of him then made a face, pointing a thumb upwards and mouthing the word, police. So he'd had to open the door to them after that. It just wouldn't do to avoid being part of the normal run of things.

'Strathclyde Police. We're investigating the death of Julie Donaldson,' the taller one said, flipping open his warrant card for him to see.

'Terrible business,' he replied, making his brow as furrowed with concern as he possibly could. 'What must her parents be going through?' he murmured, letting his voice mimic the words he'd heard over and over since the day the girl had been declared a murder victim.

'Did you know the family, sir?' This from the other one, who now nodded in the direction of the street where the tenement flats stopped and the row of terraced cottages began.

'No, afraid not, but one can only imagine . . .' He gave a sigh and shook his head.

'We're trying to find anyone among her friends and neighbours who might help,' the tall one explained, turning to leave.

'If only there was something I could do.' He smiled bleakly and sketched a small wave as he went to shut the door.

Once inside, he leaned against the door as if to keep them out. He listened as their footsteps faded away, taking them towards the close mouth; he must have been the last one in the tenement close to be door-stepped.

Julie Donaldson. He'd seen her photograph staring out at him from the front pages of every newspaper, from the TV evening news, from the homepage on his laptop. Julie Donaldson, a fifteen-year-old girl he'd met in Royal Exchange Square, not Juliet Carr, a student who'd leapt at the chance to take a film test.

His heart thudded within his chest. What were her parents going through? He'd asked but in truth he had never wondered about them, these anonymous people who lived just along his street. Had he ever met them? Somehow he couldn't make himself care about these faceless parents.

'See thon religious fella,' Arthur Pollock began. Then, as he caught the look his wife shot at him, Arthur's sense of selfpreservation seemed to kick in and he ended his statement in a mutter before slugging the last drops of beer from the can.

'We were hoping you might tell us a bit about your niece,' Detective Sergeant Cameron said, trying to keep the disapproval out of his tone. What a man did in the comfort of his own home was none of his business; if Arthur Pollock wanted to drink himself stupid during daylight hours then that was his affair. Still, it was something to bear in mind, that and the reference to Eric Chalmers. Cameron hadn't missed the man's words. They were still looking for whichever vigilante had attacked the Chalmers' home and the small man sitting opposite him fitted one of the descriptions Ruth Chalmers had given the police. But that could come later. What Cameron wanted now was something that might give a lead in this case.

'What do you want to know, Sergeant?' Mrs Pollock asked.

'Information about Julie: who her friends had been, what her hobbies were, that sort of thing.'

'Oh, we wouldn't know things like that,' the woman told him, shaking her head. 'I mean, we're a close family, but teenagers . . . well, you kind of get out of the habit of seeing them at that age, don't you?'

'What was she like?' Cameron tried again.

'Oh, lovely girl, wasn't she, Arthur?'

'Aye, lovely girl,' her husband echoed, nodding solemnly.

'Just like her mother, God rest her soul,' Mrs Pollock continued. 'Always a wee smile for you, know what I mean?'

Cameron nodded. This was going nowhere fast. He'd seen it all before: the way death seemed to magically transform the personality of the deceased. No one wanted to speak ill of the dead, particularly someone young like Julie.

'Well, thanks for your time.' Cameron rose to go but as he was being shown out of the living room, he turned. 'By the way, you don't happen to know anything about whoever attacked the Chalmers' house, do you?' The Detective Sergeant stared right into Arthur Pollock's face and the way the man's eyes slid away told him he'd got it in one. He'd be coming back here again if there was any sort of evidence to bring a charge.

Mary Donaldson folded the towels neatly and laid them to one side. Hands trembling, she sorted through the other washing: Frank's working trousers, her own overalls and the garment that had brought these sudden tears to her eyes, a pair of Julie's skintight jeans. They'd cost her the best part of a week's wages, Mary remembered. She and Julie had not quite come to a quarrel over them on the first floor of Fraser's, the girl wheedling and complaining that everyone else had jeans like that; did Mary want her to be the odd one out? Mary had bitten her lip and given in as usual. Seeing Julie's glee, however temporary, had been a relief compared to the huffiness that seemed to permeate the entire household whenever her stepdaughter had been thwarted. Now, sliding her hands over the dark blue denim, Mary would have paid a king's ransom for the bloody things if it would have brought Julie back to them.

A wave of helplessness engulfed her; Frank would never be the same man again and she was more than ever an outsider in this marriage, Julie's ghost haunting them from now till eternity.

What did happen after death? Was it all bright lights and a feeling of never-ending peace? They'd talked about it once, over dinner, just after Julie had come back from that Scripture Union camp. The girl had returned home full of a sort of joy in her spirit, Mary recalled, singing round the house, talking about all the things they'd done at camp. Being with that young man, Mr Chalmers, had brought the best out in the girl, Mary told herself. Then it had all changed again after Mr Wetherby had walked out on his family. Sam didn't believe in God, Julie had admitted to them, and Frank had told his daughter not to shove her own beliefs down their throats. The poor folk had enough to upset them as it was. And, to give her stepdaughter her due, Mary thought, she had tried to be a good pal to the Wetherby lassie and her big brother.

So where was she now? Somewhere floating out there, invisible and in a different place from them all? Or lying cold and still in Glasgow City Mortuary, no more than the leftovers of a human being?

S4 was Maggie's last class before lunch and, as the bell rang, she stepped quickly towards her door, ready to lay a hand on the girl's shoulder before the mad dash to the school canteen took them all away.

'Can I have a wee word with you, Samantha?'

The girl looking up at her English teacher was

a shadow of her former self, Maggie thought with a sudden shaft of pity. Always slim and neat, Sam Wetherby looked as if she'd lost pounds in weight. Her thin face, accentuated by the curtain of long dark hair, had the sort of appearance one associated with heroin addicts: the bone structure a mere skeleton covered in bluish skin. For a moment Maggie's resolve almost left her.

'Can you spare a few minutes, pet? I wanted to talk to you about Julie.'

The hanging head and heaving shoulders were enough for Maggie to close her classroom door and to lead the girl gently over to her desk. Out came the box of Kleenex and then Sam was noisily blowing her nose and gulping for breath between tears that were streaming down her cheeks.

Maggie wanted to take the child in her arms, comfort her somehow and tell her in soothing words that everything was going to be all right. But it wasn't. It never could be and the only comfort Maggie would be able to offer was the possible closure on her best friend's death once her killer had been caught. So she would do her bit in this investigation if she could, starting with Samantha.

'Take your time, love,' she began. 'I only want to help.'

CHAPTER 30

The forensic biologist lifted up her head and smiled. That was better. One hair from the mass of evidence bags was caught between the two prongs of her tweezers, a brittle reminder of a life that had been snuffed out years ago. The mortuary might have the skeletal remains but the grave itself had yielded up much, much more. This hair, for instance, showed that this girl had been naturally dark-haired, but examination under the microscope had given away the fact that the hair had been repeatedly bleached to make it several shades lighter. But that wasn't all the scientist had to make her smile.

When the report was finally typed out to send to the SIO, she would have a lot of satisfaction writing up the details of what flora had been discovered in and around the crime scenes. The usual specimens like rosebay willow herb and several species of fern were already there in abundance, cross referenced against the sort of soils found in the woods, but there had been a rogue among the traces taken from all three of the women's graves. One that might have gone unseen, had it not been for her meticulous and painstaking work. Soil sifting had uncovered seeds from a species that simply didn't exist in or around the park. *Ulex europaeus*, the thorny, yellow-flowering gorse, was more at home in acidic sandy heaths than in the dark shadiness of a place like Dawsholm Woods. Difficult to distinguish from whin or broom, but for someone who had made a study of these particular plants, well, the woman from GUARD knew exactly what it was she was looking at. The pods had burst on a hot dry day, probably in high summer, she thought absently, already composing the report in her head, though the plant actually can flower all throughout the year. Was this a clue as to where these victims had been prior to being killed under the shadow of these trees? Perhaps, but that wasn't her job to find out. Once her report was done, she'd be happy to know how the triple murder investigation progressed, even to the extent of preparing herself to become an expert witness for the Crown.

Humming softly, the biologist laid aside the hair sample on a clean Petri dish, a vision of a hillside aglow with the prickly, evergreen shrubs and their acid-yellow flowers.

'When gorse is out of bloom, kissing is out of season,' she murmured, remembering the old saying.

Suddenly she had an image of a man embracing a woman just moments before he put his hands around her throat. And the sharp thorns of the sweet-smelling gorse seemed to be reminders of what pain could be inflicted even in a moment of pure, unadulterated pleasure.

'They were possibly all taken for a walk by their killer before entering Dawsholm Woods,' Lorimer told the team.

The faces that looked back at the SIO showed tell-tale signs of weariness; too much overtime, too little sleep and a withdrawal from the normal routine of family life took its toll on officers after a while. So any new information that helped push things along was welcome.

'Forensic results show that both of the unknown victims were killed at a time of year when the weather was probably hot and dry; the gorse seeds in the grave soil are not native to the crime scene but may have been taken there on their clothes or shoes. And the seeds would only have been present at a time when the pods were ready to split open, again probably summer. We're not known for hot dry days in Glasgow at other times of the year,' he added wryly. 'Now we've been given a proper sort of timescale for the women's deaths; we know that Julie was killed in mid-August, victim number two was likely murdered last summer and the remains of our third woman have been dated as having been killed three years ago. Obviously they can't be exact, but the soil evidence does point towards a similar sort of time.'

'School holidays,' someone murmured.

Lorimer's head jerked up. The implication was clear: Eric Chalmers may well have had the opportunity to carry out these murders. But there was another consideration as well.

'There is the possibility that all three victims were of school age,' he told them. 'Forensic examination identifies the bones as being young adults. So far we haven't found any missing persons of that age who fit our two unknown victims.'

'Might have been school leavers,' Alistair Wilson offered. 'They aim to go to college in another city then disappear off the radar.' He shrugged. 'It happens all the time.'

Lorimer nodded. 'It certainly is a consideration. And that narrows our focus to a certain age group. More paperwork, I'm afraid,' he said to a chorus of groans. 'Find out who went missing around these times, concentrating on girls from sixteen to twenty. Then maybe we'll come up with names to put to these,' he pointed at the pictures of two sets of skeletal remains that adorned the wall, 'and figure out just what happened to them.'

Lorimer gave each member of the team the benefit of his penetrating blue stare as he swept his eyes around them. 'We have less than a fortnight to come up with more evidence,' he told them. 'After that, unless we are making real progress, we'll be faced with the prospect of a review team coming in to crawl all over us. And I for one don't relish that idea. So let's find out who these girls really are.'

'Kyle Kerrigan? That's not the lad . . . Oh, it is him. How strange,' Rosie Fergusson mused as she listened to her friend's request. The Fourth Year boy, the one whose own father had been convicted of murder, wanted to become a forensic scientist. Cathartic or what? Rosie thought, her natural cynicism asserting itself. But Maggie Lorimer sounded keen for the lad to pursue this notion and was asking Rosie for help.

'Okay, why not?' she decided. There was nothing to lose and maybe it would actually help the kid find closure from his friend's murder. Something of Solly's subject must be rubbing off on me. Rosie grinned as she flipped off her mobile. She'd have to speak to Dan, clear it with the mortuary supervisor, but it shouldn't be too big a problem. A wee trip around the place might succeed in putting the boy off any romanticised notions he had about studying pathology. But was that what Maggie had in mind?

Kenny Turner looked down at his hands as soon as he saw the photograph. Hiding his blushes, Maggie told herself.

'Quite a stunner, wasn't she?' Maggie remarked quietly. Only a brief nod came in response and, as she watched the boy's reaction, she could see the heaving shoulders that told her he had begun sobbing. Silently she passed him the box of Kleenex tissues and waited until he'd blown his nose and gathered his emotions together.

'Were you two a couple, then?' she asked softly, her tone full of sympathy.

Kenny gave a brief, watery smile and shook his

head. 'I wish,' he replied, meeting Maggie's eyes for a second before looking down again. 'There are a lot more better-looking guys in school than me. Anyway, she couldn't see past Chalmers, could she?' The voice that trembled with tears took on an edge of bitterness. 'I mean,' Kenny lifted his acne-scarred face and raised his hands towards it in a gesture of despair, 'how could I compete?'

Maggie tried not to smile back. Young love could hurt so much and a teenage lad's self-esteem might easily reach rock-bottom when he had been rejected in favour of an older man. And if that man had been Eric Chalmers, with his film-star good looks and natural charm, well, Kenny was spot on: how could he compete with that?

'But Julie liked you, didn't she? I mean, her expression in the photo . . .'

Kenny's mouth twisted into the semblance of a grin but his eyes were full of regret. 'Ach, she put it on for anyone, Julie did. Not camera shy, know what I mean? Fantasised about being something she wasn't.'

'She flirted with you?'

Kenny snorted. 'Mrs Lorimer, surely you knew how Julie was? She flirted with everything in trousers. Oh.' His face fell suddenly. 'I shouldn't be talking about her like that, should I? Not now she's dead.'

'I think it's more important to tell the truth about Julie than to mouth mere platitudes, don't you, Kenny?'

'Suppose so. Truth is, I really fancied her. Loads of the boys did.'

'But did any of them act on their feelings, d'you know?'

The boy shrugged. 'Not so far as I know. None of the ones in Scripture Union did, anyway, or at least not that I could see. And I was around her most of the time at SU camp. I'd have noticed something.'

Maggie took a deep breath before asking her next question. 'And Mr Chalmers? How did he behave around Julie?'

Kenny Turner sat up a little straighter at that, his hands suddenly clasped firmly together. 'He didn't do anything to Jules,' the boy replied, his face losing any trace of his usual jaunty smile. 'How can anyone say a bad word against him?' Then a frown appeared on his brow as another thought dawned on the boy and he looked straight at his teacher as he asked, 'Do the police think he hurt Julie?'

Maggie winced then, before she had time to respond, Kenny's eyes narrowed.

'Anyway, that's all a load of crap what she said about Mr Chalmers. Julie was going out with a guy from her own year, wasn't she?'

'She was?'

Kenny looked at her pityingly. 'Didn't you know, then? And you're their Year teacher as well.' He paused as Maggie looked at him expectantly.

'Julie was going out with Kyle Kerrigan.'

★　　★　　★

Maggie watched as the door to her classroom closed behind Kenny. His parting remark was still making her heart thump uncomfortably within her chest. Earlier, her chat with Samantha had meant a lot of listening as the girl spilled out her feelings between bouts of crying. She'd not believed her best pal at first and now she was racked with remorse, for surely Mr Chalmers must have had something to do with Julie's death? She'd lifted a tear-stained face to Mrs Lorimer, expecting some kind of reassurance on that score, but Maggie had given her none, except to say that Sam would come to terms with things in time and that it was important to let the process of law take its course. She'd been surprised at the venom in the girl's voice, though, as she'd countered that particular remark.

'It won't bring her back though, will it? She's dead and whoever killed her will rot in jail if they find him, but they won't take *his* life away, will they?'

Remembering the girl's white face and how she'd had to hold on to Maggie's desk for support as she stood up to go, gave the Detective Chief Inspector's wife serious misgivings about what she was doing. And what had she found out? Nothing much that she hadn't known before, except the fact that Julie and Kyle had been an item. How could she have missed that? Sitting back in her chair, Maggie Lorimer wondered if there was something else she ought to know about Julie

Donaldson that wasn't immediately obvious. Both Sam and Kenny had reminded her that the girl was a bit of a fantasist. Well, as her English teacher for the past three years, Maggie Lorimer had come to know that. Julie's work was full of the kind of daydreaming quality shared by few of the other girls. But had it been more than that? Was there some sort of Walter Mitty aspect to the girl's actual character? Did she really live in a fantasy world where she believed in her own daydreams? Maggie sat very still for a moment, considering this. If so, then Julie Donaldson had got herself and Eric into some very serious trouble for nothing more than a teenage delusion.

But what sort of daydreams had led the girl to Dawsholm Woods and into the arms of a killer?

DCI Lorimer listened to the voice on the line from Pitt Street. The email report would be coming in as soon as possible, he was being told, but they wanted him to have the forensic results right away.

He let the swivel chair rock him back and forwards for a few seconds as he contemplated this new piece of information. Traces of DNA matching the samples taken from both Kyle Kerrigan and Eric Chalmers had been found on Julie Donaldson's clothing. But what did that really prove? The CCTV footage showed Kyle grappling with her, clutching the victim's arm, so of course there would be traces. It had been a hot sunny day and the boy would have been sweating more than usual; his anger might also have increased the amount of perspiration on his own body. But Eric Chalmers? Why would he have left a trace on his pupil? Teachers weren't supposed to touch their pupils. At all. Even grasping hold of them in anger could have the kids shouting 'assault'. These days every last one of them seemed to know their human rights and sought to push them into the faces of anyone in authority. As a police officer who was also married to a schoolteacher, Lorimer was well aware of the repercussions of the least action from a teacher against a pupil. But had Chalmers seen Julie after his suspension? And if so, had he somehow left his DNA on her clothing?

Lorimer was left with the feeling that, despite this positive result, he was still unsure whether there was sufficient evidence to charge the RE teacher with murder.

'Yes!' John Weir punched the air as Lorimer read out the results of the DNA testing, his young face clearly delighted at the prospect of an immediate arrest.

'We are still waiting for results from Chalmers' car,' Lorimer pointed out. 'If these should come back negative we may have to rethink the man's involvement.'

'But he's guilty!' The words were out before the detective constable had time to stop himself.

'And who decides that?' Lorimer asked quietly. 'A room full of tired officers or a jury of fifteen men and women?' He was gratified to see the DC staring at him open-mouthed, an expression of disbelief in his eyes.

'We mustn't make any mistakes here,' he added. 'There's a huge possibility that these killings have been done by the same person. And *if* that's Eric Chalmers, I want evidence to link him to all three of them. Understood? We do a complete search of his house, interview his friends, his family and, yes, his church. I want everything to do with the man turned inside out and I won't be satisfied with anything less than concrete evidence to show that he's a killer. Recently, too many of our prime suspects have got away on a technicality involving DNA profiling, remember,' he growled. 'I don't want that happening in this case.'

'What about your profile, Dr Brightman?' a voice asked. 'Any joy there yet?'

Lorimer frowned. Solly was sitting in on this now, as part of the team, but the casual way this question had been asked annoyed the SIO. Some of them still felt that the psychologist's presence was superfluous to their handling of the murder case, a belief Lorimer himself had once shared. But that was before he had come to value Dr Solomon Brightman's insight into the minds of brutal killers.

'If you are asking me whether I think Mr Chalmers fits the profile, then all I can say at this stage is that there are some inconsistencies with his personality and that of a murderer who has carefully thought out his method of killing and disposing of his victims. Not that Mr Chalmers lacks an organised mind,' he continued, nodding his head so that his dark beard wagged sagely. 'There may very well be a case for thinking that this man, whoever he is, has acted upon a trigger that sets off his actions. And since we do not yet have enough information about the school-teacher's mental state, it's a bit difficult to completely rule him out.'

Lorimer clenched his teeth. He'd have been happier for Solly to have said nothing at all at this stage than to waffle on in his 'it might be but on the other hand it might not' manner. He was used to this but there were some in the room who were not, and the DCI could sense their scepticism. It was with some relief that the meeting ended and Solly left, pleading another appointment.

Back in his room, Lorimer paced around, his mind considering all the possibilities that he had laid before the team. At last he sat down heavily in his chair, rubbing his hands across his eyes as the beginnings of a tension headache manifested itself. God, he was tired! There were days like this when he almost prayed for a breakthrough, the stultifying impasses in each case causing a build-up of frustration and wasted energy.

He could do with a drink, something to deaden the awareness that they weren't making headway with either of the investigations. But 'that way madness lies', he quoted softly to himself. No officer had ever really found what they were looking for in the bottom of a whisky bottle.

He'd buy a whole damn crate of the stuff to celebrate, though, if they found little Nancy Fraser alive, he thought suddenly. And as Lorimer recalled the earnest expression of that young mother as she'd placed her last hope upon his shoulders, something inside banished the fatigue that had threatened to overwhelm him. While he had breath in his body he'd make sure his officers put in every hour that God gave them to find that child.

'Thank you,' the woman said, 'and may I ask who's calling?'

There was a short silence then a name was mumbled. 'This is confidential, right? It won't get back to me, will it?'

Barbara Cassidy arched one well-plucked eyebrow as she replied then asked for details of the caller's address. After all, she told him, they had to know where to send his fee.

When she put the phone down at last, Barbara Cassidy was intrigued; this one was surely at odds with their Senior Investigating Officer. Nobody would give a journalist that kind of juicy titbit off the record without there being some sort of grudge involved. Still, it wasn't her lot to reason why, just to type up some good copy and hope that her editor would see fit to place it on the front page. They'd already run a few column inches on the

DNA subject in the past; a couple of high profile cases had been turfed out of court on the strength (or lack) of this new sort of testing. If this Jesus-loving Chalmers were to be let off because of concerns about the validity of forensic evidence before the case even came to court, there would be a public outcry against Strathclyde Police. And against DCI Lorimer, she thought grimly, remembering the way the tall policeman had looked at her as though she were dirt on his shoes. Sort him out good and proper, she would, and have a blinder of a story to tell into the bargain. It didn't take much to whip up resentment against the Christians these days, given all their sins against wee altar boys and shenanigans among Kirk elders and their ministers. Some salient reminders of these in a well worded feature could begin a stream of invective in the letters page. And keep her editor happy.

CHAPTER 31

E ric turned on his side, feeling the edge of the sheet cold against his flesh. Ruth was sleeping now, her head burrowed into the pillow next to his, and the monitor opposite their bed sounded only the rhythmic breathing of the little child next door. It should have been a relief, this respite from the baby's girning and Ruth's exhausted sighs, but somehow the silence in the house only enlarged Eric's awareness of his wife and child, his two responsibilities. It scarcely seemed possible that in the space of two years he had become a married man and a father. Before, he had been able to choose his own destiny, or at least to follow the calling he felt had been mapped out for him. But he'd still had choices to make then, choices to heed his father's urgings and study for the ministry or to take flight to a distant land and join a mission team.

Now, as he lay watching the shadows flicking past the gap in the curtains, Eric Chalmers felt as though his life had narrowed into this small house and his little family. His job, that had once meant a real joy and an opportunity for witness, was now an essential factor in his life. It kept the mortgage paid and put food on their table, didn't it? And without that, what would happen to them all? Biting his lip, Eric knew such thoughts were born of self-pity and depression. God would provide, he knew that; he'd told Ruth as much whenever things looked difficult.

'Take no thought of the things of the morrow,' he quoted softly to himself.

And he believed these words. Didn't he? A sort of dark mist came over his mind and with it the pain of doubt. If it was all a delusion . . .

Suddenly he wanted to turn towards Ruth, to hold her tightly, to kiss her lips then bury himself deep inside her warm, unyielding body. No, it was too soon since Ashleigh's birth for that and, besides, Ruth was sleeping so peacefully that it would be cruel to disturb her.

As he closed his eyes, hoping for sleep to quieten his mind and release the tension in his body, another image came unbidden: Julie's young face looking up at him, her eyes sweet with expectation.

But Julie was dead and never again would he see her smile as she turned into his classroom, even though that memory lingered in his brain.

'Today would be fine. Not much happening down here. Aye, bring him in whenever you like,' the mortuary superintendent said.

'Thanks, it'll probably be after school hours.

Say around four-thirty? Okay, I'll call if there's any change.' Rosie put down the telephone and smiled. Right, that was one matter out of the way. She'd call Maggie at morning interval time and let her know what was arranged. Young Kyle Kerrigan was welcome to make this visit if he wanted to come into town. For some reason Solly had expressed an interest in the boy's visit to Glasgow City Mortuary and so they'd take a taxi there together. Or was he wanting to nosey around the mortuary for reasons of his own? Once into a case, her fiancé was fairly inscrutable, his thoughts centred on things like routes and possibilities as he sought to create the killer's profile.

Rosie pulled absently on the waistband of her linen skirt. She'd lost weight during her time in hospital and hadn't put it back on again yet. The pathologist pulled a face; it would be the law of natural cussedness if she were to gain a few pounds before the wedding and have to have the dress altered. Catching sight of herself in the mirror above the fireplace, Rosie considered what she saw: a slightly built woman with a halo of blonde hair above a heart-shaped face that looked paler than usual. She stuck out her tongue at the reflection, mentally telling herself that she'd need to spend time putting on some make-up before allowing that pinched-looking wee face out of doors.

It would be good to see the mortuary again, even just to say hello to all the technicians.

Everyone had been lovely – sending cards and flowers – so she'd be able to thank them in person and assure them that she'd be back among them as soon as she was permitted. And there was that matter of this murder case, she told herself. If she could just have a wee squint at the body . . . It wasn't mere curiosity on her part, Rosie told herself, simply a professional interest. Wasn't it?

'I'm going to my mother's,' Ruth told him as she folded the muslins into small squares and packed them into Ashleigh's bag. 'She said she'd come over and take us in the car.'

Eric let his hands drop to his sides. It was sensible, given all that was happening; the smashed glass would be repaired today and that meant an upheaval in the baby's room, and then the police were going to arrive with their search warrant.

'You don't mind, do you?' Ruth turned to face him, her eyes wary.

'Why should I? It's the best thing for you and Ash. And your mum will enjoy having you both.'

Ruth hesitated for a moment. 'She said we could stay for a few days. What d'you think?'

Eric pasted a smile on his face and gave his wife a reassuring hug. 'Great idea. Give you both a good rest away from all of this nonsense.'

But if he held Ruth close to him for a bit longer than she had expected, she made no comment, simply laying her head on her husband's shoulder and patting his back as though he were a child in need of comforting.

When the car drove off, Eric stood in the doorway watching till they were out of sight then turned into the house, biting back the emotion he'd hidden so well. The silence made the place seem bleak, so he switched on the radio, letting his favourite station blast out a current number-one hit. There was plenty to do, Eric told himself, picking up a discarded bib from the arm of a chair and adding it to the pile of laundry that lay in front of the washing machine.

It was while he was sorting through the coloureds and whites that the doorbell rang.

'Mr Chalmers?'

The woman smiling at him seemed a friendly sort and for a moment Eric wondered if she or the chap just behind her would produce a warrant card and ask to be admitted.

But the sudden flash from a camera told him these were not police officers.

As he tried to shut the door he could hear the woman's voice demanding, 'Tell us what you know about Julie Donaldson's murder!'

Then she was shouting, 'What d'you think, Mr Chalmers? Was it an act of God?'

Just as Eric's fingers touched the handle, he felt as if an invisible hand had clasped itself over his own, drawing him back from the impulse to throw open the door and angrily protest his innocence to this woman and to the world at large. And a small voice in his head reminded Eric that she was simply trying to provoke him into a response that she could publish, that was all.

He was still standing there minutes later when a second knock came and one of the voices outside called, 'Strathclyde Police.'

'Want to come back with me after school?' Jessica King asked casually, flicking her dark tresses over one shoulder. She and Manda were sitting in the library, side by side in the same study carrel, an open laptop showing diagrams of the human body in front of them.

'Sure. Parents still away?'

Jessica nodded, focusing her attention on the arrangement of glands within the endocrine system that they were supposed to be learning for a biology test. Manda's presence at home would help to banish whatever ghosts were lingering there, she thought. Her best friend had a knack of making everything seem fun, even their homework.

'Stay for tea if you like,' Jessica offered with a shrug that said she didn't mind whether Manda took up her offer, though her careless gesture concealed the unspoken hope that she would have company at least into the hours of darkness.

'Sh!' Manda hissed suddenly, nudging Jessica's elbow. 'Don't look now but guess who's just walked in?'

It took several seconds of self-control before the dark-haired girl glanced up from the computer screen to see Kenny Turner passing by. For a moment their eyes met and the boy grinned then dropped a wink before settling himself at a vacant laptop.

'What did I say? He fancies you!' Manda breathed into her friend's ear, stifling a giggle.

But instead of smiling or acknowledging the possibility, Jessica felt something inside her freeze: what if it were true? What if Kenny did fancy her? Could this Sixth Year boy have been the silent shadow dogging her footsteps the other night? And was it Kenny Turner, the school joker always doing mad things to make people laugh at him, who'd breathed into her ear as she'd listened for a voice on the other end of a telephone line?

Or was she now so paranoid that every attention paid to her came tagged with some sinister overtone?

Kyle crossed the road, the river Clyde behind him and the city centre ahead. This wasn't a part of town that he knew well and the sweep of tenement buildings, with their small shops hugging the pavements, came as a surprise. Saltmarket and High Street had only been names before. Glasgow University had been in this area long before the buildings in Gilmour Hill had made their presence felt and wasn't this just along the road from the place where folk had been hanged in years gone by? In a different century that could have been his father . . . Kyle shivered slightly as his imagination took him back across the historical divide. But now he was standing outside the building where more of life and death took place in reality than he could ever imagine. Mrs Lorimer had instructed him to go all the way round to the rear door.

'You'll see the front of the High Court,' she'd told him. 'Cross the car park opposite, knock on the back door and someone will let you in.'

Following her directions, Kyle strolled around the building and stopped. The High Court was a magnificent modern building in blonde sandstone, its steps and portico elegant yet austere as befitted the centre of Judiciary. Some of his mates wanted to be lawyers and were going on a visit to the courts. He couldn't see the attraction of striding around bewigged and in a black robe pontificating on the fate of some criminal or other. No, it would be much more interesting to be an expert witness whose knowledge might lead to a conviction.

There was a large van taking up most of the car park and the back door of the mortuary was open so Kyle climbed the few stairs, peering inside. Ahead of him he could see two orderlies carrying a stretcher between them. For a moment he hesitated, his glance falling on the covered figure underneath the waxed cloth. A dead person, he told himself; dead and cold. But then the reason

314

for this visit reasserted itself and he stretched out a hand to knock on the door.

Solly Brightman stood a little apart from the three other people: the pathologist, the mortuary supervisor and the young lad who was doing his best to take in all that Rosie was telling him. It hadn't been strange at all, Solly had told Rosie when she'd mentioned Maggie Lorimer's request. The boy's science grades were excellent and he obviously had an enquiring sort of mind, perfect for a career in forensic medicine. Yet Solly had been astute enough to lag behind them, observing the young man's behaviour, for the psychologist was interested in a boy who wanted to see where post-mortems took place in the aftermath of his girlfriend's murder. Was he using this visit as a way of dealing with her death? Or did death itself hold an unhealthy sort of fascination for him?

Just as he ruminated upon these thoughts, Rosie came to a halt beside the wall of refrigerated containers.

'This is where we keep the cadavers before their post-mortem examinations.'

'And afterwards?' Kyle asked.

'Perhaps. It depends on whether the Fiscal releases them for burial or cremation,' Rosie countered, shooting the boy a look. They'd already shown him the post-mortem room, the viewing room and the areas where staff worked on computers or drank scalding cups of tea. 'To warm you up after dealing with stiffs,' the supervisor had joked.

'Is Julie still in there?'

The sudden silence that followed made the boy's question seem all the more macabre.

'Yes, yes she is.' Rosie was staring at Kyle, and Solly took in the lad's quiet, almost impassive demeanour. It hadn't bothered him to ask and there was nothing callous about his tone.

'Can I see her, please?'

The psychologist caught the enquiring glance that Rosie threw at the mortuary supervisor and the slight shrug of the shoulders that was an eloquent reply of assent.

Solly watched as the boy stepped back a pace, as though to show a modicum of respect for the dead. Kyle's back had straightened and he was clasping and unclasping his hands to keep them still, a possible sign of suppressed excitement. And those eyes; how they stared as the corpse was uncovered. Was that brightness to do with unshed tears? Or did it emanate from quite a different sort of passion?

As Kyle stepped forward, Rosie lifted a warning hand. 'Don't touch her, please. We can't have any contamination.' Then, as if she too had seen something in his expression and decided she didn't like what she saw, the pathologist slid the body back into its slot in the wall. But, as she did so, a back draught caused another corpse to slide slowly out of its place in the wall.

'Woooo!' the supervisor said and they all laughed, the moment's tension suddenly broken.

Solly heard the boy thank Rosie politely and now he saw just a young man who was trying to come to terms with a difficult situation, not the boy who had devoured the dead girl with his eyes, making the psychologist wonder.

'What do you think, Kyle?' he asked, making the boy start at the sound of his voice. 'Is it Julie in there or is she somewhere else, out in a place full of spirits?'

A frown crossed the boy's face as he considered the unexpected question. 'I don't know really. Does anyone? I can't imagine Julie anywhere else, though. Not now I've seen her here.'

'And how should we live our lives if we think there's nothing after death? Hm?'

The boy turned towards him. Solly could see that he was half-embarrassed by the question but curious too.

'Don't know.' He shrugged. 'Do our best I s'pose. Try to find out answers to the questions that keep us awake at night.'

The psychologist nodded, his dark beard dipping sagely, and he then he saw the boy give an inward sigh as though relieved that his answer had met with approval. So, had Kyle given a reply that he really believed or had he simply gauged what was an acceptable response? The answer to that, Solly told himself, might well hold the key to the real reason for this young man's visit to Glasgow City

Mortuary. And was the curiosity that had been aroused a sign of some flaw in his personality? As Kyle Kerrigan made his farewells, Solly Brightman realised that for him at least the last hour and a half had thrown up far more questions about the boy than answers.

'Coming home?' he asked and was rewarded by a grateful nod as Rosie sank against his shoulder, her hands clasped around his arm for support.

Solomon Brightman was staring out of the window, his eyes not seeing the spectacular view across Kelvingrove Park and beyond the towers of Glasgow University but somewhere further away to the west. Dawsholm Woods were easily accessed from both the Maryhill entrance and the gateway from Switchback Road that linked Anniesland and Milngavie. Eric Chalmers lived so close to this place that it was almost too easy to put him into the frame for the three murders. He'd lived in that area for years, first in the Manse down in the more affluent suburbs of Bearsden then in his own home at Queen's Court right at Anniesland Cross. Solly sighed into his beard. There had to be a reason for everything, even the most aberrant behaviour. And what reason did a happily married man who enjoyed his life and his work have for killing three young women? Okay, there were the Peter Sutcliffes of this world who were also married and had committed terrible murders on a massive scale. But what he knew about Eric Chalmers didn't seem to match the same profile as these types of killers.

Solly tried to put himself inside the wood, late on a summer's night, hand-in-hand with a pretty girl.

Had the spade been there already, propped up against a tree? Or did the man holding the girl's hand always keep a spade in the boot of his car, handy for the burial of another victim? It didn't make sense to think of a schoolteacher carrying on like that. Some evidence of psychopathic behaviour would have made itself known in the man's everyday world, surely? He'd even checked the date of Julie's death to see if it had been a full moon that night. Other scientists might scoff but there was plenty of anecdotal evidence to suggest that there was a basis for believing that a full moon affected some people's behaviour. But when he'd checked, the psychologist found the moon had been on the wane that night.

And there was the post-mortem evidence to take into account. Julie hadn't been a virgin but the examination of her body had shown no signs of recent sexual activity. Just because no sexual assault had taken place didn't mean the killer hadn't wanted to perform such an act with her. Whoever he was, perhaps rape hadn't been part of his intention, unlike so many killers of young girls. Had the killer been unable to have sex with Julie? Was that it?

Eric Chalmers was a married man who'd

recently fathered a little girl of his own, not a man whose impotence might have enraged him into murder. But a younger, less experienced man might have wanted to perform a sexual act and been frustrated by his own inability. And there were plenty of young men who had been in Julie Donaldson's orbit at Muirpark Secondary School, Kyle Kerrigan among them.

Solly thought back to the boy's reaction when he'd seen Julie's corpse. His thrill of excitement had been almost tangible, palpably embarrassing for the other people there. But sex and death were closely related, the psychologist had wanted to remind them. If the sight of Julie's dead body had indeed caused sexual arousal in that boy, there was a certain amount of logical explanation for it. But he'd specifically asked to see her corpse, Solly reminded himself. Was the boy haunted by her ghost, perhaps? Had he something on his conscience? And was that his way of laying it to rest? Something was troubling the boy, of that he was sure, but the very idea that a lad of fifteen could have committed murders on young women over a period of three years was absurd. Wasn't it?

Unless – and here Solly's imagination took him deeper into the woods where not two but three figures walked slowly towards the place where one of them would be buried. Was it possible? Had there been another person there to help bury the victim, an older man, manipulative and beguiling? It wouldn't be the first time that young folk had been lured to their death by a pair of evil schemers, Solly thought. Who could ever forget the deeds of Ian Brady and Myra Hindley? It was a possibility he couldn't rule out, not until there was evidence to the contrary.

There was something about this scenario that he didn't like. This killer was far more likely to have been on his own, possibly stalking each of these young women, maybe even selecting them for something they had in common, some quality that he found attractive. Was that what he was missing? A trigger of some sort?

Profiling meant careful consideration of what you knew of the perpetrator and the victims as well as the entire plethora of information that an investigation threw up. But it also meant being aware of possibilities. This killer was a dangerous person: unstable in some way but calculating and clever. And Solly was beginning to think that this killer had never been within the orbit of Lorimer's investigation. For, the more he considered each of the people who had known Julie Donaldson, the more inclined the psychologist was to dismiss every last one of them as her killer.

'That's not very helpful,' Lorimer said at last.

They were sitting in his room, the afternoon sunlight slanting through the vertical blinds, Solly slightly turned away from the window, seated by the DCI's desk where Lorimer was perched, a cup of coffee in one hand.

'It's what I see in the paperwork that's available to us at present,' Solly replied primly. 'If I knew more about the first two victims . . .' he paused, 'it would certainly give me far more to go on.'

'Right, let me get this absolutely straight.' Lorimer sighed heavily. 'You think the women have been targeted by the same man and that he is some loner who is looking for . . . what did you say?'

'I didn't actually give it a name. I don't really know what he is looking for. We know he didn't have sex with the Donaldson girl but that doesn't mean he didn't want to. He may be trying to find fulfilment—'

'That was the word you used!' Lorimer pounced on it. 'Fulfilment. Isn't that the same as sexual satisfaction?'

'It might mean the same to him, but he may not necessarily have to resort to rape or assault to achieve his aims.'

'That's fairly unusual in multiple killings, isn't it?'

'Highly unusual,' the psychologist replied. 'There are scores of textbooks written about sexual motivation – rape escalating to murder – but I think this is different.'

'And you're trying to tell me that we're barking up the wrong tree with Chalmers?'

'I think,' Solly replied slowly, 'that whoever carried out these killings may be someone who displays psychopathic traits. And he might even

322

be in our medical system already. That doesn't fit what I've been told of Eric Chalmers,' he said, looking gravely at Lorimer.

The Detective Chief Inspector slid off the desk and began to pace back and forwards, in and out of the pool of sunlight. Watching him, the psychologist could see the deepening lines around Lorimer's eyes and the way he bit the waxy skin around his index finger: sure signs of the man's growing anxiety. There was pressure on him to come up with answers, and soon, or a review team would be put in place, taking over the whole investigation. Solly could only sympathise with the man whose tall, spare frame seemed confined within these four walls. Curiously, Lorimer's behaviour reminded him of Rosie. Hadn't she been restless recently? But was she really ready for the demands that her full-time job as a consultant pathologist demanded? Perhaps some involvement on the fringes of this case might ease her in gently, he thought.

'Are there any more forensic reports yet?' Solly asked.

Lorimer was standing over him now and Solly could see the grim expression on his face.

'So far we've not achieved very much from forensics to definitely link all three victims. The killer may have taken them to a place where there's been a lot of gorse, *before* their trip to the woods. Where? Why? And what's he doing with them?' Lorimer had resumed his pacing back and forwards. 'If you're right, we have to get our skates on. Look in all the records of mental hospitals – though we're probably going to be scuppered by patient confidentiality – for a man who has some predilection for gorse bushes and young women. That's going to be a breeze, right?' His sarcasm was so palpable that the psychologist winced.

The DCI stopped suddenly. 'Do you know how many officers we have deployed on this case right now? And how many others are trying to find a missing child? And I've got the press on my back too.'

He sat down heavily in the chair beside Solly. 'We are on the point of arresting Eric Chalmers. I just have to have one more piece of evidence to present a case against him. And if we find it in his house, well, what do I do with your emerging profile?'

'Do you think Chalmers guilty of the girl's murder?' Solly asked quietly.

Lorimer ran his hands through his hair. 'I don't know what to think any more. The last thing I want is an unsafe conviction. You know that. And, if I'm honest, Maggie's opinion has coloured my view of him. She can't see past all his decent qualities.'

'But you're worried she might be wrong about him,' Solly added.

'Worried? More like bloody terrified.' Lorimer gave a short laugh. 'How would you like to be in my shoes, arresting one of my wife's friends for murder?'

'Let's look at the timescale,' Solly began. 'The first killing takes place during the school holidays, three years ago, then nothing – so far as we know – until last year and then this latest victim. What was he doing in between these times? And why is it only in the summertime that he carries out his activities?'

'What are you trying to suggest?'

'If I were you,' Solly said slowly, 'I'd begin to look at anyone who had been around Dawsholm Park at that time: temporary rangers, students on a summer job at the Vet School. Anyone,' he paused, 'with a history of mental illness or behavioural problems.'

'Well, if you're right, it's going to be a race against time before we're landed with a review team from outside,' Lorimer told him. 'And if that looks like happening, Mitchison may well put pressure on us to arrest Eric Chalmers.'

Jessica closed the door and slipped on the chain. It was better to be safe than sorry, she told herself. Now that Manda was gone the house seemed too quiet. It would be dark soon and she could close the curtains against the night, light the lamps and put on the telly, cosy down for the remainder of the evening. Mum and Dad had texted her earlier. Their plane would be arriving in Heathrow the day after tomorrow but there was someone they had to see in London so they'd be staying over. That meant three more nights all on her own,

Jessica told herself. Three nights of waiting for the phone to ring and listening to that empty space where an unknown caller breathed into her ear.

As she pulled the curtain cord beside the downstairs window, the girl tried not to look at the trees across the road and the shadows under the street lamps, yet her eyes were drawn towards the spot where she had been sure a man had stood looking back at her. But there was nothing there, not even a movement in the empty pavement.

As Jessica cleared the remains of the pizza she'd shared with Manda the doorbell rang, a single shrill sound as if someone was putting their finger on the buzzer and leaving it there.

Jessica froze where she stood in the hallway. She was just feet away from the front door, the empty cardboard carton gripped in one hand. The girl's other hand was pressed against terrified lips as if to stifle the scream that was rising up in her throat.

The ringing sound seemed to last for ages. Then it stopped and she listened intently. At last she heard it; the sound of footsteps walking away from the door.

But, instead of a sense of relief, the girl felt only a rising panic and, trembling, she sank on to the floor, tears streaming down her face.

When the car door slammed she rose to her feet, dropping the pizza box, and sped up the flight of stairs that would lead to the landing window. All she saw was a pale grey vehicle, its red tail lights disappearing down the cul de sac. It was too dark to make out much but Jessica thought she could see the shape of a man in the driver's seat.

It was the same shadowy figure, she told herself. She knew it was. Heart pounding, Jessica ran further up the stairs to her bedroom and grabbed her digital camera. He'd have to turn and come back to reach the main road, she told herself.

By the time she'd returned to the landing window, the car was parallel with their house and just as she raised the camera, it slowed down.

The face that looked out at her from the driver's window gave a knowing smile that changed to one of anger as he saw her intention. Then he raised a hand against the flash and the car accelerated into the night as she tried to take further shots.

She looked down at the final photograph: all that was visible on the tiny screen was a blur of grey and a streak of red wavy lines.

But Jessica King didn't need a camera to remember the man's face; it was something that was indelibly etched on her memory and would stay with her all through the long hours ahead.

He wanted to take a shower, to cleanse himself from all that had happened today, as if the police had been burglars, violating his home, intruding on his privacy. It made Eric yearn to leave it all behind, go somewhere else entirely. Make a fresh start.

The telephone rang and he grabbed it, the desire to hear Ruth's voice making his eager hands clumsy. 'Hello,' he began, a smile ready on his face. But it wasn't Ruth. The voice on the other end of the line had a haish, nasal quality that set his teeth on edge.

'Barbara Cassidy, the *Gazette*. I was hoping to set up an interview with you, Mr Chalmers,' the woman began.

Eric let the silence between them linger. Was it the same voice that had screamed out at him from the other side of his door? He couldn't be sure. And what would he say to her, anyway?

'Sorry,' he replied at last. 'I don't want to talk to the newspapers.'

That was stupid, Eric cursed himself immediately. She'd put his exact words into tomorrow's edition, wouldn't she? *Murder suspect refuses to talk to the press*. He could already imagine the headlines. But would it have been any easier to say what was in his heart? Wouldn't they twist it all to suit their own story anyway? One way or another, the RE teacher had a feeling of foreboding.

And he could almost sense the demarcation lines being drawn up between those who believed him and those who wanted to see him locked up for a very long time.

The patch of ground was refusing to yield to the edge of the spade, despite the rains that had fallen steadily all night. In disgust he threw the tool away from him, hearing its dull thud as it hit the grass next to the spiked outline of the gorse bushes.

Everything suddenly seemed to be against him. The girl hadn't opened her door to him as she should have.

Wasn't she his bright angel, waiting for the kiss that would transform them for ever?

He thumped his fist against the soil where he had tried to dig the new grave, mouth open in a mask of rage.

She'd seen him. And pointed that bloody camera at him. Somehow he had to get back to her, find her on her own and then bring her here. Only then could he find sleep again.

CHAPTER 32

CLUELESS. The front page headline was repeated over and over again in several of the daily papers. It was par for the course at this stage in a missing child case, but knowing that didn't make it any easier to bear, nor was it going to help when he had his meeting with Mitchison. Would a review be suggested yet? Perhaps. The Superintendent liked to keep on the side of the Chief Constable as well as the press boys, liked to be seen to be doing something. Lorimer's mouth twisted in a spasm of anger: there were officers in this division working all hours to find Nancy Fraser but none of their painstaking efforts were making headline news, were they? And this triple murder inquiry had all of their resources stretched to breaking point. Cases didn't come neatly one after the other in this job, but in a whole ramshackle disorder that had to be tackled somehow. No sooner were you off chasing one case than another came hard on its heels, demanding equal attention. Life on the force was like that and he'd long ago reconciled himself to being able to perform the delicate balancing act that being SIO required.

The perennial promise of more manpower never seemed to materialise sufficiently to satisfy their requirements, something he did wish the newspapers would highlight a bit more.

It was now ten days since the abduction, a timescale destined to be met with a vicious reaction from the redtops who demanded results, as if the police could magically produce the child alive and well like a rabbit from a hat. Lorimer threw down the paper in disgust. The police press team could deal with this: his energies had to be saved for the task of finding what had happened to three dead women. And, anyway, finding little Nancy Fraser was officially Jo Grant's responsibility now.

DS Niall Cameron stepped into the room, one hand holding a sheaf of paper, an expression of excitement on his pale features.

'I think we've found the car!' he exclaimed. 'There's a white Mazda registered to a Miss Lorna Tulloch,' Cameron read from the newly printed page. 'Her last known address is given as Southbrae Drive, Jordanhill. That's not all that far from Yoker,' he added, trying to keep the smile off his face.

'Right.' DI Grant nodded. 'Take DC Weir with you and bring this woman in for questioning. We'll need a warrant to search the premises as well.'

Jo Grant lifted the phone to call Lorimer: he'd want to know they'd had a possible breakthrough.

* * *

331

'You're sure? That's excellent. Keep me posted after they bring the woman in, won't you? Thanks.'

Lorimer gave a triumphant glance at the newspaper crushed into his wastebin. Maybe these people would be eating their words before the next issue was out.

Southbrae Drive was in a pretty residential area leading from Crow Road up towards the leafy margins of Jordanhill Teacher Training College. The houses were fronted by well-tended gardens, blazing with colour from the hanging baskets and rows of bedding plants, now full and lush in the late summer sunshine. DS Cameron stopped the car outside the number he'd been given, noting the grey pebbledash walls and the high privet hedge obscuring the front garden. His heart beat just that little bit faster. Could Nancy Fraser have been taken here? He exchanged glances with his colleague whose raised eyebrows told Cameron that DC Weir also seemed to have considered the same possibility. As the younger man slipped on his jacket, Cameron caught a flash of silver cufflink against the snowy white shirt. He refrained from comment, but it looked as if the detective constable was doing his sartorial best to look smart on the job. Or did he have a hot date after work? The Armani label on the jacket seemed to confirm his thoughts. That looked brand-new. Lucky for some, the tall Lewisman thought. But all thoughts of his fellow officer's rigout quickly vanished as they approached the house.

The doorbell was an old-fashioned single white button set into the side of the stone wall and it gave a shrill ring as the detective sergeant pressed it. When nothing happened he rang again, leaving his finger on the button for a good few seconds.

'Looks like she's out,' Weir remarked, turning to look back at the street. 'No sign of the car, either.'

'Let's take a look round the back,' Cameron said and headed down a side path towards the rear of the house. A line of fencing with a curved gate barred their way.

'Locked!' Weir exclaimed, jiggling the latch.

'Maybe it's just bolted from the inside,' Cameron said. 'Come on, give us a leg up; can't have you messing up these new threads.'

He was right. Peering over the top of the gate, Cameron could see that the owner had bolted the gate shut. Grasping the edge of the wood with both hands, he vaulted over and landed lightly on both feet, knees bent. As he opened the gate he saw DC Weir grinning at him.

'Think you're in practice for the Glasgow Commonwealth Games, then?' he joked.

'Ach, I'll be too old by then,' Cameron replied. 'Come on, let's see what's round here.'

The rear garden contained a neatly mown lawn and a whirligig that, today, was empty of any washing. Like the front, this part of the grounds was also hidden behind hedging, but this was leylandii at least ten feet in height.

'That would screen the garden from any prying eyes, wouldn't it?' Weir remarked.

Cameron nodded then turned to the glazed kitchen door and window, obscured by Venetian blinds that were firmly shut against the outside world.

'Looks like she's away,' Weir remarked, his words receiving only a stony silence from Cameron. Stating the obvious wasn't massively helpful and they were further frustrated by having to wait until the search warrant came through.

'Hello there,' a gruff female voice made them both turn around, 'can I help you?'

Standing by the gate was a large woman in a florid print dress, an expression of belligerent curiosity on her face.

Cameron flicked an appraising eye over her: sensible woman not to come too close to two strangers, keeping her escape route handy, and was that a hefty walking stick tucked under one arm?

'DS Cameron, DC Weir, Strathclyde Police,' he told her, warrant card open for inspection.

'Oh dear, nothing's happened to Lorna, has it?' The woman's face grew suddenly anxious, though the pair of grey eyes staring at them showed a shrewd intelligence.

'We're just carrying out routine inquiries, Miss . . . ?'

'Mrs Jones. I live next door.' She pointed the stick to a direction beyond the expanse of greenery. 'Saw you arrive in your car and when you didn't come back to the front of the house, well, what was I to think?' Her walking stick was now lowered to the ground and she limped heavily forwards, one hand extended.

'Not keeping an eye on the place, officially, you understand, but we are in a neighbourhood watch scheme, at least *we* are. Lorna's a funny sort, keeps herself pretty much to herself, never bothers with community activities,' she added.

'And do you know where Miss Tulloch is at the moment?' Cameron asked.

'No idea. Like I said, she keeps herself to herself. Doesn't work as far as I know. Travels a bit, likes to go up north to that cottage of hers.'

Cameron tried to keep control of his expression at this last bit of information, asking in the mildest of voices, 'Whereabouts might that be, do you know?'

'Oh, way off the beaten track. Back of beyond if you ask me. Turn right at Ardrishaig and go along the Kilberry road until you reach some cottage or other. Hamish and I went up once, just out of interest, you know. Had some friends over from the States. Thought we'd show them a bit of the Scottish landscape. Stuff you don't see in all those tartan-trimmed calendars—'

'So she might have gone there?' Cameron broke into the woman's flow of speech before she could digress any further.

'Suppose so. I say, what has she done? Run off

with the bank manager?' A sudden guffaw made the woman's several chins roll with merriment. 'Can't see it myself, somehow. A bit long in the tooth for that sort of malarkey, I'd have thought.'

'As I said, we were hoping that your neighbour could help us with our inquiries,' Cameron repeated. 'If you should see her, please let her know we called, will you?' And handing over his card, he gave a brief old-fashioned nod before ushering them all out of the garden.

Mrs Jones turned to Cameron and Weir as they made their way towards the pavement. 'She's done something, hasn't she? I can tell,' she added, tapping the side of her nose in a mocking way.

'She hasn't had any visitors to stay recently, has she?' Weir asked.

'No idea. Sorry. Hamish and I have just got back from Tenerife. Haven't seen Lorna for over a fortnight. Why? Is she harbouring terrorists or something?'

Cameron shook his head and smiled politely, but he flashed Weir a look that told the younger man to close his mouth, a mouth that was already open to say an awful lot more.

'Crikey! She sounded just like that woman off the telly,' Weir stated as they fastened their seat belts. 'Looked like her, too. Whatshername? You know, the one that does the cooking and hunting and all that.'

'Aye, I know who you mean,' Cameron replied. And although he could remember the celebrity's name perfectly well, he chose not to enlighten Weir, for the DS's mind had made an interesting connection: Mrs Jones had exactly the same keen intelligence and awareness that shone out of the eyes of the TV celebrity, Clarrisa Dickson-Wright. And if this neighbour's estimation of Lorna Tulloch was correct, perhaps they had found the woman who had abducted Nancy Fraser. And it would be only a matter of hours from now that a search warrant would allow the scene of crime officers to search this house in Southbrae Drive, ready to take any traces for analysis. Kim Fraser had supplied plenty of material so Nancy's DNA profile could be matched. Now, thought Cameron, as they drove back to HQ, it was down to the SOCOs and their painstaking colleagues in forensics to provide evidence that the child had been here.

CHAPTER 33

'**M**rs Lorimer, can I have a word, please?' Maggie looked up from the stack of jotters on her desk, trying not to sigh. It was halfway through the third period and her only non-teaching time that day.

'Yes, Jessica, what can I do for you?' Maggie's words were out, bland and impersonal, before she realised that the girl was physically trembling. 'What on earth? Sit down here. Jessica, what's wrong, dear?'

It had taken only a little persuasion for the Fourth Year girl to let Maggie telephone the police. 'It's not something we can ignore, Jessica,' she told the girl as they sat together in the guidance room.

'Won't they think I'm being a bit of a scaredy cat?' the girl asked, anxiously biting her lip.

'Someone stalking you and making nuisance calls is taken very seriously by the police,' Maggie assured her. And if he's the same person who lured Julie Donaldson into Dawsholm Woods, they'll want to know every last detail, she thought.

But Maggie Lorimer was not about to voice that sudden idea, at least not yet.

'I thought it might be Kenny Turner from Sixth Year at first,' she told Maggie. 'He's been hanging around me and Manda since the beginning of term,' she added. 'But it wasn't Kenny, it was an older man.' The girl shuddered so violently that Maggie automatically reached out a comforting hand and patted her arm.

'It's okay. And you don't have to stay on your own till Mum and Dad get back. I'll have a word with Amanda's parents if you like.'

'Thanks.' Jessica attempted a tremulous smile. 'But I've already asked Manda and she says I can stay over at her place after school today.'

Maggie Lorimer keyed in the number on her mobile. It was Bill's direct line, but even if he wasn't at his desk there would be someone to help them. And that was an interesting little snippet of information about Kenny Turner. Why, if he'd been so adamant that he'd had no hope of a relationship with Julie Donaldson, had the boy been making overtures to the two best-looking girls in Maggie's registration class?

'I'm going up there myself,' Jo Grant told the team of officers assembled in the muster room. 'A woman with a man walking around the countryside in late summer will appear far less threatening.'

'What about back-up, ma'am?' someone asked.

'Police from Lochgilphead will be on hand whenever they're needed, but I don't anticipate having to call on them until we've made an arrest. As far as we know this Tulloch woman is on her own. Unless, of course, the child is actually with her,' she added. There was a definite sense of optimism now that the SOCOs had found traces of Nancy Fraser in the house at Jordanhill, though the fact that the DI was preparing to drive all the way to this remote part of Argyll did make some of them wonder why she didn't simply hand it over to the local force. As if reading their thoughts, Jo Grant turned a hard stare on the assembled officers. 'The press are expecting results on this one and we are not going to let ourselves down after all the work *this* team has put into finding Nancy,' she told them.

Jo cleared her throat before continuing, 'You may remember these case papers from Dr Brightman relating to child abduction. It seems Miss Lorna Tulloch has never worked due to health problems and we've managed to track down her GP who tells us that she has a history of mental illness. Okay, I know it's a long shot, but there has been an instance of a kid being taken by a delusional woman before.'

The murmur that arose made her raise a hand. '*If* Lorna Tulloch took Nancy and *if* she's suffering from some sort of mental condition, then we need a softly softly approach. We'll be in radio contact at all times,' she added, 'and we will be in constant communication with Lochgilphead as well.'

The afternoon was bright and clear as they sped down the boulevard towards the West Coast. Soon they were circling the Stoneymolan roundabout with its strange array of studded lumps of wood and ethereal birds on wires, an expensive eyesore that annoyed the Lewisman every time he passed it. Then the vista beyond Loch Lomond opened up and Niall Cameron's heart rose at the sight of these blue hills beckoning them onwards. It was the first stage of the familiar journey that took him to Skye and beyond to the green hills of Harris and home.

DI Grant seemed content to watch the countryside go by and Cameron was glad of their companionable silence, enjoying the sweep of Ben Lomond rising majestically to their right, no scrap of mist obscuring its rounded head. There was much to occupy his thoughts as the Detective Sergeant drove his senior colleague through the little town of Arrochar, the famous Cobbler gazing down at them from its craggy heights, the road circling all the way around Loch Long then heading into the depths of the hills. Had the woman brought the child along these mountain roads? Had little Nancy looked out of a car window at that deep glen with its lonely cottage as they climbed the Rest and Be Thankful? And had she gasped at the thundering torrent of water spilling down the shadowy side of this mountain, a far cry from the city streets of home? All these ideas continued to haunt him as he drove deeper and deeper into the heart of the Argyll countryside.

In less than an hour they had reached Inverary with its white houses and fairytale castle. 'Halfway there,' Jo Grant murmured, looking out over Loch Fyne and the pier where the *Arctic Penguin*, an old sea-going schooner-turned-tourist attraction, was anchored. Then the car gathered speed once more as Cameron drove along the side of the loch, taking every bend as fast as he dared, one eye always on the road ahead to see if a white Mazda might be among the oncoming traffic. At last they were past Lochgilphead and Ardrishaig, with the Crinan Canal behind them as they drove along the single-track road towards their destination.

CHAPTER 34

This summed up everything he hated about the media interfering in a high-profile case, Lorimer thought grimly, reading the *Gazette*'s feature about religious types who had targeted young girls. Despite the grainy photograph of a long-dead Irish priest, it was a deliberate attack on Eric Chalmers and upon Lorimer himself, though his own name was only mentioned towards the end of the final paragraph as if the journalist had been saving her best ammunition for maximum impact. The feeling of euphoria that had come from Dan Murphy's telephone call began to evaporate.

Lorimer read the article again and frowned. How the hell had Cassidy come by these particular pieces of information? He'd have to check with the police press officer, but even as his hand reached for the phone, Lorimer was certain that nobody had given permission for this to be made public. **SINS OF THE FATHERS** she had called the piece. Lorimer let his eyes linger on some of her phrases: *a hidden secret that was only uncovered when one of his former altar boys met him during a* *religious retreat . . . elderly priest taken into custody . . . numerous cases of both rape and murder have been committed by so-called religious men, some proved in a court of law but some still in that misty realm of uncertainty and rumour . . . scandals have continued to blot the copybooks of both Roman Catholic and Protestant denominations, whether it is, perhaps, a priest fathering a child in his diocese or a Kirk elder having an affair with a married minister . . .*

But when a man commits the murder of a young person who is in his pastoral care, then it is more than eyebrows that should be raised. Questions must be asked about what sort of persons are being trained to look after our young folk within the sanctuary of the church or any organised type of religion today . . .

Lorimer wanted to crush the paper in his hands, but he forced himself to reread the final paragraphs.

But now we have a case where the authorities seem to be shielding another religious figure from prosecution rather than taking him into custody. The Religious Education teacher, Eric Chalmers, who is at the centre of the Julie Donaldson murder, had his house completely searched by a squad of Scene of Crime officers from Strathclyde Police earlier today. So far no arrests have been made, though a person close to the investigation has informed the Gazette *that Mr Chalmers has been under close scrutiny from the Senior Investigating Officer in the case. Repeated visits have been made to Chalmers' home and his car is*

344

currently being taken apart by forensic experts to see if any traces can be found to link him with this case.

Why his arrest has not been made by DCI Lorimer, the investigating officer in charge of the case, is a matter of public speculation, but the Gazette *has discovered that the police officer's wife is not only a colleague of the RE teacher at Muirpark Secondary, but that Mrs Lorimer is a personal friend of the Chalmers family. In other walks of life a conflict of interests would immediately be noticed so why is Lorimer still in charge of this case and, perhaps more importantly, why is Eric Chalmers not yet in custody?*

'You're off the case!' Mitchison glowered at his Detective Chief Inspector. 'We'll just have to bring the review team in sooner than we wanted to,' he said, his nasal whine directed at Lorimer. 'This is a complete disaster. For one of my officers to have been named and shamed like this . . . well, I don't know what the Chief Constable is going to say about it, really I don't!' Mitchison did not deign to look again at his DCI, but examined his perfectly shaped fingernails as if Lorimer were somehow beneath his contempt.

It wasn't in his nature to grovel and the very thought of humbling himself to a man whom he truly despised made Lorimer grit his teeth, but it would have to be done.

'If I could just have a few more days, sir? We have just had some new information that might help to identify one of the victims.' The words were out and his tone was suitably beseeching. Lorimer held his breath as he caught a triumphant glitter in Mitchison's eye as the man sighed theatrically. He hadn't wanted to reveal the latest report from the pathologist yet or relate how keen Dan Murphy had been to let him know what the forensic odontology had suggested.

'Oh, well, I suppose we can give you, say, forty-eight hours. But we need a result. And I am expecting to have the news of an arrest as soon as possible. Do I make myself clear?'

When the telephone rang and he heard Maggie's voice, Lorimer's first thought was that she too had read Cassidy's piece and was calling to convey her own horror. But as he listened, the story about Jessica King and her stalker changed the tense expression on his face.

'Look, I'm coming over to Muirpark. Has the girl got her camera with her? Right. Stay with her. And tell Manson I want to talk to him as well.'

Kyle Kerrigan was crossing the playground from the PE block when the dark blue Lexus drove through the gates and curved up towards the staff car park. Following it with his eyes, the boy watched as a familiar figure emerged and closed the car door. He was supposed to be taking a message for Finnegan, but curiosity mingled with an idea that he'd been harbouring for days now made Kyle turn on his heel and follow the Detective Chief Inspector to the main entrance.

'You've got to buzz them if you don't know the right numbers to press. The teachers have all got cards that let them in, see?'

Lorimer looked down at the boy who had suddenly emerged by his side. That was Kyle Kerrigan, wasn't it? The policeman tried to conceal his shock but it was too late.

'Bit of a mess, eh?' Kyle attempted a lopsided grin as he fingered his swollen face.

'Not something that happened inside the boxing ring, I suppose?' Lorimer remarked grimly, his hand falling to his side. 'Who did this to you, Kyle? Your old man?'

'Aye, well, I kind of wanted to talk to you about that, Mr Lorimer. See—' The boy reddened suddenly and stopped.

'What is it, Kyle? If there's anything I can do to help . . .'

'See, at the police station? Remember I had that swab? Well, is there any chance you could see if my father,' Kyle swallowed hard, 'is really my father?' The boy dropped his head and continued in a mutter, 'Because he says he isn't.'

Lorimer had glimpsed the appeal in those grey eyes despite the fact that they were almost closed against bruised, puffy lids. This mattered to the boy, it mattered a lot.

'If we have his DNA on record it wouldn't be too difficult to make a comparison, Kyle. But I'm afraid it's out of the question for me to give you that sort of information.'

'Oh.' The boy dropped his gaze, looking so suddenly forlorn that Lorimer wished he could give this boy what he was asking.

'If you had your birth certificate . . .' he began.

'Yes,' the boy said simply. 'That's what my big brother said I should look for. I just thought something coming from the police would make him leave me alone, you see.'

Lorimer nodded. 'Good luck, then.'

'Oh, and it's 1066 you press.' Kyle nodded towards the door once more. 'Battle of Hastings. I'm no supposed to know that, but I do,' he said, trying to drop a wink but grimacing instead.

Lorimer watched him walk away. What was life like for all the Kyle Kerrigans of this world, brutalised by the very person who was supposed to provide care and affection? Barbara Cassidy would do well to make a feature out of that, rather than creating a media frenzy over a man who had yet to be accused of murder.

And that was something else he'd have to find time to do: begin an internal inquiry into how certain information had come to be leaked to the press in the first place.

Muirpark Secondary was like every other school in the country; any visitor had to report first to the reception desk and be given a security pass, never mind if he was a top police officer or not. As Lorimer clipped the plastic badge to his lapel,

Keith Manson emerged from his office, a worried frown upon his fleshy face.

'Jessica's with your wife in the guidance office,' Manson told him. 'Come with me.' Lorimer followed him, matching the shorter man's eager stride along the blue-walled corridor.

Jessica King looked up as they entered the room. Lorimer could see that she'd been crying but the pale face appeared composed and had lost none of the haunting quality of ethereal beauty that Maggie had earlier tried to describe.

'She's stunning,' his wife had told him. 'But entirely unaware of her own effect on people. Men especially,' she'd added.

But after a few questions it was clear that the Detective Chief Inspector was keen to concentrate not on the girl's ordeal but upon the one thing that might make a difference – some of the photographs taken as the car had slowed down outside Jessica King's home.

'Thanks. We'll be able to check this against anyone known to us,' he told the girl. 'And don't worry. If he's in our system, he won't be bothering you again.'

CHAPTER 35

'Nice,' Jo Grant remarked, turning her head as they passed a lone buzzard observing the world from its perch on top of a fence post. 'Haven't been in this part of the world before.'

'Thought you were an Argyll lass,' Cameron remarked.

'Well, my mother lived in Tobermory, but she came to the city before I was born,' Jo explained. 'I'm not a *real* islander like yourself.'

'No, I suppose not,' Cameron murmured, the lilt in his voice more marked than usual, as if being closer to home heightened his Lewis accent.

'Right, maybe we'll be able to see it today,' Cameron said shyly, glancing sideways at Jo Grant as he slowed the car down into a lay-by at the top of a hill. He stopped, let the windows roll down, then, reaching into the glove compartment, he drew out a small pair of powerful binoculars and trained them on the glittering seas below. For a moment neither of them spoke, then, 'Yes, have a look at that.' Cameron offered his companion the binoculars and Jo Grant obediently looked out to the shapes of islands beyond the water.

'Ireland,' he said. 'Not often you can make it out but on a clear day like this . . . Jura, Ghigha and Islay, do you see it?'

Jo Grant murmured that she did, before settling the glasses on her lap. Then the magic moment was over and the car was making its way carefully downhill to the lush, wooded region where the small village lay.

Even as they parked at Kilberry Inn, they could see the cottage on the other side of the road, a white car sitting on a patch of gravel under a stand of pine trees.

Niall Cameron looked across at DI Grant, watching her expression intently. 'D'you think?'

'Well, we're about to find out, aren't we?' she replied, pulling the binoculars over her head in an attempt to appear just like a normal tourist out birdwatching.

Walking down the short slope towards the white-washed cottage, Cameron felt the late afternoon sun warming his back and suddenly he understood why this woman had chosen the remote Argyll village as her bolthole. A sense of peace pervaded the area with the sound of water trickling in the burn that separated the cottage from the adjoining field, the scent of meadowsweet wafting from its mossy banks and the cloud of midges dancing under the shadow of the pines. If he closed his eyes for a moment he could be back home.

It was the child that they heard first, their feet

suddenly immobile on the edge of the road. A glance between them and a nod was all that was needed. Cameron would remain here at the front door by the car, the same white Mazda that little Sally MacIlwraith had spotted back in Glasgow, while DI Grant followed that sound of childish laughter.

As she approached the back of the house, Jo saw that it contained a square patch of grass bordered on three sides by a flagstone path. There, in the middle of the garden, a little girl was being pushed on a green plastic swing by an older woman who could easily have been taken for her grandmother. She'd seen countless pictures of the missing child yet DI Grant still screwed up her eyes against the sunlight to be sure that it really was Nancy Fraser. The woman's henna-red hair lifted in the breeze, revealing a weathered face covered in a tracery of broken veins, the skin of her neck sagging as she bent forwards.

'Hello.' Jo smiled as she walked towards them, noting the older woman's back suddenly stiffening and the way her hands clutched the two chains of the swing to bring it to an abrupt halt. 'Can you help me, please? I was looking for someone but I've kind of lost my way,' she continued, still stepping towards the woman and the little girl who was now looking uncertainly from one grown-up to the other. Jo grinned at her then hunkered down to the child's level. 'Hello, you're a lovely wee lass, what's your name?' she asked before the woman had time to intervene.

'Nancy,' the child replied, one finger going into her mouth as a shy smile dimpled her cheeks.

'What do you want?' The woman was towering over Jo now, a look of fear in her eyes. 'Come away into the house, Nancy. Granny's got your milk and biscuits all ready,' she scolded, one hand out to take the child off the swing.

But in a swift movement Jo had scooped Nancy up in her arms while that tall shadow lingering out of sight transformed itself into the familiar figure of DS Niall Cameron.

'Miss Lorna Tulloch? DI Grant, Strathclyde Police. We'd like you to come with us, please.'

Later, Cameron would tell them about how strange that return journey had been. Nancy Fraser had been placed behind him next to DI Grant, the child's car seat transferred from the ancient Mazda while Lorna Tulloch followed them in the police car behind, accompanied by the officers from Lochgilphead. They'd stopped at Inverary to let the child and her abductor use the toilet and it had been 'Granny this' and 'Granny that'; the little girl seemed to have accepted the older woman quite naturally. Only when Jo Grant had reminded Nancy that she was going home to see Mummy did Lorna Tulloch's gentle expression harden into something remote and unseeing, and Cameron had been filled with a strange sort of pity for the child's abductor. Thereafter she had been silent, letting Jo and the child chatter to one another as they were led back to the cars taking them back towards Glasgow. There was no sense of triumph as they'd made that two-hour journey back in the early evening sunlight, he'd tell his colleagues. Simply a feeling of immense relief and an overwhelming anticipation to see mother and child reunited. They'd called Lorimer with the news so it wouldn't only be Kim Fraser at HQ waiting for their arrival.

As he saw their cars swing through the gates of the police car park, Lorimer wondered what fate awaited the elderly woman. Just what was her story? That was something he'd want to know, despite the matter being pretty much out of their hands after today. Other people's stories went on and what became of them could affect choices he might make in other cases in years to come. Lorna Tulloch was seriously delusional – of that there was absolutely no doubt – but, from what he'd been able to glean from Cameron, she'd taken good care of Nancy and the child had even seemed quite fond of this stranger who had claimed to be her grandmother.

There were more officers than usual lining the corridor where Kim Fraser waited to see her child, their eyes filled with the sort of emotion most people didn't associate with hardened cops.

'Nancy!'

'Mummy!'

Lorimer saw DS Cameron and Jo Grant stop at the doorway, Miss Tulloch between them. He could see the woman's thin arms hanging by her side, thin and old and brittle. A childless woman, drained of the sap of youth, she seemed shrunken and shrivelled into herself, her dark red gypsy hair curiously at odds with her pallid complexion. He'd shaken his head as Jo had produced the cuffs; there was no need to restrain her now.

As Kim Fraser hugged her child to her, crying, smoothing her hair and saying, *Nancy, Nancy* over and over again, she glanced up at Lorimer who was standing there, one hand on the older woman's arm.

'Is that?' Kim left the question unfinished as she stared at the person who had caused her so much anguish over these past ten days. There was a sudden silence as the two women faced one another. Then Jo Grant nodded to a pair of uniformed officers to lead the prisoner away, and the moment was past.

'You did it.' Kim Fraser looked up at the DCI. 'I knew you would, Mr Lorimer!' The girl's face was covered in tears but a huge smile shone through them as she hugged Nancy to her.

'Not me, Kim. DI Grant, here, has been in charge of the case lately,' he said. 'And it was down to a whole team of people, I promise you,' Lorimer assured her. 'As well as a lot of good old-fashioned police work.'

Kim shook her head. 'See if they newspaper folk

355

ask me, I'm going to tell them. Youse didn't give up on me, Mr Lorimer. Not once. And I cannae thank you all enough for bringing her back.' The girl's glance took in Jo, Cameron and the others who lingered still in the corridor.

Lorimer swallowed as Kim Fraser burst into a fresh bout of weeping.

Then Nancy piped up, 'What's wrong, Mammy? Are ye no pleased tae see me?' Everyone laughed at the child's innocent remark and Lorimer could see one or two of his officers wipe away a sudden tear.

'It's hard to believe.' Lorimer shook his head, putting down the two case files with a thump.

Solly shrugged his shoulders; the vagaries of human nature came his way so often that very little seemed to surprise the psychologist. But it was one of those quirks of fate that the very case file he had originally shown the Detective Chief Inspector should be replicated by the woman from Jordanhill.

'Never had any children of her own,' Lorimer said, his voice betraying the sympathy he could not help but feel for Lorna Tulloch.

'Nor have you and Maggie but that doesn't make you want to go out and steal someone else's child,' Solly reasoned. 'Normal, healthy people may fantasise about what having a child may be like but only a very few will act on that fantasy. She did believe that she was the child's grandmother while they were together. But whether she is suffering from severe delusions or not is a matter for the clinical psychologists to decide.'

'What do *you* think?' Lorimer shot him a look.

'I only saw her for a short while after your people brought her in. She was certainly withdrawn. Hard to tell if she was feeling guilt at her actions or pain at being bereft of the child with whom she had so obviously bonded.'

'And what will happen to her now?'

'Well, there are the charges of child abduction to deal with but she will be undergoing rigorous assessment prior to that. To see first of all if she is actually fit to plead.'

'And is she?'

Solly shook his dark curls. 'I doubt it. Her previous psychiatric history suggests a personality that simply cannot cope with certain aspects of reality.'

'But she could drive a car, look after two homes, plan a child abduction!' Lorimer protested.

'Yes,' Solly agreed. 'And once she had the child she was perfectly happy, taking care of her, playing with her as a real grandmother would have done. In fact,' he mused, 'she may have given that little girl a nice break from city life.'

'How can you say that! The poor wee thing must have been distraught at being taken away and parted from her mother. I know Kim Fraser was beside herself with anxiety.'

'Small children adapt far more quickly than you might imagine,' Solly told him mildly. 'And your DI did say that the child seemed to be well cared for and not fearful in any way.'

It was true, Lorimer thought. The woman might have committed a terrible crime by snatching Nancy Fraser, but she had shown genuine affection for the little girl and there were no signs that she had harmed her in any way. What had it been like for Nancy the day she had been abducted, though? Had she screamed and cried out? Had she sobbed herself to sleep on the first night, missing her own mummy? That was something they might never know.

Solly smiled at him. 'Nancy's fit and well. There are no little bodies buried in the woods. And Lorna Tulloch will be taken care of by those who know what is best for her future.'

Despite the benign expression on Solly's face, Lorimer shuddered. It had been a case where his expectations had been to find the child dead somewhere, the victim of child molesters, perhaps. Or worse, not finding her at all, leaving that young mother in the never-ending hell of uncertainty.

'Yes.' He sighed at last. 'It's been a fantastic outcome. And I suppose you're right about the Tulloch woman.'

A vision of her henna-red hair came to his mind, the face pale and expressionless. Who could tell what thoughts had been percolating through that disturbed mind? But it still saddened him to imagine her spending the rest of her life locked away in some institution, far away from the hills of Kintyre.

CHAPTER 36

Please say you recognise him, Lorimer prayed as he approached the head teacher's office once again.

Jessica's digital photographs had now been cleverly enhanced by their experts at Pitt Street and her stalker's face was fairly clear. They were still continuing to work on the blurred second photo to see if any identifying marks could be found on the car. If Jessica's stalker was indeed the killer of Julie Donaldson and the other young women, then Muirpark might be the missing link. It was too soon to reveal the information that had come from Dan Murphy concerning the remains of the two unidentified victims. But Manson might just be able to help him on that score.

At last he was sitting opposite the stocky figure of Keith Manson, a china cup of lukewarm coffee in front of him. He'd listened politely to the head teacher as the man had catalogued the problems facing the school and staff in the light of Eric Chalmers' suspension, plus his own secretary, Jackie, suddenly being called away to look after a sick mother, but this was not what he had come to discuss.

'Did you ever have exchange students from Eastern Europe at Muirpark?' he asked.

Manson's eyebrows shot up at the sudden change of topic. 'Well, yes, we did as a matter of fact. Should have had one last year but, let me think, yes it must have been three years ago. What was her name? Anna something . . . I'd have to look it up for you,' he said. 'She was pretty homesick, I do remember that. Wanted to go back straight after the summer term instead of . . .' Manson pulled open the drawer of a filing cabinet and began to rifle through the thickly stacked papers. 'Should have it on computer, but we lost a lot of stuff when we upgraded to a new system last year. Bloody technology!' He gave a quick smile of satisfaction as he drew out a pink folder. 'Here we are. Anna Jakubowski. Came from St Petersburg. Parents weren't too happy when she extended her visa and stayed on here to study, after all.'

Lorimer gave him a sharp look. 'Where did she go?'

'That's the funny thing. She never kept in touch. The organisation she'd come over with sent us mail from the Jakubowskis to see if we could forward it to Anna. But of course we couldn't. She simply seems to have disappeared. The details are all in here,' he said, handing the folder to Lorimer.

'Did she have any particular friends at school? Anyone from the staff, maybe?'

Manson looked at him sharply. 'The Modern Languages department pretty much took her under their wing,' he said. 'But,' he paused for a moment, his eyes clouding over, 'I do remember that Eric Chalmers was very good to her. He and Ruth took Anna to their church during her stay.' Manson looked away for a moment, biting his lip as if he had already said too much.

'That was before Chalmers was married?'

Manson nodded. 'But quite a few of the staff showed her hospitality as well,' he added quickly. 'My wife and I had Anna to stay over a weekend so we could take her up to visit St Andrews.'

'Did you ever see the girl in the company of this man?' Lorimer asked, showing Manson the digital print from Jessica's camera.

'Sorry, not that I remember. And I've got a good memory for faces, even if the names sometimes escape me,' Manson assured him. 'If Jackie was here she could probably help you.' Manson shrugged an apology. 'But I do remember that the travel organisation assumed Anna had had some sort of rift with her parents.' Manson frowned suddenly. 'But she had seemed so keen to go home. Girls!' he exclaimed. 'Always changing their minds.'

But Lorimer didn't reply. Already his own mind was quickening: perhaps someone else entirely had made up Anna Jakubowski's mind for her.

If Dr Murphy's information was correct, the dental evidence of the older skeleton found in Dawsholm Woods might very well show it to be that of the Russian girl.

'You started to say that the school should have played host to another student last year. What happened?'

'Oh, that travel company got it all wrong. Sent her to a different school altogether in the end, I believe. In fact one of their reps handed in a pile of stuff at the start of this term. Not that we're considering taking anyone else,' he added.

'Do you happen to have her details on record by any chance?'

'Could have. As you can see we're not good at throwing things out,' Manson added with a wry smile as he turned back to the bulging drawer full of files.

'Can't remember her name at all, but it should be in here. Yes.' The head teacher pulled out a sheet of paper. 'Jarmila Svobodova, if that's how you pronounce it. She was a student from Prague. Do you want to take a copy of this with you?'

It hadn't taken long to establish that Anna Jakubowski had neither left the UK within the last three years nor had she taken up the college place that had been offered to her. Could they obtain a sample of her DNA from Russia? Lorimer thought. Talking to the tour organisers had been a complete waste of time; their personnel had changed over the passage of time and there was nobody who was either willing or able to help Strathclyde Police. And the Czech girl had arrived in Scotland in early May last year. But where she had gone after that was a complete mystery. Yes, the agency had given all that information to the police at the time but they weren't responsible for the girl's whereabouts once she had arrived, were they? the man from the agency had protested.

It wasn't what he'd anticipated when he'd first looked at these young women's remains in Glasgow City Mortuary, but now they needed help from officers who could act quickly, Lorimer told himself, justifying the call he was about to make to Interpol.

'Yes, I'd say she could be from somewhere like the Czech Republic,' Murphy told him.

Lorimer was standing by the pathologist's side as they looked at the bones lying on the table.

'Slightly different dental work. And the type of amalgam used in that filling,' he pointed a small probe at a molar in the gumless row of teeth, 'I think it's what they use over there, if my memory serves me correctly.'

'So there might be a forensic link between them?' Lorimer asked, his face suddenly hopeful.

'Sure, you already think so,' Murphy answered, grinning. 'Or you wouldn't be making detailed inquiries into missing European students from around the time we estimate they were killed, would you, now?'

'Last summer and three summers ago,' Lorimer murmured. 'If that Russian girl who was at Muirpark Secondary School *is* our first victim, then is this Jarmila Svobodova?' He looked at the remains of the other girl that had been found in the woods. 'And where did he meet them?'

It was going to be one of those days that broke all the rules about standard working practices, Lorimer thought to himself, driving back across Glasgow city centre. Already he'd put several things in motion but before he could make an arrest, he had to have the final pieces of the jigsaw in place. Mitchison was champing at the bit to have Chalmers under lock and key, and the press situation was raising the tension levels to bursting point back at divisional headquarters, the last place Lorimer wanted to be going right now. Solly hadn't yet come up with a clear profile but that was simply one more tool in the box, the DCI reminded himself. The psychologist's methods were not infallible and he shouldn't let past successes cloud his judgement in this case. Nor should he let Maggie's opinion sway his thoughts. If evidence was found in Chalmers' car or in the house then he'd be first in line to arrest the man. Just because the media wanted to hang him out to dry didn't mean he *wasn't* guilty. But then there was Solly Brightman's other suggestion, one that was being followed up right now, and he'd have to see what progress was being made in that direction. And now that they had this photograph, some identification was possible. If the person that had been stalking Jessica King was indeed their suspect.

He wasn't hiding himself away, this man, whoever he was. He'd followed Jessica on foot as well as arriving at her home by car. So did this mean he was a local man?

There was something twitching at the edge of his brain, a memory flickering from the TV report on the Soham murders. Hadn't the killer appeared at the crime scene, unable to keep away from what he had done? And was there any possibility of creating a circumstance that might bring this particular killer out into the open?

As he drove up St Vincent Street, past the grand pillars dominating the Physician and Surgeons Hall on the rise of the hill, Lorimer gazed at the skyline ahead of him. The blue was fading over the city, pale grey clouds appearing just above the river. He was out there somewhere. Several summers had brought him into the parkland and the woods, and this summer wasn't over yet.

And if Lorimer didn't have the chance to find him now, how many more young women might he lure towards their death in summers still to come?

'He's guilty as sin!' The man's voice dominated the babble in the closely packed staffroom.

'How can you say that?' Sandie Carmichael protested. 'He's one of your own colleagues! How are you going to feel when he comes back to school and knows what you've said?' she stormed at Herriot.

'Could be he'll never set foot in this building again,' another voice piped up.

'Aye, and even if he is found innocent, who'd want to come back here after all of this muck raking?' someone else remarked, in a tone of disgust.

'What happened to good old-fashioned loyalty? That's what I want to know,' Sandie continued hotly. 'Eric's been a great colleague to all of us. And I dare anyone to say otherwise!' The Business Studies teacher picked up her bag and marched out of the room, leaving a low buzz of talk behind her.

'Oh, Maggie, thank God for someone sane,' Sandie began as she fell into step with her friend. 'You should hear that lot in there.' She cocked her head back at the staffroom door. 'Soon as they scent something vulnerable they're howling their heads off like a pack of jackals.'

Maggie sighed. 'I know. It's horrible.' She paused. 'Did they say anything about me? After that newspaper article . . .'

Sandie laid a hand on Maggie's shoulder. 'Remember what you're always saying to the kids? Don't believe everything the papers tell you. Look, Maggie, they're not really out to get Eric. Or you.

They're in the business of selling newspapers and all they want is the biggest sort of scandal-mongering they can legally get off with.'

'I suppose so. It's just that I feel so personally involved now.' She broke off, unwilling to reveal the news about Jessica.

'Don't worry.' Sandie patted her kindly. 'That husband of yours will find out who killed Julie. I know he will.'

But as Maggie Lorimer turned into her own classroom, she failed to conjure up a similar feeling of optimism. If her husband and his team didn't find another suspect, what was to become of Eric Chalmers?

The database containing DNA profiles was not something that Lorimer searched on a regular basis but it hadn't proved too difficult to find what Kyle had asked for, he thought, tearing off the relevant sheet of perforated paper from the machine. Kerrigan Senior was Kyle's father in name only, not his biological father at all. But how was the boy going to react to this news when he found his birth certificate at the registry office? And what use would he make of it? Lorimer folded the paper and put it in his inside jacket pocket. If he could only bend the rules just this once? He gave a snort of derisory laughter, making the uniformed policewoman passing by look up at him, a question in her eyes. No, what he'd told Kyle was true; he simply couldn't reveal privileged information like this.

'Sir?' DC Irvine was approaching him from the other end of the corridor, a look of excitement on her face. 'We've got an ID on the stalker's car,' she told him, waving the sheaf of papers she held in her hand. 'And a name and address. Adam Russell. And see the address? It's the same street as Julie Donaldson!' she exclaimed as DS Wilson joined them, peering over Lorimer's shoulder.

'He's already been questioned in a door-to-door,' Wilson remarked.

'Aye, and so was Peter Sutcliffe before they caught him,' Lorimer retorted. 'Come on, get a back-up organised. We're going after him right now!'

CHAPTER 37

The shadows were beginning to lengthen, he noticed. It would soon be time to leave and move back to a warmer place for the winter months. Even his dreams had begun to take on elements that they'd say were not in keeping with reality. He sniggered. Reality! It was a word they loved to use as if he were not in touch with life in all its forms. He knew more about the real world than they ever would, these closeted academics with their white coats and theories.

Perhaps it was a sixth sense or his own heightened awareness of things, but before he even heard the car door slam, he was out of the house, all he needed in one capacious overcoat pocket. Smiling to himself with the thrill of it all, he headed down the flight of stairs leading to the back court, away from the two figures that had turned into the close.

They'd come for him several times before and he'd let them lead him away, limp and unprotesting between their solicitous arms, some drug working swiftly in his veins.

He wasn't going to let himself be trapped like that again.

It might take them less than three minutes to find that he'd gone. But in that short time he could be round another corner, through a lane and into the maze of back courts, zig-zagging his way from Crow Road all the way to the Botanic Gardens and the safety of his secret place.

A whinny of laughter left his lips as he sped along the dusty pavement, his coat flying behind him.

Turning another corner, a gaggle of school kids gaped at his mad dash along the street, one shouting out an obscenity that he pretended not to hear. Once on the main road he would slow down, he told himself. Then he'd simply disappear. For who would notice someone like him among the mass of humanity going about its lawful business?

'He's gone,' Irvine said, swinging the heavy door back and forward in her hand as if testing its weight. 'Didn't even bother to lock it behind him.' She broke off as Lorimer raised his hand then put one finger to his lips.

How long have you been away? Lorimer thought, entering the empty living room. As he looked around, the desolate, sagging furniture seemed to tell its own tale of a life that was past caring about the comfort of material things. But perhaps it could tell him something else. Hunkering down, the detective ran his hand lightly across the surface of the nearest sofa, years of use permanently moulding the seat cushions into twin craters. The side of his mouth gave a mere twitch as he felt one side of the settee warm, the other stone cold.

'He's been here just minutes ago,' he said quietly, making DC Irvine spin round then look warily over her shoulder at the door to their left.

She opened her eyes wide, motioning towards the doorway.

Lorimer nodded once and stood up slowly. He would go in first.

'Police!' The word burst from his mouth as he slammed through the bedroom door, fists ready to repel any attack.

'Shit!' Lorimer turned back into the room. 'Let's look in the other rooms. No, you stay here!' he commanded, already halfway through into the corridor.

His footfall was entirely silent as Lorimer crept into the bathroom, but there was no sign of Russell. The kitchen too was empty, but he prowled around anyway, eyes devouring the work surfaces until he spied a kettle. It was still warm and further inspection found a dirty mug in the sink and an ashtray with one fag end still smouldering.

Irvine was right beside him now. 'Get on the radio, will you?' Lorimer asked. 'Put out a description of Russell. He can't be that far away.' Then he stopped, biting his lip as he made a mental map of the area. 'Tell them he's possibly heading in the direction of Dumbarton Road or back up to Jordanhill.'

Immediately Irvine turned away, the radio already at her lips.

Lorimer was back in the main living room now, looking out of the window fronting Crow Road. They had only the merest details about Adam Russell so far – a single photograph from Jessica's camera that might be anyone. It would be nothing short of a miracle if he was spotted in the next few minutes.

Straightening up, the DCI looked more closely at the room. It was something he had learned to do early on in his career as a detective. Reading the homes of people could give all sorts of clues as to their character as well as what they liked, and how they lived; things that might lead to building up a fuller picture.

Everything in this room was old and worn out: the furniture was in a state of collapse, the curtains at the window looked as if they hadn't been washed for years and as he put out a hand to shake the grey material, a cloud of dust rose into the air. Above him a pleated plastic lampshade hung at an angle, its edges nicotine-brown. There were burn marks on the carpet and worn patches near the edges of the chairs and settee. Lorimer moved towards an ancient sideboard, a cheap-looking piece of furniture that had a pair of ornate tarnished handles on either door.

Pulling them open, he saw a mishmash of boxes sitting on top of a pile of table linen crammed up against an old sewing box, loose threads spilling from its bulging sides with a pile of papers pushed into the remaining space. Some of the boxes looked as though they had been there for decades, the cardboard curled at the corners and several layers of sellotape binding them together. Fingering them, he could feel how thin and papery the tape had become over the years and he guessed that these might have belonged to Russell's parents. He'd start with them first. A label attached to the top of one box lid gave the address of a Glasgow department store long gone, the watery blue writing underneath addressed to Charles Russell Esq. Opening the box, Lorimer saw a heap of black and white photographs, reminding him with a pang of a similar cache stowed away in the attic of his own home, family stuff to be sorted out on the promise of a rainy day that had yet to come. His mum had always insisted on writing people's names on the back with pencil, he remembered, turning the first photograph over in his hand.

It was a portrait of a young woman looking towards the camera, sitting rigidly upright as if fearful that the felt hat decorated with a plethora of fruit and flowers might slip from her head. A studio portrait, he thought, seeing the sepia-coloured stamp on the back and the pencilled words, Wedding day, 1946. Russell's grandmother, perhaps? Lorimer sifted through the rest, searching for an image of Adam Russell, something more up to date, though with the advent of digital photography anything he found here would still be a few years out. And he hadn't noticed a computer in any of the rooms.

Lorimer flicked through the heap of photographs, discarding them into the box lid, until he came to one that took his interest. It was a colour photograph of a small child wedged between a man and woman sitting on a beach towel. He turned it over to see the words, Ardrossan, 1984. He turned to look at the people on that beach, frowning. If it hadn't been the Russells themselves, other names would have been pencilled in, wouldn't they? And it fitted. Adam Russell had been born in 1979 so the little boy in the picture would have been about to begin school. He was smiling into the camera, hands clasped in front of him as if someone had instructed the boy to strike a pose. His parents (Lorimer assumed) had their arms around one another, little Adam squeezed between them, and were staring at whoever it was that had been taking the picture. The man had the look of someone who had been ill: the skin on his face hung from a slack jaw and the eyes were redrimmed. The woman, however, was quite the opposite. A florid-faced female with ample bosoms rolling out from her print dress, Adam's mother exuded the sort of jollity that Lorimer associated with naughty seaside postcards.

He put the photograph to one side, sifting through what was left of the pile.

'No joy, sir. They don't think there's sufficient description to identify him anyway,' Irvine said, coming into the room.

'Okay. Look, I want to see if we can find anything

375

while we're here,' Lorimer began, looking up at his detective constable. Seeing the worried expression on her face he added, 'We'll have a search warrant by the end of play today. Russell must have seen us coming. He fair got off his mark. So until we catch up with him, I'm not about to waste a chance like this. See if you can find a computer or a laptop anywhere. Okay?'

Irvine's anxious expression was not lost on the DCI. She didn't like anything that wasn't strictly by the book. Lorimer grinned to himself, remembering the first time he'd seen one of his own senior officers take liberties with the rules.

There! Lorimer picked up a photograph of an older Adam Russell and held it carefully between his fingertips. He was looking at a young man in his early twenties, Lorimer reckoned, turning to see what was written on the back, but for once the paper was blank, no date to verify the man's age. Russell was standing on a pavement, his back against a black metal railing, part of a red sandstone building visible behind him. To his left Lorimer could see the edge of what looked like an academic gown and part of a man's dark suit. And though the photographer's own shadow was cast over the picture, he could read an expression of irritation on the man's face as if he'd been a reluctant subject; in fact, one hand was slightly raised as if he had thought about obscuring his features from the camera. He was wearing a dark grey lounge suit and a white shirt, though the tie had been loosened and the top shirt button undone. Lorimer's eyes fell again on the building and the railings, something gnawing at the edge of his mind. Then he had it. The Barony! It was the building near to Glasgow Cathedral where students from the city universities held their graduation ceremony, he remembered. Was that the reason for Russell's apparent displeasure? He'd not graduated with his peers yet he'd gone along to see their success. And he'd kept that photograph. Why? Was it a reminder of what Russell himself had failed to achieve? Lorimer sat back on his heels, wondering. A graduation photo would have been something to have put on top of this sideboard by proud parents, but there were no framed portraits at all, just this box of snaps all mixed up together.

There were a few more photos of Russell, showing a younger man in various poses, but none as striking as the one beside the Barony, nor as recent. But it was good enough to show to the girl in Maggie's Fourth Year, just to confirm his suspicions that she had been stalked by this man. Lorimer rifled through the pile of photographs, almost discarding one of a class group taken in a school hall when something about it made him pause. That shield on the wall above the boys and girls standing facing the camera: he knew what it was. Holding the photograph a little way from him, Lorimer took a deep breath. It was the main hall of a place he'd been in very recently – Muirpark

Secondary School. And if there was a group photo, perhaps there would also be a single one of the boy in his uniform? Sure enough there was a colour snap in a brown card frame of a young boy of around twelve, his blue eyes staring intently at the photographer.

Slipping all three photographs into his wallet, Lorimer walked out of the room to join Irvine in the search for a laptop. If they found one, it could be a big help. He had a sense that some of the pieces in this jigsaw were beginning to fall into place. But right now they needed more clues about the missing man and where he could have gone.

CHAPTER 38

It was never quiet here, but that was all right. The rumbling from the Glasgow Underground like subterranean thunder reminded him that there were others, like him, deep below the surface of things, travelling into the night.

It was always night here, the constant darkness a cloak to protect him from prying eyes. Sometimes the scutter of tiny feet would alert him to the rats whose habitat he shared, but they didn't bother him and he had no reason to go after them. The tunnel bent away from the daylight after only a few yards, any residual light fading from the slime-covered walls and plunging into a blackness that was thick with soot. Deep within this place, the earth smelled cold and lifeless; denied the essential light, nothing here could grow, not even an etiolated weed searching through a crack in the bricks.

He was safe. A sigh broke from his chest and he leaned his back against the tunnel wall, reassured to feel its solid surface. In a few minutes he would walk deeper into the tunnel until he came to his secret place, but for now simply being here away from the brightness of the day was enough. Besides, what was happening out there in the world no longer mattered to him.

Except, a little voice told him, that elusive girl, the one whose lovely eyes haunted his dreams. The one that he still had to find.

Kyle took the paper in his hand, eyes following the lines of printing, lips parted in concentration. Then he looked up. 'It's right enough then?'

The registrar's clerk nodded her head, folding her arms across a minuscule bosom in a gesture that still managed to express disapproval.

Kyle turned away. 'Right. Thanks.'

As he walked away from the imposing building there was so much more that he wished people could say, like *he's been a father figure to you* or *he's been the one who brought you up, looked after you,* but he would never hear anyone utter phrases like that, especially when they were so blatantly untrue. Tam Kerrigan was a thug and a brute. His constant denial of parental care towards Kyle didn't even give him the right to be called his father, despite the fact that the charade had been played out over fifteen years.

'Wonder who he is?' the boy muttered, looking down at the words 'Father unknown'.

Kyle nodded to himself. Was there someone he could ask? Gran, maybe? And what would he do now, move back in with her? Probably. But there was something else he would have to do first.

* * *

'We do have their permission,' Solly told him. 'Unusual, I'll admit, given the patient confidentiality that normally surrounds these cases, but I managed to persuade them that there were sufficient grounds for releasing his entire file.' He coughed and gave a little smile. 'Actually it turns out that I know Russell's psychiatrist. Gave him some help when he was researching a book,' Solly added.

Lorimer was sitting beside the psychologist in his West End home, the evening sun pouring through the huge bay windows that looked down over the city. Solly had been busy, it seemed, since they had found Russell's out-of-date appointment card tucked away in a bedside drawer.

'Adam Russell has been attending this particular psychiatrist as an outpatient for several years,' he told Lorimer. 'He was first treated the year after dropping out of university.' He turned to look into the detective's sharp blue eyes as he paused. 'The same year that both his parents died.'

'Ah.' Lorimer's eyebrows rose as he digested the significance of that statement. 'Do we know what happened to them?'

'According to the notes, the Russells were both alcoholics. He'd been treated for depression and she had a heart condition,' Solly said. 'They were found dead in their car somewhere down the Ayrshire coast. Let me see.' He frowned, turning over a page in the document he had laid upon his lap. 'Yes. Outside a town called Ard-rossan.'

'Ardrossan,' Lorimer said, automatically correcting Solly's pronunciation of the word.

'The verdict was suicide. They'd both inhaled carbon monoxide. Hellish thing to lose both your parents like that,' he added thoughtfully.

'Are you saying that was what tipped Russell over the edge? Living with two confirmed alcoholics can't have been easy. Maybe the strain of it all got to him eventually.'

'Or perhaps he had a biological predisposition to self-destruction,' Solly sighed. 'That's one of the theories attached to his earlier notes. There was some evidence of self-harming after his first stint as a patient.' He frowned. 'My friend confided in me that he'd been a bit suspicious of the patient's motivation. Wasn't at all convinced he was the genuine article. Might have been faking it, he said. But that was never actually written down in the notes.'

'How did his referral to a psychiatrist come about?'

Solly shrugged. 'No record of that, I'm afraid. We'd have to find his original GP and ask.'

Lorimer took the file from Solly. The police had been given only the rudimentary facts on Adam Russell on a need-to-know basis but now that Solomon Brightman had managed to winkle out the man's entire case history they had much, much more to go on. DC Irvine had discovered the laptop shoved under Russell's bed, its tangle of wires concealed under a dusty sheet. Back in HQ all its secrets would soon be revealed. But now he had to read the history of a man who was out there in the city somewhere, a man who might well be guilty of much more than stalking an attractive teenage girl.

Eric was praying. The room was still warm from the late afternoon sun and there was a rosy glow washing the cream-painted walls of the nursery. He'd chosen to come up here as a way of being closer to Ruth and Ashleigh and now he was kneeling beside the nursing chair where mother and baby had spent long hours together. Sometimes Eric had come upon them quietly, lingering in the doorway as Ruth sang to her tiny daughter, rocking the chair back and forth, a pang of wonder in his heart that these two people were his family. He'd stand still, listening, before slipping away undetected, leaving them to those special moments that seemed to enclose them in a little world of their own.

His prayers were for them, of course, and for all helpless creatures that needed the Lord's protection, a list that went on for so long that sometimes Eric felt a kind of despair at this world with all its ills and troubles. But tonight he must not weaken. He must be strong for what lay ahead.

CHAPTER 39

She'd come home late from school, wearied by classes who had decided to act up all afternoon. Sometimes, Maggie thought, it was a conspiracy they all hatched during lunchhour to be as bad as they possibly could. Or, then again, maybe it was simply too many E-numbers wreaking havoc with young systems already full of swirling hormones. Whatever the reason, she was tired and had wanted nothing more than to run a bath and soak away the day's irritations.

Chancer had rubbed himself all over her ankles, almost tripping her up until she'd emptied some food into his supper bowl. Now he was washing his orange fur, perched daintily on the edge of the bath, seemingly impervious to the steam that rose from the water's surface. Lying back into the warmth, Maggie sighed. Jessica had gone to stay with Manda and her parents so that was one less thing to worry about. The day's events slowly disappeared as she let her thoughts drift.

Kyle Kerrigan seemed to be a bit happier now for some reason that she couldn't fathom. He wasn't the same boy she'd known last session, but then he'd been through so much, hadn't he? And poor little Samantha Wetherby, Julie's best pal; how was she coping? Maggie's lips gave an ironic twist. Why was it she cared so much about the kids in her class? From their point of view, Mrs Lorimer probably ceased to exist once the final bell had sounded every day. Was it because she had never had children of her own? Was that it? Sinking further back into the soothing warmth of the bath, Maggie smiled at her own introspection. Sandie's tales of her teenage son were designed to be completely off-putting, but a little baby . . . The memory of Ruth Chalmers and baby Ashleigh swam into her mind, the softness of the baby's downy skin, her sheer vulnerability and Ruth's protecting arms. That was what she had missed, wasn't it: the desire to nurture, to care for another human being. Well, teaching gave her that opportunity, didn't it? And now that she had taken over the Scripture Union club, wasn't she in a position to look out for the kids a little bit more?

The vision of Kenny Turner came to her then, making Maggie sit up, the water swishing around her waist, droplets streaming off her bare shoulders. Had she been right to delve into matters that were really none of her business? Finding out from him about Kyle and Julie had been a nasty shock. But was this feeling of unease caused by her suspicions about the boy's relationship with Julie or guilt that she was dabbling in things best left to people like her husband?

With a sudden shiver, Maggie recalled Eric's face as she had come upon him that day, Julie tearing away from him. What had that all been about? And were her protestations about the innocence of the tall, handsome RE teacher really justified?

'It won't do, you know Your reputation is going to be tainted for ever, let me tell you. And how you can expect to have the trust of parents again is beyond me.'

Eric Chalmers sat gazing at the tall man in the wing chair whose eyes refused to meet his own. It had been a mistake to come over here, but he had never given up the hope that his father would see things from his point of view. Perhaps this time, he'd told himself, he'd show some sympathy. But as usual none had been forthcoming.

'What do you suggest, then?' Eric asked, trying to keep his voice as neutral as possible, hiding the thickness in his throat.

'Take your wife and child as far away from here as possible. Start again somewhere else. If that Manson fellow is prepared to give you a decent reference then take up another teaching post. All you're trained for, after all,' the Rev Chalmers added, his bitter tone edged with spite.

'Wouldn't it have been worse right now if I had been an ordained minister?' Eric asked quietly.

'Hah!' His father pointed the stem of his pipe towards Eric. 'For the first time in my life I'm actually glad you never took up the ministry. Just think of the damage this would have done to the Church!'

Eric sat silently, his eyes wandering over the man who sat before him. His thin craggy features still had a sort of classical refinement about them, though the tilt of his head was more haughty than noble. It could have been a Shakespearean actor sitting there, spouting his fine words. And hadn't there always been a bit of that in his father? Wasn't he known for some memorable sermons, words rolling off his lips as if he was inspired. But it had been an inspiration born of a love of the English language and the sound of his own remarkable voice rather than anything holy and sacred, Eric thought with a pang of sorrow. Rev Chalmers' own reputation was based on a lifetime of Sunday morning performances, rather than any quiet, unseen pastoral work.

'Is that all you have to say, Father?' Eric asked at last, rising from the hard-backed seat he had chosen in this familiar room with its book-lined walls and soft lighting. He'd been ushered into the study like one of his father's parishioners on a matter of business, not as the son of the Manse.

'You have never bothered with my advice before, Eric, so I don't see why I should waste my time trying to warn you now. But I'll say this,' again the pipe was jabbed in his direction, 'if you're not careful it's more than your job you'll lose once this matter is finished.'

And turning away towards his desk, the Rev Chalmers began to read over the contents of a paper. It was a gesture meant to convey that he had uttered his final word and Eric was now dismissed.

Back out in the cool night air, Eric walked slowly past the snug rows of houses along the street, catching glimpses of a well-lit interior or the flicker from a television set. Other people would be going about their ordinary lives, watching the news, having a drink, talking over the day's events with their families. He swallowed hard, determined not to let any self-pity overwhelm him, but he could not banish a sudden sense of loneliness.

There was still no sign of his car being returned and he had walked over the hill from Anniesland so now he would return the same way over Switchback Road. As Eric drew close to the brow of the hill, his eyes were drawn to the dark mass of trees flanking the opposite side of the dual carriageway. Dawsholm Park, where he had fed chaffinches as a boy and scattered peanuts for the squirrels, now seemed to Eric Chalmers a place of ineffable sadness. And, like his childhood, it would be forever tainted with memories impossible to forget.

Lorimer stood looking around the incident room. Blown-up pictures of Julie Donaldson and the skeletons of the other two victims were alongside enlarged passport photographs of the missing girls, their young faces gazing out hopefully at a world that they had expected to enjoy. Now these images were stuck on the board side by side with the men who might be in the frame for their murders. The latest photos had been enlarged and copied so that Adam Russell's face was now part of this collage. The DCI had dismissed the rest of the team before utter exhaustion set in; he simply couldn't afford any mistakes being made at this crucial stage. But Lorimer had remained there alone, thinking over what he had read in Russell's case notes.

Adam Russell had been on his own ever since the death of both parents, continuing to live in the family home. It was a stone's throw from the Donaldsons' house and easy walking distance from Dumbarton Road, from where he could catch a bus or the Underground into the city. After giving up on his film and media course at university, he'd drifted into a series of jobs, none of which had lasted very long. And he'd been treated for depression, several episodes of anxiety following as the years passed and his condition justified the prescribed medication. Lorimer sat down at the nearest desk and turned once more to the thick, well-thumbed document he held in his hands.

'Personable . . . charming . . . plausible,' the words seemed to leap off the page at him. Russell had told stories to his doctors about his responsible career as a professional make-up artist, a tale that did, however, hold a grain of truth. The notes showed that he had been employed on a casual basis at the King's Theatre and also at a funeral parlour, his skills evidently sufficient for someone's purposes. But most of what he claimed to be was based on a tissue of lies. Make-believe, perhaps. Or would a psychiatrist call it something else? Delusions? Most of the man's income over the past few years had derived from Social Security benefits; flimsy papers typed up by his visiting officer were stapled to several of the pages, showing dates and figures, his continuing illness regularly assessed to justify his claiming invalidity allowances.

The DCI was used to reading background reports on criminals whose behaviour suggested a lack of mental capacity and who might not be considered fit to plead, but this file had him puzzled. Russell did not seem to fit neatly into any sort of category. The man appeared to be perfectly capable of looking after himself and leading an apparently normal life. Nowhere was there evidence to suggest a pattern of violent behaviour except for the episode where he had claimed to have self-harmed.

So why had he run? And why had he stalked Jessica King?

Lorimer rubbed his eyes; they were gritty and beginning to sting with tiredness. He was certain there must be something within this file, something that would give him an insight into this case.

It came to him quite suddenly, not so much what was there but what was missing. He'd read them over and over, almost dismissing the thin paper pages as irrelevant. But now he saw it: several dates when Russell should have been in receipt of benefits were blank. He turned over the pages again and again, but there was nothing to show the man had been in paid employment. And it was at the same time for the last three years in early summer. So what had he been doing?

Three years ago a girl had arrived in Scotland to stay and Muirpark Secondary School had been her host. Then last year another girl had come. Both were now missing persons. Was it their mortal remains now lying in Glasgow City Mortuary?

He had worked in a funeral parlour. Was there some link there? Peter Sutcliffe, the Yorkshire Ripper, hadn't he been a mortuary attendant? Lorimer's head buzzed with unanswered questions.

Then he thought back to what Maggie's head teacher had told him and his hand stretched out towards the telephone.

Manson was at home and not best pleased to be disturbed by the sound of the DCI's voice. But he did provide the name Lorimer was looking for.

The offices were closed for business, the recorded voice told him, but there was a mobile number he could ring in an emergency.

'Mr Clark? Detective Chief Inspector Lorimer, Strathclyde CID,' he began, wondering just what the man on the other end of the line would make of a call at this late hour. If Derek Clark was surprised he was too polite to show it and within minutes Lorimer was ringing off, thanking the man for his time.

It was the sort of moment that he relished, the clarity that came when all the pieces finally fell into place.

The agency had been happy to employ the young man, himself a former pupil from Muirpark, and they had had no hesitation in renewing his services each year as an escort for their overseas students. Mr Russell had been paid in cash, but that was all right, surely? Clark had asked, obviously anxious that his firm had not transgressed any of the legal requirements of employing casual labour. There had been a moment's silence after Lorimer had mentioned the names of the missing teenagers, though. Not our responsibility, had been Clark's final response.

'Where are you?' he asked aloud, staring at the picture of Russell standing awkwardly against the black railings, his hand raised in a blur, lips slightly parted as if to protest. The SOCOs had scoured the man's flat once a warrant had been obtained but no forensic results would be shown until tomorrow at the very earliest.

Lorimer heaved himself to his feet. There was no way Russell would return to the flat now but he'd posted an unmarked car across the street to keep watch just in case.

It was time to go home, catch some sleep. Maggie would be waiting as usual and the thought of her welcoming smile when he walked into their home quickened his step as he went out of the incident room, leaving the faces of all those different people staring blankly into the night.

CHAPTER 40

The leaves that had been drifting slowly from the trees in the last lazy days of summer now whirled downwards, scattering across the grass, the frenzied wind whipping at the branches. Autumn was almost here now, this early morning chill edging the breeze with a memory of ice and snow from the high peaks further north. All sounds seemed concentrated within the trees themselves, like a roar of an aircraft repeatedly taking off into the darkness. Wave upon wave of gusts made the ancient oaks sway under the flying scraps of clouds, the moon appearing fitfully like a ghostly face leering out from a veil of grey, torn cobwebs.

But the noise made him feel strong, excited, as though it were endowing him with special powers. As he sat on the stone by the tunnel's mouth, Adam felt as if he were the only person alive. And wasn't he named for the first born man, the special son of God? The wind in his face made him think of the hot blood running through his veins; though in truth his bare hands were numb from the cold. It was almost time to hide himself away once more, deep within his cave, his kingdom. The all-night grocer's had provided enough rations to

394

keep him going for days and he had plenty of spare batteries for his torch, should he need to use it.

A movement to his left made him start but it was only a squirrel scampering down from the foot of a tree trunk. The animal froze suddenly as if aware of the man's intention. Then, just as Adam stooped down to pick up the stone, it whisked around the bole of the tree and out of sight. He stood up then, angry with himself for letting the beast escape. The moment's fury made something in his stomach churn and he tasted sour bile in his mouth. Looking over his shoulder, Adam decided to risk one quick dash into the bushes to void his bowels.

Minutes later he was walking down the old railway tracks, his feet keeping time with the carillon of echoes from the noise of the wind outside.

Lorimer woke early and, despite so little sleep, he felt more awake than he had for days. All night the wind had howled around the house, the straggling fronds of climbing rose beating against their bedroom window, making him feel as though he had been just on the edge of wakefulness. As if recalling a vivid dream, Lorimer remembered the events of last night and a quickening sense of purpose made him slip away from Maggie's warm body.

It had to be Adam Russell.

All the bits fitted together, even to the profile that Solly had at last produced. A white male in his twenties to forties, was the first line on the psychologist's report, the description applying to a vast sector of society but in particular to every profile Lorimer had ever read of a serial killer. Dressing quickly, Lorimer made up his mind.

'Ye-es?' Doctor Solomon Brightman reached for the handset, his head still muzzy with sleep.

'It's me. Can I come up?'

'Lorimer?' There was barely a pause as the psychologist registered the note of excitement in the detective's voice. Something must have happened if the DCI was at his door at this hour.

Ten minutes later the two men were sitting opposite one another, a steaming pot of one of Solly's herbal brews on the table between them.

'Russell was diagnosed with some depressive type of illness, okay?' Lorimer began. 'Nothing so specific that he presented himself as a danger to the public. On the contrary, according to these case notes,' he tapped the file he was holding, 'the man was an exemplary patient, completing all the necessary programmes so that he could cope on his own, taking all the relevant medication.'

'Right, I read all of that,' Solly said, his brow creasing in an uncharacteristic frown of annoyance.

'The focus of the notes was always on Russell's well-being,' Lorimer said grimly, lifting up his cup and taking a sip, then grimacing at the taste. 'How can you drink this stuff, Solly?' he asked, setting the cup back down. The psychologist smiled briefly and shrugged.

'Anyway, all these notes tell us is how he responded to such-and-such a diagnostic test; how well he did jumping through their various hoops. There's nothing to suggest that he might be a stalker, or anything more sinister.'

'Well, why would his case workers look for things that weren't there?' Solly replied mildly.

Lorimer looked at him sharply. 'Listen to what I found out last night. Every summer this man's been employed by an agency to help with the overseas students who went to various schools, including Muirpark Secondary. Acting as chauffeur, taking them around the city to familiarise them with the place and seeing that they were conversant with things like automated cashpoints and transport facilities,' Lorimer told him, watching as Solly's eyes grew wide with understanding. 'Then, as the summer came to an end, Russell's health always seemed to take a turn for the worse and he was back on some form of medication.'

'Right,' Solly agreed, nodding his dark head sagely, 'that's interesting. And this agency . . . they didn't check up on his background?'

Lorimer shook his head. 'They spoke about him like he was their favourite employee; Russell seems to have been a plausible sort of character, right enough.'

'Hm. Plausible *and* someone who liked to play the system. There have been cases where—' He broke off as he caught Lorimer's exasperated sigh.

'Listen. Each summer there was a different group of students to show around. And I'm certain that two of them were murdered.' This time it was Lorimer who paused to let his words sink in.

'If it is Anna and Jarmila whose remains are lying down in the City Mortuary, then are you trying to say this establishes a pattern? What about the missing summer?' Solly asked doubtfully.

Lorimer fixed his blue gaze on the psychologist. 'Maybe we simply haven't found a fourth body yet,' he said.

'Right, you know what you've to do,' Lorimer told them. 'We've got less than a day before a review team takes this away from us so get cracking. I want Russell found and I want him brought in.'

There was a murmuring of approval as they all left the incident room. Something was happening at last and the collective adrenalin rush was almost tangible.

He'd handed the team a variety of actions: to find out what else Russell's neighbours knew about the man, to make a search among his GP's records and more detailed enquiries about his parents, as well as looking for clues about where he might have gone. The car Jessica King had photographed was also missing and if they could trace that it would give them something else to examine. Not for the first time Lorimer breathed a prayer of thanks to whatever authority had decided to create such a plethora of CCTV cameras in and around the city. And, he thought, if he could swing it, a TV bulletin would also be going out at lunchtime today with a picture of Russell and a plea to the public to come forward if they had any sightings of the man.

As he waited for the line to connect him to the Chief Superintendent, Lorimer drummed his fingers on the desk, thoughts racing about his new suspect. If he had his way, the lunchtime news would have an exclusive feature, something that would piss off the press, though it might just make their evening editions. Eric Chalmers had suffered trial by media for so long now that his was a household name and letters to the *Gazette* had poured in, showing a marked division of opinion. At Muirpark the teaching staff seemed to be at one another's throats arguing about his involvement in this murder case, Maggie had told Lorimer sadly, her voice tight with emotion. So she would be jubilant if he could finally prove that her friend was innocent.

Suhayl scratched his head, wondering. Had that been the same man he'd served during the wee small hours: the one with the big black coat and the unsmiling eyes? Suhayl, who was a poet by choice and a greengrocer by necessity, regarded the television screen closely then scribbled down the telephone number on the brown paper bag he'd snatched from the end of the counter. It was him, he was sure of that: same height, same face, same pale washed-out complexion. Nodding to himself, Suhayl picked up his mobile from its place by the till and began to punch out the number.

'Where did you say you are, Mr Kamar?' Lorimer swung his chair around, studying the map of Glasgow on his wall as he listened to the Asian grocer's words. 'And you saw him crossing over . . . ?' Lorimer's eyes took in the area around Great Western Road where the Botanic Gardens met the junction of Byres Road and Queen Margaret Drive.

Suhayl Kamar stood in the doorway of his shop, one hand holding his mobile against his ear, the other describing patterns in the air as though he were explaining things to a visible companion. 'Yes, he went up to the side of the gate and disappeared just like that. One moment he was in the street under the lamp post, the next he had vanished. So he must have gone into the gardens, sir. There is no other explanation.'

Lorimer put down the telephone. They were having a fair number of calls but this was the first that had merited being put through to him personally.

It only took a few minutes to establish the grocer's claim. CCTV footage had three sightings of Russell – one near to the grocer's shop, one within the park itself and the third way over near the disused railway track. Grabbing his jacket, Lorimer swung himself out of his chair and headed for the car park.

He knew that area, he thought, heart pounding. He'd spent time there as a youngster, snooping around the old tunnel with his pals. But he'd always been too afraid to enter the claustrophobic darkness after that first time.

Now was it some strange quirk of fate drawing William Lorimer back to a place that had haunted his dreams ever since?

CHAPTER 41

Kyle sat down heavily on the bed. Packing all his belongings into that battered case had taken longer than he'd thought. Twice he'd yanked the whole lot out again and twice he'd repacked it more carefully, folding things smooth so they would fit. He hadn't realised just how much stuff he actually owned. But now it was done and the case was on its side next to a bulging duffle bag and his school satchel. It only remained to do one last thing.

He'd imagined this moment over and over again, remembered Jamesey's words. *Pit the heid in him*, he'd told his wee brother, grinning. Wee *half-brother*, Kyle reminded himself. Not a full-blood relation. And he knew he could do it. Knew he could take the man on, hold him back and smash his own head against that girning face. In his mind he could hear the crunch of bone as Tam Kerrigan's nose met the impact of his head: a real Glasgow Kiss. He could almost smell the blood, see the look of surprised anguish in those piggy little eyes as he stood back, triumphant over the man at last. He knew he could do it.

'Whit's goin on?'

Kyle looked up, his reverie vanished in an instant. Da stood there, hands by his side, a belligerent expression on his unshaven face.

'Whit's a this?' Kerrigan pointed at the luggage on the floor.

'I'm going to live at Gran's,' Kyle told him, standing up, surprised at how calm he felt now that this moment of confrontation had actually arrived.

'Oh, aye? An who says you can?'

'I do,' Kyle replied, watching the man before him. Was that a look of uncertainty in his eyes? He'd been taught to look for signs of weakness in an opponent and he could see plenty right now. Tam Kerrigan's awkward stance, the looseness around his jaws that spoke of recent hours at the bottle, but, above all, a sort of wariness in those bloodshot eyes as if he was seeing something in Kyle that hadn't been there before.

And Kyle knew in that moment exactly what that was. He no longer feared this man, no longer felt the need to give him the grudging kind of respect due to a father. And somehow that sense was being conveyed to the wiry little man who stood licking his lips, clenching and unclenching his fists.

He just needed to come at him. Just once. And Kyle could smash him, finish him for good, leave him with the taste of blood and defeat in his mouth.

'Whit's a this aboot? Ye're leavin yer faither?'

Kyle shook his head. 'You're not my father. You've told me that often enough, haven't you?' He took a tentative step towards the man and had the satisfaction of seeing him raise his fists protectively. 'D'you know what? I've been up to the registry office to collect my birth certificate so I *know* you're not my father.'

Kyle was panting now, the adrenalin coursing through his body.

Just one lunge, one sweet Glasgow Kiss . . .

'Ye wee toerag!' Kerrigan made a move towards him and in a flash Kyle had him by the wrists, forcing him back, feeling the feet slip against the linoleum floor until he had him pinned against the bedroom wall. Kyle felt the strength ebbing out of the smaller man as he held him there, forcing him to look into his eyes.

'You-are-not-my-father,' he said, gripping the skinny wrists in his hands and glaring into a pair of watery eyes that belonged to a stranger. And in that moment he sensed Tam Kerrigan had known it all along, years of resentment building up, making him lash out at the unsuspecting boy. And for a brief moment he felt pity for this old man, pity mixed with a feeling of disgust.

Kyle let him go and stood back.

'You will never lay a finger on me again. D'you hear me?' Kyle asked quietly.

Kerrigan nodded, speechless now, rubbing the places on his wrists where Kyle had grabbed him, then looking away from those piercing grey eyes that had held him every bit as effectively as those strong boxer's hands.

But it gave him no satisfaction to see the older man flatten himself against the wall, cringing as Kyle bent to pick up his bags and head out of the door.

As he walked out of the close, wee Tracey-Ann from downstairs was sitting on a faded blanket, rocking her dolly to sleep.

'Ur ye goin yer holidays, Kyle?' she asked.

'No, hen,' he told her. 'I'm away for good.'

'Aw.' Her little face crumpled for a moment as she looked at his suitcase. Then the child gave an exaggerated sigh, something she'd seen her own parent do a million times before. 'Ta-ta, then, Kyle,' she said and smiled up at him before turning her attention back to the dolly in her arms.

'Ta-ta, wee yin,' Kyle replied, swinging the duffle bag over his shoulder and heading down the street for the last time.

He knew exactly where he was going. Hadn't he seen it often enough in nightmares? The darkness that would always swallow him up until he woke, trembling and lathered in sweat. William Lorimer had known and despised his weakness, this engulfing claustrophobia, this thing that had haunted him since childhood. They'd left him there, deep within the tunnel and run off, laughing as he'd stumbled on, going the wrong way until he was crying with fear, huddled against the wall, terrified of the train that was going to screech towards him, its huge metallic bulk crushing him to death.

He had emerged whimpering at last, the daylight never more welcome, to find the big boys had gone and he'd had to make his own way home, snotnosed and tearful. But the incident had left its mark and Lorimer could still not enter an enclosed space without an elemental sense of terror.

The grass around the tunnel's mouth was flattened on one side as if something like a large stone had been removed. Looking around, Lorimer saw it: rolled away against the wall, its flat top perfect for someone to sit on. Stooping down, the detective saw a glint of silver. Instinctively he drew out a handkerchief and picked it up, examining the folded piece of paper. It was the inside wrapper of a stick of chewing gum, folded and refolded then shaped into a circle. Lorimer could just imagine the tall blonde man sitting there, running the metallic paper round and round his finger. He recalled the reports from Russell's neighbours, confirming what the police had feared: Adam was a man with problems, one fellow had said. He's got a medical condition, another had whispered, touching the side of her head. Solly's profile of a man with psychopathic traits seemed to be emerging from the shadows at last.

Some sixth sense told him that he was in there. Waiting.

Heart pounding, Lorimer took a step towards the tunnel's gaping mouth then began the long walk away from daylight into darkness.

Breathe in, breathe out, he told himself, taking a gulp of sooty air and counting to four, then exhaling on a count of eight. Relax, breathe, relax, breathe, the rhythm of his inner voice soothed the trembling that lay somewhere under the surface; the trembling that threatened to break loose and overwhelm his body in a full-blown panic attack.

It was not long before the light disappeared completely and he had to feel his way forwards, one hand on the wall to his left, taking careful footsteps, making no noise except for these breaths that seemed unnaturally loud.

He stopped suddenly, the rumble from the Underground train rising, screaming like a banshee somewhere close at hand, its vibration forcing Lorimer to cringe against the wall. Then it was gone, brakes screeching and some moments of silence before it set off again, its rattle disappearing into another underground tunnel.

He could imagine them for a moment: ordinary people marching up the steps, away from the cold tiled walls curving overhead, the draught of air billowing at coats and skirts as they climbed up and up into the daylight at street level. And somehow they gave him comfort, these nameless, ordinary people. Wasn't it his job, after all, to protect them from places like this and from the sort of danger that lurked somewhere just ahead?

Then he heard it. A single sound magnified by the darkness. A foot scraping against the metal rail.

So, Russell was in the middle of the tunnel. And coming towards him. Had he heard Lorimer's own football, sensed another human being inside his hiding place?

Instinctively Lorimer reached into his pocket, feeling the shape of his mobile phone.

Then a sudden image came to him of how you lost a signal whenever the Glasgow to Edinburgh express entered a tunnel. It would be of no earthly use down here, would it? He'd be unable to call for back-up and he hadn't told anyone where he was going. And what if Russell had a weapon of some sort?

Lorimer waited for the panic to begin but nothing happened. Instead he stood waiting, ready for the man who approached him, unseen in the blackness, his sense of hearing heightened by the loss of his sight.

On and on he could hear Russell coming, his feet sliding now on the rails, a curse muttered under his breath. And in that moment Lorimer knew that he was still an unknown factor in this man's reckoning. If he kept perfectly still, hardly breathing at all, Russell might come right up to where he was standing.

Adam could feel the place where he had secreted the torch batteries, a space in the wall where a few bricks had been dislodged, feeling the place with his hand, a blind man searching for a familiar shape. He'd counted the number of sleepers along the track, stopping when he came to the thirteenth. Thirteen bits of timber between the gap where he slept and the place where he kept his stash: thirteen, his lucky number.

Then he screamed, an echoing wail that filled the blackness as something large and heavy fell on him, forcing him down.

His face struck the edge of the rail, teeth smashing against the metal, and then another kind of darkness began to descend as he heard a voice somewhere far away calling his name.

Lorimer sat outside the tunnel, waiting. It had taken all his strength to drag Russell's inert body out into the daylight and now he was lying on the grass next to the DCI. His face was a right mess, streams of blood pouring from the wound on his forehead, covering his neck in one dark red patch, his teeth jagged and broken in places.

But he was breathing all right. Lorimer had felt a pulse. The ambulance was on its way and in a matter of minutes he would be joined by a squad car.

He looked up to see an old man approaching them across the expanse of grass, his elderly dog loping by his side. It looked like a cross between a black Labrador and a greyhound, Lorimer decided, gazing dispassionately at the animal's greying muzzle.

As he saw them, the old man stopped, hesitant, unsure what to do, what to say.

'He's had an accident,' Lorimer explained, seeing the fear and doubt in the old man's eyes. For a moment the policeman wondered what he was thinking, this vulnerable stranger who had come across such a bloody scene. Did he think that Lorimer had attacked the man lying on the ground? Well, he supposed he had, flinging himself sideways into the darkness, taking the man by surprise.

'Now see here.' The old man brandished his walking stick at Lorimer, taking a brave step towards the place where the policeman was sitting. But just at that moment he turned as the ambulance's siren whined close by and Lorimer stood up.

'It's all right, sir.' Lorimer took out his warrant card and held it so the old man could see. 'Everything's under control.'

The man's face cleared and he gave a stiff little nod. 'Right, officer,' he said, touching a finger to his forehead. 'Come on, Holly, good girl.' Then Lorimer watched as the pair of them moved away as the sound of the siren grew louder.

What was courage? Was it being brave enough to face your worst nightmares, or something like this: an old man with a stick facing up to some stranger who might have been a violent mugger?

Lorimer shook his head, pondering as the ambulance drew up.

If he lived to be as old as the man walking sedately across the grass, dog by his side, he'd still have things to learn about humankind.

CHAPTER 42

Lorimer parked the car at the end of a long line of vehicles snaking all the way from Clydebank Crematorium to the garden of remembrance over the hill. Keith Manson had gained the permission of the educational authorities to close Muirpark today and, judging by the crowds already outside the low-lying grey building, most of the senior staff and pupils were in attendance. Lorimer glanced across at his wife, clad all in black as befitted the occasion. Maggie's head was bowed and she didn't look at him as he clasped her hand. There was nothing left to say between them. Every suspicion that had pointed towards the RE teacher had proved unfounded. Maggie had been right in her unwavering support of Eric all along.

They had arrived fifteen minutes before the funeral was due to begin but it was obvious that they would not even come close to the crematorium, never mind gain access to the building. Luckily the Glasgow weather was on its best behaviour and a late summer sun warmed them as they took their place beside the line of mourners. Others were walking back from the overflow car park to join them and Lorimer could see that any latecomers would have to stand across the path from the main drive, a good fifty yards from the main entrance.

It was unnaturally quiet given that so many young people were assembled in the crowd but then the solemnity of the occasion had probably rendered them silent. So much had already been said about Julie; now was the time to give her some respect.

Lorimer's height allowed the advantage of seeing over the heads of the other mourners and he began to pick out a few familiar faces. In among a crowd of other lads, Kyle Kerrigan stood facing the place where the funeral cortège would arrive. There was something different about the boy today, Lorimer thought. Perhaps it was the dark suit, making the boy appear so much older. Or was it that quality of stillness in his manner? So much had happened to Kyle over the past few weeks that it was no wonder the DCI noticed some indefinable change in the lad.

His eyes roved past the youngsters and Lorimer caught sight of some of Maggie's colleagues from school. There had been such a bitter division of opinion among them. Were any of these people, standing so silently, examining their consciences and regretting harsh words spoken against Eric Chalmers? Or were they too ashamed to show their faces today? Attendance at Julie's funeral wasn't compulsory, Maggie had told him, but from the hundreds of people lining the pathways, it did look as if the entire school population had made an effort to turn out.

At last the hearse glided into view, followed by two shiny black Daimlers. All that could be heard were the murmurs from the funeral directors as Frank Donaldson and his family were ushered from the cars. As Julie's flower-covered coffin was carried inside, Lorimer could feel Maggie's fingers tighten on his grasp.

It was not until the funeral party had made their way inside, leaving the crowds to wait patiently on the paths, that Lorimer heard the first sounds of girls weeping. Then the loud-speaker allowed them all to hear something of the service beginning with the Twenty-Third Psalm. At first he thought it was coming from a distance, but then the man beside him began to sing and gradually the entire crowd had joined in the familiar words, their voices growing in strength, resounding in waves until the organ within the crematorium could no longer be heard.

'Wow!' Rosie said softly, the glass of water halfway to her lips. 'That sounds awesome.'

Maggie nodded her head, still too full of the morning's events to articulate her feelings. It had been Lorimer who had described the funeral service at Clydebank to Solly and Rosie and he had tried hard to capture the unique atmosphere

414

as all these people had raised their voices together.

'It was,' he agreed. 'And afterwards it took an hour for us to get out of the place. You wouldn't believe how many folk were there.' He shrugged as if to say that it had been beyond him to judge the numbers of mourners. Silently he recalled the aftermath of the funeral.

An attendant had come along to speak to the drivers, telling them it would take a good while to have the place vacated and not to keep their engines running. Maggie had sat in the car, the window rolled down to give her some air, her face pale with the strain of it all while Lorimer had strolled up the hill away from the lines of vehicles waiting their turn to leave. Up there in the garden of remembrance, he'd stood looking out over the river Clyde and the span of the Erskine Bridge. To his left the City was shrouded in haze but further west the river glinted in the sunshine, the hills beyond etched against a sky the colour of forget-me-nots. It had only been days since Cameron and Jo had made that journey, bringing the little girl home with them. But standing there on the day of Julie Donaldson's funeral, Lorimer had felt it was another lifetime ago.

'What's happened to Lorna Tulloch?' he asked Solly, his mind suddenly back to the here and now.

'My sources at the university tell me that she is still undergoing assessment. But,' the psychologist paused, looking directly at Lorimer, 'they don't expect her to be fit to plead.'

'Poor cow,' Rosie said suddenly. 'What kind of existence can she expect to have for the rest of her life?'

'Oh, I don't know,' Solly replied, 'it takes a special sort of person to do psychiatric nursing. She'll be well cared for, believe me.'

'Right, must be off.' Lorimer rose from his seat opposite the psychologist and immediately Maggie was beside him, her hand slipped into the crook of his arm.

'See you both soon, I hope,' Rosie told them. 'It's only another three and a bit months till the wedding, you know, and Maggie and I have *loads* to plan.'

Lorimer grinned. The pathologist's voice was full of enthusiasm for her future with Solly and the day that had filled them all with so much sadness suddenly seemed that wee bit brighter.

'Are they okay, d'you think?' Rosie asked, her head cuddled into Solly's shoulder. They were standing by the huge bay window that overlooked the street below, watching as the Lexus swung away from the kerb.

'Lorimer and Maggie? Oh, yes, they're fine.'

'Fine? Is that a professional opinion, Dr Brightman?' Rosie teased.

'You want me to make the right psychological noises, do you? All right. Maggie's bound to be feeling a bit adrift. After all, one of her husband's murder cases coming right to her classroom door will have left its mark. That's something she's certainly not used to dealing with.'

'But she's good at supporting him with other stuff, isn't she?' Rosie asked thoughtfully. 'I mean she's often moaned about having to re-heat his supper late at night. But she still does it; cooks loads of great soups and things. Waits up for him as well, I guess.'

Solly nodded and smiled. 'Maggie's a good wife,' he agreed. 'Having a husband whose working hours are dictated by criminals with no consideration for mealtimes or wives waiting at home can't be easy. But,' he paused and drew Rosie to him in a gentle embrace, 'she loves him.'

'Will I be a good wife, d'you think?' Rosie murmured into his dark curls.

Solly traced a finger down her forehead and tapped her nose. 'Oh, I don't know about that.' He smiled wickedly. 'I rather think you might be quite a naughty little wife.'

Rosie giggled as his arms came around her waist. Then she gave a sigh of pleasure as Solly led her away from the window towards the bedroom door.

EPILOGUE

Adam was dreaming with his eyes wide open. He saw the girl laughing as she came towards him, her mouth parted in a smile. And he knew what he wanted; a kiss, just one kiss from her dead, cold lips. Sometimes the dreams changed and he was falling again into blackness, waking to feel the broken teeth against his gums. They'd made a decent job of fixing him up in the prison hospital. And he was beginning to learn how to work the system. They hadn't let him do any programmes yet, but he would and in time he'd convince them that he was well enough to go home. The other things had been blotted out of his mind, helped by the drugs he'd been given. No memories lingered of being in that police cell, questioned by that tall man with those staring blue eyes. Adam's mouth curled into a smile of contentment. They couldn't take away his dreams.

'You came close to it, though.' DS Alistair Wilson wagged his head at Lorimer. 'Another day and we'd have been crawling with some snotty-nosed review team trying to tell us how to do our job.'

Lorimer laughed, whisky clutched in one hand,

418

his third of the night. Wilson was right, it had been a close thing. But Russell had been easy in the end, confessing everything to them, even telling how he'd lured the girls, his victims, with promises of stardom.

The police officers had watched, fascinated, as the man had become by turns a film director then a make-up artist, changing his persona as the tale unfolded. It had been like watching a human chameleon. And his hunch had been correct. A fourth body had been unearthed from a culvert near the river, somehow undetected by their geophysics lads. Lesley Reid, a wee lassie who'd been missing from home, assumed to have taken the usual route down South after a row with her father. One of how many who slipped through society's cracks? Only once had Lorimer seen a shadow cross the man's face; the mention of Anna had troubled him and he'd looked away from Lorimer's blue gaze. Someone more skilled in the ways of the human mind would have to delve deeper to find out just what had made him kill his first victim.

Lorimer looked around at the officers in the pub, laughing now that the case was over. Not minding too much that Russell had been declared unfit to plead, just glad that places like Carstairs Mental Hospital were there for the mad, bad and dangerous people who were deemed unsafe outside its heavily fortified grounds. DS Cameron, drinking his orange squash, was having a discussion with young John Weir. That one was worth the watching, Lorimer thought. Weir had been unable to meet his eyes lately and he was tempted to think that the Detective Constable might be the one who had been responsible for those leaks to the press. He couldn't prove it, but the DC's recent request for a transfer would be met and some other poor blighters would have the dubious pleasure of John Weir's limited experience.

It was almost time to go home. Maggie would be waiting and she would be able to update him about Eric Chalmers. The RE teacher had left Scotland last week and would even now be settling into a mission in Malawi, his wife and baby daughter with him, beginning a new life together. He'd do all right, Lorimer thought, remembering the man's easy smile and firm handshake when they'd seen him off at Glasgow Airport. There was strength in this man, something courageous that had nothing to do with his physical stature. How many folk would have had the guts to visit Frank Donaldson the way he had? No charges, he'd insisted. The man had suffered enough and he'd forgiven him for the random act of vandalism that had frightened his young wife.

Lorimer drank the last of the whisky and signalled to the barman. It was his shout, his tab, his party that he was leaving.

Walking into the chill night air Lorimer hailed a taxi, a glow of pleasure warming him. Soon it would be the two of them together at home, just himself and Maggie. And looking out at the city lights glittering against the wet Glasgow streets, he couldn't imagine a better way to celebrate.

ACKNOWLEDGEMENTS

I would like to thank the following people for their help in researching this book and bringing it to completion.

Suzy and Chris Aldous and the staff and pupils of Balfron High School and Lornshill Academy; Ann and Les Aldous; Valerie Penny and the staff and pupils of Bathgate Academy; Bob Fawkes, Head Teacher, Park Mains High School; Detective Inspector Bob Frew, Strathclyde Police; Dave Savage and his staff at the Argo Centre, Drumchapel; Gabrielle Vogt for help with offender profiling; Dr Jennifer Miller for suggestions regarding forensic biology; the staff at the Macaulay Institute for inviting me to their Soil Forensics Conference; Jenny Brown, my fabulous agent, for her guiding hand; my lovely editor, David Shelley, for his unstinting support; Caroline Hogg for keeping me right on all manner of things and also huge thanks to all the other superb staff at Little, Brown. Lastly to my ever loving Donnie for his encouragement and suggestions (not all of which I accepted, but I do listen, honest!).